SHATTERED VEIL

AN
ASTORIA ROYALS
STANDALONE

Deborah GARLAND

ALL RIGHTS RESERVED

Shattered Veil ©2024 Deborah Garland

WARNING: The unauthorized reproduction or distribution of this copyrighted work is illegal. No part of this book may be used or reproduced electronically or in print without written permission, except in the case of brief quotations embodied in reviews.

This is a work of fiction. All names, characters, and places are fictitious. Any resemblance to actual events, locales, organizations, or persons, living or dead, is entirely coincidental.

Edits by:
Julie K. Cohen
Suzanne McKenna Link
Zoe Neft

Model and Discreet Covers Designed by
The Author Buddy

Published by Deborah A. Garland
www.deborahgarlandauthor.com

ASTORIA ROYALS STANDALONE EDITION

Award-Winning and Amazon Top 45 Author Deborah Garland presents brand new Irish Mafia romances set in the Astoria Royals world but can be read as standalones.

All Astoria Royals Romances are perfect for dark romance readers and each romance promises a happy ever after. With a wee cliffy to the next book.

Your mental health matters, so please read the TWs located in each book as well as Deborah's website.

Grab the Standalones:
Reckless Obsession
Shattered Veil
Illicit Temptation

Astoria Royals (Brides and Sinners):
Sinful Vows
Savage King
Sleeping with the Enemy
Deal with the Devil
Ring of Truth

FROM THE AUTHOR:

Thank you to all the readers who have loved the Astoria Royals Mafia Romances. This was supposed to be the last book in the series. But after I created the Astoria Royals Special Edition Series of standalones, I decided to write one more book.

This is Balor's story and if you think you know him, you don't. And I hope that's a good thing for you to be surprised by the quiet, nerdy hacker, who has a very dirty side and keeps dark secrets.

Shattered Veil contains themes that might trigger some readers:

First and foremost, the heroine is a domestic violence survivor. Thanks to so many women who've told their stories, I've learned no two are alike. I myself am not one. Ella's story and her experiences are her own and told in a generic way and not meant to represent anyone.

Second, one of the villains in this story, and the DV abuser is a police officer. His profession was carefully chosen to represent the extra threat a woman faces in that situation and the challenges for the hero (a mafia boss) to retaliate without retribution.

Third, this story contains an on-page suicide from a secondary character (not an O'Rourke-obviously). I won't give anything else away except that this character was given a chance at redemption and took a cowardly way out.

Additional Trigger Warnings:

Foul Language
Explicit and Graphic *Consensual* Sexual Situations
Graphic Violence (Including on-page murders)
Kidnapping/Abduction
Torture (Including torture of a pregnant woman to induce a miscarriage that is not successful and NOT by the MMC)
Deceased Parent
Terminally Ill Parent
Marital Abuse (Not shown on page)
Prostitution

If these themes bother you, please skip this one, or read with caution.

Your mental health matters!

Enjoy Shattered Veil!

DEDICATION

To the women who underestimate the quiet, nerdy guys and end up being railed beyond their wildest imagination...

And to all women who had the strength to leave an abuser. You're the real hero!

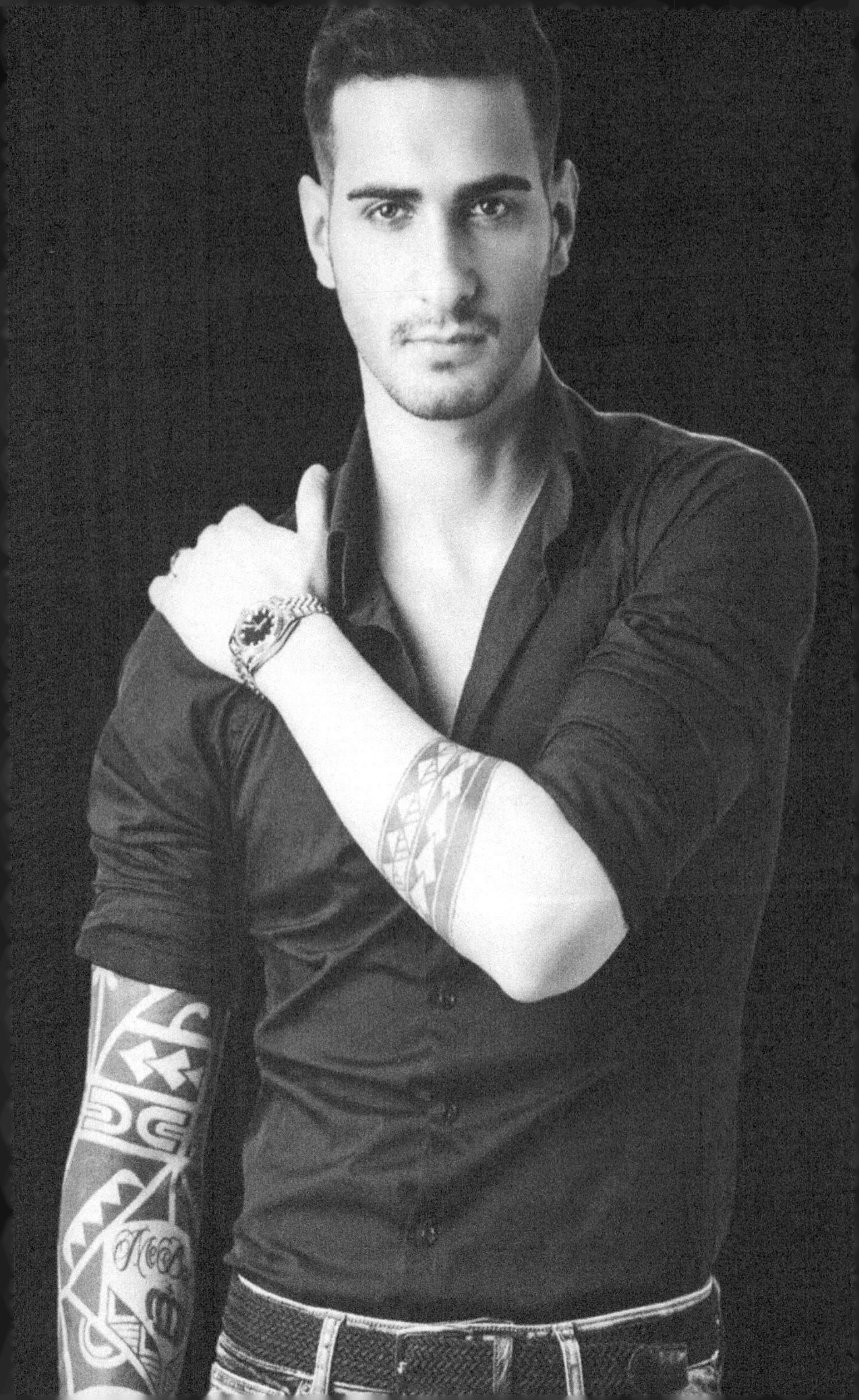

PROLOGUE

January Broadcast Message on all Dark Web Channels:

Iceman claims responsibility for the large-scale ransomware attack last week that brought financial markets to a halt, grounded airplanes, and darkened social media during the holiday season, igniting global outrage and panic not seen since the recent pandemic.

This stunt netted Iceman millions in ransom money.

Before any copycats sharpen their claws with opportunistic bad ideas, take note: the UN has created a new task force and will hold a symposium next week in Sydney, Australia.

It's Invite Only to top global firms and a few renowned, heavily vetted technical experts.

The goal? Not to find Iceman. He's a ghost and possibly a consortium of Iron Curtain hackers banding together to wreak havoc across the globe. They're probably pissed off from the incessant Artic weather, lack of female company, and raw fish.

It's rumored that the notorious and elite cyber sage known globally as Maverick—yes, the irony—will be walking among us next week under his alter-ego, whoever he may be.

Watch your backs, hackers.

Together, this global elite power unit will work to reverse-engineer the ransomware code and destroy Iceman's life's work, so citizens of the world can get one good night's sleep.

Until the next tragedy strikes.

See you Down Under…

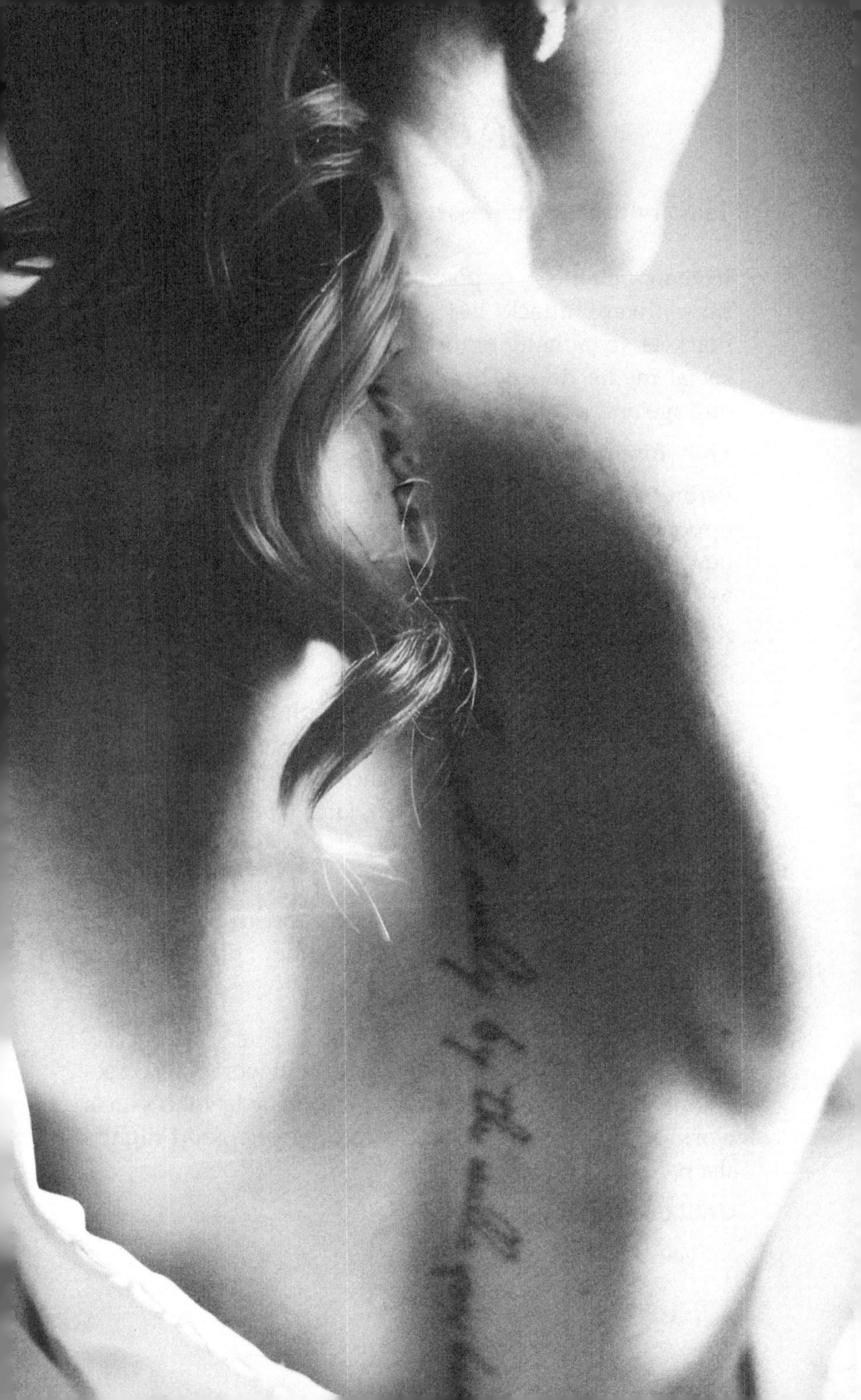

CHAPTER ONE

ELLA

"Excuse me." *Jerk*, I add on the inside to the entitled prick who set his duffle bag on my seat.

My first-class airline seat from Sydney to New York.

True, *I* didn't exactly pay for it. My father did.

Dad got delayed, so he sent me ahead. Alone. Tonight. Without notice. I came back to our apartment after a date and he had my suitcase packed and a car service waiting to whisk me to the airport.

My father has always been secretive. After years of circular answers, I stopped asking questions.

My original seat was a few rows back, where I had both seats to myself until the flight attendant asked me to move so the airline could upgrade a couple on their honeymoon. They'll probably get naughty for the thirteen-hour flight from Sydney to Los Angeles.

And I haven't had good sex in nearly two years.

My reassigned seat is currently occupied by Jerk's bag. Rude. Is the overhead compartment not good enough for him? So what if it's a quality leather duffel with a rich, earthy scent I can smell from the aisle?

That seat he's hogging probably costs seven grand.

After I clear my throat, the jerk looks up at me and pulls something out of one ear.

"What?" he snaps.

He's wearing dark horn-rimmed glasses that would make an ordinary man look like a geek. But this guy has sculpted cheekbones and the square jaw of a Hollywood heartthrob. Good Lord, did I score a seat next to Liam Hemsworth's body double?

Makes sense. We're about to depart Australia for Los Angeles. Following this long flight, I have a five-hour layover in L.A. before the final leg to New York. I'll be in the air for the better part of the next two days and I'm not in the mood.

"Your bag," I say, folding my arms.

"Yeah, it's *my* bag," he drawls in a sexy Irish accent that tingles my nether regions and erases Liam Hemsworth from my mind. "Can I get a glass of McCallan?"

I blink, ready to call him a jerk out loud when I realize he's mistaken my navy wrap dress for a flight attendant uniform. A dress and high heels aren't the most comfortable thing to wear for a twenty-hour flight, but I didn't have time to change.

"I don't work here. That's my seat." I point.

"Your seat?" The hot jerk's gaze cuts across my body in a stare I feel.

Panic swells in my chest that he's some hotshot who can pull rank and toss my ass in coach.

"Yes, mine." I jam my thumb behind me. "They moved me next to you to bump some newlyweds into first class."

Jerk makes a gagging noise.

"Is that reaction for sitting next to me, or the newlyweds?" I ask.

He rolls his eyes. "The newlyweds, and marriage in general."

A rich, handsome man who doesn't want to get married. How original.

The real airline attendant appears. "You need to take your seat, Miss."

"I'm trying." *This jackass won't let me.*

These insults are going audible next.

The jerk removes his glasses, and now, I'm staring at the most handsome man I've ever seen.

Figures. Most insanely good-looking men are jerks.

"This seat was supposed to be empty," he says, low and gravelly while yanking the bag away.

"I'll store that for you, sir," the attendant offers in a

purring kitten voice.

Clearly, she's noticed how stunning the man is, too. I bet that Irish accent opens a lot of legs.

Jerk scoffs a laugh. "I don't let women carry my luggage."

Smoothly, he rises from the oversized airline seat like a phoenix rising from the flames. Daunting. Impressive. Majestic.

My eyes follow him until he reaches his full height of what's got to be over six feet tall. The extended headroom on this ultra-jumbo jet designed for cross-global flights doesn't block his head.

The attendant leaves to assist another passenger, and I stare at the jerk lifting his bag. His red button-down shirt with an asymmetrical gray collar and matching turned-up sleeves hugs his torso and thick biceps.

"Excuse me," he says, trying to get into the aisle to put his bag in the adjacent closet situated between each set of rows.

I step back, agog as that deep voice seeps into my bones.

He gives me a once-over again, this time in a way that suggests he realizes my dress isn't a uniform.

His eyes flare and his jaw muscle jumps. "Can I put your bag away?"

I fist the handle of my ordinary carry-on, a Coach tote holding my laptop. "No, thank you. I have work to do." My palms sweat more with every flicker of those green eyes.

The attendant returns. "I need you to take your seat, Miss, or—"

"*Relax*," the jerk snaps at her.

I should probably stop referring to him as that.

"And I want my McCallan. *Now*."

I can tell by his tone—which isn't harsh, just insistent

with quiet power—that he's used to getting his way.

"Yes, sir." The flight attendant snaps to attention. "And you, Miss?"

"I would adore a glass of red wine."

I bend at the waist to tuck my bag in front of me, and when I look up, the man's eyes bore into mine.

He shuts the closet and says, "Would you like the window seat?"

Shocked that he'd care to offer, I shake my head. "No, thank you."

The idea of being confined and pinned into a tight space triggers me.

"If you change your mind." He swaggers back to his seat, his scent wrapping around me.

Spice, mint, and leather.

"Thank you." I finally plant my ass into the comfy seat of buttery-soft leather.

Settling in, I tuck my arm close so I don't hit his. But that's unnecessary because First Class seats are huge, while narrow coach seats are for making new friends.

Or enemies.

My body relaxes and melts into the luxuriously, overstuffed seat. Movement next to me yanks my attention toward my neighbor sliding those dark horn-rimmed glasses back on again. The Clark Kent/Henry Cavill vibes have me nearly sliding off my seat.

I sigh, and all movement next to me stops.

The sexy Irishman hits me with a volcanic expression.

I quirk an eyebrow. "Yes?"

"Is that how you sound when you come?" The honey-over-gravel thing is real.

Mixed with the brogue, I'm *ready* to come. But I blink at him, feigning outrage. "Excuse me?"

"You heard me." He takes more liberty with his once-over this time. "It's nice to see someone dressed up for a flight. The pajama look really grates on my nerves."

I pinch my skirt. "This trip was last minute. I was..."

Embarrassment floods me. On a date. A bad one. But bad dates with men I'll never see again are a thousand times better than what I went through with my ex.

"Anyway. How would I know how I sound?" God knows I haven't had an orgasm with a partner in years.

I get myself off, but it's pathetic to cry out masturbating. Although, Jerk here will flash into my mind next time and it might make me more vocal.

"Me, I love a screamer," he offers unsolicited. "Whimpering my name because you're so mindless with pleasure is my kink. Among other things."

Is this happening? I just met him. I don't know his name and we're discussing orgasms. And kinks!

"Wow," I laugh. "Before we continue this conversation, how about first telling me your name."

After a pensive stare, he says, "Balor."

Damn, that's a sexy name.

"Balor," I whisper, liking the way it rolls off my tongue. "Like valor."

"I don't mind the comparison." He smiles like I've pleased him somehow.

"Nice to meet you." I extend my hand but he makes no move to shake it.

"I don't...like people to touch me. Nothing personal."

I lower my hand. "None taken. Though doesn't no touching make sex hard? No pun intended." God, shut me up. Now!

"I manage." His wicked smile confirms he has absolutely no difficulty in the sex department.

"Anyway, my name is—"

"*Don't* want to know." His quick retort deflates me and the entire conversation ends abruptly.

Back to Jerk...

The captain makes his announcements, disappointing me with his flat American accent. Although, after six months in Sydney, listening to carbon copies of Hugh Jackman started to get old.

I'm glad to be going home and getting my life back on track. A new job awaits me and my best friends, Hannah and Val, are meeting me for brunch tomorrow. Or is it in two days? Crossing over the international date line confuses the heck out of me.

"Sorry, folks," the pilot comes back over the loudspeaker. "We're in for a long wait on the tarmac. I'd tell you how many planes are in front of us, but I can't count that high."

"At least he has a sense of humor," I say. "It must be obscenely high."

"Don't need obscene humor. I need to get the hell home." Jerk pulls out his phone, taps away, then slides it back into his pocket.

"This is the captain, again, folks. Strike my last transmission. We've been advanced to number two. Flight attendants, prepare for take-off."

Jerk closes his eyes and rests his head with a sly grin ghosting his full lips.

What the heck?

Who *is* this guy?

CHAPTER TWO
ELLA

Three hours later...

Despite the sexy come-on from Balor before take-off, he's not said another word to me.

Bummer.

His sleek silver laptop with a brand logo I've never seen sits on his tray table. His long, sexy fingers swipe across the stainless-steel keyboard like it's a piano and he's Marc-Andre Hamelin.

My laptop isn't high-end or fancy, but it works well enough to update my resumé with the special ed teaching I did in Sydney. I pray I can get my job back at Fredericks Elementary next fall. Especially after the mess I made.

When the laptop battery craps out, I dig into my bag and panic, realizing my charger is in my checked luggage.

I groan.

"There's that noise again," Irish guy mutters. "We have ten more hours to go."

"Did you say something?" I play dumb.

His fingers stop moving. "You heard me."

"Do you do this a lot? Openly proposition strange women on planes?"

"Did I proposition you?" He goes back to typing.

"It sounded implied."

"Implied doesn't count." He turns to me. "If I want to do something about those groans that are making me crazy, you'll know."

I glance around and wonder if the plane went down, and this is my version of heaven.

Yeah, let's go with that.

Being on an airplane provides one of the few breaks from modern life. Unless it's a private jet where rich people make calls like they're sitting in an office.

Commercial airline travel provides an escape.

"Am I? Making you crazy?" I ask playfully.

Annoying him is fun.

"Your fucking perfume is." Balor's blunt answer startles me.

"I'm not... I'm not wearing perfume."

His gaze swivels my way. "Then it's just how you smell that's got my blood moving in a different direction."

Oh my God. *My* blood just moved in a different direction.

Is he flirting with me? Or toying with me? Or maybe it's an honest-to-God pheromone thing.

"And you didn't answer my first question," I say. "Do you do this a lot? Hit on strange women on planes."

"No," he says firmly. "I'm usually on my private jet. Alone."

Now this makes sense. Unless he's some *Tinder Swindler*.

"And this jet, is it in the shop?"

He closes the laptop, his jaw tight. "Okay, butterfly. Let's talk."

"Butterfly?"

"Your wrist tattoo." His eyes lower to my left wrist.

"You caught that?" I pull down my sleeve with a ruffled cuff.

"I saw the roses on your ankle, too."

I glance down and notice the cut of my black leather slingbacks expose the three colorless blooming roses that start at my ankle and cross over the top of my foot.

"Seriously, why are you dressed so formally for such a long flight?" He keeps his attention on me.

"I was on a date." My downturned voice gets a look of sympathy.

"And?"

"The date ended. Then I got a call about a job and this

was the first flight available."

I'm purposely cagey since my father and I are both starting new jobs with the same company. Mine's an assistant gig he got for me. It's nearly impossible to get a full-time teaching job in the middle of the school year.

Balor frowns. "A job that pays well enough for a last-minute, first-class ticket from Sydney to New York?"

I hesitate to tell him my father picked up the tab. "Yes, sir."

A deep chuckle rumbles from his chest. "Don't call me sir. I *like* it."

I lean closer. "Are you... A *sir*?"

"I'm a man."

"Yes, that's obvious. I mean are you one of those Doms?" Thank you, *FSOG*–now every woman secretly wants one.

"No." He turns his head. "I don't have time to train subs."

Because there's so much sex in the D/s relationship, especially new ones, it's an arrangement that requires a serious time commitment.

"Too busy for a relationship, eh?"

His eyes flicker back to me. "Are you Canadian?"

"No."

"I thought you said 'aye.' That's what my brothers and I say when we mean yes. So, *aye*, I'm too busy for any kind of relationship or commitment. I use..."

Hookers? Escorts?

My core tightens as my nipples flare to life. I've heard of people hooking up after meeting on a plane. This could be my turn. Good Lord, an idea hits me.

He clears his throat. "Never mind."

"Oh, no. You need to finish that sentence. Because if you mean paid company..." I slink my hand toward him and stroke his forearm. "Whoa, what's this shirt made of?"

He cracks a real smile, finally. "It's Poplin. All my shirts are made with it."

"It feels amazing." I smooth his sleeve again, hypnotized by the softness and impressed he only wears custom shirts.

He stops me with his warm palm over mine. "I said, I don't like to be touched."

"Oops." I pull my hand back.

His lips say no, but his eyes sparkle with curiosity. "And if you touch a man like that, he might interpret that as consent."

"With a...woman like me, consent is irrelevant." Oh my God, did I just say that?

"A woman like you?" His eyes drink me in. "Butterfly, are you a..."

I bite my lip and choose my words very carefully. "I can be whatever you want me to be."

"Are you getting off in Los Angeles?" His gruff voice bottoms out.

"I am." My pulse thunders in my ears. "If you get me off there."

His face turns to granite, eyes blazing. "Where do you live?"

"New York City."

He frowns again. "And you were just on a...date in Sydney, Australia?"

I smile, swallowing nervously. "Yes, sir."

He leans into me and with an invisible barrier or propriety torn away, he says, "Did he come inside you?"

The immediate dampness between my legs startles me. A wave of arousal, something I've not felt in years, washes over me. It's like a rebirth and it hits hard, strong. After what I went through with my ex, I never thought I'd experience this spark again.

And damn it, I want more. It's the most alive I've felt in forever.

My thighs tense, my core tightens, and my nipples stiffen, the tender buds scraping against my lace bra. Fire simmers in my veins, igniting an insatiable longing I'm desperate to satisfy.

Unable to form words, I only shake my head, wondering how such an undeniable attraction can blossom so fast and powerful out of nowhere.

"Answer me, butterfly."

I shake my head.

"Why *not*?"

Shit… Can I keep going? Let this lead to a one-night stand that I really need *and* mix it with a hooker fantasy?

If my poor father only knew what he set me up for.

But I'm twenty-seven, and I love sex. Or I did before Wesley Brennan. It's been six months since he hurt me for the last time, and I'm finally beginning to feel like myself again.

This sexy stranger is the gasoline I need to get my flame roaring.

"He…didn't pay me enough."

"Jesus *fucking* Christ. How much…" Balor leans in.

"If you own a jet, I'm sure you can afford it."

"We can make use of that five-hour layover in Los Angeles," he utters. "In bed."

"Can you last five hours, sir?" I whisper.

"I can last. How do you feel about getting back on this plane limping and sore after what I'll do to you for five hours, butterfly?"

CHAPTER THREE

ELLA

I'm still shaking from his response and unable to form a comeback.

"Now sit there like a good girl with your legs crossed, so I can get some work done," Balor growls playfully.

"You realize that's another ten hours?" I yawn, already sleepy from the wine and the meal served shortly after take-off.

We're somewhere over the Pacific Ocean, in between time zones, but it's past midnight in Sydney.

"Right," Balor acknowledges. "I'll get some sleep eventually."

"I wouldn't leave that up for chance. You don't want to be tired when we land, especially if you want your money's worth."

He guffaws sharply. "Don't worry your pretty head. I'll have my money's worth."

"Okay, then, I'll just tire myself out."

"By making yourself come?" His brazen dirty talk spoken so effortlessly spikes adrenaline in my veins.

The captain lowered the cabin lights fifteen minutes ago. The seats are arranged on a diagonal, and to my left is a storage closet. It's as if the airline's interior designers knew what happens on these mega-long, transcontinental flights.

"I admit, when I'm tossing and turning, a good O helps me sleep."

"*Show me.*"

"Show you?"

"Show me what you do to yourself. Close your eyes."

Inhaling a deep breath, I let them slip closed.

I can't believe I'm doing this.

"Open your legs." His deep rasp burrows inside my

chest. "Are you wearing panties?"

"Yes, sir." I wonder if he'll snatch them off me and steal them.

"Reach under your dress."

Swallowing, I gather the skirt in my fist and glide my other hand up my thigh.

"Reaching," I whisper. I shaved my legs for a date that turned out to be a bust.

This is my reward.

"Touch yourself over the panty fabric, right in the center."

"Oh, God," I murmur, deep and sexy.

"How does it feel?"

"Warm. Wet."

"Fuck," he whispers into my ear. "Slip your fingers inside the top."

I've read how men love pulling a woman's panty to the side and sliding inside. Interesting how he likes the idea of me getting myself off by reaching inside my panty.

"Yeah," I moan on an exhale.

"Finger yourself. Is your clit hard?"

I never thought of my clit in terms of being hard but holy shit. "It is."

"You sound surprised."

"I never noticed it before." I swallow roughly. "Or it's hard just for you."

When I tip my head closer to gaze into his deep green eyes, he gently nudges my chin away. "Too close," he rasps.

That should turn me off, but it has the opposite effect. It feeds into the fantasy.

I want to hear him say my name, but it's best we keep this anonymous. He sleeps with escorts, and unless I want a side gig hooking, I won't be seeing him again.

"Play with your clit, butterfly," he says with a little

more force.

"Do you like fingering yourself?"

"Mmm, especially when I need to wet my clit."

"Fucking, aye." His sexy groan greets my breathy gasps.

"That accent of yours makes me wet."

"Christ, you look so sexy, playing with your cunt. Are you close, butterfly?"

"So close. Keep talking that dirty talk. Tell me what you want to do to me."

"Be a good girl and make yourself come with those sexy fingers. I need the taste of your cunt to be *your juices* when my tongue buries between your legs. Not the man you fucked earlier. You're mine now. I want to hear you moan when I sink my cock inside you and stretch you."

"Oh, God…"

"Are you coming?"

"Right there. Tell me… Tell me how you want me to come."

"I want you to come on my face, then I'm going flip you over and sink my dick inside your quivering cunt. Make you come again with my fingers in your ass and feel that tight, wet pussy squeeze my dick so hard. Christ, it will feel so incredible strangling all the cum right out of me."

I whimper as my clit pulses harder than I think it ever has. "Finger in the ass. I want that."

"Not just my finger, butterfly. You'll take my cock there, too. And fucking love every inch."

CHAPTER FOUR
ELLA

After the explosive orgasm, I remove my hand from under my skirt.

"Taste yourself," my narrator growls before I have a chance to wipe my fingers on a left-over dinner napkin.

"Maybe you'd like to taste me." I wiggle my damp fingers close to his lips. "Oh, right. You have that no-touching thing."

"Excuse me," he says, leaving his seat.

The door to the first-class passenger bathroom closes and locks with a click.

I picture him in there, beating off. Smiling, I sigh, exhausted from the tension slowly leaving my body as blessed sleep claims me.

When I wake, I have no idea where the hell in the world we are, but a quick look out the plane window shows water as far as the eye can see. We're still somewhere over the Pacific Ocean.

We took off at nine-twenty-five p.m., Sydney time with a scheduled arrival in Los Angeles at five p.m. My connecting flight is a red-eye to New York.

I wonder how many brain cells I'm destroying with all this recycled air.

The attendant graces me with a platter of food placed on the tray table that pops out from the side of the seat.

Clearing my throat, I say, "I didn't order anything."

"I ordered for us," the voice next to me pipes up.

Balor appears rested, with a fresh shave and shaggy hair perfectly styled. Horrified at how ravaged I must look, I curl up under the blanket someone put over me.

The attendant hands over the same tray of food and he takes it.

"What did you order for us?" The covered dishes entice

me to sit up.

"Belgian Waffles with all the works."

"Ooh." I sit up fully and grab my utensils. "What the hell time is it?"

"That's irrelevant since whatever the hell time it is will change in a second at the speed we're flying."

"Are you some kind of engineer?"

"Close, I went to MIT." He easily reveals that tidbit but recoils like he didn't mean for it to slip.

I lay a hand on his arm. "Don't worry. I really don't give a shit where you went to school or what you do for a living or that you can afford a jet and these glorious custom shirts."

He narrows his eyes on my hand, but with a lip quiver, he ignores it. Gifting me with a smile, he says, "I like how you think. Now eat."

"Is that a command?"

"Aye." He lifts his silver dome cover.

Breathing in the warm cinnamon aroma, I can come again. And the exquisite presentation makes it so picture-perfect, I almost don't want to touch anything. Almost. It's hard to believe that people line up to make those cheap waffles for breakfast in hotels.

Two thick and crispy waffles sit stacked on a plate surrounded by dainty silver containers filled with whipped cream, mixed fruit, syrup, and powdered sugar.

Thank you, Daddy.

For sending me ahead *and* buying me this first-class ticket. Otherwise, I'd have never met this guy who dirty talked me into an amazing orgasm and ordered me waffles the next morning.

This feels like a date. The kind I've always dreamt about.

"I'll be right back." I unbuckle myself and smooth my dress.

"Where are you going?" he asks with a sharp alarm in his tone.

I halt, slipping my shoes back on. "To the bathroom to freshen up."

"You look fucking gorgeous. Eat first."

"Are you always so bossy with your dates?"

A forkful of waffles layered with each of the toppings stops right at his gorgeous mouth. "*This* is not a date."

"Too bad, because you'd certainly be getting lucky."

"I will be getting lucky in about two hours."

"I'm getting lucky right now." I grab the top waffle, take a bite, and sigh at the warm crunchy texture.

That earns me a stifled laugh. "Not to be rude, but how much do you charge that you can afford a last-minute first-class ticket from Australia to New York?"

I nervously play with the whipped cream. Charge. Money. To sleep with him. Right.

I'm a better liar than I thought. He really believes I'm a hooker. It's tempting to tell him no charge, but that could turn him off. He could think there are strings attached.

But I have no idea what a hooker who can afford first-class air travel charges for a five-hour fuck. *Pretty Woman* plays in my head. She asked for three grand for five days or something like that. But those were 1980's dollars.

"Considering I'm off the clock, so to speak, and it's all gravy, let's say one thousand dollars an hour?"

He coughs into his juice. "That's it?"

"You'll be paying for the room?"

"Aye."

"And the transportation to and from the hotel?"

A bushy eyebrow lowers. "Is this some kind of volume discount?"

"Exactly." My stomach unclenches. "I don't usually stay more than two hours with a...client. Five hours..."

"Five hours of unbridling fucking? Still one thousand

an hour?" he says, pursing his lips dabbed with left-over sugar I want to lick off his mouth.

"Uh-huh." I lean in, but he snaps back.

"What are you doing?" His sharp tone startles me.

"You have a smidge of sugar on your mouth." I point. "I wanted to clean you off."

He exhales and wipes his own mouth with a fancy napkin. This no-touching thing is real.

"Terms and conditions, butterfly."

Narrowing my eyes, I return to my waffles. "Go ahead."

"Once we're in the room, and I'm a paying client, I touch you. You don't touch me. Except your mouth on my dick. No kissing."

I want to argue that the arrangement sounds odd and pretty cold, but he thinks I'm an escort. "Okay. Anything else?"

"I come anywhere on your body I want. I take you on your hands and knees. No face to face." He leans in closer. "And I'll pay you ten grand."

CHAPTER FIVE

ELLA

We land in Los Angeles, and it feels good to move my legs again. I'm warm and tingly, anticipating five hours of mind-blowing sex with the gorgeous mysterious man hovering behind me while we wait to get the hell off this plane.

But if anything can kill a sex buzz, it's deplaning and elbowing your way through a crowded airport terminal.

First-class passengers leave first, but that means shit once you're off the plane. Balor, who still hasn't offered me anything past his first name or asked for mine, steers me forward with his hand on the small of my back.

I touch you. You don't touch me.

With mirrored shades on, he speaks low into his phone and next, an agent escorts us to an express lane in LAX customs.

We whisk through in record time and step outside the airport where a sleek, black limo awaits.

Balor opens the door for me but before I can get in, he puts an arm out to stop me. "We're clear about what will happen when we reach the hotel?"

"Absolutely," I say, hiding my nervousness.

"You understand I'll be paying you for your company? This isn't a date."

Sleeping with me is a business transaction, and he's making sure to not give me the impression that he's swept away with emotion or excitement.

I flick my gaze at the mirrored lenses, aiming to look him directly in the eye. "Will that make you fuck me harder?"

"Get in," he growls.

I've only been in a stretch limo once for prom with eight other kids. I duck inside and scoot across the rear bench closer to the other door.

Anticipation flickers in my chest. And foolishness, when Balor lowers into the bench seat smooth as a panther.

He closes the door himself and glances around looking for me. "There you are." His low drawl sets the tone, his intention clear.

"Here I am." If this *were* a date, I would expect to be kissed.

Looking at those lips, I'm tempted to knock a few hundred, or heck, a thousand off my fee, if he would agree to it.

"Lean against the door and spread your legs." When I hesitate, his eyes darken. "Problem?"

"No. I thought we'd wait until we reached the hotel."

"We only have a few hours, and the things I want to do to you can take days. Now open your legs. I want to taste you."

I glance at the raised partition between us then lift my leg. Balor grabs my foot to direct my leg to the back of the bench seat. When I'm open wide to him, he kneels on the floor between my thighs. I emit a quick squeal of surprise when his warm hands sear the skin of my thighs as he yanks me towards him, tipping my hips provocatively.

With a quick flick of his wrist, he tears off my panties.

"These stay off and you're not getting them back." He burrows his nose into the lace fabric and inhales deeply. "Fucking sexy."

"Keeping the panties costs more." I wiggle, getting even more wet watching him.

"Looks like I'm starting a tab." He stows the panties in the inner pocket of his jacket. "Just so we're clear. You and this cunt are mine until we reach New York. I'm the only one touching you until then."

As if I'd turn tricks in the airline bathroom.

"Touching?"

"You're being a brat," he says through clenched teeth. "I like that."

Without another word, he lowers his face to my sex and runs his tongue along the entire length.

"Oh, God." I grip the back of the seat.

"I'll make you scream so loud he just might hear you." He grips my ass hard and goes at me with his tongue. His pace is unrelenting, devouring me like I'm the first or last pussy he'll ever lick. "Fuck. This cunt tastes sinful."

The flicking of his tongue against my clit has me dazed, but I jump when he slides a finger inside me.

"Yes, right there," I whimper.

"Christ, this is tight. Who the hell are you fucking?" He works me with one finger, then two. "I need you to come. I want you dripping down your thigh when I throw you onto the bed."

With his fingers pumping in and out of me, it takes just a few more sucks and licks before I feel the beginnings of an orgasm.

My muscles throb, and knowing I can't cry out like I want to, I grab his head instead, my nails gently grazing against his scalp. "That's so good."

"Jesus," he groans, ignoring that I grabbed him. "I can't wait to feel this tight cunt pulse around my cock."

He licks me through my powerful orgasm. I spread my legs wider, and let him continue to feast on me.

The limo stops and Balor looks up, his chin shiny with my arousal.

"Good timing." He roughly tugs down my skirt. "You're mine. No one fucking sees what's mine. I like that you don't dress like a cheap whore. You're classy. I *really* like that."

"I like that you like it." I sit up and try to gather my sanity.

Coming in hot, he brushes his lips against my ear. "Tell me you're mine."

"I'm yours."

"Now close those fucking legs."

The dirty talk and rough demands get me excited all over again.

The limo door opens, and I tug my skirt out of my ass crack. The driver leers at me and irritation spreads across Balor's face. Surprisingly, he doesn't give the driver shit.

He's clearly wealthy and no stranger to limo drivers, but I appreciate how he keeps his cool.

In the lobby, Balor flags down a woman in a uniform holding an iPad and wearing a headset.

"Wait right here. Do not move," he commands me.

I suspect he doesn't want me to overhear his last name.

He slips the horn-rimmed glasses back on, and the woman clutches her chest as she checks Balor in. After a few nods, he signs the iPad with a stylus and she hands him keycards.

She motions left, but he crooks a finger toward me first.

I feel judged when the woman eyes me, and for the first time, I don't like this game we're playing. But Balor and I still have to sit next to each other for the long flight to New York. Backing out would make it a horribly awkward slog across the country.

I dismiss the look and square my shoulders. I've already come this far and I want, no need, this sexy man to fuck me.

As I move toward Balor, I decide I don't care about the money. I don't intend to take it. The next few hours will get me over an emotional hurdle.

This fantasy is what I need to start a new chapter of my life after what I went through with my ex. A chapter where I'm not afraid of a man touching me.

We get into the elevator and he cages me against the

wall. His hands stay on the satin wood and not me. His green eyes give meaning to the word emerald.

When I look away, he barks, "Eyes on me."

I flick my gaze back to meet his, a twinge of exhaustion flooding me. But I hide it.

"Who do you belong to?" he whispers.

"You."

"Who *owns* you?"

"You." My thighs clench at his visceral tone.

"You, what?"

"You, sir," I purr.

The elevator door opens and he gestures for me to step out first. He carries both his duffle and my bag with one hand and takes my hand with the other. It's a surprising gesture that feels instinctive. The sensation of his warm palm intimately brushing against mine startles me.

He keys into a room at the end of the hall. My jaw drops, taking in a luxury suite.

"Go into the bedroom, get naked, and lay face down on the bed." Balor tosses our bags on the living room sofa.

Right, he only takes women from behind. Picturing getting railed that way heats me all over.

I flick the ties on my wrap dress, taking in his fiery gaze. "Repeat that?"

"Brats get fucked harder."

With my dress open, I hold back a smile, twirl the tie, and dance into the bedroom saying, "Promise?"

Inside, I don't get anywhere near the bed, when Balor comes up behind me, roughly pulling the dress off. The fabric turns into a makeshift rope, which he uses to bind my hands together.

"Remember the rules, I touch you," he whispers to me from behind. "You don't touch me. You touched my head in the limo. I let that slide."

"I like touching you. And you liked it, too. Don't be

so…" I push my ass into his groin, startled at the thick pipe in his pants. "Rigid."

"I like you. Okay. I'll play your game." He shucks the dress away and closes his hands around my waist. "Put your arms up and back around my neck."

I reach behind and grip his shoulders as I grind some more against his erection. Good Lord, the size of it.

"I want you naked." He unclasps my bra and tosses it across the room.

I'm completely naked. And he's fully dressed.

That's when things get crazy…

CHAPTER SIX
ELLA

I'm sure the hotel bed is luxuriously expensive, but it's the last thing I have time to notice as I get railed senseless by a sexy, brutish stranger who won't let me touch him.

"Take my cock into this greedy cunt of yours. Fuck, you take me so deep." Up on my hands and knees, he pushes in and out of me with a steady rhythm even as his knuckles caress my spine. "I've never felt anything like this cunt wrapped around my dick."

I've lost track of time and space and days...

Just as he promised on the plane, he plows me like there's no tomorrow, and for me, there isn't. Just this crazed euphoria where I've lowered my inhibitions and my walls. All I want is to absorb his unbridled energy.

Warmth tingles down my spine and my core tightens until it's throbbing out of control.

"Aye, come with my cock inside you. Who's making you come?"

"You." Panting and drooling, I drop facedown into the bed cover and arch my back.

The movement pops my ass higher and makes him swear. "Fuck. You're gonna make me come so hard and spill so much cum inside you." He leans forward, his chest against my back, his taut pecs slick. Or is that dampness? "Jesus fucking Christ, I never do this. But I have to really feel this cunt. How much extra to take you bare? I have to come inside you. *How much?*"

Are those even menu items? "Um."

"I'm clean, baby. So fucking clean. How much to fuck you raw?"

"It's so good. I don't care," I grunt. "Just do it!"

He wrenches out of me, my arousal dripping down the back of my thighs. I'm impatient with need, although it's only a moment before he thrusts back inside.

"Oh my God, are you bigger?" I moan.

"I am now. Fuck, I'm gonna lose it. Chriiiiist," he groans and starts pulsing inside me.

Feeling a gush of warm liquid fill me, reality clears the sex fog. What the hell am I doing? I'm out of my mind. I'm not even on birth control!

"Take every bleedin' inch of my cock," Balor grunts with each hard thrust. "Damn you, it's too good."

When he collapses against my back, his heart hammers so hard I feel it.

"My God, you're a..."

I wait to hear slut. "I'm a what? Say it." Distress fills me, waiting to be called something awful because that's how I feel right now.

"A fucking angel." He peppers my back with kisses.

Relief washes through me. I twist around, wanting to hug him. Just to say thank you. But he backs away.

Hiding my disappointment, I roll over and close my legs.

Balor barks at me, "Show me."

"Show you?"

"Show me what I did to you." He motions for me to spread my legs.

As soon as I comply, he dives forward and licks me clean with such voracity, I come again from the sheer dirtiness.

"Good girl," he mutters and then sits back. "Jesus, you're amazing."

Me? He could be a model carved from marble with that chest and those abs of utter perfection.

"I'm glad you think so." My eyes stray to Balor's body. Too many shadows. I roll over and flick on a lamp. "I have to see you better."

He stands up stark naked, breathing heavily, gazing at

me with wicked thoughts written all over his gorgeous face.

He pauses as I look him over. Each arm has dark, banded tattoos that I know hurt. "Like what you see, aye?"

"You have no idea." I sit up and pull a pillow in front of me, feeling not so perfect. But few women can achieve the cut look I'm staring at.

He doesn't seem interested in my body other than my pussy. And that's fine by me.

"Are those washboard abs from a few hundred sits-up a day? Or smoothies?"

He laughs. "I have a martial arts training regimen."

"Ahhh." I take a deep breath as he holds my gaze. "Are we done?"

"Not even close." He stretches, giving me a show I'll never forget. "Get into the shower, butterfly, so I can fuck your ass."

***

Three hours later...

"I ordered room service," Balor says, pulling up his pants over his still-swollen dick.

"You ordered me breakfast without my input." I wobble from the bathroom in the softest robe, ever. "Now you chose dinner for me? I'll knock a grand off if I can get a say for one damn meal."

"You don't like bacon cheeseburgers?"

My stomach growls loudly, and I clear my throat trying to cover it.

I plop onto the bed of tangled sheets as I wait for my heart to stop pounding after the incredible sex we just had in the shower and then the gigantic bathtub with jets. "You got me pegged."

His jaw ticks at that word. "Most people love cheeseburgers."

"You?"

"I don't eat red meat."

"You don't know what you're missing."

A loud knock at the suite door startles me and I sit up.

"Get dressed, take your time. I'll take care of the food."

Ugh, I have to put that damn dress back on. It's been how many hours? I lost track.

I have extra panties in my carry-on, but I skip them in case Balor wants access to me. I'm thinking he's not done with me. We have another five hours on our flight to New York.

I brush my teeth, and using the hairdryer, I tousle my long auburn waves, then fix my makeup. What's left of it.

Dressed and reinvigorated, but sans panties, I stroll into the suite's main room, alarmed to see a strange man standing there.

"Um, hello. Who are you?" I blink, wondering if I missed something.

"Name's Trace." His Irish brogue sounds deeper, sultrier but he's just as striking as Balor.

"Oh... Kay... Where's—" I flush with embarrassment, thinking the mysterious stranger who fucked me for five hours straight probably gave me a fake name.

"He had to leave."

"Oh? Will he be back?"

"He's taking his jet back to New York."

Trace's words slice through me. Balor *left* me here. And didn't say goodbye. Man, that...hurts.

I recall him saying he had a jet. Guess he wasn't lying.

Panic swells in my chest as I check the time. The plane takes off in about an hour, but thankfully I'm only five minutes from the airport. My bags are already checked for the flight, and FAA regulations won't let them take off if my ass isn't in a seat.

I just hope Balor or whatever his name is didn't stiff me

with the hotel bill.

"Something came up and he's needed back in New York straightaway." Trace holds out an envelope. "He sends his apologies."

I look down at it but don't take it from him. It's probably the ten grand Balor offered to pay me even though I asked for five.

Glancing at the room service cart, I notice only one dome, nerves rattling through me.

He planned this.

He only ordered food for me. I was hungry earlier, but now I don't think I can eat.

"I saw him twenty minutes ago. Why didn't he just tell me himself?"

"Like I said, lass. Something came up."

"Lass?"

"An expression. An endearment."

"And my...friend. He's your..."

"Boss."

"Are you a bodyguard?"

His cheek ticks. "Not for long."

Bingo.

"What are you, six-four?"

"Six-five."

"Were you on the plane?" There's no way I'd miss *this* guy.

Trace looks around and considers if I'm worth an answer. He thinks I'm an escort.

"No. I had to do security for his sister." He clears his throat, like something caught in it. "A team in Sydney guarded Mr..."

I wave him off, lightheaded at this point and not sure if I care to peel any more layers from this embarrassment.

"Thank you for the message. You can...leave." I shake my head and lift the dome, amazed at how good that cheeseburger looks. There're even French fries cooked to a golden-brown perfection, wrapped up in a steel cone, with a slice of cheesecake on the side.

Trace waves the envelope. "Are you taking this, lass?"

I scoff. "By all means, leave it on the dresser."

This part of being a whore isn't fun.

"I'd feel better if you took it. Can't have any misunderstanding."

"Fine." I step forward and finger the envelope, the thickness messing with my head.

I look up to say something, but Trace is gone, the front door clicking shut behind him.

Sitting with my goodbye hamburger, I take a bite. "Jesus, that's good."

But it's also huge. Not that my mouth has any trouble accommodating huge things shoved in it anymore.

Why did I hope sex with Balor, or whoever he is, meant something?

He stuck to his T's and C's. And I did, too. No kissing. No face-to-face. In the shower, he plowed into my ass with my face against the wet tiles. It was the best thing I've ever felt.

I eat until I'm full then gather my things to leave.

In the lobby, a concierge manager waves me over. "Miss?"

Oh my God, Balor didn't pay for the room, and I don't know his name. I'm also carrying an envelope of cash in my purse.

I'm guilty of a real crime. He *paid* me for sex. I could get arrested.

"Yes?"

"A car to the airport has been arranged for you. It's right outside," the woman says.

I relax. For a second. "Thank you. And the suite?"

"Taken care of."

"Tip?"

"Also taken care of."

My heart feels like an anvil and my throat catches. "I'm not a... You know. We were on a flight together from Sydney. He was charming. I was just living out a fantasy."

"We don't ask questions of our guests."

"Can you tell me Balor's last name?" I ask, feeling like an idiot.

Her eyes flicker, signaling I had the right first name, but she also looks shocked that he gave it to me. "Sorry."

Swallowing, I nod. "Thank you. And I mean it. I'm not a paid...you know what. I'm a teacher. I was living in Sydney, working with special needs children and..."

When her eyes glaze over from disinterest, I shut up.

"Your car, Miss."

I glance outside and see a shiny limo waiting. "Thank you."

As the black stretch pulls away from the hotel, I sneak a look in that envelope. My breath leaves me when I count hundred after hundred. This has to be at least *twenty* grand.

Twenty-freaking-thousand dollars.

But no note. No thank you. No it was nice knowing you. Or fucking you.

The ride back to the airport is quick, and my thoughts blank out as I go through all the steps until I'm in a first-class seat again. Even if Balor hadn't dumped me, there was no guarantee we'd be sitting together again. Although, if he had the power to move us up in the take-off line as he did in Sydney, he could get his seat moved. Or mine.

When a shadow drapes over me, my spirits lift, thinking it's him. He changed his mind. It was some kind of test to see if I got all clingy or started crying.

"I got the window," says a voice with no accent, and it

feels like acid dripped on my skin.
　Hope. Smashed.
　"Sure." I tuck my legs, the row tighter on this plane.
　A portly man in a tracksuit sits next to me.
　I should have bought that seat for an imaginary dog with all this extra money.

CHAPTER SEVEN
ELLA

Under a sharp winter sun and during brunch at my favorite Upper West Side bistro the following day, I give my best friends a rundown of my Trans-Continental activities with a hot stranger. Capping off with the fat wad of cash his *bodyguard* left me.

"You did what?" Hannah blurts.

"*How* much?" Val's eyes widen.

"Was the sex any good?" Hannah doesn't wait for me to answer questions one and two, just starts firing off more.

"You could have been killed," Val scoffs.

Funny, I hadn't considered for a moment that Balor would hurt me. Living with an abusive boyfriend taught me all the signs. Balor exhibited none of them.

"Well, I survived, and since I'm sort of rich right now, brunch is on me, girls. Cheers!" I lift my mimosa and clink the glass to each of theirs. "Besides, I can step off the curb and get hit by a bus."

"Have you heard from Wesley since you've been back?" Val asks, making the sick connection from getting hit by a bus to my abusive ex.

Or she drew the short straw.

"No." I shake my head.

I'd met a handsome cop in Times Square on New Year's Eve, just over one year ago. But on Valentine's Day, Wesley didn't give me a box of chocolate, he gave me a black eye—the first of many—for coming home late.

It was followed by a sincere, emotional apology.

I took the route of forgiving and being supportive, especially when he admitted to a drinking problem and promised to go to meetings.

He whisked me away on a romantic weekend in

Vermont, but when we got back, everything I owned was moved out of the apartment I shared with Hannah and into Wesley's house.

The committed gesture threw me off since we'd only started dating. But I bought into the ruse. Every bit of it. I believed every word. I stupidly thought I was in love. His parents were dead and he had no family. I wanted to help him. I knew being a cop was difficult. Having the strength to take what he dished out from the stress of police work made me feel like I was helping him do his job better.

I thought of my mother and how she sacrificed so much to help people in a dangerous country.

Things were good with Wes for about…two weeks after I moved in with him.

He kept drinking and started cutting me with a knife, branding me as his.

"Now who will want you?"

Every ugly incident was followed by apology after empty apology.

Trapped in his world, I lived in fear every day and considered how to escape. How to tell someone. How to ask for help. I worried that with him being a cop, no one would believe me. Conventional ideas got tossed out the window.

I lost my job teaching special ed at a private school after missing so much work. That plunged me into a pattern of co-dependency.

Because I usually had a black eye, swollen lip, or a slight limp, I kept my distance from my father all those months. If Dad saw the bruises, he'd strangle Wes. Or bankrupt him by using his cyber skills to hack into Wesley's accounts. Dad's side programming gigs always sounded downright shady, and I was afraid that Wesley's retribution would reign down not just on me, but Dad, too.

When my father mentioned his company was sending him to Sydney for a six-month assignment, I saw the chance to save myself. I packed a small bag, showed up at his apartment with a busted lip, and begged him to take me with him.

He wanted to kill Wes, but Dad knew better than to mess with a cop. You mess with one, you mess with them all. My father's dark secrets in the wrong hands would hurt him.

It pained him to have to protect his sketchy life over my well-being. But I understood. Going after Wesley was a lose/lose decision.

Six months in Sydney helped me recover, and toward the end of our stay, I gave dating another try. That bad date had soured my mood, but being all dressed up on the plane led to Balor noticing me. And talking to me. Even if he mistook me for an escort. He gave me the greatest night of my life.

Not only hadn't I been afraid, but my mind also opened to the unbelievable pleasure I could receive from a man's hand without the fear of pain.

Now I have all this extra cash to throw around, but I don't have to worry about rent. Not that freeloading is my brand. Having nowhere else to live here in New York, I agreed to move into Dad's luxury apartment in Midtown Manhattan. He thinks I'm broke. I can't explain where my sudden wealth came from. Plus, I don't feel comfortable living alone yet.

Even as a cop, Wes can flash his badge and tin his way into any building. I feel safer living in a high-rise with top-notch security and an intercom system to give me a heads up.

But I can't be afraid of my ex forever. I'm not his girlfriend anymore. It's not a he said/she said domestic dispute. I'm a civilian. And if he bothers me again, I won't hold back reporting him this time.

I doubt he'll go near me. I kept my phone, my socials, and my email. There's been no messages. It's like he disappeared. Wes doesn't use social media. Most cops don't—to avoid retaliation.

Except for an email he uses for work, he's nearly off the grid.

"Are you going back to Fredricks Elementary?" Hannah asks, knocking me out of my thoughts.

"They filled my spot again. I can apply in a few months for the next school year. My dad got me an assistant job with his new boss." I stick my tongue out to signal my distaste for the pity position and working for some hot-shot data security manager as his assistant.

"Your dad got a new job?" Hannah asks.

"A week before we left Sydney, he dropped a bombshell on me," I say, pushing the quiche around on my plate. "He quit his job at World Trade Bank and got hired by a private company here in New York. Said his new boss recruited him at a technical conference he went to about the global outage right before Christmas."

"That outage was unreal," Val says, clutching her phone.

"I know."

"A new job will keep you busy." Hannah smiles.

I can't move back in with her since she lives in an unmanned building, and Wes knows Hannah still lives there. I would never put her in danger.

"When do you start?" she adds.

"Next week when Dad gets back." I exhale.

"It won't be that bad," Val says.

"Easy for you to say, you bake cookies out of your apartment, taste test your products, *and* make a killing."

The girls keep talking, but I begin getting stressed about where to deposit the money Balor gave me. I heard banks track transactions over ten thousand.

I'll have to open several accounts, or keep several thousand tucked away in my bedroom. Who knew having money could be this exhausting? Thinking about the money leads me back to thinking about Balor.

God, I can't get him out of my head. I'm considering asking my father to do a little hacking to find out Balor's last name from his Sydney to L.A. flight info. I just haven't come up with a reason why I need to know the name of some random guy who sat next to me on the plane.

Since Wes, he's been very protective of me.

If Dad finds out Balor mistook me for a hooker and then left me in a hotel, my father would destroy him with a single keystroke.

CHAPTER EIGHT
BALOR

Several blaring alarms rouse me from sleep. Since the flight from Sydney, my sleeping has been so fucked up again and I feel like a truck hit me in the middle of the night. I've needed two alarm clocks and both phones, regular and burner, to wake my ass up every morning.

I'm tempted to just send them all against a wall to shut the hell up, but then I realize it's Thursday.

Fuck.

Moments later, my regular cell phone rings, and I grouse at the caller.

"Aye, Trace," I answer. "I'll be down in a few minutes."

Although after I shower, masturbate, and figure out what to wear, it will be closer to forty minutes.

But Trace works for me and doesn't give a shit how late we are.

Forty minutes later on the dot, Trace Quinlan arrives at my townhouse in Downtown Astoria to drive me in my new Rivian, a state-of-the-art and expensive-as-fuck electric SUV, to the weekly meeting with my brothers.

Now that I'm awake, I'm teeming with energy over the devious plan I nailed, but I have to keep it to myself right now. Kieran, my oldest brother and the head of our family, will have me committed.

I hired Corvin Snow—aka Iceman—the cyber-terrorist responsible for the biggest global hack in decades, the one that shut the world down a few days before Christmas.

When our credit cards stopped working and we briefly lost access to funds right before Christmas, I mentioned Iceman in a fit of fury. I don't think my brothers will connect the name Snow to Iceman. They'll just think Snow's another Russian hacker I found behind the old Iron Curtain.

As the Chief Technology Officer for World Trade Bank, Snow showed up to the cyber conference in Sydney last week. The exclusive event brought the best tech talent from all over the globe to deal with *his* massive ransomware outage.

He waltzed around like a rockstar. All while hiding his true identity.

I'm keeping Snow a secret from my brothers until I find a way to hack *his* private databases and grab the ransomware virus code for myself.

That's too sweet of a weapon to pass up. Not that I would use it to hurt innocent people the way Snow did. But something that powerful will come in handy one day, considering I work for the mob.

I admire Snow's talent and his balls. Iceman is good, but I'm better. I just don't have a death wish to blow up the world.

I could not believe Corvin Snow's gall to walk so casually among people he fucked over. My team unmasked him before I got to Australia. I never would have gone to that conference, but I knew Snow released the ransomware and that he'd be there.

Other companies at the conference went on a recruiting frenzy that week given how they were hit. But I walked away with the brass ring. Corvin Snow is now the Lead Project Developer for O'Rourke Technologies, a startup LLC my brother Eoghan, our consigliere, created for my new business venture.

Weapons.

"Damn, it," I grumble, remembering I have to get one of Eoghan's HR paralegals to send Snow all the paperwork he needs to fill out in order to work for us.

No one tried to recruit *me* at the conference. I'm locked into this life with my brothers and no amount of money, perks, or vacation time, of which I get very little, will lure me away.

I'm pretty sure Lachlan, our psycho enforcer, would kill me if I tried to work for someone else. Even if I am his brother.

Divona, my childhood home, comes into view, and for the first time in years, I get a prickly feeling as a raw memory of my da hits me out of nowhere. Where the hell did that come from?

It's like my walls have crumpled, but why?

The iron gates open when the guards see Trace and we climb the long driveway with pink trees and wavy beds of pink and white Chrysanthemums on both sides.

The Rivian stops and I hop out, confidently pushing the kitchen door open even though I don't live here anymore. Kieran used to take meetings out of his high-rise office, but after marrying Isabella, the Italian princess who gave him two sons, he does our weekly family meetings from Da's old office.

I greet Patricia, Kieran's house manager, and sit my ass in his office where I wait another fifteen minutes alone. I have sleeping problems, and yet I'm the first one here.

"Fucking autocorrect keeps changing pussy to puppy." Lachlan wanders into the office, typing on his phone and bumping into shit.

Lach is six-six, and I'd bet on a bull in a china shop to make less of a mess than he is right now.

"What are you texting?" I ask him, kicking chairs out of his way.

Shaking his head, he shows me his phone.

I want to kick your puppy.

"Whose *pussy* do you want to kick?" I ask, afraid of the answer.

"What?" He snaps up, then looks back at his phone, grumbling. Steam coming out of his ears, really. "I meant kiss."

"Please tell me that's Katya." I rub my temples, but I really don't care to think about any of my brothers' poor wives getting railed.

"Who the fuck else's puppy would I want to kick?" he laughs, typing into his phone again.

His wife Katya is pregnant, and Lach is the worst expectant father I've ever seen. And I've seen some doozies since Kieran and Riordan both have wee-ones now. They turned feral protecting their wives the further they were into their pregnancies.

Kieran and Riordan finally stroll into the office, tension humming from them.

"What's up?" I ask.

"It's official. Griffin, Connor, and Shane are leaving us," Riordan announces, his tone tight. "We just got off the phone with Ewan."

It's the end of an era. For the first time in almost fifteen years, a Quinlan won't be working for an O'Rourke. Their oldest brother, Ewan, was one of our da's hitmen back in the day.

I should feign surprise, but they'd kick my ass if I didn't know that the Quinlans will soon be working for the Greek mafia in Manhattan.

"Shane will be missed," I say. "He helped us out of several jams the last couple of months."

"Their cousins, Trace and Rhys will be working for them, too," Kieran adds with a hint of sadness in his voice.

Trace Quinlan has been my bodyguard/driver for the last few months, but I've sent him to work a few events for my sister Shea in East Hampton. I can find another driver, and although Trace came in handy a couple of weeks ago, I don't want a full-time bodyguard anymore.

My brothers fall into a conversation about the Quinlans, and our history with them, while I tune them out and think of that escort I fucked in Los Angeles. The leggy redhead I had to taste won't leave my thoughts.

What are the odds that a high-priced escort would be in the first-class airline seat next to mine?

I used to be ashamed of only using sex workers. But I have no interest in relationships and work ungodly hours. Even if I casually dated, someone would end up hurt when they wanted more and I came up empty.

My work schedule leads me to mull over one of Corvin's hiring conditions. A last-minute request. One that didn't sit well with me, but having Snow under my watchful eye had me saying yes.

Hire his daughter as my assistant.

I never had an assistant in the traditional sense. That's two hiring packages I have to send Eoghan, who manages everyone on our payroll. Legit and not so legit. Snow sits on a razor's edge in between. The compensation package I threw at him made his jaw drop. He's got a lot of secrets and sins.

And a wicked gambling addiction.

I hope his bank statements don't look too fucked up because Eoghan will run a background check on him. Plus, World Trade Bank sponsored his work visa. He's not a U.S. citizen and still maintains a damn Russian citizenship.

I kick Eoghan's chair to get his attention. I need to speak to him privately after this. But he's another love-sick eejit staring at his phone.

All my brothers have fallen like bricks for women in the last two years.

"I filed those drone patents," I say to a room full of men who are glued to their phones. "I plan to blow up the White House on Friday."

Fucking nothing.

"I also spent twenty-thousand dollars on a five-thousand-dollar hooker." Why twenty-grand? It was the most I could get as a cash advance at the hotel and she deserved it.

I had these crazy thoughts about asking to see her again. Maybe even offer her one of those thirty-day contracts to live in my house and suck my dick the minute I step in the door. Something I've never done.

I never sleep with the same woman twice. Although, many try to get into my bed a second time.

That's why I called Trace, who was in Las Vegas with his brother, Rhys, guarding Eoghan and Jillian. I needed him and the goddamn O'Rourke jet to get me the hell out of Los Angeles before I did something stupid.

I couldn't sit on a plane with that woman for another five hours to New York. She was too tempting.

I didn't even trust myself to pay her. I made Trace do it. A dick move, but she's an escort. She didn't care as long as she got her money.

Only, something felt really off with that woman. Maybe it was the long flight and changing time zones. She seemed so fucking into me and my dick, it confused the hell out of me.

Tempting my fate, I left a note with my burner phone number on the last hundred-dollar bill in the envelope of cash.

Christ, that butterfly was the hottest sex I've ever had. Deep down, I paid her all that extra money so she wouldn't have to immediately sleep with someone else.

The idea of *anyone* else's face in that sweet pussy clenches my jaw so tight, it could break. My blood pressure roars in my ears and the compulsion to commit murder floods my veins thinking of someone else touching her.

The murderous visuals in my head of some other *John*, dead on a hotel floor, his dick out, are way too real for comfort.

I never even got her name. By choice. I could have hacked into the airline's manifest, but the mystery is that itch I'm dying to scratch.

I've used only my hand and the memory of her to satisfy me.

Fuck me, I don't know why.

I glance around the room and my spine stiffens. Is falling in love contagious?

No, thank you.

Especially not with an escort. Not when my brothers moon over their pure wives and how it drove them fucking nuts seeing virginal blood on their cocks. I'm pretty sure it's what made them feral.

Not me. I prefer to be in control of myself.

A text message pulls me out of my thoughts.

Corvin: Are we still meeting for dinner this Saturday, Mr. O'Rourke?

Me: Aye, I made reservations. I'll drop you a pin.

Getting a table anywhere on a Saturday night requires hacking skills these days, but I made a call and got a table at my favorite Italian restaurant.

Corvin: Excellent. I asked my daughter to join us for dinner so you can meet her in a casual setting.

Fuck, the assistant I don't want.

I'll do anything to trap Corvin Snow in my web. The ransomware code he developed allows someone to hack into any server with no trace. Snow is a walking financial weapon of mass destruction.

Despite making three million a year, Snow confessed over a few too many whiskeys in a Sydney bar that WTB had terminated his contract. The bad blood with such a prestigious bank wrecked him. There he was, drunk and threatening to drain his former employer of a cool billion before fleeing to Bora Bora.

I talked him off the ledge and offered him a job for five

million. No way would I let him disappear into the shadows.

I even used his daughter as a selling point. And a guilt trip.

How would she feel if you disappeared?

He kept details about her close to his chest. Just that her mother died when she was young. He stroked a silvery-white beard, telling me how he raised his daughter himself. And that she'd dropped by the conference a few times.

For all my spying on Snow, I hadn't seen a young woman with him. I must have kept missing her.

Me: Look forward to meeting your daughter.

Not really…

CHAPTER NINE
ELLA

Estella:
Ricardi's on the Park. Tonight at 7 p.m.
Dress nice.
Dad

His handwritten note on my bedroom door draws a smile from my lips. He left early this morning for one of his typical freelance computer jobs. I worry how his new employer will feel about his extra-curricular activities.

With shady people.

With our hectic move back to New York City, Dad hasn't mentioned anything about the man who hired him. He's still utterly incensed from getting screwed over by World Trade Bank.

Even if they did pay his mortgage here in the city for the six months he worked in Australia. And even though he already has a new job—with a bigger paycheck.

His pride will be his undoing.

At night, he sits at his desk in the office until the wee hours of the morning working on his laptop. I hear him speaking sometimes, and I'm guessing that's part of his contract hacking work. When not speaking Russian, drips and drabs of his conversations make my blood run cold.

Looking at my closet, I exhale in frustration. I fled the States six months ago with the clothes on my back, leaving everything behind in Wesley's apartment. Slowly, I built up a new wardrobe in Australia designed for comfort. And warmer weather.

But it's late January in New York. And freezing.

Now I have to start all over. It's exhausting. Not to mention expensive. Somehow using the money Balor left me makes me feel dirty. I don't want to look down at everything I bought and feel used.

Charging him was a joke, I never intended to take his money. But I certainly wasn't leaving that cash in the hotel room.

Shaking those thoughts way, I check the time. It's getting late.

I also have nothing to wear. The navy wrap dress I wore on the plane, the one Balor peeled off me, is the only thing I have that's appropriate for a nice restaurant like Ricardi's. But that dress has cum stains on the ass area.

Even if it were clean, I'm not wearing that for another man. Even if that other man is my new boss. Memories flood me about Balor again. I felt so connected to him. Odd, since I'd gone out on several dates in Australia attempting to once again feel safe with a man and not cringe or feel sick.

Balor made me feel comfortable. Maybe it was the safe confines of our airline seats, like we were in our own world. So intimate and special.

Sadly, I was wrong. He left me in a hotel suite. Sure, he was thoughtful enough to arrange a limo for me so I wasn't stranded at the hotel. But he didn't even stick around to say goodbye.

Pawing through my closet, I pull out a dated red, white, and black color-block sweater dress I found in a box of old clothes. Dad brought it from our house in Connecticut, a Tudor passed down from my mom's family.

Slipping on the sweater dress, I'm pleased with how it hugs my curves, and its crew neckline looks professional.

Whoever the hell this new boss is, I won't tempt him with cleavage. Sleeping with a stranger was daring and perhaps reckless enough. I won't sleep with a boss.

When I step into the living room at six-thirty, Dad spins around from looking out the balcony's double French doors. "Estella! You look beautiful."

I hate how old that name makes me sound, especially with his heavy Russian accent, but it was my Baba's name, his mother. "Thank you. Can you please introduce me as Ella?"

"If you wish." He hugs me. "How are your friends?"

"The same." I nod and don't return the question because I don't think he has friends.

Not here in New York, anyway. Maybe back in Connecticut where I grew up.

"Are you hungry?" Dad asks me, adjusting his tie.

"I am. I ordered us an Uber," I say, checking my lipstick in the mirror.

"Always taking care of me. You will do well with Mr. O'Rourke."

Hearing his boss's name for the first time stills me. "O'Rourke?"

Irish...

Dad rubs his chin. "Did I not mention his name?"

"No." My throat tightens.

Balor was Irish. Spoke with an accent. A sexy one I'll never un-hear.

"Mr. O'Rourke is sophisticated hacker like me." Dad sits me down on a wing chair. "Before we go, there is something I must warn you about his family..."

***

My jaw hangs open in the back of the Uber as we ride to the restaurant.

The O'Rourkes are Irish Mafia.

I didn't hear much after that.

Didn't need to. Although, I wanted to scream at my father. How could he get into bed with the *mafia*? Then he told me how much he was making, and that he would purchase me my own apartment. My heart raced at that, but I don't want to be handed some luxury condo.

Not when I want to teach special-needs kids in a

moderate-income school district.

I'll spread my wings and live on my own again soon. And in a place I choose when *I* feel safe.

Spread your legs...

That voice, that sexy brogue is stuck in my head.

Oblivious to my shock, Dad chats with the Uber driver, who, upon hearing my father's thick accent, started talking with him in Russian.

A language he never bothered to teach me.

My father saw a lot happen in his life. He's tough Russian stock. My mother was an American doctor from Darien, Connecticut, treating sick kids in Moscow. They fell in love, got married, and moved back to Darien where they had me.

Unlike Mom, the sight of blood makes me squeamish. But I inherited her giving spirit. I love teaching and the nurturing aspect of Special-Needs Education.

Inside the Uber, I fix Dad's tie. "Are you sure about taking this job?"

"I did my research," he says, holding my hand. "They are dangerous people, but fair to those who are loyal. That made the decision easy for me, after the way those..." He curses his old boss under his breath. "Plus, if we earn their trust, the O'Rourkes will protect us. Protect *you*."

"I don't need protecting." Not at *that* price.

My father's phone buzzes, and he takes it out of his stylish wool overcoat. "Oh, he is there and has table for us."

"Is this an interview? Or do I have the job?"

"It was part of my negotiation."

"I could have found a job myself, Dad."

He smiles at me with soft eyes. "After that beast laid his dirty hands on you, I would prefer you to acclimate back into this city under my watchful eyes. Once I am more comfortable with the O'Rourkes, I intend to mention—"

"No!" I gasp.

Wes is a cop, and the O'Rourkes are Irish Mafia.

From what little I know, mafia bosses are all brutal. And when ranked in viciousness, the Irish leave other syndicates in the dust. Cruel mafia against a psycho cop? The streets will be stained with blood.

"I'm living in your apartment with you, working with you. I'll be safe. I *am* safe." I consider my situation differently.

If Wes was a decent cop—and by *decent* I don't mean honorable, I mean not fucking clueless—he should know the O'Rourkes are mafia. And if he bothers me, he'll see I'm associated with them and back off.

End of story.

The Uber pulls up in front of one of those quaint restaurants with low ceilings and exposed brick. Dad holds my arm as we descend a few steps down to the entrance, but I'm nearly knocked over by the wonderful smell of basil and garlic.

"Ah, I see him," Dad says.

My phone vibrates, and I'm conditioned like a dog with a treat to look at it.

When I see it's an email from Fredricks Elementary, I open it immediately, not even thinking.

"Estella," Dad whispers in my ear, leading me into the restaurant. "Put your phone away."

"Just a second, Dad. I have to read this one email." I keep walking, eyes down, my fingers scrolling.

Ella, hi!

I heard you're back in New York. I'd love to meet with you about a part-time aide position for the rest of the school year. The kids miss you so much. I hope to hear from you.

Sara

My heart pounds. I don't need this job with Dad!

By now, he's let me go. I glance upward to search for his shock of intense dark hair and wide shoulders, ready to tell him my news. I rush to catch up and stop when I see my father open his arms, greeting the man who I suspect is his new boss.

All this trouble Dad went through and now I have to tell the guy I can't work for him?

I expected a man who's my father's boss to be hunched over with wrinkled skin. At the table, a much younger man with adorably messed-up shaggy hair, sharp jaw, and dark rimmed glasses stands up from a curved booth and my stomach drops.

Every muscle tenses, and I can't breathe.

No…

No, no.

I freeze and nearly fall over in my stiletto-heel boots.

Green eyes land on me and the handsome face morphs, mirroring the same shock rolling through me. Until the look of surprise melts into a glare.

It can't be him. The man on the plane was a breathtaking god. This is Manhattan, though. The place is crawling with gods.

Balor…

His piercing stare drags back the memories of how he took me in that hotel bed. Sure, we only did it from behind. But the memory of him and his grunts when he thrust into me, his face pushed into the back of my head with one hand around my throat, whispering the filthiest things in my ear, crashes back to me.

Every night since, I relive how he buried his face between my legs and licked me until I came again and again, wringing me of every sane thought. The shower we took, still from behind, flashes at me. How he slid so deeply into my ass. Even though it was my first time.

He thought I was an escort, and an escort doesn't say

no so…

He thinks I'm an escort!

How am I going to sit here and have dinner with him and my father?

My father. Oh, God.

I slept with my father's new boss, who's also my boss, *and* Irish Mafia! Dad can fly into a rage on one of his typical reckless impulses and some guard somewhere will shoot him.

Trace. I spin around looking for the six-five bodyguard, but don't see him. Perhaps that's on purpose.

God, this is awful. I plaster a smile on my face as I approach the table, drawn in by Balor's stare.

I give my head a shake to communicate: *Please don't say anything. Please!*

"Mr. O'Rourke," the name ominously slides off my father's tongue. "This is my jewel. Estella."

Thrusting my hand toward him to play the part, I say tonelessly, "Nice to meet you, Mr. O'Rourke."

My robotic, flat greeting draws a frown from both him and my father.

"Same here, *Estella.*"

"Ella." I roll my eyes. "I go by Ella."

Eventually, I'll have to explain why I have a different last name.

Always cautious about anti-separatists and KGB loyalists, Dad wanted me to have my mother's last name. Reyes.

With a dry throat, I search the table for water and grab a glass. Like I just ran a marathon, I chug the water, some of it dripping down my chin. I grab a cloth napkin to wipe my mouth and find Balor O'Rourke staring at me.

Any hope of un-seeing this stunning man naked in that hotel room vanishes. He broke his rule and let me run my lips across every warm inch of skin and all his rippling muscles. He's tall, but not bulky, just lean as hell.

It's all I see, and I want to see it again.

And never will because he's my boss.

I put down the glass and follow my father's lead when he holds out one of the wooden seats across from Balor. He's perched inside the banquette seat against the brick wall, with an unobscured view of the entire restaurant.

Of course, a mafia boss doesn't sit with his back to strangers.

Balor's stare weighs on me as I lower into the chair. His heavy-lidded gaze carries the secret of how he held me down to suck his cock. Again, and again.

"Ella!" He jumps up and points. "Sit on the banquette seat with me, please."

"What?" I ask, my heart pounding.

"I don't want your back exposed," he murmurs.

Dad smiles. "You are very wise. Thank you for considering her safety."

"My pleasure," he growls, frowning at me.

He's angry because he thinks I'm a hooker who's lying to my father.

It sparks a chuckle in my throat.

"Something funny," Balor says, low and warning-like.

Something will be.

He steers me to the seat and his touch sends goosebumps across my skin.

"Nothing, *sir*," I drawl and his expression turns volcanic.

CHAPTER TEN
ELLA

A waitress comes to the table, all smiles and drooling over Balor. "Can I get you started with some drinks?"

Strong. *I* need something strong.

Balor lifts the drink menu, his thigh drifting toward mine. "I would adore a glass of red wine."

I choke on a sip of water.

I said that on the plane. He's mimicking me.

"Anything particular, sir?" the waitress asks, purring at him.

She's either angling for a tip or a date.

Sorry, honey, unless you double as a hooker...

"Ella *loves* red wine," Dad says. "I raised her with a European focus on wine and food."

He gave me my first sip of wine at sixteen.

Balor leans into me, his hip now fully pressed against mine. "Then Ella should pick. See anything you like? *Ella*?"

He's taunting me now to say his name and out the fact that we've met before. I'm smarter than that.

I tilt my head and narrow my eyes with a grin. Glancing at the menu, I go right to the bottom of the list of Reds.

"We'll have the Romanee-Conti Grand Cru 1990."

My father's jaw hits the table. "Estella! Are you mad? That is an insanely expensive bottle of wine!"

The waitress shifts awkwardly, and I hear a gurgle of glee in her throat, considering the tip this dinner will fetch her.

"Really?" I say and take a closer look. "I thought it said one hundred dollars. I mean, wow, twenty-thousand dollars is a lot of money. Right...*Mr. O*?"

Boy, does that fit him.

My father's breathing goes erratic. He stares at me with an expression that says: *You are out of your mind, teasing a mob boss.*

I'm teasing the man who screwed me and left me with a stranger who gave me an envelope of crisp hundreds for my services.

"Twenty thousand dollars is nothing to me," Balor teases back. "I'd pay anything for something so…sweet."

Shit, I could have asked for more money.

"If I may, Mr. O'Rourke." Dad grabs the menu, attempting to save both our lives. "We will have the Mondavi Late Harvest Reserve."

My eyes lower to the menu, and scoff at the sixty-dollar price tag.

"And please, give me the bill for it."

"Snow, don't insult me." Balor smiles across the table at my father. Underneath, his hand squeezes my thigh. "I can afford a sixty-dollar bottle of wine. And we both know I can afford the Grand Cru."

"I cannot accept such an expensive gesture," Dad says, his shoulders back.

He likes to be pampered and praised but only if no strings are attached.

The waitress stomps away mad, and I wouldn't be surprised if our meals come with a side of spit.

With Dad checking the menu for the least expensive dinner, I reach under the table to knock Balor's hand off my thigh and scooch away.

Only, his hand closes around the bottom of my sweater dress.

"So, Ella…" Balor yanks me closer. "I would love to hear about your work experience."

He thinks I'm a hooker and that my father doesn't know.

"I have lots of experience…years of experience," I play

along.

"Years?" He rests one elbow on the table, the other hand sliding under the hem of my dress.

Angling my body, I add, "Right after college. I got a call about a great opportunity with a little boy."

Balor snaps, *"What?"*

My father looks perplexed. "Ella is a special-needs educator."

Somewhere *teacher* fell out of favor in our lexicon, and I missed it.

"A special-needs educator." Balor annunciates the words, repressing a laugh because I'm certain he thinks that's the cover story I gave my father.

"She is," Dad insists. "If I can be open since we are in intimate company, I thought she could do better with her Yale education."

"You went to *Yale*?"

"Lux et Veritas," I say, figuring the motto translation *Light and Truth* really applies here.

"What did you study at Yale?" Balor asks.

With a smile on my face, I say, "Chemistry." And because I have a death wish, I poke him in the chest.

I won't bore Balor how I focused my studies on brain chemistry and wrote papers that led me to summer clinics working with severely autistic children.

Mixing liquid chemicals lost its flare for me after one semester when I burned myself.

I got my first tattoo, the roses across the bridge of my foot after the skin grafts didn't do shit for the burn scars. That fueled my healing journey this summer, covering all of Wesley's scars with other tattoos.

"Sounds like you're overqualified to be an assistant," Balor says.

"She needs a job, Mr. O'Rourke."

"And she can have one."

I really don't *need* this job, no matter what it pays. The part time aide position at Fredricks is enough right now. Dad never spoiled me. He passed down his strong work ethic. This thing with Wes upended our life, and now Dad will throw money at anything to keep me safe.

Or throw me at a mob boss for the same reason. That's what Dad thinks I *need*.

But I don't...

"Actually, Dad." I smile at Balor and look away, waving my phone. "Sara from Fredricks *just* emailed me as we were walking inside. They have an open aide position with a little boy for the rest of this year."

I have no idea what Balor O'Rourke planned to pay me and right now money isn't my main concern. Dad wants me safe. I want my life back. I'm tired of hiding and being afraid.

Balor's shoulders relax like he didn't want me working for him anyway. Oooo, that stings.

The waitress comes with the bottle of red wine and does the showing, the opening, and the tasting ritual. Balor takes a taste, and to my surprise hands me the glass.

A smudge from his lower lip catches the light and to tease him, I turn the glass around and sip from the same spot, leaving a lipstick stain.

I smile, handing the glass back to him, and then go weak, watching him sip again from that same spot.

The waitress pours two more glasses, refills Balor's, and takes our orders.

"Getting back to Ella working for you." Dad sounds flustered but when his phone rings, his jaw tightens. "Excuse me, Mr. O'Rourke."

"By all means. Take your time." Balor is polite, though I expect he'd be offended by his new employee taking a call. But with Dad out of earshot, Balor turns his attention to me.

"Ella, Ella, Ella," he breathes out my name on a lustful sigh.

"I'm *not* an escort, okay," I whisper.

He visibly swallows, disappointment shadowing his eyes. He only sleeps with escorts, and I just put myself in the no-go column.

Now I'm disappointed.

"I paid you twenty thousand dollars."

"I only asked for five. And can we discuss the jolly green giant you sent to deliver it to me?"

"You mean Trace?" He smirks.

"Does your bodyguard always pay your escorts?"

"Trace is temporary. I usually don't have a bodyguard." He pulls at the collar of a crisp cerulean blue button-down shirt with the sleeves rolled up to show off his tats. Thick bands of ink, a test of pain endurance, are sexy as hell on him. Those are his only tattoos. The rest of his body is like untouched snow. "He was on my brother's security detail in Las Vegas that day. It was an hour flight, so…"

"Lucky for you. And you can have the money back. I just came up with a fee because…" My cheeks blaze with embarrassment.

"Yeah?" He sits back. "Let's hear this one. Why did you lie?"

Biting my lower lip, I say, "You wouldn't have wanted me."

Scoffing, he tugs on his collar. "I wanted you, trust me."

"Because you thought I was a hooker." I take a sip of wine and then say, "I figured I'd never see you again, so why not?"

"There's more. You're holding back."

Balor's heated gaze fuels me, and opening up to him is easy. "I love sex and wanted to fuck you."

He squeezes his glass, muttering foreign curses under his breath.

"And since I'm somewhat of a behavioral expert, can we peel back a few layers? Why only hookers?"

"*Escorts*," he emphasizes. "Fully vetted, fully tested, high-price, discreet *escorts*."

I squirm, remembering how he begged to take off the condom and come inside me. Of course, I was clean, too, after being tested in Australia, fearing Wes was cheating on me on top of everything else.

But I'd stopped taking birth control. I called my gyno and asked for emergency contraception. He's backed up three months, so his nurse approved three refill packs to hold me over until I can see him.

"Okay. But *why*?" I press Balor about the escort-kink.

"Because I have no time or interest in a relationship. If your father told you anything about my family and what we do, then you understand I can't set myself up to be ambushed or blackmailed by strangers. I use a solid escort service because *I have needs*."

His words spark electric, and I tingle.

"I don't want a relationship either right now." I bite my lip, stopping myself from opening up about Wesley. Being bold, I add, "And I have needs, too."

"Jesus, you're so damn tempting." Balor gulps down his wine. "I need a scotch."

"If I remember correctly, we had a good time."

"We did. *I did*." He puts down his glass and eyes me with a hooded glare. "I would love nothing more than to sink my cock into that wet cunt every night." I blush as he laughs to himself. "I should have known you weren't a sex worker."

"Why do you say that?"

"You were so fucking tight, and no one's... Clawed at the sheets and moaned like that. I wondered if it was an act."

"It wasn't." I don't care if I sound pathetic, at least I'm being honest.

"And that shower, fuck." He growls. "Had you done anal before?"

I smile, shaking my head.

"Jesus Christ," he grumbles, breathing heavily. "Did you like it?"

"I loved it," I whisper. "With you."

He pours more wine since the waitress is nowhere to be found. "I take it you didn't see my number?"

"Your number?" My heart seizes.

"On the last bill in the envelope, I wrote my burner phone number." He rubs a hand down the back of his neck.

I laugh. "Because you thought I would need a refill once I hit the last hundred?"

"I guess." He smiles. "I wasn't sure why exactly."

He wanted me again, but only if he paid me.

I'm so damn tempted to say, *Gotcha*, and tell him I really am a hooker but don't tell Dad. Then Balor can keep plowing me.

There is something so sexy, so elegant, so raw with quiet power about this man. I could really fall for him.

Oops, I think I already have.

CHAPTER ELEVEN
BALOR

Fuck.

Fuck.

Fuck.

Knowing Corvin Snow's screwed-up past and dark secrets, I have to question if he sent his daughter on that plane to…

What?

Get me to fuck her?

Ella excused herself, and I'm alone at the table. Left here with her scent that I tried so hard once to get out of my system.

Her flushed cheeks and confused sable brown eyes melted my immediate spark of anger. Now I'm heated, but for a very different reason.

She loves sex *and* doesn't want a relationship.

Where did this woman come from?

She's supposed to be working for me, which adds a layer of bullshit I don't want to deal with. But I really really really want to fuck her again.

She woke up something inside me and I've been going crazy wondering why. Now I know. She wasn't a hooker. I mean escort! It was all real. And it's been so long since anyone came on my cock who wasn't being paid, I forgot how intoxicating that is.

Here I thought she was some new breed of sex worker, mixing the meet-cute experience with white-hot sex.

I can't get her smooth skin out of my mind, that sweet scent that was all her and not bottled. My cock is so hard remembering how I felt thrusting into her tight cunt. Those breathy gasps, head hanging down, taking me so damn deep. I can't get the vision of her plump ass that begged to be held and squeezed and fucked out of my head.

She tamed that wild mane of mahogany hair tonight. Smoothed it and pulled it back to the nape of her neck. That long, creamy column calls out to my hands to close around and control her breathing while I fuck her.

Lust floods my veins, and I'm seconds from going into the men's room to stroke my dick and relieve this ache. But Corvin just went in there, and that will be awkward.

The man's not stupid. He'll put two and two together. He leaves me alone with his hot-as-fuck daughter, and now I'm whacking off?

I will tonight for sure in a hot shower, soaping up my cock, and fisting it like her tight cunt.

Or…I could call my escort service.

But fuck, I don't want someone else. I want Ella and need to find a way to get her into my bed.

CHAPTER TWELVE
ELLA

I return to the table right after Dad, and a moment later, our food arrives.

Over the meal, Dad bores Balor with a little of his background. I can tell by the way my new boss barely responds. But when Dad talks about my mom, Balor's interest piques.

He lifts sympathetic eyes to me. "My mother is very sick. She's in Ireland right now."

"Were you born there?" I ask, wiping up left-over marinara sauce with the most scrumptious bread I've ever tasted.

"Aye. She wanted her last days to be there."

My heart tugs for him. My mom died in a car accident. It was traumatic but quick. To watch your mom die must be so much more painful.

"Mr. O'Rourke," my dad interrupts us.

"Corvin, call me Balor. Mr. O'Rourke makes me sound old."

"Balor," my dad says humbly. "I hate to lay something so vital on you. And Ella, do not hate me."

My breathing stops. "Dad, no…"

"Ella suffered abuse at the hands of her previous boyfriend."

"Oh, God." I cover my face.

"What?" Balor utters, his tone sharp as a blade. "Who?"

"That's not important." I shake my head. "But it's true and why I went to Australia with Dad on his assignment for the bank."

"This ex of yours hurt you so bad, you had to escape to the other side of the world?"

I hesitate to respond because he sounds so deadly. "I just needed to get away," I whisper.

"It is why I want her to work for you," Dad interjects.

"You *are* working for me, in my command center every day where you'll be safe. I appreciate the honorable career you want, but your father is right. Until..."

"Until?" I'm stunned, my stomach twisting.

"Until we know Wesley will not bother you again," Dad clarifies.

"Wesley?" Balor says, his cyber brain clicking on.

I assume he's a hacker like my dad. Balor will go home and hack away until he finds Wes. I tremble at the idea of him finding out my ex is a cop. I don't want Balor to do anything that will put his *mafia* family's secrets at risk.

"Let it go. It's done." My eyes plead to Balor. "I'll work for you. Just tell me when to report and where your office is." Working in a command center sounds daunting.

Balor smiles and sits back because he's won. "You'll find out."

The check comes and even though my father tries to pay for it, telling Balor it's the least he can do after the incredible salary and a signing bonus I knew nothing about, Balor takes care of the bill.

Seeming happy, Dad stands up and excuses himself to tip the waitress, something he always does when dining with a colleague who pays.

As soon as my father is out of earshot, Balor slides closer to me.

"What did he to do you?" His eyes roam my body. "I didn't see any scars. Thank fuck, I might have lost it. Especially when I thought you were..."

Because Johns and pimps beat up hookers.

"Black eyes. Busted lips. Cuts." I refrain from showing him all the places, but each body part Wes hurt tingles in pain when I mention them.

"Black *eyes*. Both or more than once?"

"Both... And more than once." My throat goes tight.

"Cuts." He fingers my shoulder. "The tattoo under your left collarbone?"

I'm not broken, just mending and ready to live...

"And my wrist." I raise my hand to show him the butterfly again. "The heart on my hip. The spiderweb on my thigh. All my tattoos cover the scars from his abuse."

"He let you tattoo over his scars?"

I shake my head. "I got them all in Sydney. It was a way to heal. To blend the pain of the needle and watch evidence of my weakness vanish."

"You weren't weak. Men who abuse women are." Balor looks ready to murder someone.

"I felt so trapped. And scared. I know...who you are. Dad told me about your family."

His eyebrow raises. "Did he now?"

"You can trust me," I whisper. "My father isn't exactly on the up and up."

Balor leans in. "Last name of your ex. Now."

I exhale. "No."

He growls. "Not many people tell me no. I have a first name. I can find him. And—"

"It will come back to me. He'll..."

"No one is getting near you again. You're living in a secure building." How he knows that can only mean he vetted Dad. "You'll be working for me. And one whiff of that scumbag coming close to you, you're getting a bodyguard."

Overwhelmed, I hold my chest. "I don't want to live like that."

"Better than being dead."

"I never thought he'd kill me."

"Most DV abusers don't intend to kill. It's all about controlling their victims." His fists tighten. "All too often when the victim fights back that's when they end up dead."

"You sound like you have experience with this." I clear my throat. "Did you have another girlfriend who—"

"No. I never had a girlfriend." He rolls his eyes. "Second grade. Maybe. She never answered my note."

I snort into my hand. "Thank you for making me laugh."

"I'm serious. Your father told you who I am. Who my family is. We respect women."

"He also said you're loyal to those who offer their loyalty in return."

"That's correct. Will you be loyal?" he asks quickly, but bites back a frown.

"I'll be loyal. In every way." My hand reaches for his leg, but he grabs it.

"Ella... It's not that I don't want to fuck you again because I do." Shockingly, he presses my hand on his groin. "Feel that? That's how much I want you."

"I'm not looking for a relationship. Especially now," I say. "I'm only twenty-seven."

"I told you I only..."

"...screw escorts. Got it." I sit back and pick up my water glass.

"That *and* I'm your boss." With a final once-over, he slides away and doesn't touch me for the rest of the night.

CHAPTER THIRTEEN

ELLA

Hannah and I stroll through Central Park Sunday morning with steaming lattes in hand.

"Everyone at the Warwick is excited about the owner's wedding. Even if that's breaking many hearts." Hannah, who's a housekeeping manager for the swanky hotel, sips her drink.

She manages the corporate executive floor at the Warwick, where she pulls in a grand a week in tips alone.

I stifle a brief sting of jealousy. I miss working at Fredricks Elementary in Manhattan, which is close to Dad's apartment. Now I have to commute to Astoria, Queens and work in a command center. I don't even know where Astoria is.

"Sounds like you have a crush on the hotel owner," I say, wanting some solidarity with an inappropriate relationship.

Hannah's face contorts. "Are you kidding? He's mafia. I wouldn't touch that with a ten-foot pole." The word mafia falls off her lips with disdain but oh, so effortlessly.

My father whispered it like *Voldemort*. They who shall not be named.

"Not all mafia is bad," I say, dreading telling her about my new job.

"They kill people," Hannah shrieks.

"Some people deserve it."

Hannah stops walking and stares at me. *"What?"*

The look of disgust in her eyes changes my mind about my dad's hesitancy to speak the unmentionable. Hannah is my best friend, but in this instance, loyalty to Balor and his family rings louder. "Never mind. I am dying to tell you something, though."

"Oh my God, what is it? Is it Wes?" Panic hardens her

features.

"No! The hot guy. From the plane."

Her mouth forms a little O. "He called you?"

I don't want to point out that he didn't have my number because he didn't ask for it since he never planned to see me again. Only...now I know he left me *his* number, which I've been meaning to fish out of the envelope, but it's buried in my closet.

"No. But...I saw him."

"Get out! Where?"

"Last night. The dinner with my father and his new boss."

"Shut up!"

"Apparently, he's my new boss, too."

"What about the school?"

Shaking my head, I pull her out of the road and sit down on one of the benches. "I heard from Fredricks' HR. They can only offer me something temporary and part-time, but Dad is freaked out about me going back there since that's where I met Wes."

"If Wes wasn't a cop, I'd disagree because it's important to be strong and independent. But he's right." Hannah nods. "Wes is insane, and since you ditched him, just seeing you again may set him off."

"I know." I hug her. "But are you following the bouncing ball? The job my dad got for me is with *him*. The guy from the plane. That's mine and my dad's new boss. I had hours of crazy, intense sex with him."

Her eyes go wide. "Oh, God."

That he was. It wasn't my woozy, airplane-air-tainted brain that made me fall into bed with that *certified* god.

And not a *Conan the Barbarian* warrior god with biceps the size of tree trunks, or a Viking god.

No, Balor is sleek, muscular perfection.

"Yeah." Shaking my head, I add, "I guess it wasn't that

huge of a coincidence. Turns out he was at my dad's conference in Sydney."

"Does your dad know you guys hooked up?"

"No. It's not the having sex part that I think would flip my father out, it's that he slept with me because he thought I was an escort. And did all those...dirty things to me. Things men do *only* with hookers." I see Balor's face every time I close my eyes. "And now I'll see him every day."

Smiling, Hannah says, "Maybe it will spark something real between you two."

"I kind of threw out the idea to him last night. After he said the dirtiest things to me."

"Then he's on board for some fun. You're adults."

"He seemed cautious. Working for him only gives him slight pause."

He's mafia and does whatever the hell he wants, I say in my head, already loyal to keeping his secret.

"But he *only* sleeps with escorts so he won't get attached."

Hannah wrinkles her nose. "Sounds like he's got commitment issues."

"I'll say." Balor is wound tight, but I can't help wondering if I could loosen his threads.

"What are you doing with the money he gave you?" Hannah asks.

"I offered to give it back. He refused." I shrug.

"How much will the new job pay?"

Laughing, I suck down the last sip of my latte. "I don't even know. I'm kind of a clean slate. I don't have any debt or expenses. Dad's private health insurance plan covers both of us. I don't have a car."

"Your job is likely a piece of cake that pays well. With the bonus of looking at a hottie all day."

"That's one hell of a silver lining." I loop arms with

Hannah to pull her up from the bench with me.

"My latte is cold." Hannah tosses her cup. "Let's get refills and head to Val's apartment and taste-test some of her sinfully delicious cookies."

I stop dead in my tracks.

"Balor said the same thing about my…" I point to the ache between my thighs.

CHAPTER FOURTEEN
ELLA

A car picks up my dad and me from his apartment on our first day working for O'Rourke Technologies.

No, not a car. A tank. An elegant, massive SUV, the color of steamed milk with chestnut trim on the doors.

My smile fades when the driver emerges, and I nearly fall into my father. I'm paralyzed by the same towering, brutally handsome man who handed me an envelope of money two weeks ago.

"Ella, it's okay. This is Balor's bodyguard."

Yeah, I know that, and he might have seen me naked.

God, this is embarrassing.

"Corvin Snow." My father reaches for the bodyguard's hand.

I try to stay upright while my cheeks heat in utter embarrassment. The man paid me off like a hooker.

"Trace Quinlan," he says, wearing a finely cut double-breasted suit.

"Hi. I'm Ella." *And I'm not a hooker!*

Trace shows no emotion, and for a second I wonder if he doesn't recognize me. Christ, how many of Balor's women with fucked-up hair, smeared makeup, and a body wrung out from sex does this man see?

Does he pay all of Balor's escorts for him?

My stomach twists, making Balor's taste for paid sex feel even more real and sordid.

I hate it for some irrational reason.

Dad helps me into the SUV, and Trace closes the door.

"Are we getting picked up like this every day?" I whisper to my father.

"I expect so." Dad smirks, loving this royal treatment.

Why is Balor kissing my father's ass like this? Is there something else going on?

"If this music bothers you, let me know." Trace's deep, thick accent hits me in the chest and shatters me to pieces.

"This is beautiful," Dad says about the classical music.

I wish it were heavy metal to drown out all the screaming in my head telling me to jump out of this car. It was hard enough to face Balor after our encounter. This further deepens my shame.

Talk about a rough first day at a new job.

CHAPTER FIFTEEN

BALOR

My personal gym, located adjacent to my office in the command center, with its large windows provides a panorama of the city and allows the early sun to light the space.

Working out is part of my morning routine. Today is no different. Sweat coats my entire body from timed rounds of jumping jacks, push-ups, and side-leg kicks. I count in Mandarin, learned from a Master on a retreat in Hong Kong several years ago. Counting, I try to focus my mind and not think of Ella, that she'll be here in the building near me, all day.

Flexing in extremely low lunges, I close my eyes to concentrate and balance. Even though in my periphery, I'm tracking all motion past the glass partition on the office side.

A door to the gym opens, and there she is, in a plaid skirt and boots. Fuck, those legs wrapped around my waist while I fucked her felt so good.

The vision breaks my chi, and I catch myself before I tumble.

"You told me to let you know when she got here, boss," Trace says, standing behind her.

I lift my head, sweat pouring into my eyes. "Thank you."

The way she stares at me makes my body feel different than when any other woman I'd been with looked at me. Because my escorts are *paid* to look at me like that.

But I don't buy them to ogle me.

And looking back, I can't be sure if any of them had or hadn't. Ella eyes me up and down. Her lids flutter as her gaze reaches my waist, and it triggers something visceral inside me. Even in that L.A. hotel, her stare unraveled me.

Right there, I should have known she lied to me about being an escort.

Ella tugs her purse strap against her shoulder. "I didn't want to bother you. But your bodyguard insisted."

"My workout ran late." I stretch. "You can go, Trace," I say to him, but my gaze fixes on Ella, realizing she looks horrified. "What?"

With Trace gone, she says in a strained voice, "I'm *so* embarrassed. That man... He was the one who gave me the money. My father was with me this morning, Balor."

Fuck. "Trace didn't say anything, did he?"

Even as I ask, I know he didn't. A military guy who barely speaks would never betray a boss.

"No. It just messed me up in the head. My father... He's going to find out."

"He's not." I suck in a breath. "And if he does, I'll handle it. We're adults and we had no idea who each other was."

"Right, tell him you thought I was a hooker."

"You led me to believe that," I argue, low and controlled.

The bitter words kick up my memory of those hours, away from the world in a hotel room, where I fucked her so damn good and deep. My cock stiffens, and I want to push her against the mirrored wall, spin her around and fuck her again. Watch her eyes roll into the back of her skull through the reflection while I enter her.

"Yes, but I don't want him to find out." Ella exhales and looks away. "Are you done?"

"Not really, but—"

"Finish." She glances around. "This is a pretty sweet gym. Is it for employees?"

"No." My forehead crinkles, realizing I sound like an asshole. "My guys...don't work out. They're the types who have coffee for breakfast, Red Bull for lunch, and fast food for dinner."

"The ones in the skinny jeans I passed to get here?"

"That's them. I'll introduce you if you want. But…"

"But?"

I breathe and straighten my back. "Hang on. Let me finish this last stretch."

Balancing on my left foot, I bend my right leg so my foot is pressed against my inner thigh.

"Standing lotus?" Ella asks me, pacing like a caged lioness.

"Standing *half* lotus," I answer.

"Well, you can't do full lotus standing," she laughs.

"True." I soak in the glorious tension as my hips release and then change legs.

"Is all this how you get that body?" She waves a hand at me, pointing from my legs to my chest.

"And a strict diet. Which brings me to a conversation I want to have with you."

Her jaw drops. "You think I need to go on a diet?"

My left leg snaps down. "What? No."

Her face reddens as she hugs herself. "I know I've put on a few pounds."

"A few pounds? Where?" I approach her despite being drenched in sweat and possibly smelling bad. "I think you're goddamn perfect."

"As…what?"

"A woman."

"But you only date—"

"I don't date. I pay for sex," I growl. "I pay professional women to suck my dick, spread their legs, and then leave."

Her breath hitches. "I didn't leave. You left."

"I know." I turn around and grab a towel. Changing the subject because we can go round and round on this one, I say, "Bear with me, butterfly. Your father told me you needed a job. I never had an assistant."

"You don't have to keep me. I have another job offer. I'll tell my father—"

"No." I think about the ex who abused her, and I see red thinking of someone hurting her. "Your father was right. You're just back in town. I don't think it's wise for you to work in a place where that animal can find you."

"Ever?" She clutches her throat. "I worked on a Master's thesis while I was in Sydney. I want to teach, Balor."

The way she says my name almost brings me to my knees.

"Just until I know your ex has forgotten about you."

Although, what I know about abusive types is they rarely give up and walk away. Too often, the woman ends up dead. A shiver runs through me. Fuck. No.

She blinks. "My father, I get. But why you? Why do you care?"

That's what I'm figuring out.

Breathing heavily, I say, "I don't know. I just do."

"Is it wise that I work for you if you have these feelings?" She folds her arms, using my hesitation to get out of this job.

"They're not feelings, they're..." Fuck, I don't know how I feel.

My heart's been racing since she stepped into this gym. Her smile melts something inside me and awakens a part of me that wasn't exactly dead. I've just never felt alive like this before.

Until now.

"I don't know what I need as far as an assistant," I say to get out of my head. "Why don't we figure it out as we go?"

Shrugging, she says, "That works. What time do you want me?"

Now... "Huh?"

"To start every morning. Dad said he starts at eight."

"Eight is fine."

"What time do you get here?"

"That...changes." I toss the towel and turn away, facing a problem I've been having for months.

Sleeping. My mind is a running engine. I can't shut it off. I eventually fall asleep but it's never for very long. Which is why I agreed to Trace, who I need more as a driver than a bodyguard.

"Where's your office?" Ella asks.

"Next door." I push a button and steer her through the secret panel that opens to my very utilitarian office.

Ella wanders to the large plate-glass window overlooking my datacenter filled with servers and storage units, her face in awe.

"What are you? IBM?" she jokes.

"You're not the first person to compare what we have to IBM."

"That makes me feel...smart."

"You are smart," I correct her, forcibly. "The way you speak and carry yourself."

"Yale will be proud."

Fuck, I almost forgot that. My brothers and I tout our Ivy League educations and here I accidentally have a contender for top grad working for me. I'm about to ask her something about Yale when my office door flies open and Shane busts in like he usually does.

"Yo, Maverick, Sectors 1 and 2 aren't reporting."

I go still when Shane calls me by my code name. I need to remind him and the others in my command center to nix that with Snow around.

I step aside and let Shane see Ella and his face drops. "Errr."

"Maverick?" She catches on. "Wasn't he a fighter pilot

for the Navy?"

Shane and I exchange glances. She must not know her father goes by Iceman. The first correct thing that man did. Kept his sins out of his daughter's head, so she can't be kidnapped for intel.

Thinking about her getting kidnapped makes my vision blur with fury.

The global select team, including me, were never able to hack Iceman's code. There wasn't enough time, and it was too complicated. But enough tools and tips were shared for geniuses to keep at it.

Rather than churning endless nights trying to hack it, I carved my own foothold. I *hired* Iceman and will give him projects that will reveal his code. Even if it's in pieces.

"It stands for being an innovator, a rebel," I say, covering myself.

She nods. "Oh right. In the literal sense. Cool."

When she turns back to the window, I punch Shane in the arm.

"Sectors 1 and 2, you said?"

"Aye."

Ella turns around and her eyes dance up and down Shane's frame, igniting the kind of jealous rage I thought I was immune to.

"Anything I can do to help?" she asks. "Whatever it is you're talking about?"

If this were any other situation, I would shove an unwanted assistant at Shane so fast...

But not Ella.

"Unless you want a career in cyber security, you—" I stop talking when she waves me off.

She wants to teach.

"Shane Quinlan, this is Ella Snow." I make the introductions. "I'll meet you in your office in a minute, Shane."

She fidgets when I say her name but smiles at Shane.

"Quinlan? Are you Trace's brother?" she asks.

"Cousin. And it's nice to meet you," Shane says to Ella and leaves, flashing me a knowing smirk.

"Can you do me a favor, butterfly?" I grab my gym bag from the chair near my desk.

Her cheeks swell at me calling her that. "Depends on the favor."

"We're in agreement that what happened between us, every piece of it, the plane ride, the hours we spent in the hotel room, and how much I paid you stays between us." I hate that I sound like some pervert coach, harassing his progeny.

"And the shower," she whispers, her eyes trailing over me again.

That shower sex was the best of my life. "Definitely the shower. Everything."

"Of course." She exhales.

"Good, who you fuck is your business."

"Exactly." Pain in her eyes floods my veins with rage.

Why hadn't her father done anything about her abuse?

Watching her with her father, I see Ella controls her own life. But she smartly heeds warnings about her safety.

I love sex and I wanted you...

"How are you doing?" I ask her, moving a tendril of dark auburn hair from her face.

"I'm good. Still adjusting to the gravitational pull of the earth from this hemisphere."

My eyes go wide. "You feel that too? The difference? I thought I was crazy!"

"I can't say if you're crazy. Leaving me in a hotel room—"

"I'm sorry," I say with my eyes on the floor.

I don't explain why I left though, and she doesn't ask because she accepts that I blew off a hooker.

Damn... That's cold.

"And what will be my duties, Mr. O'Rourke?"

"You can call me Balor around here. Everyone does." Knowing I probably stink, I say, "I need to take a shower."

Her jaw tightens. "My duties wouldn't have anything to do with that, would they?"

Testing boundaries, I approach her. "Depends."

Getting sucked off in the shower is something I'd highly enjoy. Something in her eyes tells me she would. Because she likes me. And can fall for me, the way I can fall for her.

Then, I remind myself that I don't do relationships. What I saw one night traumatized me from ever wanting one. Something no one else in my family knows.

If only Ella would agree to something no-strings. But I saw her heart and her passion. She might think she could do it, but when she catches feelings, I'll hurt her.

"I'll explain more of what I need when I get out of the shower. In the meantime..." I glance around and think of something for her to do. "Why don't you order us some breakfast? There's a menu on my desk with stuff circled that I like. Order yourself anything you want."

"What about your guys?"

"I've never seen them eat food for breakfast." I shrug, skimming the waistband of my workout shorts.

"I'm sure they do. If you spend hours cooped up in your office, how do you know?" She strolls to the door. "I'll see if they want something."

Before I can say no, she's gone, taking her scent with her.

I know what I want. I want her in my shower and my bed. I have to figure out how to make that happen without getting my heart involved. Or hers.

***

After three days of Ella being in the office, it's like all

the geeks I hired have developed a Casanova side. They flirt with her shamelessly, clearly not aware of proper office protocol.

The only woman on my team is Camryn, who's as nerdy as them.

Watching my nerds get their alpha on over my woman unsettles me. My woman. Damn, I like thinking of her as mine.

It's time to break up this party.

I catch her in the breakroom making cups of coffee for the team's afternoon caffeine fix. I come up behind her, wanting to press my thick, relentless groin against her ass.

I should fire her. Let her take that job with the school and give her Trace. Of course, what I'm about to suggest is only going to bring us closer. And me to the edge of doing something I know I shouldn't.

"Can I talk to you for a second?"

She whips around. "Oh, God. You scared me."

Her complexion goes white and next, she's shaking.

"Did he attack you from behind?" My voice is low and deadly.

She sniffs. "How did you know that?"

"Because fucking cowards do that. And men who hit women are fucking cowards." My crass language, vein pulsing, and lips snarling don't make me sound tame.

But Ella doesn't look at me with fear. She has no reason to be afraid of me. She trusts me. And I love that. It's blind trust. I had her in a hotel room and could have done anything to her. If there was an evil bone in my body, I had an opportunity.

"I really want to hold you right now, but it's not appropriate."

"I know… Boss." Her sadness guts me.

How the fuck did we get here? Oh, right. I hired her cyber-terrorist father to work for me so I could take him down.

"He'll never touch you again. I promise you."

"You sound so…primal." She exhales. "But you can't promise me that, Balor. I won't be put on lockdown or shoved behind guards because that'll mean he won."

Fuck, I love her strength.

"And you've not heard from him?"

"No. He's…" She hesitates. "He has a lot to lose since I'm no longer under his control."

I'm sickened by what happened to her. I *will* find and punish that prick. My chest tightens and a thickness in my throat makes me heave. I've never killed anyone. Never had to. Never wanted to. I deliver intel to my brothers, who use my evidence to assassinate our enemies.

That's my role. But this… This hatred of a man I've never met and the desire to see him suffer and die at my hand will eat me alive, turn me into someone I don't want to be.

"I'd like to talk about you working for me," I say to Ella.

I need to get out of my head or I'll strangle my plants.

"Did I do something wrong?" She bites her lip.

Fuck, I want those red velvet pillows wrapped around my dick so badly.

"No." I touch her arm, needing more contact or I'll go insane. "Ordering food for us all day and making coffee isn't something I really need."

She nods. "I understand."

"But there is something I can really use you for."

Her eyes widen. "Yeah?"

It's thrilling to think she'd agree to be my no-strings, plaything. God, the fun we could have.

"If you've noticed I don't always make it into the office by eight."

"Or nine. Or ten." She smirks. "Late nights with the

ladies?"

I push her against the breakroom wall, my control snapping. "No. There's been no one else, Ella. I... I can't." Rolling my eyes, realizing I'm making it sound like I can't get it up, I clarify, "I can't be with anyone else. Not while I still have your taste in my mouth."

And what I'm about to ask is only going to make her a bigger temptation.

I might be a genius, but I'm a masochist too, apparently.

CHAPTER SIXTEEN
ELLA

The following Monday, Trace tells Dad he needs to find his own way to work. Grumbling, he orders an Uber. God forbid he takes the subway.

Trace then brings me to a three-story brick townhouse in a very chic Astoria neighborhood.

Last week, Balor confessed to having horrible sleep habits, ones that make him impossibly late every morning. He's even missed appointments.

"It's a lot for me to admit that I need this," he confessed, blushing.

Then he assigned me the duty of waking him up. In his bed. And making sure he's awake and into the shower.

Trace parks in the driveway and lets me inside the house through the kitchen. My jaw drops at the size of it. On the island is an envelope, and inside is a key to the house. Along with a bunch of passwords and pins.

I'm flattered by how much Balor trusts me.

Trace tips his head to me and disappears into a room behind the kitchen after fisting a Red Bull from the pantry.

Past the kitchen, through a living room with a fireplace, I find the staircase near the front door.

Swallowing, I climb, mentally counting the steps. It's something I do to reduce stress. At the top of the stairs, a landing stretches out.

Which bedroom is his?

He never told me. A few open doors suggest those aren't the rooms. I take Balor for a *sleep-with-the-door-closed* kind of guy.

"Just make sure I'm awake. I sometimes take a pill and the morning is all fog and blur," he added last week.

I reach the second of the two closed doors. The first was a bathroom. So clearly, this one is Balor's bedroom. He's sleeping on the other side of this door. Resting my head on the raised panels door, I take deep breaths as my fingers close around the cool steel lever.

My breath releases when it opens. It occurs to me that I've never woken up anyone. Not even my dad. After bad dreams that made me cry, he came into my room.

I certainly never woke up Wes. My only moments of peace, other than being at school, were when the prick was asleep. Or at work.

Balor's body comes into view and all I want to do is climb into bed with him. Wake him up with my mouth.

This sounded pathetically easy a few days ago, but it's ridiculously hard because Balor is sleeping naked.

Lying on his stomach, he's twisted in the blankets that barely cover his thick legs and sculpted ass.

My God...

Slowly, I approach the bed, breathing in the scent of musk, spice, and mint.

"Balor," I whisper, gently nudging his shoulder.

His skin feels so warm, and I want to keep touching him, but he lurches up, still on his stomach. Shockingly, a gun appears from under a pillow, and next, I'm staring down a barrel.

"It's me!" I cry out, frozen.

A bright green eye finally opens, and he shoves the gun back under the pillow. "Christ." He rolls over and yanks the covers up. "What time is it?"

"Seven." The time he told me to be here. "Did you sleep okay?"

"I don't know." He's groggy and adorable with his hair mussed up.

I could gawk at him like a love-sick schoolgirl, or be the mature assistant he needs. "Come on. Up. Shower."

"Yes, ma'am," he says seductively, staring at me with heavily-lidded eyes.

Then he pushes the covers away and stands to his full height.

Completely naked.

His glorious, thick, veiny cock is hard and bobbing.

He expects me to look away, but I stare into his eyes and then work my gaze down his body. It's nothing I hadn't seen before. By the time my eyes reach his cock, his hand is wrapped around it.

"Can you handle this?" he asks, gravelly, deep, and so very male.

"The gratuitous inappropriate nudity?"

"Aye. This job. Me. Like this. Every morning."

"You don't see me running away, do you?"

He leans in bringing our faces close. He just woke up, but his breath is sweet. "Good girl."

"I just didn't think I'd need a bulletproof vest."

"I'll never hurt you. Ever." He spins and ambles to his bathroom.

The view from behind and his round, hairless ass is almost as good a view as the front. I stare. And tonight, alone in my bed, I'll remember this and make myself come.

As Balor closes the bathroom door, our eyes catch and he smiles. "Make us some breakfast, butterfly."

Heated and clouded with lust, I manage to navigate the stairs and not fall down the entire flight.

In the kitchen, I open the stainless-steel fridge and without any requests, I get creative. I take out eggs, cheese, and veggies.

By the time Balor comes down, showered and dressed, I've plated two veggie omelets. I remember he said he doesn't eat meat.

He struts in wearing an MIT T-shirt under a hoodie and faded jeans. "That smells amazing."

"Not as amazing as you," I mumble to myself, reaching

into the fridge for orange juice.

As I turn back, I nearly drop the container.

He's practically pressed into me. "Did you say something, butterfly?"

"Nope."

"Lying to your boss? That deserves a dose of dirty punishment."

"I wouldn't dream of it." I bite my lip. "Juice?"

"Sure. I also need a protein shake for after my workout."

"Absolutely. What do you—" I'm pointing inside the fridge, but he snags my hand and leads me back to the island.

"Eat before it gets cold."

"Okay." I pick up the fork, watching him take a seat on a stool on the other side. "I toasted up sunflower bread I found in the pantry."

"My favorite." He takes a bite.

"Who shops for you?"

"I have a housekeeper who comes in every day around noon. She makes up the bed. Does laundry. Cleans. Shops."

"I see. Do I need to help her with anything?"

"No. She takes care of the house. You take care of *me*." The visceral annunciation makes my core throb.

"Right."

***

The next two days go the same way.

On Wednesday morning, I make protein waffles topped with fruit and a side of fried tomatoes. But Balor doesn't come downstairs. I wrap up the food in foil and place it in the warming drawer, then climb the stairs to find him.

In his bedroom, he's standing in a towel, slung low on his hips. The sight is nothing short of phenomenal.

"Problem?" I ask.

He spins around, and God, I wish that towel would fall to the ground. We can be friends with benefits. Because all I want is his cock. He's a great man. But I'm not ready for a commitment yet.

"This is the worst part of my day. Picking out what to wear. Too much to think about."

Taking this as a challenge, I step past him into the apartment-sized walk-in closet. Stacked wardrobes are filled with jeans, dress pants, casual pants, track pants, and suits.

I enjoy getting the hang of cooking and experimenting with breakfast recipes. But dressing him *will* be the favorite part of my day.

Nothing has a label, which means it's all custom.

Don't get me started on the ties. There are only a handful because he doesn't wear one to the office, but they're the softest things I've ever touched in my life.

His hung-up shirts rival the best layout at Barneys or The Armoury. Rows of crisp linen and raw silk long-sleeve shirts take up a whole wall. One section is drawers of neatly folded polos, bright white undershirts, graphic T's, Henleys, and in one drawer alone, MIT merch. Sweatshirts, logo T's, joggers, and zip-up hoodies.

One wall houses his shoes. Loafers. Oxfords. Monk straps. Boat shoes. Top brand sneakers. And hidden in the back, combat boots.

The faint blue and white paint splotches suggest they may be from the paintball craze. Because this man certainly isn't painting houses.

I never thought about being a stylist, but I love dressing up Balor. Once he's put together and comes down to eat, I smile watching this handsome man beautifully dressed move through the kitchen pouring his coffee, thinking *I did that.*

I catch his lingering stare that speak volumes about how much he wants me. But he hasn't touched me.

"I saw something on the schedule about a meeting a few hours north of here?" I say, fixing his tie.

His eyes bore into me. "We're visiting a semiconductor factory."

Like other meetings, I manage his phone. In the passcodes he handed over without hesitation was his home screen lock pin.

I'm floored by his trust in me. Or it could be he knows I don't have the slightest clue what to do with a stranger's phone.

A man in a suit greets us at the factory, and a few minutes later, I realize he's the CEO who works out of Hong Kong. He flew in to meet with Balor, personally.

This had been scheduled before I started working for Balor, and all I saw on his calendar was: Chip Warehouse Walkthrough.

For a hot minute, I thought we were going to Frito Lay.

After the standard tour, I'm handed a hazmat suit and minutes later, we're in a quadruple-locked lab. It doesn't take me long to figure out that they're making custom semiconductor chips to Balor's specifications. He talks freely around me, and my chest tightens when it all comes together.

I smile and nod, feigning boredom, all while my insides are twisting.

Balor is building weaponized drones.

We peel out of our hazmat suits an hour later, and when my legs tangle, I nearly fall on my face, but Balor catches me.

"I got you," he drawls, his hands around my waist.

Damn, that feels good.

"You got me? Who's got you?" I say with a smile.

He laughs and tugs the rest of the ugly plastic suit off

me. "Superman fan, huh?"

"Sorry, Batman. I'm team Clark Kent. The movies, though. Not the comics."

"I collected comics when I was younger."

"They're probably worth a lot of money."

"I guess." He shrugs. "I would never sell the comic books that got me through tough times."

"Tough times? You?"

He pushes those dark, thick glasses up his nose almost robotically. "I was bullied as a kid."

This floors me. "What suicidal moron bullies the son of…"

Balor tilts his head, alarm darkening his eyes. "There were a lot of us in my family. People lost track."

"Some say it builds character." I straighten my spine.

"And an enemies list," he says low. "I got hurt rather bad my freshman year at MIT. My brothers… Took care of it."

"And do you…" The air leaves my lungs. "Take care of people?"

"Aye." He waves his phone. "Revenge via technology."

I relax. I can deal with the mafia connection if his hands aren't stained in blood. I don't know if I could date a killer. I know that appeals to some women who crave alpha men who will burn down the world for them. After what I went through with Wes, I'm not sure I could ever trust that a man prone to violence would not turn that anger on me.

Lost in my head, I catch on that the assistant for the CEO says her boss would like to have dinner with us. Balor fidgets and politely refuses.

They'd treated us to lunch already.

"It's getting late, and there's a storm coming," Balor mentions the heavy snowfall the meteorologists have been promising all day.

I'd forgotten about it, but looking up at the sky, a swirl of angry gray clouds takes my breath away.

Moisture in the air thickens, and the temperature drops quickly.

We're at least one hundred miles from Astoria.

With Balor's hand on the small of my back, we leave the building, a glass façade that had sparkled against the blue sky earlier.

"Did the CEO travel twenty-three hours just for that two-hour tour?" I ask Balor.

"Aye. I insisted. That's how I know he's taking my business seriously."

At Balor's SUV, I notice my skirt twisted getting in and out of that hazmat suit.

When I adjust the zipper before getting into the Rivian, an electric land yacht, Balor does a double-take at me.

"What?" I ask.

"I don't want to sound rude. But did you wear that same outfit a couple of days ago?"

Horror floods through me, and my cheeks flare with heat. "Um. Yeah?"

"Are you telling me or asking me?"

"I... I don't have many winter clothes left right now."

"Left?"

My face heats up. "All my things are still at Wes' house. I basically fled with the clothes on my back and my passport."

Fury boils in his eyes. "What's his address? I'm going there right now to get your belongings."

And just like that, I could turn this guy into a murderer. Because it would come down to that, knowing Wes.

Shaking my head, I say, "No. I'm sure he threw it all away. That shows I mean nothing to him."

Balor opens the rear door to the Rivian. "Get in. Now."

"I'm serious—"

Two thick fingers land on my mouth. The heat we generated those few hours weeks ago roars like kerosene from a single touch. "So am I. Get. In."

Giving up, I slide into the backseat, and when the door closes behind Balor, Trace pulls away.

"Please," I beg. "I know you're powerful. And your family is..."

"Deadly."

"Look, he's a cop, all right," I blurt and wait for the flicker of hesitation in Balor's eyes. "I don't want to make trouble for you."

"Where is he a cop? What precinct?" Balor's face goes rigid.

"He bounces around. He's a sergeant of a special unit, I forget which one."

Rubbing his knuckles, he says, "We have cops in our pockets."

"Have you ever tried to pit one against a fellow officer?" I whisper. "They protect their own."

Balor's jaw tenses. Shaking his head, he murmurs, "You promise you haven't heard from him?"

"Yes, I promise." I nod exaggeratedly.

"Then buy more clothes for yourself." Balor strokes the ponytail that falls over my shoulder. "Do you need a day off?"

"It all happened so fast six months ago. When we got to Sydney, I only had a few hundred dollars in the bank. Working as a special-ed teacher doesn't pay much. Dad gave me his credit card, and I bought clothes there. But it was summer."

"Spend the money *I* gave you. I gave you twenty thousand dollars."

"I don't *want* that money." How can I explain the pit that landed in my stomach when I took it?

"Why?"

"I screwed you because I liked you and I *wanted* you. I didn't want to be paid."

Trace cackles from the front seat.

"Pipe down, Quinlan."

"Aye, sir."

Men like Balor who travel with guards and drivers have to trust the people who see them behind the veil.

"You liked me?" Balor sets his gaze back to me, speaking softer. Lower. Just to me.

"Of course." I inhale and struggle to speak. "Didn't you...like me?"

You fucked me like you did.

His eyes slip closed. "I did like you. It felt different. I eventually figured out why."

"Because I wasn't really a hooker," I mutter under my breath. "Do you still...like me?"

I'm tempted to remind him of the bulge I often see in his pants. But I'm old enough to know men can fuck women they hate really well, too.

Not that Balor hates me. But men can fuck without emotions on the turn of a dime.

"I do like you, Ella."

"Then—"

"Balor, 5-0, coming up on my rear," Trace says, stoically. "Lights and sirens."

I freeze. 5-0. Cops.

"What?" Balor leans into the front compartment from the back seat where he and I usually sit when Trace drives us around. "We're not even doing sixty."

"Balor..." I whisper. "Cop."

"It's okay." He squeezes my hand. "Quinlan, your heat's registered?"

"This one is."

"Pull over."

Only, there's a loud pop and the car swerves hard to the right. The last thing I see is the center median coming up in the windshield.

CHAPTER SEVENTEEN
BALOR

"Hold the fuck on," Trace says, and swings the Rivian across three lanes with the cool air of a military pilot pulling the nose of an aircraft up out of a dive.

He cuts off several cars but manages to avoid hitting them. Then he pulls to a hard stop when we reach the right lane shoulder.

Ella shakes in my arms. "No. No, no."

Kissing her forehead, I say, "Stay in the car. Do not get out."

"Quinlan, out. You and me." I push the door open, thankful I'm not on the roadside with traffic screaming by.

Trace and I strut to the back of the SUV to see my left rear tire is flat.

"I heard a pop," he says to me. "I think they shot the tire."

I study the dark blue cruiser with *State Trooper* printed in yellow sitting a few car lengths behind us. I don't see cameras.

Shaking my head, I say, "Okay. Get back inside the car. Lock the doors. Protect Ella. Whatever it takes, man."

"Aye." He spins around, obeying my command.

The light bar on top of the cruiser still flashes, but the trooper kills the sirens. The cop remains in the front seat, talking into his radio transmitter while looking straight ahead.

At me.

Ella's ex is a cop.

They protect their own.

I don't worry about facing a police officer in Astoria, but I'm not in Astoria right now. The trooper, in a solid black uniform and an enormous hat, gets out. He struts toward me with a baton dangling in his fingers.

"Something wrong, officer?" I ask.

He stops and tilts his head at my flat tire. "You got a blowout."

"You had your lights on before the blowout. We weren't speeding."

"License and registration."

"I wasn't driving. My bodyguard was."

His right cheek twitches. "Who the hell are you that you need a bodyguard?"

"Someone with enemies." I cross my arms.

"I'd like to look at your vehicle."

My heart pounds with rage. "Sure thing, but just an FYI, my bodyguard is carrying. He's licensed."

"Thanks for the warning." He struts past me.

"I'm calling for service," I shout out to him.

"Don't got a spare?" he says over his shoulder. "Or are your nice hands too good to change a flat?"

"My nice hands earn me a nice living. So yes, sir."

That answer turns him around and he just stares at me. It rattles me because I can't download his brain to figure out what he's thinking.

His head swivels toward my rear window briefly. "Did you know tinted windows are technically illegal?"

"Then I would suggest your detectives go after car dealers. It's an option I paid good money for." I block his view of the rear door. "My assistant is in the back seat."

"Is she carrying, too?"

"No."

"You got an assistant, a bodyguard, and a two-hundred-thousand-dollar SUV. Who the hell are you?"

"Someone important, officer."

When he steps around me to speak to Trace, I take out my phone and call Shane.

"It's me. I'm on the highway. Find my car and tell me where the hell I am. I have a flat. We had 5-0 on our ass.

Trace heard a pop, then a tire blew out."

"On it," Shane says and then informs me of the town we're in.

"Something is off here, Shane."

"I'll call a tow truck," the officer says, handing Trace back his license and carry permit, but no ticket.

Thank fuck.

"That's not necessary."

"Just offering assistance. That's what we're here for. To help. Protect and serve," he annunciates.

I don't know if I'm wired because I have Ella and everything is firing inside me to protect her, or if this guy is fucking with me.

"Yes, officer," I grind out and watch him walk back to his cruiser. "Did that sound off to you, Shane?" I murmur into my phone.

"What's his plate number?" he asks and I read it to him. "Okay, his station house is a few miles away."

"I don't want some random service truck touching my fucking car."

"Trace will fix the tire. He's not delicate, trust me. He's a warrior. He and Rhys make us look like spoiled brats."

"Aye. See you soon." I end the call, but a wicked chill cuts through me.

Tiny flakes fall on my home screen and blot into pinpricks of water. I look up and mutter, "Aw, fuck."

The snowstorm.

***

Trace changes the tire, but minutes later, the trooper is back, advising me the highway is closing and I need to get off at the next exit.

Now we're stuck in the beginning of a monster blizzard.

I won't risk the ride downstate, and I can't ask my brother's helicopter pilot to pick us up in a violent snow squall that's expected to quickly blanket the whole county.

Looks like we're staying in a local hotel.

We drive to the nearest one with a great rating and find the check-in line fills the lobby. The highway closure means every other stranded motorist is looking for a room, too.

Trace talks on his phone and keeps an eye out since this place hasn't been scoped out for a stop. I don't expect anyone here to know who I am, let alone want to hurt me. Unless I act like an asshole and bully my way to the front of the line and make parents with crying babies sleep in their cars by demanding three rooms.

We finally get to the check-in desk, and the clerk is sweating. "Can I help you?"

"I need two rooms. I have two employees with me." I hand over my driver's license with a one-hundred-dollar bill behind it.

The guy, who's young and clean-cut, pulls his tie and says, "I only have rooms with a king bed. We're keeping the two queen rooms for families. We're all out of cribs and roll-away beds."

I blink, taking that in. "The one-bed rooms are fine."

The guy processes everything and hands me the keycards. "We're ordering pizzas and warm food platters for everyone. They should be set up here in the lobby in a little while."

Nodding, I say, "Thank you."

I strut toward Trace who's clearly guarding Ella for me.

She's on her phone but hangs up when I get closer. "I spoke to my dad and told him we were staying the night."

I freeze, hearing her mention her dad. "Did you tell him which hotel?"

She casually shakes her head. "He didn't ask."

"Did you tell him about the State Trooper pulling us

over and the flat?"

"No. Just that the highway is shut down."

Her father hasn't called or messaged me. His daughter is an adult, and she works for me. He has no idea about Los Angeles, and hopefully hasn't tracked my credit cards to find out which hotel I'm in. Or that I'm registered in two rooms, each with one bed.

Now, either I look like a bossy perv and shove Trace in a room by himself so I can be with Ella, my assistant, or I attempt to share a bed with a six-five ex-Irish Defences alpha.

"I'm sorry," Ella says, sounding guilty and it guts me.

"You didn't cause the snowstorm," I tell her with a hand firmly on her waist. "This isn't your fault."

"Yeah, but I wouldn't be here if my father hadn't forced you to hire me." She gazes out at the snow quickly piling up.

I hate the pain in her eyes from thinking she's caused this problem I have.

Is it a problem?

Either I make her sleep alone, with me, or with Trace. Fuck this, I *need* a third room.

Angry over this impossible choice, I turn back to the front desk, but a manager gets on a loudspeaker and says, "Folks, I'm sorry. There are no more rooms. We're full up."

CHAPTER EIGHTEEN
ELLA

"Here." Balor hands Trace and me packaged toothbrushes and travel-size toothpaste tubes from the gift shop.

"I keep a set in my purse." I wave it off and hope he returns it so someone else can use it. Or gives it away.

I started keeping them on me the first time Wes locked me out of the house. I rode the subway for hours a few times, waiting for him to cool off.

I'd been too embarrassed to crash on Hannah's sofa. I didn't dare go home to my dad, who would have seen bruises and flipped out.

Balor steers me to the elevator. "They're putting out food in a little while. Get settled in your room and meet me back down here in the lobby."

I go still.

My room.

Balor and I aren't sharing a room. Why did I think we would? I hoped it, but...

"Here." He hands me a keycard. "Do you want Trace to go with you?"

"He's your bodyguard," I say, brushing a hand through my hair, wondering what I look like after such a long, trying day.

"I don't need a bodyguard. My brothers insist."

I like that his brothers take his safety seriously, but it also makes me wonder why they insist. Is Balor in some kind of danger he's not telling me about?

"Where are you going?" I ask.

"You worried about me, butterfly?" He pinches the collar of my coat. "I'll stay here and grab us a table to eat. You *need* food, Ella."

"Honestly, a bag of chips—"

"You're eating." Balor hovers over me. "You barely ate lunch. And chips are hardly a meal."

My heart flutters that he'd notice how much I'm eating. Or not eating. I've not mentioned that spikes of nausea attack me throughout the day. And I'm scared to death of what it means.

"There are a lot of people in this hotel. I don't know how much food they are putting out. I want to make sure you get a meal."

Nodding, I spot Trace rocking on his heels a few feet away, wearing shades and scanning the room. Sure enough, as we speak, the lobby is filling up.

"Trace, here's the key to our room. Please sweep both." Balor hands him the second keycard.

"Aye, boss." Trace takes it and struts toward the elevator.

I turn to walk away and Balor tugs on my arm. The force sends my forehead straight for his mouth where he plants a kiss on my skin.

"What was that for?" I ask, swallowing hard.

"I... I don't know," he whispers harshly. "It's just so damn hard not to."

Not sharing a room is his way of keeping a distance he's fighting.

"I'll be right back." I turn, and when I'm not grabbed this time, my heart sinks.

Trace and I ride the crowded elevator and on the fourth floor, others mill around with little kids, looking for their room. Trace takes the lead and strolls confidently down the right-hand hallway. At an alcove with two doors, he stands to the side.

"It looks like you're right next door."

Nodding, I key my way in and wonder if Balor hears me try to make myself come later, will he knock down the wall to get inside and help me finish?

***

Twenty minutes later, I'm back in the crowded lobby, and Trace launches into full bodyguard mode. He's visibly rigid, glaring at anyone who comes remotely near me and Balor.

While Balor saves us a place on the food line, Trace steers me toward an open table with his hand on the small of my back. He's protecting me. But he's Balor's bodyguard. Does Trace see what I mean to Balor by protecting me like this?

Trace Quinlan still makes me uneasy. He not only saw me in a robe after Balor fucked me, but he paid me for the sex we had. Now, here I am. Balor's assistant. But sleeping in a separate hotel room.

Riding with Trace each morning, I never thought to bring up what happened in Los Angeles, but now that we're in this hotel situation again and with Balor several feet away, I feel like I need to set the record straight.

"You know I'm not really an escort, right?"

Jaw tight and his thick body in a military posture, he says, "None of my business, lass."

"Fair enough. But I'm not. I just told Balor that to have a little..." When I fade off, Trace finally looks at me with a cocked brow to finish. "A little fun. A fantasy."

"Fantasy," he says in a deep timbre. "Fantasy about sleeping with a rich, powerful man?"

"No." I smile. "Getting lost with a stranger. Or... Being away from the world and not caring about anything."

"Do women...like that?"

If I'm still around next December and there's a holiday grab bag, I'm tossing in bundles of romance novels for Trace and the others at the command center. Tip them off about what women want.

"The accent does it for me, too." I wink.

"Accent."

"That brogue. Yours is deeper than Balor's."

"He's lived here in America since grade school. My brother and I just moved abroad around six months ago."

"Makes sense." I nod. "You were in the military in Ireland?"

"Aye." He stiffens and just as there are so many American wounded warriors from two decades of war in the Middle East, Trace might have scars. Emotional or even physical.

I imagine this tall and broad man with damaged skin under his suit. Marks from an honorable duty to serve. Unlike my scars, which are permanent memories of how I couldn't fight back.

Etching my own skin with tattoos was the only way I knew how to take back my power.

Shaking that away, I go to ask Trace some more questions about the tattoos I see snaking up his neck, but Balor joins us at the table.

Trace stands when Balor sits down. Looking at the plates of food that he made for us, I smile. It's everything I like.

"Quinlan, sit," Balor says, handing out wrapped plasticware that feels cheap in my hands.

I can only imagine how a billionaire feels using this crap.

"You two, eat." Trace adjusts his suit jacket. "There're too many people here for me to relax."

"They're poor schleps like us who got caught in the storm and had to find refuge off the highway. No one's even looked my way." Balor is next to me, our legs bumping. "I also hacked into the cameras here and sent feeds to Shane. If anyone does something stupid, Lachlan will track them down."

In a lethal murmur, Trace says, "If something happens, I hope Lachlan will let me and Rhys help."

Even Balor stops what he's doing based on Trace's tone. "That would be up to Lachlan."

Who in the world is this Lachlan character?

Trace's jaw twitches. "I'll be able to eat better when you're back in the rooms."

"The food will be cold then, Trace," I argue, even if it's kind of cold now.

"They have microwaves," he says, looking straight ahead. "Not that I'd mind if they didn't."

I don't know everything about fitness, but at six-five, that man must require several thousand calories a day. We had lunch with the CEO, but Trace stayed with the car. I assume he ate on his own somewhere in that small town.

Balor elbows me. "Eat. Don't worry about him."

Jealousy laces his tone, and I smirk, yanking the plastic wrapper away from the fork, knife, and spoon.

The hotel put out heated trays of baked ziti, wings, Swedish meatballs, eggplant rollatini, and at least thirty boxes of pizza.

Balor grabbed a little bit of everything.

"Oh, there was salad?" I ask, seeing someone walk by holding a plate overflowing with dark, leafy greens.

"Aye, I guess." Balor stabs a tiny meatball, looking at it with suspicion. "I don't know a lot about women, but handing one a salad unsolicited is a quick way to get kicked in the balls."

I choke a laugh around my chicken wing. "I wouldn't kick you in the balls. I wouldn't kick anyone in the balls."

Balor turns to me. "Not even your ex?"

Every muscle in my body tenses. "It never occurred to me. I'm not a violent person."

Balor grumbles. "The asshole counted on that."

He eats with more force like he's annoyed. I hope not at me. He brought it up.

"I'm getting some salad." I scoot away before he or Trace can stop me.

I'm no one, so I don't need protecting the way Balor does. He's mob royalty and a billionaire.

Seeing more plates put out, I juggle two and make one for Trace.

Returning to the table, I shove it at him. "Eat, Trace. Please. You have to be hungry. What good will it do if something happens and you're light-headed?"

He glances down at the heaping plate I made for him. With a faint smile, he takes it and sits down to eat. "Thank you, lass."

I devour my entire plate of salad while Balor speaks on his phone. It's been ringing since we arrived.

One by one, each brother calls him, offering to drive up to collect us.

Over and over Balor tells them the roads are closed. He hangs up, and then another call comes in and it starts all over again.

"Your family cares about you." I nudge him.

He nods, rolling his eyes. "It's because I'm one of the youngest."

"And how old is young?"

"Thirty-five. My sister Shea-Lynne is just a year older than me."

Trace visibly tightens his fork hearing Balor mention his sister.

Balor and I hold each other's gaze, and the depth in his eyes suggests he wants to open up more. I lay my hand on his thigh and watch his eyes flutter. I'm ready to ask him what bothers him about his brothers, but he cuts me off.

"My brothers are not used to me being out of reach. Lachlan often needs my help with intel if someone he dragged to the black site isn't cooperating."

"Black site?" I've heard that term in movies. "And what

does *isn't cooperating* mean?"

Balor's body goes rigid, and his green eyes penetrate me.

"Never mind," I say, figuring it's best I don't know.

"It's the place we take people who deserve to be punished for betraying us." The calmness of his voice scares the living hell out of me.

"I see."

"It's nothing you need to worry about." He wipes his mouth. "My brothers forget how much they need me until I'm not around. They put Shane through the wringer while I was in Sydney."

Mentioning Australia thickens the tension around the table.

"Or..." I smile. "Your brothers *care about you*."

"Errr, I think it's the former."

Trace stands up with his empty plate and heads back to the serving trays for another round. I smile, glad I got him to eat.

"I'm sure it's both." I toss my plastic fork into the center of an empty paper plate.

"Have you heard from your dad?"

"Since I called him and told him I was here with you? No."

"I just think considering what you went through he'd—"

"*I lied to him, Balor*. I didn't tell him the truth about the abuse until we left for Sydney." I cover my mouth for a second. "I worried if my father found out about Wes, he'd try to hurt the bastard. Not kill him of course. My father isn't a..." I hesitate to say killer, sitting with a mob boss. "I worried Wes would have him investigated. I think my father's side work isn't always on the up and up." I wait for a reaction from Balor but get none.

"Go on." Balor probably investigated my father and

knows more than me.

Or Dad is *that* good at covering up his shady side-gigs.

"I explained when we prepared to move back here that he had to let what happened with Wes go. My ex isn't worth having his life torn apart."

"I'm not afraid your dick ex could tear *my* life apart." Balor leans in, eyes above his horn-rimmed glasses. "I can run circles around anything that bastard might try to do to me."

I think about that, but I just don't trust what kind of connections Wes has.

Still, I smile at those green eyes and wonder if Lois Lane felt this way getting close to Clark Kent, only to see Superman behind the glasses.

And thrilled at how the Man of Steel punched a hole in the world to stop it from spinning just to save her.

CHAPTER NINETEEN
BALOR

"I need to stretch my legs." Ella stands up and without waiting for a word from Trace or me, she strolls away.

Maybe she wants some space. We've been together since seven a.m.

I, like many other people around me, am glued to my phone. She isn't. It makes me jealous how she can live in the real world, while I'm sucked into cyberspace and the dark web.

Even if it's all in service to protect my family.

Ella moves languidly and explores the otherwise banal lobby with a few pops of colorful pieces of art on shelves of a massive bookcase on the opposite side of the dining area.

Outside, the snow piles up. A custom feed on my phone from the New York State Highway Department posts alerts and updates on snow removal plans.

It's bad. Plows are grounded until the storm slows down. According to the weather reports, there's a blizzard warning until sunrise.

The main highway is closed but they left smaller two-lane parkways open for local traffic. Still, they're too treacherous to risk a journey home.

Why risk it when I have a roof over my head and a warm bed? Which bed, though?

Good Christ. What the hell do I do about this bed situation?

"Balor, can I speak to you?" Trace's voice lifts my head.

"What's up?" I look up at him.

"I didn't want to say anything in front of Ella." His words ring ominous.

"About?"

"The rooms you secured for us." He pulls at his tie.

"Is there a problem?" Not that I can do much about it.

"There was only one bed." His voice gets low.

"I know," I say, nodding. "They saved ones with two queen beds for families and gave me ones with a king and sofa."

"There wasn't a sofa, and I'm pretty sure that bed was also a queen-size." He clears his throat. "I'll post outside your room and nap against the wall if I get tired."

I exhale, knowing I would never make a guard sleep on the floor. Ella nailed it on the head earlier. What's the point if they're exhausted and stiff?

Stiff.

I hide a chuckle. Two months working for Lachlan and he's got Trace and his brother, Rhys, trained like attack dogs who will turn away comfort.

Trace clears his throat and looks over at Ella, who's plopped down into a wing chair and sipping from a can of soda.

"It's none of my business, but you and Ella…" He must have seen something in my eyes because he doesn't finish that sentence.

"You're right. It's none of your business." I suck in a breath and harness the right way to feel about Trace's intrusive and assuming words.

Griffin, Connor, and Shane work for my brothers and me. We've been aligned with *those* Quinlans for decades. They are as close to being our brothers as any other souls could be. Kieran was supposed to marry their sister, and we would have been bonded by that vow.

Norah Quinlan dying suddenly broke that alliance in name only, but spiritually, the Quinlans were always a top tributary family over any other Irish clan in Astoria.

Breaking the tension, I say, "Trace, I'll stay in Ella's room. It's been a long day. We all need our sleep."

Not that I plan to get any sleep if she's next to me.

"I'll tell Ella about the arrangements." I give a squeeze to Trace's arm. When I stand to get the feeling back in my legs and Trace doesn't follow, I ask, "Are you coming?"

"I heard a man on the food line mention he's a Marine who lost both legs." Trace lifts his pant leg, showing me scarred flesh. "I was lucky. I'd like to buy the man a drink and see if he needs to talk. Opening up helps."

It makes me wonder what the hell Trace went through with the Irish Defences that he would seek out an American stranger to talk to.

"You're officially off duty, Trace. Shane hacked into all the cameras. We're safe." I shuffle toward the television area, hiding a smirk.

Trace wants to spend his night hanging out with a fellow wounded warrior, while I'll be in the room next door, balls-deep in a woman I've been dying for since I left her in that hotel room in Los Angeles.

CHAPTER TWENTY

BALOR

I stroll toward Ella who's watching a wall-mounted television on the opposite side of the lobby. Away from all the food. Away from me.

I can't stop thinking about her. Or whacking off in my shower to the memory of her mouth every damn morning. Because every morning, she wakes me up as part of her job and then leaves the bedroom.

It's time to be honest with myself. She's the real reason we're still in this town. My brother's helicopter pilot has enough skills and could have made the trip. The idea of being snowed in like this, pushing the world and my responsibilities aside for another night alone with Ella pulses through me, my cock aching for her.

Every time I set eyes on Ella, my axis shifts. There's something there. Something hidden, drawing us together, and I don't know what it is.

But I'm her boss and pursuing this obsession with her might turn into a nightmare HR lawsuit. For all the precautions my brothers take to stay off law enforcement's radar, to shatter the carefully constructed veil we live behind for sex is something I'll never live down.

But, Christ, look at her. I'm shockingly aware, with the snow falling, trapping us in this moment, my busy world can stop. Maybe I can get out of my own way and take what I want if Ella is willing to submit to me for one more night.

A dark chuckle tickles my chest. *One night. Yeah, right.*

The idea of taking her in the dark with only the glittering, reflective glow of snowflakes has my cock so hard, I'm making deals with the devil on my shoulder to get what I want.

I don't know where any of this is coming from. No woman paid to suck my cock and go away has made me look back a second time. Yet Ella's dazzling smile every morning waking me up and her soft laugh as we talk over breakfast have me questioning my reality.

Did that plane fly into a chemtrail and rearrange my soul?

But another honest point I need to reconcile is that her father has stopped me from crossing the line with her. That man has darkness behind his eyes, and it's shocking Ella doesn't see it.

That's her dad, I get it. It took me years to see my father for the monster he really is.

Fuck, I can't push this away anymore.

Ella looks so lovely sitting there. Her rich, mahogany hair and dark brown eyes sing to me. And for all that strikes me about her, she's utterly ordinary. She doesn't stand out, and that suits me just fine. The glam look of an expensive whore lost its luster. I want real. And Ella fits that bill.

She fits *me*.

As if she's attuned to me, she lifts those beautiful eyes when I get close. She drinks me in, and her smile lights me up like no other woman.

Paid or not.

"What's up?" she asks, batting her eyelashes.

Without thinking, I grasp her tiny wrist, the pulse beneath the butterfly tattoo dancing against my fingers.

"Can I talk to you?"

She hesitates for a moment but then nods. "Sure."

I help her out of the seat and steer her down a quiet hallway that leads to the pool.

"Is everything okay?" Ella's eyes look tired, a little red, and her makeup is smudged.

Fuck, it's almost nine o'clock at night. Her obvious

exhaustion gives me pause because I'm revved up and ready to launch. Is this a mistake?

"Depends." My gaze lowers to her body.

That cute short skirt and tight sweater caught my eye this morning, and I feel like shit for asking if she's wearing the same clothes over and over.

That scumbag making her run off and leave everything behind stirs an irrational deadly fire in me that I see in my brothers' gazes every day.

Bloodlust I thought I was immune from. Now I see I just needed a woman of my own to light the fuse.

"Depends on what?" Ella responds coyly.

"How do you feel if I sleep in your room tonight?" I can't bottle up what I feel for her anymore.

I'm tired of dreaming of her every night, reliving our hours lost in pleasure in that L.A. hotel room. I've had enough of walking around rock hard, aching in frustration with every pulse of my cock for her.

"You know there's only one bed." She swallows, her throat working.

"I know." My sight goes hazy for a moment, picturing her swallowing my cum one more time.

"If we're in the same bed, I don't know if I'll be able to sleep." She sucks in a breath. "And I thought we shouldn't... You're my boss now. It's...wrong, right?"

"What if I take the choice away from you?" The need to kiss her again is almost unbearable.

Cute white teeth sink into her lower lip. With bright pink cheeks, she says softly, "I... I didn't want to be alone tonight."

Fuck, all the time I've wasted worrying about this and I could have stripped that short skirt off those luscious thighs and buried my head between them sooner.

"Come on." I take her hand and lead her toward the elevators.

"Where's Trace?"

"Having a beer with a wounded warrior," I mumble.

"He seems like a good man." She visibly tenses. "Even if he is a little terrifying."

"Trace is deadly. But I trust him."

"So do I," she says with a smile.

The elevator arrives, but to my bitter chagrin, we don't have the car all to ourselves. Families with kids who'd been in the pool pile in, wrapped in towels, dripping on the vinyl floor.

I never felt the need to breed, which allowed me to sink into the lazy habit of paying for sex. No one to explain a three-day work bender to fix a technical problem.

Ella wants to go back to her teaching job. All my brothers' wives work in some capacity.

When a mom catches my eye, she says softly, "The pool tires them out."

"I'll bet," I say and bury my face into Ella's hair. "I know what will tire me out. Wet and dripping is part of my plan, too. In bed, with you moaning beneath me."

At our floor, the hallway lights flicker. Spending the night in a hotel far away from Astoria on short notice is one thing. Losing power is something else. No Wi-Fi and no way to charge my phone is like rubbing my skin with steel wool.

Ella squeezes my hand, and if anything can get me the hell away from my phone for several hours, it's her.

She makes me feel alive. The air moves differently when I'm with her, and it terrifies me. Because she's not someone I can pay to get on her knees to suck me off and fuck me.

She can leave me, for good. She can't be controlled with money.

"Good thing I'll be here with you tonight." I open her door and steer her inside. "If the power goes out, the electronic locks won't work.

Wryly, she flips the deadbolt. "Old school, right here."

"Clever girl," I growl.

The darkness makes her gasp, and it looks like they're reserving power. "Wow."

"Hang on." I fire up my phone's flashlight.

I bang out a text to Trace.

Me: If you have an extra piece with you, please drop it off to Ella's room. The door locks might stop working.

Trace: 10-4

The deadbolts offer a decent amount of security, but nothing beats the cold steel barrel of a Glock should every other protection measure fail. Choking up, I see Ella's ex being that maniac who would kick in a door.

Ella opens the drapes and a glow from the auxiliary lights outside floods the room. Snow reflects off the glass and drenches the room in soft shadows.

"There's a balcony." She pulls open the door and spins in the falling snowflakes, sticking her tongue out.

Christ, she's beautiful.

"Too bad all the patio furniture is covered in snow." She adorably twirls again.

I join her outside, the snow catching in our hair. "Then I need to get you hot and naked out here."

"I can make snow angels and melt all the snow, you get me so hot, Balor." She grips me and kisses me so hard, it's like two electrical charges firing off.

I'm the one who can melt steel.

"Now, show me the highway and I'll clear the roads!" she says coyly.

"No. You're mine tonight." I press my lips to hers.

"Wow, this is happening."

"It is. If you don't want me, then—"

I don't get another word out when I'm pulled down and our mouths collide in a ferocious, greedy kiss.

I had her in the shower, completely naked and dripping wet. I've been losing my mind ever since.

"You know I don't have pajamas with me," she says, lust in her sweet voice.

"Neither do I." I start unbuttoning her sweater. "And if you did, you wouldn't be wearing them. Not with me."

CHAPTER TWENTY-ONE
ELLA

I shiver, and Balor insists we go back inside, where he secures the balcony doors behind us.

"I can't wait anymore," he says, backing up to the bed, my skirt bunched in his hands.

I can't believe this old plaid micro-mini skirt got Balor to look at me differently. I'd been flirting with fire to see if I could rekindle what we had in Los Angeles. Even if that was stupid because he's my boss now.

More than that, he's a powerful man in a family of killers.

The way his gaze tracked me all day makes that familiar quiver of heat deep in my core roar to life between my legs.

Those hours in Los Angeles with a 'stranger' fulfilled a fantasy and got me over my fear of being alone with a man. Being in *this* hotel room with Balor means something completely different.

Something's at stake, although other than my heart, I don't know what. I could totally fall for him. But he's a billionaire mob hacker who prefers escorts. I'm... I'm just me. A schoolteacher.

"Earth to Ella," Balor teases me with a soft growl. "What's my butterfly thinking?"

That Irish accent warms my chest.

But Balor's vision goes dark whenever the subject of Wes comes up. My ex hasn't bothered me since I got back.

Tonight feels so right for Balor and me, I don't want to voice any concerns.

"I'm thinking of which side of the bed to lay on so you can fuck my mouth." I glance down at my body, shocked at how my nipples have stiffened.

"It doesn't matter... I'll find a way to fuck your mouth

no matter what position you're in," Balor hums in my ear, cupping my ass.

Kissing my neck, he's paralyzed when light suddenly floods the darkened room.

A loud whir of air hits the windows and vibrates the glass.

Gasping, I jump back.

"What the ever-loving fuck?" Balor shoves me behind him. "No. *No. No. No!*"

A ginormous luxury helicopter lands in a field of grass north of the parking lot.

"What is that?" I ask him.

Balor spins around, a vein in his neck pulsing in anger. "My brother's helicopter."

***

Balor's brothers sent their helicopter for him.

When I specifically heard him tell them no.

I loved the idea of getting naked with Balor again under the glow of white shimmering snow through the window. Now that's ruined.

Anticipating another hot night with Balor, my panties are freaking soaked. I use the bathroom to calm down and fix myself. When I finish, the room door is open and deep male voices filter in from the hallway.

I edge out and follow the sounds coming from the second room where Balor is with Trace.

The bodyguard stands there in a white ribbed tank top with a gun holstered under his left shoulder.

"I'll stay here tonight with the Rivian and drive back when the roads open," Trace says.

"They can give this room to anyone stuck in the lobby," I say, putting on my coat.

"I'll let them know," Trace says to me with a bow to his head.

Gripping my hand, Balor adds, "We'll see you

tomorrow."

The bodyguard slips his dress shirt back on. "Aye."

Balor and I walk hand in hand down the hallway to the elevator.

I glance back at Trace who's smiling at us.

At least this time I'm leaving with Balor instead of being left behind.

CHAPTER TWENTY-TWO

ELLA

The next day, Balor picks me up himself in a sleek black Lamborghini. Last night, the helicopter smoothly cut through the falling snow and landed us safely on a Manhattan helipad.

He dropped me off at my apartment around ten p.m. My dad, who monitors satellites for Balor, knew the helicopter was dispatched to airlift us out of that small town. If I didn't go home...there'd be some explaining to do.

Instead of driving us to the command center this morning, Balor parks in front of a high-end boutique on Mayfair Street in Astoria. This city didn't get any snow compared to the blizzard we saw so far north yesterday.

"Today, your job is to buy new clothes," he says from the front seat.

"Great. I love dressing you." I unbuckle myself, wishing I can stay in this amazing car.

He barks a laugh. "I like you dressing me too, but this time, the clothes are for you, butterfly."

"For me?" I pinch my leggings, cheeks heating with shame. "If I embarrassed you yesterday by wearing old—"

He stops me with a finger on my lips. "Shhh. No. Not at all."

All I have to do is open my mouth and I'll be sucking on his fingers.

He helps me out of the sports car and whispers against the curtain of my hair, "You don't embarrass me. You can never embarrass me. Don't you see yourself?"

I'm spun around and my reflection, *our* reflection, shines off the store's glass front doors.

"I don't know what I see," I confess.

"Your looks had nothing to do with what he did to you. If anything, he was probably jealous because you're so goddamn beautiful, he thought he needed to bruise you so no one else would want you. But you know what?"

"What?" I ask, quivering.

"I want you," he utters. "Every inch of you. Bruised skin. Healed skin. Tattoos to cover his sins."

"Balor," I go breathless. "You want me, but you're…"

"I'm your boss." Icy anger seeps into his tone, his inner struggle apparent.

"For now," I challenge him, because I don't *want* this job.

I want to go back to Fredricks Elementary.

Balor stares at me, pensive, with the weight of the world, or at least a mountain of problems, playing out on his face. He's figuring it all out. Me and him. How we make this work.

I can't push, especially since I don't know what I want or what I can give, emotionally speaking. All I want is something physical with Balor because he makes me feel alive.

"Are you coming with me?" I ask.

"Where?" He strokes my ponytail, twisting it in his fingers.

"Inside? Shopping?"

"You want me to?"

I'm aware it's Thursday, the day he meets with his brothers. "If you've got somewhere else you'd rather be."

"There's nowhere else I'd rather be."

A woman emerges from the store and waves.

Balor scoops my hand into his and steers me to the entrance doors. "Erin, thanks for meeting Ella here."

"She doesn't work here?" I turn to Balor.

"I'm a stylist for Shea-Lynne O'Rourke. Brides mostly." Erin beams at Balor.

"I'm not looking to get married. But I do need to refresh my wardrobe." I refuse to repeat where all my other clothes are.

"I can help you with that." Erin opens the door. "Balor, I got this."

I stiffen, thinking he'll leave me.

"I'm staying. For a while. To make sure she's comfortable." His arm winds around my waist.

Erin's face turns pensive like she knows his history. "As you wish."

The name of the store doesn't sound familiar and it's not a chain. Once inside, the high-end fixtures and displays, rival the snazzy Manhattan boutiques. The designer brand names suggest how precious I am to Balor. That he wants me to have this level of luxury. And the help of a stylist to rebuild my wardrobe.

My eyes slip closed, hating that I'm being treated like an injured kitten. I'm off my game because Wes can be anywhere. In Sydney, I felt more like my old self and used my strength to heal from the superficial wounds.

Now my father and Balor want me on lockdown. Am I not seeing the potential danger the way they are?

My fingers tighten around Balor's hand, and he reacts to the change in pressure. "You okay?"

"Uh-huh," I choke out, but I'm having a panic attack.

"What do you need, hun?" Erin asks, swiping an iPad.

"A little bit of everything," I say, feeling overwhelmed already.

"Give us a minute, Erin." Balor tugs me aside. "What's wrong? Talk to me. I'm here."

"I want... I want to scream. I hate this. I hate having to do this." I sniff.

"Say the word, and I'll drive to his place. You can watch me beat the piss out of him first and get your clothes after."

"That's not the answer."

"How much did you tell your father about what Wes did to you?"

"Not much."

"You kept it bottled up?"

I nod.

"You didn't want him to worry."

I nod again.

"Let me make something clear right here, right now. I can handle worrying. You don't have to be strong for me." He glances around.

Following his gaze, I spot other women shopping, glancing at us.

"Fuck, I should have shut this place down for you."

"Can we leave?" I ask, my voice small.

"No. You're doing this." He brings me into a dressing room. "Go ahead. Let it out. Scream. Cry. Throw things. Punch something. Punch *me*."

Tears build up and once they leak, I can't stop them.

It starts as a choking sob, but Balor holds my face. "Come on. Wail."

"I don't want anyone to hear me."

"Why not? Who cares? I don't. Stop protecting him. When Erin asks why you need all this. Tell her. Don't feel ashamed. Shame *him*!"

My rage builds to a frenzy, a volcano erupting inside me. In the corner, I spot a mannequin. A male one. It's dressed up in a baseball hat, a stupid striped shirt, and Bahama shorts like someone is taking it on a boat for crying out loud.

I storm up to it and start punching it. Screaming at it. Kicking it. *"You bastard. I hate you. I hate you."*

This goes on for I don't know how long, until Erin peeks into the dressing room. "What's going on?"

She probably thinks I'm yelling at Balor and is ready to

call one of his brothers.

Balor pulls me against his chest. "She's letting out some bottled-up anger."

"Are you that hard to work for?" Erin asks.

This makes me snort a laugh into his chest. "No. He's the best boss."

Erin fidgets, knowing she's not getting the full story. "Oh."

Straightening my back, I say, "I walked away from everything I owned eight months ago to get away from an abusive situation."

Erin nods. "I've worked with survivors in the past. I have a checklist for building a new wardrobe."

The sense that I'm not alone in my trauma takes so much weight off my shoulders.

"She can have whatever she wants." Balor kisses me on the cheek. "Just don't buy anything too revealing. No one sees what's..." He bites his lip.

Mine? Is that what he wants to say?

I can't get it out of my head. Not to mention what we almost did in that hotel room last night before we were whisked away by men in a helicopter who turned out to be Trace's cousins.

Balor's brothers weren't on the helicopter, but with the raging storm, it made sense not to risk mafia bosses, especially three who are new fathers, according to Balor.

Erin asks me a series of questions about my schedule, my life, and my fashion goals. I answer with Fredricks Elementary in mind for next fall. Waking up Balor can be done in jeans and T-shirts, or naked like him. God, I wish.

Erin shows me a graphic with an entire wardrobe laid out by piece. It's a starting point of what I need. The knot in my stomach loosens. I'll actually walk out of here feeling like a new woman.

"If we agree this is what you need then we shop until

you find pieces you adore. Then match them up with coordinates," Erin says. "What kind of skirts do you like?"

I nod and swipe to see the options. "Pencil. Flare. Mini?"

"One of each," Balor insists. "No minis."

"Three of each," Erin chimes in. "One mini. She has nice legs."

"Ten of each," he snaps. "If you see it and want it, it's yours."

Balor's phone rings and his jaw twitches when he glances at the screen. No matter how many times he ignores the calls and sends a text, it keeps ringing.

"You should answer it," I say and with a nod, he does.

"Jesus fucking Christ, Riordan. *What?* I know what day it is," he says, stomping away.

Erin steers me back through the store, folding anything I want to try over her arm. When I see her struggling, I think it's time to see how these work on me.

I catch Balor making his way through the store, looking for me. Waving him over, I say, "I'm going to try these on. Can you help—"

"I have to go," he says abruptly.

"Oh." Breathing deeply, I say, "I'll go with you. We can do this another day."

"No. You need to do this right now."

I need to look better, got it. I need to look less like a homeless person. Got it.

"Okay." I wave him off, figuring my outburst must have scared him.

Out comes a credit card. A sleek black one. "This has no limit. Buy whatever you want."

I'm uncomfortable with him picking up the tab, especially with all the money he gave me.

That money I earned.

"No. I can pay."

"I brought you here. I'm paying." Balor's phone blares to life again. He rips it out of his pocket and hisses into it, all gruff and talking in Gaelic.

Buying me things is just another form of control. My emotions are all over the map. My mood swings are nothing like I've ever seen. I don't know what's wrong with me.

"Go." I push him away because I don't want him to think I need him like this.

I expect him to kiss me on the forehead, but with Erin watching us, he's stock still. Next, he's playing with his keys.

"I'll pick you up in a few hours."

***

Shopping is an annoying slog without Balor.

Maybe it's irrational, but I'm hurt. I thought shopping was a romantic gesture when it wasn't. When Balor had the chance to leave me, he took it.

He doesn't want a relationship, and I clearly have baggage from my last one.

With his credit card in my hand, I take advantage. I load up with the maximum outfits Erin's program recommends and then do a lot of damage in the perfume and jewelry departments.

It's childish and I'll probably return it all, but right now, I'm angry and hurt. This shopping spree is the only thing that feels good because I know the final bill will get his attention. Force him to react. Show me how he feels about me.

"Oh, and you'll need a gown," Erin says, knocking me out of my thoughts.

"A gown? For what?" I ask.

"The O'Rourkes attend a lot of fundraisers, galas, auctions, shows."

"With their wives and girlfriends," I say on a painful

swallow since I'm neither.

I don't want to be his wife or *anyone's* wife. But I'd like to be his girlfriend to get some more benefits. But he doesn't want that.

Erin steers me to a sea of beautiful gowns. She digs into the racks and produces several in my size. Black, white, pink, yellow, and light green.

"Knowing the family, I recommend you buy at least one," she says.

I glance at the price tags and laugh. "One? I'll take them all."

CHAPTER TWENTY-THREE
BALOR

"I'm going to Dunbar Valley in a few of weeks to check on Cormac," Lachlan says at the meeting in Kieran's office the minute I walk in.

Late.

Did I mention I'm still irate over Griffin commandeering the helicopter to fly in a blizzard to lift me and Ella out of there like we were stuck in a war zone?

Messing up my chance to sleep with her again.

Either from what Lachlan just said, or me storming in, frustrated, the room filled with my brothers becomes deadly silent.

"Are you taking Darragh?" Riordan asks, watching me take a seat like he's expecting an apology for cursing at him.

"He asked to come," Lachlan says. "I warned him, I'll be recruiting new guards and assassins while I'm there. It won't be a glamorous trip. He still wants to make the journey."

"Good," Kieran agrees. "It will mean a lot to Cormac to see his twin. As the father of twins, I look at Cillian and Matteo and can't imagine they'd ever go through what our brothers went through. What Darragh went through for Cormac."

That kicks the emotions around the room until the door to the office opens and we all spin around.

"Hey, hey." Shea peeks her head inside.

After smiling around the room, our sister's eyes land on me with a slightly wider one. We've always been closest.

Lachlan jumps up and twirls her around like she's five. With his six-six frame compared to her petite body, she might as well be.

"Am I interrupting anything?" Shea grins, knowing we'd stop anything for her.

"What do you need, love?" Kieran says.

"My guard isn't working out," she says, sounding frustrated.

"What do you mean, not working out?" Lachlan already sounds murderous. "Did he lay a hand on you?"

"No!" She slaps his arm. "He's distracted lately. I think he's having an issue with his wife. Look, don't kill him, okay? Just assign him somewhere else."

As if we'd trust a distracted guard with marital problems to protect anyone in the family. I doubt Lachlan, who manages all the guards, will kill Soren, but he'll spend some time at the black site being *reminded* of his lifelong oath to protect us and keep our secrets.

"Take Trace," I offer.

"No." She noticeably stiffens. "When you sent him to back up my guard for the big party I hosted last summer, he…"

"He did *what*, Shea?" Lachlan tilts his head. "I was there. With Katya. You didn't say anything."

"Because I'm a big girl and I don't need a guard," Shea argues, eyes narrowed at Lachlan. "No one bothers me in East Hampton."

"You *will* have a guard, love." Kieran stands to his menacing full height and gets serious with her. "Either that or your ass moves home to Astoria. They plan parties around here, too. If you're going to live seventy *fucking* miles away from me—"

"Fine." Shea backs down immediately.

Kieran rarely uses that tone with her. But it's because he loves her. We all do.

We take a break and after each brother hugs and kisses our only sister, I hang back, her eyes finding mine in between the doses of adoration.

My brothers exit the room, leaving my sister and I alone. The meeting came to a halt when she arrived. We don't talk business around Shea.

When we're alone, she says, "Are you coming to the gala?"

"Aye."

"Bringing a date?" she asks with her arms crossed.

My throat goes tight. "Um."

She knows...

"Really, you're not bringing this delightful bowl of sunshine?" She holds up her phone and shows me a photo of Ella with her stylist Erin.

"I haven't asked her."

"And she's shopping with your credit card?" Shea adds.

My phone rings, and I don't recognize the number. Setting my phone to ghost mode, I answer it. "Alo? Who is this?"

"B. O'Rourke?" A man says, using the name on the credit card I gave Ella.

This should be good.

"Aye. I mean yes." I answer all kinds of security information when I assess this call is legit. "How much? Six hundred and twenty thousand?"

Shea gasps, reminding me she's standing there.

The man on the phone mentions a few line items over one hundred grand classified: Jewelry.

I think this has to be some kind of joke. Or mistake. I can go into my account and reverse the charge. When I see Ella, I'll find out what she bought. She may not even know she's been charged this much.

"Sir?"

"Aye, that's my assistant who's mad at me. Put the charges through."

"Assistant?" Shea asks, watching me put my phone

away, ignoring the sweat on my brow.

I have the money, but Eoghan pays our bills. I'll hear it from him.

"Aye, she's my assistant. She had an issue with her ex. Left all her clothes at his place and didn't want to go back to get them."

"Why aren't you going to get her things?" Shea asks, the enormous sum Ella spent forgotten.

"You know me well." I stroke my forehead. "He's a cop. That's a delicate hornet's nest to shoot at."

Shea nods, understanding.

"Have anything else you want to tell me about her?" She sounds concerned. "You just spent close to three quarters of a million dollars on her."

I tell my sister everything. Usually.

"There's a lot to tell, and I don't know where to begin." I sit down, the seriousness of the situation hitting me.

Feelings I am struggling to both deny and push away.

She looks down at her phone. "Do you like this woman?"

"Aye. I do. That's the problem."

"And she's not a..." Shea's the only one of my siblings who knows I only sleep with escorts.

That shopping spree would make perfect sense to her.

"No," I answer.

She exhales. "Thank goodness that phase of your life is over."

"I'm figuring it all out," I say, so she doesn't worry about me.

Christ, I do the same thing that I pushed Ella to stop doing just a few hours ago. We're made for each other, all right.

Nodding, Shea looks around the empty office.

"Any word on Cormac?" she asks, sadness in her voice.

"Lachlan's going to see him in a few weeks."

"Really?" Shea lights up. "Do you think he'll let me go with him?"

"To an Irish torture camp? Are you out of your mind?" I say, seeing red.

"With *Lachlan*," she annunciates his name. "I'll be fine. I'm going to ask him right now."

I watch her bounce away, defiant and feisty.

Oh, Trace Quinlan is going to have his hands full with her…

CHAPTER TWENTY-FOUR
BALOR

With Shea gone, the weekly meeting resumes. This is my shot to tell them Corvin Snow is working for me. I'm comfortable mentioning it since he hasn't breached my most secure sites in the three weeks he's been working for me.

"What's up with you?" Eoghan asks me, looking at my lap.

Jesus, do I have a boner?

I admit, watching Ella punch that mannequin, taking back her power, yelling, and screaming in the store was sexy as hell. It turned me on.

Then spending so much of my money?

She can spend every penny of mine, but now I have to fuck her to punish her, deliciously.

"Balor?" Eoghan nudges me.

"What?" I ask him, shifting my legs.

"Your knuckles are white?" He frowns. "Something wrong?"

"Balor?" Kieran calls out to me.

"I'm fine." I turn back to Eoghan. "Can Jillian come by my house? I want her to meet my new assistant who'll be…" I stop when jaws tip open all around me.

"Assistant?" Lachlan crows.

"I'll get to that." I wave off the curious gapes and return to Eoghan. "I want Jillian to work with her, she's privy to the weapons project and can help with the patent filings. We toured the chip facility yesterday."

"You got stuck Upstate in the snowstorm until late at night." Eoghan cocks his head. "Was that *assistant* with you?"

"Aye, and Trace," I say to get him off my back.

Kieran covers his face. "The weapon patents, Balor."

"I have the final specs from the manufacturer. Jillian can update the patent applications."

"Balor, I'm not Jillian's secretary," Eoghan pushes back. "If you want a meeting with her, call her yourself."

"You've changed your tune about her now that you're married," I scoff. "You acted like you owned her and controlled every facet of her life a month ago."

"That's how I got her to marry me. Now I can dial things back." Eoghan smiles.

At least I haven't gone off the rails the way Eoghan did with Jillian. He's lucky he didn't get arrested for the shit he pulled with her.

Even if it worked.

I don't have to go all psycho stalker with Ella.

She wants me. I want her, too, but I'm blocked. I'm stuck. Chained to the only way I know how to be with a woman. No feelings. No strings.

Being with Ella every day these last couple of weeks and not being able to touch her has the emptiness gnawing at me. I can call my service any time. Any second. Right fucking now, and have a beautiful, sexy woman sucking my cock in ten minutes.

Only every time my dick gets hard, I think of Ella. And it's her cunt I imagine when I jerk off.

Fuck, I'm in trouble.

"Whatever," I snap at Eoghan. "I'll call your wife."

Eoghan's lips twitch. "Never mind. I'll do it." He stands up and leaves the office.

He's too fucking easy, but I'm thinking he's using this as an opportunity to have phone sex with her. Those two are addicted animals.

"How is this new assistant working out?" Riordan asks, breaking me from my thoughts of Eoghan.

"Fine, but I have something more important to announce." I stand up to take command of this meeting.

"I found Iceman."

My words wipe the perpetual grin right off Lachlan's face. "Where?"

"I hired him when I was in Sydney."

"What?" Riordan shrieks. "He nearly breached our network."

"I know better than all of you what he did. He did it to hundreds of businesses and financial websites. It wasn't personal. He cast a wide net and our sites and accounts got swept up in it." I take a breath. "His name is Corvin Snow."

With Eoghan conveniently out of the room, I don't have to worry that his HR paralegal mentioned that name to him.

"How do you know it was him?" Kieran asks, sitting back. "I assume he didn't admit it."

"Of course not. I tracked his digital fingerprints and his signature code entries. And I have state-of-the-art backups that not only prevent attacks, but reverse-engineers them. I had a special team tracking him down. Then he had the balls to show up at the global conference three weeks ago." I sit down. "The bank he was working for didn't renew his contract. So, I scooped him up."

"Why in the world would you want a man like that anywhere near our network?" Kieran asks, anger in his eyes.

"I'm logging his keystrokes. I threw a ton of money at him and have him doing bullshit coding to see his skills firsthand." I take a breath.

"What's your end game?" Riordan asks, leaning toward me, looking concerned.

"To learn his methods. The thing about serial criminals, they keep it all bottled up when they're actually dying to talk about it. He thinks he's in a safe space right now. Only a few of my most trusted developers know who he really is. They're gushing over him. He's eating it up and spilling more and more to them. I'll have that ransomware code he wrote, or at least the framework, in a month."

"You're playing him," Riordan says. "How do you know he's not playing you?"

I don't. But I'm fairly certain.

"Trust me. He's got an ego the size of the Empire State Building. I've been feeding into that. I gave him an office. I took him to dinner. I invited him to the fundraiser gala next week."

"That may work for a while, but he'll eventually get bored and want more," Kieran says.

"Or get on your nerves," Riordan adds.

"I'll have what I need from him by then. But there's more." I stare at eyes like mine except different colors, eager for me to continue. "His *daughter* is my new assistant. It was a condition he made for me."

I don't know if the tone of my voice changed, but the way my brothers' eyes widened when I said *daughter*, I might as well have played a video of me fucking Ella for them.

"Daughter?" Kieran drawls.

I go to answer, but Eoghan comes back in, zipping his pants. "Jillian will be at your house Monday morning."

"Great." I put my head down but lift it at the silence. "What?"

"I asked you about hiring the man's daughter." Kieran's voice is low and sounds miffed from being interrupted.

There are fucking five of us, what does he expect?

Shaking my head, I say, "I only agreed to hire his daughter because he told me she got abused by a boyfriend six months ago. She moved with Iceman to Australia when he got an assignment there. He's worried about her. He's got issues, but he loves his daughter. And well…" I close my eyes ready to light the bomb I dropped. "I fucked her in Los Angeles without knowing who she was." I won't mention that I mistook her for an escort or that I gave her twenty-thousand dollars.

Who I fuck is my own damn business, and I've always been discreet. Although the way Eoghan smirks at me suggests he's figured out what my large cash withdrawals have been for.

"I'd only found out about her ex after I agreed." I don't mention he's a cop. Yet. "I want to keep her close to me so the eejit ex doesn't get any ideas that he can hurt her."

"Close, as in on your cock? She works for you," Eoghan says with unmitigated gall, considering the crimes he committed in Las Vegas with Jillian.

I glare at him.

"Her father has no idea?" Lachlan says, playing with a knife.

"Snow didn't crash Kieran's plane recently, did he?" Although that might be the least of what Snow would do to us if he knew we were on to him.

Or what he'd do to just me if he knew I slept with his daughter.

He sees her as fragile and vulnerable. I see her as strong and taking control of her life. Pushing away the fear. Not letting that prick win.

"I just want Snow's ransomware code." I look around the room, knowing my brothers trust me to keep them safe this way.

"Then what?" Eoghan asks, crossing an ankle over a knee. "What are you doing with Iceman after you get what you want from him?"

"We kill him," Lachlan sneers. "What do you think?"

My stomach twists because Lachlan killing Snow is the force field that will keep Ella and me apart forever.

"I don't think that's necessary," I immediately argue

out of the ache in my body to make Ella mine.

Lachlan stands to his full height. "You hired a madman with cyber skills that could decimate us. And you're screwing his daughter."

Anger floods my veins, but I keep my cool. It's my signature position in this family as the smart one, the sane one. Just as they fear Corvin Snow after seeing what he did before Christmas, they secretly fear me as much.

Mafia families are notorious for infighting. Some dons put hits on their own brothers.

We've never come close to falling apart like that until women came into our lives. Eoghan stood outside this very office last month threatening to disappear with Jillian.

Fuck, it's in our blood to bond so viscerally with a woman once she gets her hooks into us. I thought I was immune. And never more wrong about anything in my life.

"I'm insulted you think I can't protect us. His virus hit us. It hit everyone. Your damn credit cards didn't work because of the shitty banks. Unless we want to start our own bank…"

"Nooooo," Eoghan groans.

"Exactly. I'll deal with Corvin, and as far as his daughter—"

"Balor," Kieran interrupts.

"What?" I stop talking because he's in charge.

"I know you can protect us. But being overconfident is a blinding mistake we can't afford. We all have faults. No one here is perfect." He turns his glare at Lachlan. "You think you are, Lach. All those scars on your body say otherwise."

"Kieran," I keep fighting.

"I'm sorry, Balor," he says in his savage tone. "We kill Snow once you have his code. He'll be a liability. Lachlan, he's yours."

I feel like a wall of bricks just fell on me. Any thought of making Ella mine has gone up in flames and Lachlan is holding the fucking can of gasoline.

CHAPTER TWENTY-FIVE
ELLA

Breezing through my apartment before leaving for work on Friday morning, I open the front door and trip over a ginormous box.

"Son. Of. A. Bitch." I peel myself off the hallway carpet.

Glancing up and down the corridor, I twist around and look for a label on the box. Surely someone left this at the wrong apartment. I'm not expecting anything.

Or is it for my dad? More of his secrets that will get him into trouble.

I don't see any shipping labels on the box. In fact, it's in rather pristine condition. Like, no way did this go through the postal system.

It's also not taped shut. Just folded closed. My heart swells, thinking it's a box of puppies or kittens. I yank open a flap, disappointed when I don't see any sweet furry faces looking up at me and crying out for love.

After the last few days, I can use some puppy kisses or kitten cuddles.

The box is packed with clothes.

The colors and the fabrics register, along with the scent. Mine.

These are *my* clothes.

The ones I left at Wesley's house.

Shaking, I pick through them with mixed feelings of dread, reminding me of what I went through. I ran off, leaving all of these behind on the battlefield.

A door opens a few apartments away, and I bolt around, ready to scream, expecting to see Wesley strolling toward me. But the neighbor with his Yorkie leaving for their morning walk waves to me.

This box means that Wesley knows Dad and I are back from Australia. That he knows I'm here. And got into the building. My heart pounds thinking he was probably standing at our door just moments earlier. In the back of my head, I knew it was only a matter of time. Closing the flap, a thick envelope catches my eyes. Touching it, dread fills my heart. It's thick.

I lift the box and bring it into my bedroom. My father can't see this. He can't know Wesley was here. He'll tell Balor and a war will break out.

The envelope, like the box, isn't sealed, and I see it's stuffed with a wad of notebook pages torn out from a book filled with Wesley's handwriting.

Bile rises in my throat. I can't read this. I *won't* read a word. He's either apologizing again or threatening me. I want to burn these pages along with the clothes that will only remind me of the person Wesley abused.

I shove everything into my closet and close the door.

When I get back into the living room and open the front door again, a tall man in a suit stands there and I scream.

"Ella, it's me," Trace gently grips my upper arms. "I've been waiting for you."

"I'm sorry." I nearly puke, my nerves are shot. "I'm running late."

"What's wrong?" He glances around and whispers into my ear. "Is someone in the apartment? Just nod, you don't have to say anything else."

"No, no. I'm here by myself," I say.

Then again, I'm not sure. I'm not sure of anything anymore.

"Do you have everything?" He spins around, seeing my work bag and purse on the floor.

"I do." I quickly lift them and press it all against my chest.

Trace stays silent on the ride to Astoria, and I do breathing exercises to calm down.

In the driveway of the townhouse, he says, "I have a

meeting with one of the other O'Rourke brothers. I'll be back to drive you both to the command center afterward. The boss knows."

Nodding, I get out and use my key to enter through the kitchen like I normally do.

Since yesterday, Balor's been distant.

My heart breaks when he stays in bed after I wake him up and doesn't give me my usual show.

God, I'm addicted to seeing him naked.

He doesn't even mention the money I spent at the store yesterday. It's like he doesn't care.

I consider mentioning the box Wes dropped off, but I'd only do it to get a reaction and make myself feel better.

Instead, I close the bedroom door and amble down the stairs, feeling sorry for myself. The sight of a stunning blonde at the front door knocks me from my pity party.

Shocked, I open the door. "Yes?"

"I'm here to see Balor." The bombshell stands on the front steps, staring at the green goop stain on my shirt from Balor's morning smoothie.

The hair on the back of my neck stands up immediately and my instinct is to push this woman down the eight concrete steps she and her high heels climbed to reach the front door.

What if she's a sexy assassin?

For one, Balor doesn't have an appointment right now. Not here. He never takes appointments at his house. And from what I gathered, not many people know he even lives here. We leave out of the back kitchen door, and the Rivian has tinted windows.

Taking matters into my own hands, I step outside, and close the door behind me. I immediately regret it because it's chilly.

"What's this about?" I ask with my arms folded.

Her perfect forehead wrinkles. "He's expecting me."

"Is he now?" I quake in her perfect appearance.

Long, ice-blonde hair, hazel eyes, strong cheekbones, and makeup so striking yet so subtle you'd think she wakes up with rose-glow cheeks and bronze shimmer swept across her almond eyelids.

She's gorgeous and smells nice, and that's when it hits me like a freight train. She's *got* to be an escort.

How could Balor do this to me? He hired someone to show up while I'm here working? And what am I supposed to do while he's with her? Wait for him to…finish?

God, that visual makes me so dizzy that I grip the banister feeling sick.

"Are you all right?" she asks.

"Yes." *No, I'm not all right.*

I've fallen for my boss. He's mafia and doesn't *do* relationships. Only escorts. And I'm staring at a woman he's paying to fuck. In his bed. Where I just woke him up. In sheets I roll around in when he's in the shower.

Don't get me started about how I secretly sniff his pillows.

"Sheesh you're freezing, let's get you inside." She reaches for the doorknob. "Shoot, it's locked."

"What?" I spin around. "Oh shit."

"Who are you?" the woman asks.

"I'm his assistant." I ring the bell, cringing that Balor is going to find me with his date locked out of the house.

"Are you sure? And you don't have a key?"

"I didn't think I needed one," I say tartly. "He's not expecting guests."

"I'm not *a guest*. I'm here to work. I'm Balor's—"

The door swings open, and my heart sinks seeing Balor with wet hair. Water droplets dot every inch of his amazing naked body wrapped in a towel.

"What the hell is going on? Oh hey, Jillian." Balor's

tune changes seeing *her*. "I thought you were coming on Monday?"

He knows her. She's got to be one of his usual sex workers.

All the tension from Wes dropping off my clothes, being in my building, and outside my door when I was showering catches up to me. Seeing Balor's bare chest looking at this woman has everything spinning.

I don't know what happens next because everything goes black.

CHAPTER TWENTY-SIX

BALOR

I'm wearing nothing but a towel, still dripping wet from my shower when Ella collapses. I catch her, but I'm barely able to keep the towel from slipping off. If Eoghan drove by and saw me standing on my front steps like this in front of his wife, I'd have a lot of explaining to do.

"Jillian, what the hell happened?" I ask.

"I rang the bell, and she wouldn't let me inside. She asked me who I was and what I'm doing here."

"I didn't mention you were stopping by. Eoghan said Monday."

"It sounded urgent."

Panicking, I reach down to lift up Ella, still grasping my towel. "Jillian, turn the hell around."

I let the towel fall and stark naked, I briskly carry Ella into the house and lay her on my sofa. With her settled, I snag a throw blanket and tie it around my waist.

Jillian comes in and closes the door. Holding the towel, she says, "Am I interrupting something?"

"Of course not. She works for me."

"In your house. While you're in the shower?"

"She's a personal assistant. This is my house. I shower in my locked bathroom. I wasn't bathing in the kitchen sink. I was upstairs and heard the doorbell." Interrupting a killer jerk-off session imagining her gagging on my cock.

"Right." Jillian nods. "She locked us out."

"How?" I check Ella's pulse but don't know what I'm feeling for. "Never mind. It's not important."

I crouch down and feel that she's still breathing.

"Did she throw up?" Jillian strokes her forehead, nudging her chin at a giant green splotch on Ella's shirt. "Poor thing."

"That's my smoothie, I think. She doesn't keep a

change of clothes here." I put that on the to-do list.

Heck, I'm ready to move her in. Her father makes my skin crawl, and I hate her living with him. *I* figured out who he is, so I'm sure others will, too. Someone dangerous who can show up at his apartment and hurt my Ella. Not to mention her fucking ex who's out there with a badge *and* a gun.

"Does she have a temperature?" Jillian asks. "Feel her forehead."

"She's a little warm." I stroke both of Ella's cheeks.

"Lay her on her back and raise her feet with a pillow to get the blood moving back toward her brain."

"Ella, baby." My body sears hot as I nudge her awake.

"I'll get some ice for her head." Jillian dashes off, her high heels clicking against my ceramic floors. "Maybe take that stained shirt off, if she feels a little warm."

Shaking my head, I gently lift the stained T-shirt over Ella's head, smiling at the cute lace trim camisole underneath that doesn't appear wet or stained. I toss the shirt and lay her out on my sofa, tucking one of the pillows Shea bought under Ella's feet.

Smoothing her hair, I stare down at her, worry and panic consuming me. But also, visceral possessiveness crawls through my veins.

"Here." Jillian hands me a towel soaked in cold water and a bowl.

I don't ask how she found everything.

Gently, I press the towel to Ella's forehead.

"Ella, baby, open your eyes. Deep breaths, baby. Deep breaths. You're okay. I'm here."

She gasps awake and coughs, clutching me. Her nails digging into my skin wakes up something primal in me.

Mine.

CHAPTER TWENTY-SEVEN

ELLA

"Ella, baby, open your eyes. Deep breaths, baby. Deep breaths. You're okay. I'm here."

A smooth voice with a sexy Irish lilt floats into my ears and it feels like velvet rubbed on my brain.

"I love you. Please don't leave me," I murmur to the vision I'm dreaming about.

"What?"

The sharp question pops open my eyes.

Balor's beautiful face fills my vision. His wide shoulders and outstretched arms hold me. My eyes skate down his chest. His bare chest.

Next to me, his leg is propped up. His naked leg. And he's practically on top of me.

I sit up and press my lips to his mouth, a soft moaning escaping me.

His full, moist lips stay fastened against mine, but he doesn't open for me, or…

Oh, God.

I pull back and focus better. "Hi."

"Hi."

"Hi…boss."

Laughing, he says, "We're well past that."

"I'll get her some juice," a feminine voice says from behind me.

I jerk up to watch the sexy blonde in high heels and a tight dress with a killer hourglass figure sashay to the kitchen.

And Balor's naked.

Pushing him away, I notice the blanket around his waist. "I'm sorry I interrupted."

"Interrupted what? You passed out."

"Your date with that… That woman."

"What woman?"

I get to my feet and point. "With that whore!"

"What?" the woman shrieks.

"That's my brother's wife, Jillian," Balor whispers.

"Wife?" I immediately wish I could sink through the floor.

Just evaporate.

"Aye." Balor pulls me against his chest, his bare chest. "Keep breathing. It's just a misunderstanding."

"God, I feel awful." I still don't know what's going on.

That woman is someone's wife, so I shut the fuck up before I make matters worse.

"My other brother is a doctor," Balor says. "Do you want me to call him? You scared the fuck out of me." He sounds so sincere and worried.

"I don't need a doctor." Maybe a shrink because I'm losing it over this man.

"Did you eat anything today?" Jillian asks me.

"No. I usually wait for..." I bite my lip. "Balor and I eat breakfast together."

"Do you, now?" Jillian smirks at Balor over his shoulder.

"She's my *assistant*." He sounds guilty and pinches the bridge of his nose. "Part of her job is to come here in the morning and make me breakfast. And other stuff."

It'd been working perfectly for a couple of weeks. Yet that woman looks at us like we're crazy.

That woman...

I make eye contact with Jillian and mutter on a rough exhale, "I'm so sorry."

"Why would you think I'm a whore?" she asks.

"Um." My eyes stray to Balor who's gone crimson.

"Just a misunderstanding." He slides his gaze to me, covering my ass.

"A beautiful woman knocks on a..." I motion to his

sister-in-law, who's *a mafia wife*. "A powerful man's door. I'm sorry."

"Aw, you think I'm beautiful," Jillian coos. "Thank you."

"Okay, now let's get you something to eat." Balor helps me sit up.

Jillian crouches in front of me. "I poured you some juice."

"Thank you." She seems to like me now because I called her beautiful.

"Ella, Jillian is working on the weapons project for me," Balor says. "She's filing the patents."

I close my eyes. "God, I'm so sorry."

"I should have told you she was coming by," Balor says regretfully. "The dates got mixed up."

Shaking my head, I say, "This is your house. You don't have to clear guests with me."

"No. She was coming to meet me *and you* for business. I just...forgot."

I tug on the blanket. "That's why you need me."

We stare and the world falls away. God, I want him to kiss me so badly.

"Balor, I'll leave the applications on your dining room table. Let's schedule a proper meeting to talk about them."

I push to my feet. "No. Don't reschedule for me."

Balor stands up, clutching the blanket. "It's not that urgent."

"Why the fuck are you parading around half-dressed in front of my wife?" A man in an exquisite blue and gray herringbone suit sways toward us from the kitchen.

"Who... Who are you?" I ask.

"That's one of my brothers." Balor looks at the man, stepping in front of me. "Eoghan, calm down. I was in the bloody shower when these two birds locked themselves out on my front step."

Brother... One is more gorgeous than the next...

"Go put some fucking clothes on," Eoghan barks.

"Eoghan, my love, your brother has a blanket around his..." Jillian slides her hands over his shoulders. "I don't want to see anyone's you-know-what but yours."

To my shock, Eoghan takes her mouth with reckless abandon like we're not in the room.

"Jesus Christ," Balor grumbles, and pulls me away.

We climb the stairs with our hands linked. In his bedroom, he sits me gently on his bed. "Tell me the truth, how do you feel?"

"I got dizzy. I thought she was here to... Be with you. I saw you in a towel, I thought that meant you were waiting for her. My heart just went offline." Tears clog my throat until I'm sobbing like a child.

What the hell is wrong with me?

"Oh, butterfly." Balor holds me. "I'm sorry."

"I thought that was payback for me spending so much on your credit card. I don't plan to keep most of it. Especially the jewelry. I'll return it all later today."

When I stop crying, he wipes my eyes. "You'll do no such thing. I told you to buy what you need *and want.*"

His shower-fresh skin smells so good and his warmth melts against my cheek.

God, this is embarrassing.

I bet if Balor *had* ordered an escort, she'd look exactly like the woman downstairs.

And I'm sitting here with no makeup, yoga pants, and I smell like a kale smoothie.

I gulp down the last of my pity tears. "I almost...outed you. Your tastes."

He exhales. "I think Eoghan knows what I'm into."

Am into. Present.

"Have you...since we—"

"No."

"Why?"

We lock eyes, and his stare holds so much weight that it makes my lids heavy.

"Never mind." I break away. "I need the bathroom. I need... Holy shit, where's my shirt?"

"It had something green on it, I took it off you." He runs the fabric of my cami between his fingers. "I noticed it was an old shirt. Same as these stretch pants. Why aren't you wearing your new clothes?"

The box left at my door earlier flashes before my eyes. I have so few clothes that weren't in that box. But that will open a conversation about how much I spent on clothes he technically bought for me. Clothes I really don't want. But I also don't want a wardrobe from my past.

What do I want?

"I don't need anything fancy to work. I'm just waking you up and cooking breakfast," I say to get out of my head. "I'll let you finish getting dressed."

Balor's fist tightens the blanket slung around his waist. His face turns hard as granite, his gaze straying to the bedroom door. "As you wish, Ella."

I stand up and look at the closet. "Your clothes are hanging up on the back of the door."

He steers me to his bedroom door, but his eyes widen when the sounds of moaning fill the hallway. "Fuck," he mutters. "Use my bathroom. Please."

"Why?" I ask, but the image forming in my head is a clue.

"They're having sex on my couch."

CHAPTER TWENTY-EIGHT

ELLA

The following Monday, Balor and I robotically stick to our routine. On Friday after my medical emergency, Trace drove me home and I didn't hear from Balor all weekend.

I also haven't looked at the box or Wesley's letter. But it's haunting me. I can't stop looking over my shoulder. I've also decided not to tell Balor or my father. It's none of their business.

Either of them.

This morning, I woke up Balor as usual and after I picked out his clothes, I left the bedroom.

Something feels so off with him. With us. We came so close to fooling around again and now he barely looks at me.

When the doorbell rings this time, I jump. But I smile seeing Erin, the stylist. "Hey, good morning."

"Hi, good morning to you, too. I'm dropping this off for Mr. O'Rourke."

I take the thick black garment bag, noting how heavy it is. "What is it?"

"His new tux. I had it tailored for him a few weeks ago. He didn't need it until now."

He needs a new tux *now*?

"Oh, right." I play dumb. "And that's for…"

"The Youth Music Program Fundraiser Saturday night." She smiles. "All the O'Rourkes are going. I hear Mr. O'Rourke, the oldest brother, insists on the whole family attending. You know, show their strength. Their bond."

My throat tightens. I get what she's saying one hundred percent. I've pieced together that there are eight siblings, seven men and one sister. One brother is in Ireland as well as their parents. The six brothers who live here in Astoria and their five wives are a lot of damn O'Rourkes. A formidable group to screw with. Since they're…

Mafia.

I wonder if Erin knows exactly who she does these stylist services for. She looks happy as a clam and not the least bit afraid.

"Well, I have to go. I have Mr. O'Rourke's… Another one. I have a bunch of tuxes to deliver. See you soon." She gives me a once-over. "You look nice. Do you like your new clothes?"

"I do. You were a great help. Thank you." I smooth my new gray houndstooth pencil skirt with blue stitching.

Remembering how Jillian looked in one, I pushed aside my pride and wore the one Balor bought me. With a cashmere cardigan and a lace camisole underneath, I feel polished. And stronger.

I love how Balor looks at me when I'm dressed nicely.

After closing the front door, I take the garment bag upstairs.

Yesterday, Sara at Fredricks Elementary contacted me again. They can't find an aide who's a good fit for that little boy. She really wants me to take the position.

With these thoughts in my head, I walk into Balor's bedroom without knocking. No point. He'd tell me to come in even stark naked. But he's not in his bedroom, and his bed is still unmade.

I hang up the tux in his closet and then stand over the bed.

The messed-up covers look so damn sexy. I wonder if he's brought one of his paid women here and fucked them in this bed. God, that hurts. I know he's not been with anyone since me, but that won't hold.

And I'm not sure I can bear it when his control breaks. Last week's meltdowns proved that.

I pick up his pillow and smell it. The scent knocks me over. Woodsy, spice, and mint. I figured out that's his shampoo.

A noise from the bathroom draws my attention and I tiptoe that way. A door separates the toilet from the vanity and shower.

Running water stills me. He's in the shower. God, his body is amazing. I know I shouldn't do this, but I push the door open slightly. A voice muffled behind the glass catches my attention.

"God, yeah. Take my cock," he groans.

Oh shit...

I know he's in there alone. That means he's pleasuring himself. My core clenches, remembering his cock. Long and thick. Veiny but beautiful with a wide pillowy head that's perfect.

"Let me fuck your ass, it'll feel so fucking good..."

I close my eyes and my heart pounds. He did that to me in the shower.

Oh my God, is he imagining me?

CHAPTER TWENTY-NINE
BALOR

"God, yeah. Take my cock." I close my soapy fist around my throbbing dick, imagining I'm thrusting into Ella.

Christ, she took me so good in that L.A. hotel suite. Again, and again.

I wanted you.

I liked you.

I may have paid her, but she spread those legs out of pure desire for me.

Which meant all those fucking moans were real.

With my hand on the tile wall to steady me, I pump harder than usual, needing release. "Let me fuck your ass, it'll feel so fucking good…"

No fucking teasing where this is going, like when my hand finds my swollen cock in the middle of the night and I just tell myself, one stroke to take the edge off.

I'm so wound up after she wakes me up, I can't get into this shower quick enough to relieve the ache of my constant fucking erection. The morning she passed out after I knew she was all right, I showered and came all over the glass twice.

That minx has my mind by the balls. And in the gutter every hour I'm awake. Which is why I started taking pills to help me sleep.

I can't fucking take it.

I'm full-on fucking my hand when movement catches the corner of my eye. My bathroom door is open when I'm sure I closed it.

Out of respect, since I gave Ella full reign of my house.

It's her, I see the outline of her body. Jesus, she's watching me. The glass is clear but the steam and the rivulets of water make for a very erotic show of me jerking off.

I should shout for her to leave. I should turn around. But damn it, I don't want to. It's been torture to keep my hands to myself, to hide what she's doing to me.

Fuck, why is she watching me? That takes balls.

And damn, that gets me even harder.

Testing her, I keep going, full frontal.

I stroke the underside, massaging the fire traveling up my cock that will end in a deluge of cum. I feel it. I fucking feel it.

I struggle to see what she's wearing. Is it one of those new outfits I bought her? Has she finally accepted that I want to take care of her?

The possessive O'Rourke side claws its way into my brain, telling me to take her and dominate her the way I want. The consequences of Kieran's death plan for her father have strangled me since he gave the order at our meeting.

Knowing I'm being watched, I slowly work my hand up and down the entire length, trying to control my orgasm, and see how long Ella can take. How long will she stay and watch?

"Fuck, yeah," I groan as the pumping tease tightens my balls.

My leg muscles tense as my cock twitches. I alternate the pressure to keep going. And damn, it's so fucking good.

But it'd be better if her lips were around my cock.

Eyes glued to the figure in the doorway, I remember how Ella's tight cunt felt, and my hand squeezes the same. A mistake because now I'm on the edge, slipping from my control.

This is fucking nuts. What the hell are we doing?

I drop my hand and slide the shower open. "Don't you dare move. You want to watch me make myself come?

You want a better view?" I step out and move toward her.

Water sluicing down the side of my face, I leave a trail of puddles on my floor tiles, but I don't give a fuck.

Ella's eyes are wide and she's frozen. Either out of fear or heady with need to watch me finish.

Standing over her, I feel the water dripping from my face. It lands on her cheek, and fuck, I want to lick it.

"Get me off," I growl through clenched teeth. "You're no whore. You're better than any whore I've had. Stroke my cock until I come because I want it. *You* want it."

Ella doesn't touch me, though. Her hooded chocolate eyes go wide with... I know that look. It's beyond desire. It's beyond want. It's need.

"I said, make me come. Or leave." I give her an out.

Ella swallows, her throat working.

I grip her neck. "Do that again. Swallow."

The fucking muscles, taut and corded, blow my mind.

"I..." She groans, the vibrations driving me wild. "I want..."

"Whatever you want right now, take it. I'm yours. Right now."

"I want to taste you." Ella presses her lips against my bare, wet chest.

Her hands stroke the parts she can't kiss. Further and further down until she gets on her knees in front of me.

Jesus fucking Christ.

CHAPTER THIRTY
BALOR

Ella's hand wrapped around my cock draws a hiss from me like I've never uttered before. The feel of her fingers tightening around my length weakens my knees, and I have to slam my hands on the vanity to hold me up.

"You want my cock in your mouth, aye? Then take it. Suck it. Get me off."

After a teasing lick up and down, she takes my entire length into her mouth, and I nearly blow right there and then. Her hands cup my balls and it's a fucking metaphor come to life because she has me by the balls.

Her mouth is a fucking vacuum, and for a second, this is the whore action I expect. The perfect blow job. Her cheeks hollow out sucking me so hard, it borders on pain. But it feels so fucking sweet.

"Hold the fuck on." I grip her hair as I thrust deeper into her throat. I fuck her mouth, my balls slapping her chin. "Fuck, take me deep down that throat."

I plunge in and out of the warmth of her mouth, so far gone now. I want to feel my cock contract in her sexy mouth.

There's nothing I love more than coming down a woman's throat. Being milked. But I have to teach Ella a lesson. She thinks she wants me. She thinks I'm confused. Fuck, I am.

Time to change that.

I fuck her mouth so hard, hitting the back of her throat, that the vibration of her gags makes it feel even better. When I'm ready to bottom out, I yank my cock out and come all over her face.

Squeezing my dick, I watch the ropes of cum glaze her beautiful cheeks and lips. Her jaw hangs open to catch my release. Molten lava pools in my abdomen, heat scorching up and down my spine, every cell and every inch of me on fire.

"Is this what you want? You think you want me? This is who I am, Ella. This is the kind of sex I like."

The last drop hits her chin and my sanity returns, only its razor sharp. I lift her up, my breath ragged against her face.

"I'm not sweet, Ella," I whisper, licking my own cum off her face. "I'm difficult and moody."

When her face is clean and she's thoroughly horrified at my words, I walk her back into the bedroom.

"God, yes," she hisses because she thinks now I'm going to fuck her and prove how brutal I can be when provoked.

I want that so bad. I want to be balls-deep in this woman again. And now the reasons I can't are piling up.

That's when my O'Rourke bloodlust takes control. The minute we can't have something, we will kill for it.

I'm better than that. I can control this insanity.

Eyes closed, Ella lets me steer her, our feet moving in sync even though she's walking backward. It's a smooth dance, but I have to do this.

I reach my bedroom door. "Open your eyes."

She doesn't immediately realize what I did. The way she looks at me scrapes my insides. And it's pure. It's real. I didn't pay a dime for what she just did, or the way she gazed longingly at me. How she was ready to throw down with Jillian out of jealousy.

Fuck, that was so hot.

My throat tightening and air hard to find, I crash my mouth down on hers.

Her tongue immediately meets mine in a seductive swirl while I plunder her lush mouth. She whimpers and moans. And this is just a damn kiss.

But it's more.

It's the end of the line.

It's goodbye. To whatever the hell we had.

I stop and look at her swollen lips. Those big, hopeful eyes will be the death of me. I gently swipe away a spot of cum I missed, although I'd love nothing more than to have her walk around all day with my release on her gorgeous face. I soften my spine and rest my lips on her forehead.

"Look what you make me do. This… This is all I know. You don't want me. I promise you. This is for the best."

Lachlan is going to kill her father, and she'll never forgive me. Her bitter hatred will gut me to my very core.

Feeling tears in my eyes, I grip her shoulders and push her out into my hallway.

Then close and lock my bedroom door. For the first time in three weeks.

CHAPTER THIRTY-ONE
ELLA

What the hell was that?

Shaking, I hold on to the wall as I make my way down the hall. The staircase wobbles in my vision, and I'm afraid I'll tumble.

You don't want me.

This is who I am.

On the lower level, I go into the bathroom to wash up and catch my face in a mirror, a face Balor just ejaculated all over. His words ring loudly in my ears. I expect to be horrified with myself. Letting a man do that to me.

But I'm not.

Damn, this is who *I* am!

And I love it. I love us—if this is who we can be together.

I consider marching back upstairs and making him finish what he started or at least address what's going on between us.

That's what men like him expect. Women to line up and exist in their world on their terms.

I need to shake this guy up.

Shake...

I head to the kitchen to make his smoothie and breakfast only for him.

He comes down dressed in the clothes I laid out for him, and I stiffen my spine, pretending what he did to me didn't happen, or that it meant nothing to me.

"Here's your smoothie," I say to break the silence.

He slips on his glasses and stares at me. Like he's waiting for me to have some kind of tantrum. We play chicken for a few seconds. Seeing who will crack.

"And I made your breakfast. It's in the oven."

"Thank you," he says quietly.

I blink but don't break.

"I have Jillian's notes for the patent applications. I'd like to work from home the rest of the week. If that's okay with you." I fold my arms, sounding light and breezy as if nothing happened.

A muscle in his jaw jumps to suggest he doesn't like when I'm unavailable to him. "If that's what you want."

"I think that's what I need," I say, rubbing my cheek.

His face reddens. Before he can add any harsh words, I pull my work bag over my shoulder.

"If you need anything else, call me." I don't wait for a response and sail out the front door.

I rush to the end of the block before Balor can come looking for me and drive me home himself. Ducking into a deli, I order coffee and an Uber.

Will he fire me? I'm leaving that door open because I want that aide position at Fredricks Elementary.

I might have just forced him to slam that door in my face the way he did in his bedroom.

CHAPTER THIRTY-TWO
BALOR

"She's going to kill him," Lachlan says, holding back his signature cackle.

In the lobby of The Orchid, I watch my sister in a full-length, low-cut, lavender evening gown snap at Trace who's been, for the lack of a better phrase, up her ass since we arrived.

The idea of him doing anything with my sister's ass stirs a fire inside me. But Shea's an adult and knows better than to sleep with one of her bodyguards. That compromises her protection.

And if she remotely likes the guy, she's putting him in danger, too, because I can't be sure Lachlan would hold back from taking out a guard who touched her.

Consensual or not.

"Did she talk to you about going to Dunbar to see Cormac?" I ask my brother.

Lachlan's face turns to granite. "She sure did. And you can guess how that conversation went."

"You said *no*. She said *please*. You said *no* again. And then she pouted?"

"Three out of four. She said, '*Fuck you, I'm going.*'"

I laugh, wiping my eyes behind my glasses. "She really does not take gobshite from us anymore."

"That's what worries me." Lachlan's voice gets low, his eyes on his pregnant wife.

Katya sits on a plush velvet banquette with her sister, Ana, neither of them looking like ice-cold Russian Princesses anymore, but instead, strong Irish Mob wives.

Even if Ana is technically the Bratva underboss.

Priscilla and Isabella, who've become close friends, stand a few feet away talking to two other women in gowns. Riordan, Kieran, and Darragh hover at the bar nearby, two other men in tuxes with them, the husbands of those women, I assume.

I can't help but do a discreet facial recognition scan and learn the men are... Cops. High-ranking inspectors. Hmmm.

My eyes search for Eoghan and Jillian, who are grinding on the dancefloor alone, their hands all over each other. I never got an apology for them fucking on my couch. I don't expect I ever will.

It's striking how at this large event, I feel alone. Moreso because it's my own doing. Fuck, this week without seeing Ella every day hollowed me out.

Wanting my mind off her, I say to Lachlan, "Are you seeing Ma and Da when you're there?"

"Aye."

I wonder if I should go with them. Take a vacation. I know I'll worry about Shea being there, even though Lachlan and Trace's protection is more than she needs.

"Will you be...all right going back to Dunbar?"

Lachlan's eyes darken. "Of course."

"Lach, it's me. It's okay if that place will freak you the fuck out."

He was sent there as punishment for going against Da when he was eighteen and it made him into the vicious killer he is today.

"Nothing freaks me the fuck out." He stares at Shea and Trace again. "Trace is ex-Defence Forces, you know that, right?"

"Of course I know that. I vetted him." I don't get the reference until it hits me.

Dunbar Valley is filled with Irish terrorists.

"I don't think it's a good idea for Shea to be there."

"You tell her that. I'll assess the situation when I get there." He narrows his eyes at me. "Do you think for one minute I'd let something happen to Shea-Lynne?"

"Of course not."

As much as I worry about her, since the cyber-attack and hiring the terrorist responsible, all while trying not fuck his daughter, I've been wrapped up in my own world.

A hand skates over my shoulder, and Lachlan's eyes widen. My heart soars, thinking it's Ella. I spin around and my stomach twists.

"Petra." One of my... I can't even think of the word because her hand on me feels like acid.

But I'm not rude to women. I gently take the hand off my shoulder and after a squeeze, I return it at her side to remind her: Do. Not. Fucking. Touch. Me.

Not sure why she thought a gala would change that.

"Balor." She bats jet-black fake eyelashes at me. "It's been so long."

And there's a reason for that. I wasn't short of female company since the last time we were together. I don't go back for seconds, and she wasn't enough for me to break that exception.

Only Ella was.

"I've been busy," I say with a sting in my voice.

Lachlan chuckles under his breath and strolls away, gliding like a goddamn panther. Impressive for his size.

Petra doesn't give him a second glance, playing her cards perfectly. Women can't help but stare at Lach, whether it's fear, lust, or some sick combination of both. He kept many beds warm for years until he developed a thing for Katya. A fascination we never knew about until he crashed her wedding and killed the groom.

"I'll be done with Ares Zervas at the end of this month," Petra tells me.

Ares' name gives me pause. The head of the Greek Mafia strolled in here earlier, but I hadn't noticed Petra on his arm.

And the way she says *done* makes me sick. I'm well aware the women I screwed had dicks in them right before and right after me. It was part of the kink, the filthy side of me that I indulged for way too long.

I just got fucking lazy.

Paid sex brought temporary relief to the constant tightness in my chest, and I was always planning my next hooker fix. Until my last 'lady of the night,' who turned out to be a complete fabrication, but completely banished that loneliness. Now, all I want is Ella.

I lean in close to Petra and her breath hitches, likely hoping I'll also break the no-kissing rule for her. "Listen to me and take my advice carefully. When you're done with Ares, I suggest you stay the fuck away from him."

Zervas is a brutal psychopath. I don't like Petra, but I don't hate her. She played her part and doesn't deserve to be killed sucking Ares' dick when someone retaliates for his crimes.

"I'm always careful. In fact, I—"

"I'm done talking to you. Walk away and have a good evening." I level a glare at her.

Stunned, and her throat bobbing in embarrassment, she strides toward Ares, who doesn't acknowledge her. I'm surprised he'd bring a... Whore... I almost finished the thought, but what does that say about me?

Petra doesn't take Ares' hint and loops her arm in his.

Ares may not object to her touching, but the expressions of the men around him change in her presence. It's subtle as fuck, but I see it.

And it sickens me to think if anyone saw me with Petra or any woman like her, that was how they looked at me when I didn't notice.

With the cocktail hour winding down, the flow of guests slows to a trickle from the entrance. A shock of dark hair and a thick white beard catches my eyes and I smirk.

Corvin took the bait. Not bait in the way that I plan to out him, but he's soaking up the royal treatment. I'm laying it on thick to get him comfortable, so he lets his guard down.

I briefed my brothers that I sent him an invite and passed around a photo of what he looked like. I asked them kindly to not only hide the shock of seeing him on their faces, but also not to lunge for the guy.

That request was directed at Lachlan mostly and my exact words were: *Don't shoot the fucker on sight.*

They have to trust me. Shane's specialty team is tracking everything he does. If Shane, who's as good as me, maybe even better in some areas, is making sure this guy doesn't fuck with anything of ours, I sleep better at night.

Not that I'm sleeping again. Despite what I take. It's torture dragging my ass out of bed because Ella isn't there. I've grown so reliant on her.

The best I've felt and the most productive I've been recently was waking up every day to her gentle nudges on my shoulders. The instant shot of energy made me soar every morning—but along with that, I had the burning need to pull her into bed and fuck her.

One day this week, my housekeeper found me passed out in my bed at noon. Which startled the fuck out of me, and her, because the sheets were gone. I was naked and hard.

I'm ready to greet Corvin when I spot a slender figure in a pale green satin gown on his arm.

Ella.

I didn't recall Snow's invite having a plus one.

She gatecrashed this event. Her fiery spirit turns me the fuck on.

God, I missed her this week, and seeing her loosens the

knot in my chest.

I glance at my brothers and for the first time feel this soul-rattling chasm between us. Even a little pissed off that their brutal, savage ways are keeping me from what I want. Ella.

Before I can do anything, I feel the weight of my brother's green-eyed stare. Kieran. The boss. Our king. His stare wrecks me, a faint smile lifting from his lips.

It's gotten back to me here and there that my brothers fear me for what I can do to them. The way Kieran regards me, I see respect in his eyes. He'll listen to me when the time comes to decide Corvin's fate. Unlike the other developers and hackers who work for me, Corvin sits in a league of his own. A dangerous intersection of knowing our sins as a Mob organization and having the technical ability to obliterate us.

It never mattered to me who my family killed. It's not indiscriminate. There's always a reason. Lachlan isn't as insane as people think. He's calculating and precise. But he wants Corvin's head when this is done. Taking Ella as my own changes my trajectory about Corvin.

There has to be a way to control him. Find that intersection in the Venn diagram where he can live and be trusted.

Lachlan wants to gut him because he's a menace. Something I'm struggling with because of one little wrinkle. I'm falling hopelessly for his daughter.

If Lachlan gets his way, Ella will be alone in the world and at the mercy of some psycho fucking cop.

I'm the one who can protect her.

Right now, I have to address what happened earlier this week.

Damn, I miss her.

I finish my drink and hand the glass to a waiter before striding over to greet them both.

Ella catches my eye and the hitch in her breath does me the fuck in.

Getting closer, I see the dress has a gently-scooped neckline with a tempting glimpse of her ample cleavage. Dainty straps with beads contrast the definition of her shoulders. And that thigh-high slit heats my blood. I've never seen her wear anything revealing. Jesus, that slit makes her legs look like they go on for days. She's a stunning beauty in that dress with her soft waves of dark mahogany hair cascading past her shoulders.

Corvin sees me and smiles, clutching Ella's hand in his elbow. "Mr. O'Rourke. I hope you don't mind, I brought Ella."

"I actually bullied my way in here," she confesses.

"If you need me to pay for her plate," Corvin offers.

I hold my hand up. "We always buy full tables. It's fine."

My gaze collides with Ella and the room feels like it's on fire.

"Thank you, Mr. O'Rourke," Corvin Snow showers me with this syrupy admiration that has to be an act.

Or he could be grateful not to have been caught for the cyber takedown of the century and is now happy to hide behind my fucking skirt for protection.

"My *pleasure*," I say with my eyes right on Ella.

Pleasure...

"We will get out of your hair and mingle," Snow says and sweeps Ella away from me.

Anger floods my veins, but I smile through it, determined to keep an eye on her.

"She's here?" A feminine voice whispers in my ear from behind.

Closing my eyes, I face my sister. "Aye."

"And her father works for you, too?"

"They came as a package deal before I realized who she

was. And considering what I did to her..."

"Do you think her father would object to you dating her?"

"Dating," I scoff and wave to my brothers. "Have you not figured out that O'Rourke men don't date? They *possess*."

"So be different." She nudges me. "I can tell you like her. You didn't blink an eye approving her shopping spree. And I saw just now how you looked at her."

"Why are you watching me?"

"Maybe looking for the signs." She shrugs.

"Signs?"

"Of how a man who's crazy about a woman is supposed to look at her." Her tone worries me.

She's isolated working in East Hampton. She can marry whoever she wants. Kieran refuses to arrange a marriage for her. But her last name must give many men pause. And those who want to marry her because of who she is, is not someone she would want.

I don't tell her that I know all about her and Archer Crest because she'll never forgive me for spying on her. And that I know it's over between them and he broke her heart. Something else I can't share with anyone because I really only talk to my brothers, and they'll kill him.

"It will happen, Shea. When you least expect it," I say, wanting her to have hope, and then I kiss her on the cheek.

Smiling, her eyes widen as she lets out an, "Uh oh..."

"What?" I follow her gaze, and fury consumes me seeing Ella in the arms of another man.

CHAPTER THIRTY-THREE
ELLA

I let Geoff Bracken take my arm and lead me onto the dancefloor.

Even if it meant letting my father introduce me to a man I don't want, I was coming to the gala if Balor would be here.

Dad already frowned at me dating *a cop,* who many already think are too violent. But he held back the *I told you so* when I showed up at his apartment, broken and terrified.

Not that polished rich men don't hurt women. Domestic violence knows no boundaries.

Balor made a point to tell me he wasn't one of those men. That he *and his brothers* were dead set against mistreating women.

Shoving his dick into my mouth and coming all over my face aside.

Geoff runs a hedge fund, according to my dad in the blatant setup disguised as a casual introduction.

I smile, waxing on about living in Australia for six months and teaching special-needs kids there. He wrinkles his nose, figuring out he's dancing with a working-class girl and not a princess looking for a prince.

God, I miss Balor, but he greeted me so coldly before. I overstepped the other day, watching him shower. He may have been teaching me a lesson, but I loved it. I want us to play more like that. I made it clear that I'm not looking for anything serious.

After a few more minutes of Geoff's grating voice and self-boasting, I'm sick and thinking how I can escape him.

A deep voice sails over my shoulder. "I believe that woman belongs to me."

Geoff's eyes widen and he swings me around. "Excuse

me?"

"Your dance partner." Balor stuns in his new jet-black, double-breasted tux. "She belongs to me."

"O'Rourke, is it?" Geoff's snippy tone signs his death warrant.

"Aye. You know who I am?"

"Everyone knows who you are. *And* your family. You think you own this city?"

"I don't think we do. I know we do. Now —"

"Geoffrey, Balor O'Rourke is my boss," I jump in to avoid bloodshed. "And *my father's* boss. I'm working tonight and he needs to talk to me. That's what he meant."

Balor holds his hand for me to take, his razor-sharp glare taunting Geoff. "Are we clear?"

"Fuck off, O'Rourke."

Balor's glacial scowl deepens. "Take your hand off her, or I'll take it home as a souvenir."

The icy tone and the gory threat should appall me. I'm freaking turned on.

Geoff drops my hands and shoves his into his pockets. "Whatever." He spins and hikes toward the bar.

Being free of Geoff's grimy hands brings air back into my lungs.

"Try not to kill him," I say to Balor to show I'm not afraid of him. That I completely get who he is and what his family is involved in.

"I don't kill people. I told you that." He pulls me into his chest, but we're on the dancefloor so he shifts his legs as if we're dancing.

"I don't care if you do." I shrug. "You won't hurt me."

"You sure about that?"

"Yes."

"Why?"

"I've seen evil. Stared it in the face. That's not you. I trust you," I whisper.

His features rearrange as if I've handed him a diamond mine.

"You *should* trust me." He bites back another comment. "Did your father introduce you to Geoff?"

"Yes, of course."

"I'd like to think your father doesn't know that Geoff Bracken is in the middle of a vicious divorce with the pregnant wife he cheated on."

"What?" My extremities go cold, questioning my father's intentions with me.

I know he never wants me near Wes again. Does he think a rich philanderer is okay so long as he doesn't hit me?

"Perhaps your father doesn't know about the mistress." Balor exhales with tightened frustration like he's trying to give Dad the benefit of the doubt.

"I think my father is just old school," I say to save him. He's still Balor's employee and being paid an enormous salary. I don't want to make Balor doubt his judgment.

"Why else did you really save me from Geoff?" I pull the pin and drop that grenade to challenge him.

He visibly swallows. "I'm...working through issues."

A twist of excitement twirls in my belly as I finger his lapel. But the *working through* hits a nerve. "Issues, such as the desire to only sleep with a paid escort so you can keep your heart out of the equation?"

"Something like that." His jaw tightens when he drinks in my stare.

My heart jumps into my throat, and I can only hope he means me.

For me.

"How do you feel about that?" he asks. "That I want to get past my hang-ups."

Not wanting to seem too eager, I play it cool. "I think progress that leads to healthy relationships is a good one."

He barks a laugh. "That is the most benign bullshit safe answer I've ever heard."

"I'm not sure which adjective there I should argue. After this week—"

He jerks me closer, cutting me off. "I'm sorry about the other morning."

I bite my lip. "Which part?"

He huffs. "All of it. I shouldn't have gotten so damn inappropriate with you."

"Inappropriate? You crossed inappropriate by putting on a show for me in your shower."

"The blood in my veins was roaring through my ears that morning. I didn't catch or didn't process anything you said," he gets low and gravelly. "Did you like what you saw?"

"Yes," I say on a breathy moan.

"And what I did? All of it?" His smile implies the cum facial he gave me.

"Yes," I whisper.

"Fuck." He lowers his head. "Ella..."

"I think we need to be honest about this working situation. You don't need me, but I am needed at the Fredricks school. Even if I'm just an aide right now. This position will allow me to apply next year to get my old job back."

I don't need his permission to take the aide's position. But my father arranged for Balor to hire me. I'm trying to be mature and respectful about my responsibility.

"What are the hours?"

Excitement pulses through me. "Nine to twelve, Monday through Thursday. And they're closed for all major holidays."

"What about transportation?"

"I used to take the subway there."

"That's not happening." Balor shakes his head. "How

about we do our thing in the morning because *that part* I do need. You're making a difference, getting my ass in gear every morning. It's been a terrible week without you. After you finish with me, I'll drop you off at the school and my new driver—"

"New driver?" I glance around to locate Trace, who I saw earlier.

"Trace is my sister's bodyguard now. I have a new driver, Denton. One of my brother Kieran's guards."

"Oh." It hits me that no matter what, his brothers want Balor protected. And Balor wants me protected.

"I'll have Denton pick you up at noon and bring you back to the office to catch up with me."

Excitement hums under my skin. I want to hug him. I want to kiss him. I want to fuck him.

Balor's lips part to say more but they slam shut. My heart aches when he puts some distance between us, but he doesn't let me go completely.

"Snow," he says over my shoulder.

I shudder that my father might have been watching me. "Dad?"

"What happened to Geoff?" He turns to find his so-called friend.

"The guy with the pregnant wife?" Balor snaps.

My father goes ashen. "He's getting a divorce."

"To be with his whore," Balor says. "Not a person I'd let a woman I care about spend time with."

Dad's eyes stray to our linked hands, but we're dancing. And Balor is my boss who admitted to saving me from a creep.

My father might also be aware of Balor's proclivities when it comes to sex and knows, or thinks, he'll never make a move on me. Or Dad thinks Balor is mob royalty who is waiting on a princess to become available.

Even if my father thinks something is going on, Balor

is *his* boss and chewing him out will get him fired. Or worse.

"I didn't realize," my father says. "Ella, I just got a call from a...client. My side work, that you approved, Mr. O'Rourke. I need to leave. I'm sorry."

"No problem. You're not on the clock. You're free to do what you want," Balor says icily.

"Can you make sure Ella gets home safely?" Dad asks gently.

"Of course," Balor responds.

"I'll walk you out, Dad." I go to break free, but Balor doesn't let go of my arm.

"You don't need Ella to walk you out, do you, Snow?"

"No." Dad's gaze cuts from Balor to me. "I trust you, Mr. O'Rourke."

"As you should," he says with a deadly tenor.

"I will be staying at our house in Connecticut for the rest of the weekend." My father kisses me on the cheek, where he whispers, "Be careful."

I nod and watch him go. With him out of earshot, I glance back at Balor. "He told me to be careful. Am I in any danger?"

"He told you to be careful with me?"

I nod.

"And he whispered it so I wouldn't hear, but you told me what he said to you. *Why?*"

His question carries a lot of weight, so I choose my answer carefully. The O'Rourkes honor loyalty. From what I've seen they're loyal to each other first. There comes a time when a woman has to break from her father and give herself over to a man, make him her priority, and steer her loyalty to him.

"Because I believe you want what is truly best for me." Even if it's not him. But he seems willing to open his heart to me.

"Good girl," Balor breathes into my skin, kissing me on the forehead. "I have one more question for you, Ella."
"Yeah?"
"Are you coming home with me tonight or not?"

CHAPTER THIRTY-FOUR

BALOR

In my arms, Ella nods tightly, agreeing to go home with me. My cock swells so hard and so fast, I might bust a nut in these tuxedo pants.

I take her hand and steer her off the dancefloor. Reality slams into me seeing my family at the two reserved tables filled with powerful people my brother, Kieran, wants to impress.

The one thing shared by every one of my brothers' wives was the look of sheer terror in their eyes taking us all in for the first time.

Ella stands tall, composed, showing no signs of being frightened.

But right now, Ella isn't my wife or fiancée, not even my girlfriend. She's a woman I fucked who's now my employee and that's what they'll see. My staff *is* my business. I don't follow rules anyway.

While Ella doesn't appear afraid, I decide to pass on introductions to the members of my family she hasn't met.

"Wait here, please," I say, stopping at the edge of the dancefloor near the lobby doors.

Her eyes stray over my shoulder. Nodding, she gets that I'm saying goodbye to my brothers without her, but she doesn't call me out on it.

"I need to get my purse from Dad's table and use the ladies' restroom," she says, light and breezy.

Nodding, I lean in and kiss her cheek. "I will come find you, if—"

"Balor," she breathes, sounding desperate for me. "I want this more than you know."

That stiffens my cock like iron.

I squeeze her hand. "Good, because I'm fucking you all night until you beg me to stop."

Her jaw drops at my blunt words. "Not face down this time?"

"No. Go get your things." I wink at her.

When she turns and struts away, I stride across the dancefloor, heading straight for Kieran.

He's the only man I feel any obligation to explain myself.

"A word," I utter to him, his eyes locked on me when I approach him.

"Of course." He shows his unwavering respect for me, given my contribution to our empire.

"I'm leaving. I'm taking a woman home with me." I raise my chin. "Snow's daughter. The assistant who works for me."

His right eyebrow raises. "Does her father know?"

"I don't care."

"You should care if you think he's dangerous."

"I'm not worried what he can do. I'll make sure he doesn't hurt us. Trust me."

"I trust you with everything we have, Balor. You know that, right?" Kieran's trust weighs heavily on me.

"And if we take down Snow, I want Ella with me, at my side. No prejudices." I glare at him.

"You won't have any from me." He stands at his full height.

"I don't care for long drawn-out goodbyes."

"You do the Irish exit better than any of us." He grips the back of my neck. "Have yourself a good night."

"I plan to."

After tossing nods to anyone at the tables looking my way, my eyes search for Ella. I stop, seeing her speaking to Jillian and Eoghan near the bar.

Eoghan fists a whiskey, and it's the first time his hands have been on anything except Jillian's ass. She's pregnant and sips from a tumbler of sparkling water.

Without any tension from the day they met, it pleases me the way Ella smiles and laughs with them. Whatever the hell they're talking about.

Joining them, I immediately slide my hand around Ella's waist, catching Jillian's eyes.

"Our wedding celebration invites go out next week. Am I putting you down as a plus-one, Balor?" she cheerfully asks me, referring to the big party they're having because they already got married in a Vegas wedding chapel last month.

"Absolutely," I give my response about bringing Ella with no hesitation.

"And bring her out to Shea's house for the bridal shower," Eoghan says, sounding all-in on these wedding plans.

"Send me the date again so we can look at our schedules." Turning to Ella, her jaw hanging I open, I say, "Ready?"

"Uh-huh." Ella smiles, squeezing my hand.

"Have a good night," I say to Eoghan and Jillian.

Ella stops at the coat check and picks up her calf-length wool coat. I help her into it and lead her toward the exit. The valet brings around my Rivian, which I drove myself.

I lift Ella into the passenger seat, snagging her dress so it doesn't catch on the door. "Let's stop by your apartment to pack a bag."

"A bag?" she chirps the question.

"You're staying with me until Monday."

"I am?"

"Aye. That's what I want. Don't you?"

"My dad…"

I check my phone. "He's already on the West Side Highway."

"How do you know?"

"Because I'm tracking his phone," I say, staring at her.

"Are you tracking mine?"

"Aye. You work for me."

Nodding, she sits back. "I'm okay with that because I have nothing to hide."

"Good girl."

We stop at her building, and I offer to walk her up to the apartment, but she waves me off. Her building is secure. Snow assured that because he's got enemies.

She returns less than twenty minutes later with a stylish white leather tote bag, but still in her dress and those heels I want wrapped around my head as soon as possible.

After she gets in, I lean in and breathe against her neck. "That gown looks beautiful on you."

"You bought it."

That gets me so fucking hard, I can't control myself.

"And I'm glad you left it on because now I get to be the one who tears it off your body."

CHAPTER THIRTY-FIVE
BALOR

Inside my townhouse, I hold Ella against the back of my front door, my hot breath sending a shiver through her that I can feel.

"Let me be clear about something, Ella. This isn't just for tonight or this weekend. I've gone insane these last few weeks wanting to sink my dick into your pussy. I need to make you understand, you're mine." I rub my cock between her legs, bunching her dress in my hands.

"Balor," she cries out, feeling my hard cock.

I'm fucking desperate for her, but I step back.

"Turn around," I command.

She spins, breathy moans falling from her lips.

"Hands on the back of the door," I growl and skate her dress zipper down.

Inches of tawny skin come into my vision, and memories of how she made me feel in L.A. wreck me. But it tastes sweet because I get a do-over with her.

"No bra?"

"It's a tight dress."

"Yes, it is. It fits you like a second skin." I lower the fabric, shimmying it past her hips and my chest tightens at the tiny black lace thong hugging her hips and flossing her ass.

I crouch, following the fabric until her gorgeous ass is in my face.

"Balor," she moans.

"Step out of the dress, hands stay on the door."

Gently, she kicks the gown away.

On a whimper, she says, "Balor, I want to tell you something."

I freeze and run my hands along every silky inch of her spine. "Turn around."

She boldly faces me, standing there topless with bouncy, full breasts, and pink nipples that I take into my mouth. "You're making this hard for me, Balor."

"Hard? This is hard for you?" I bring her hand to my swollen groin.

"I'm serious." Her tone snaps my attention.

"What do you have to tell me?"

"That night in the hotel... When you took off the condom."

My stomach clenches. "Talk to me."

"I wasn't on birth control. I should have told you no or told you I wasn't on anything. I went to the doctor a few days later, and I'm on the pill now." She lowers her head.

I lift her chin to look into her eyes. "Thank you for telling me. I was wrong to pressure you. I just couldn't... I needed to feel you."

"And now you can. I haven't been with anyone else, Balor."

"Neither have I. If you're okay with it, I don't want to use anything with you." I lean in. "Ever."

"Ever," she repeats, her voice cracking.

"Now that we've settled that. Get your ass in my bed." I grab the two fleshy halves of her plump butt that have been teasing me for weeks.

She sashays past me, topless in a thong and high heels.

Admittedly, my escorts have done this, and it meant nothing. I was paying them.

Ella is here because she wants to be here.

We reach my bedroom where I lift her and throw her onto my bed.

She cackles deliciously and sinks into my thick comforter.

"Spread your legs and play with your pussy, while I undress."

Her fingers inch down her stomach and slide into the

thong. I'm hard as steel as she pulls it aside, giving me a glimpse of the pink, glistening wetness.

These fucking threads can't get off my body fast enough. I want to be completely naked.

"Look at me." I stand there soaking in her stare.

"You are the hottest man I've ever seen." She rears up on her elbows. "How do you get cut like that?"

"Pain. Sweat. Effort," I rasp.

I dip my knee into the mattress, her scent of arousal hitting me and making my mouth water.

I cover her body with mine as she wraps her legs around me. I kiss her, strikingly differentiating what this is. She's mine to fuck in a deeper, visceral way than any woman being paid.

Ella's lips are so fucking sweet, and she kisses me like she craves me as much as I crave her.

"I can kiss you for hours, but I want to taste a different set of lips." I work my way down her body until only the scrap of lace separates my mouth from her cunt.

I tear it off, and the sound of fabric ripping hitches her breath.

Tossing the shredded lace aside, I bury my head between her legs and lick her pussy, wanting her to cream all over my tongue.

"This sweet cunt is mine," I mutter and slide two fingers inside her. "Come for me."

"It's yours," she moans and comes in my mouth, tightening around my fingers, strangling them.

I suck on her clit, making her cry out, her heels hitting my back.

I stop and yank off the shoes, forcibly throwing them across the room.

"Are you mine?" I ask her.

"I'm yours."

"Tomorrow will you be mine?"

"Yes."

"And the day after that?" Like a man winning at the casino, I keep feeding the machine to win some more.

"Every day. Please. Fuck me."

I line up my cock up with her dripping entrance and push the tip in.

"Oh, God," she moans.

"Yes, that's me." I pull out to wipe her wetness over her swollen throbbing clit.

"Right there."

Slowly I ease inside her, every inch unraveling me. "Be a good girl. Take my cock into your sweet cunt."

As I slide in deeper, her stiff nipples look so fucking inviting. I lower my mouth to lick and suck each one until I'm fully seated inside her.

"Chriiiiist," I mutter.

I knew fucking her again was going to be the end of me. I just didn't think getting her into my bed would be so life-changing. Taking a woman like this. Face to face. Kissing her is monumental.

"Wrap those legs around me, squeeze my hips."

"Mmmm." She fits me so perfectly.

I fuck her like an animal, needing to get this one climax out of the way so she understands what she does to me.

"You're dripping all over my balls, baby."

"It's so good." She finds my eyes. "Kiss me. Please."

"I love how you beg." I take her mouth, ravenous for her silky lips and tongue, imagining how it will feel on my dick again.

Even in my ass. Don't even ask me what *that* costs. My Ella will do that for free.

"Balor!" she calls out my name, her soaking wet pussy strangling my dick as she comes again.

I kiss around her moans and pull out.

I flip her over and run my lips along her spine. That

tattoo of Russian letters trailing down the length of her right oblique muscle intrigued me the first time I saw it, but I didn't ask.

Now, I *have* to know.

"What does this mean?" I stroke the etchings on her skin.

"I don't know. My father gave me a printout and told me to show it to the artist. It's a Russian proverb."

Something nags me about that, but my cock is too hard and needs to be inside her again.

I continue running my fingers down her spine until I reach the crease of her ass. I took that hole in the shower, bare, except for some lube.

My nails leave little scrapes on her skin and marking her ignites a flame in me like gasoline.

"You look sexy as fuck on your hands and knees dripping for my cock." I separate her cheeks.

She gasps, thinking I'll take her that way, but I just lower my mouth and lave her hole with my tongue.

"Oh, yes. That's so dirty. I love it." She grabs the sheets.

I line up my cock with her drenched slit. And slam back in.

After licking my finger, I slide it deep into her ass.

She climaxes again immediately around my cock. I'm not sure how long I'll last.

She's so jumpy, flinching and moaning at every touch, every one of my moves. I fucking love that. I roughly fuck her as her moans turn into high-pitched squeals.

My control slips. "I'm so close, baby. I'm going to come inside you and fill you with my cum."

She mewls as my hips slap against her plump, sexy ass. The sound embeds into my brain. Her cunt tightens on my cock with such a perfect, sexy force. I'm reaching my limit. I'm on the brink of my release. Every muscle tenses as I thrust faster and deeper.

"I'm close. Do you have another orgasm for me, baby? I want us to come together."

She whines with her head down as I slip a second finger into her ass. "Yeah, that'll do it."

"You've wrecked me, baby. I'm gonna come."

She drenches my balls, her arousal dripping down her thighs.

I'm about to fly over the edge. Stronger than ever. Catching her turned head, cheek pressed to the mattress, naked, open, taking my cock and my fingers in her ass do me in.

"Fuuuuck," I cry out, pumping faster in rhythm with her cunt spasming around my sensitive cock.

I use what's left on my fingers to push my dripping cum back inside her cunt and coat her hole. My cock hardens instantly. I slip the head of my cock past the quivering ring of nerves.

"Yes, please. Fuck me there."

She opens for me and I bury myself deep inside her ass. I keep her hips tilted and power-fuck her.

Climax after climax rushes through me. Cum gushing from her hole slicks out and my thighs are drenched with the juices from her dripping pussy mixed with my hot cum.

I should have gotten soft hours ago.

Not even close.

CHAPTER THIRTY-SIX

ELLA

Locked in my bathroom at home, I stare at the positive pregnancy test.

The gala was two weeks ago, and I should have started my period the day after. When it didn't come, I shrugged it off to all the sex Balor and I had that weekend.

Since that night, without the pesky hindrances of blood or cramps, we've gone at it like rabbits. Mostly when I arrive to wake him up.

Now that morning wood is all for me. I ride him in his bed and then he takes me in his shower.

I started working at Fredricks Elementary again, and I finally feel like my old self. Only better, because I don't have a psycho boyfriend I'm afraid to go home to or bruises to cover with makeup.

Is Balor my boyfriend? It feels odd to think of a thirty-five-year-old man, who's *in the mafia,* as a boyfriend.

And since we're not public about our relationship, labels haven't come up. I've not told my father because Balor is his boss and Dad can be a little...brusque when he's mad. I assume he would only see another powerful man trying to take advantage of his daughter.

But Dad *needs* this job. It's steady and safe. Freelance gigs can dry up at any time or get him into trouble. Worse, hurt him. I worry he'd forget all that and...

I don't know what he'd do to Balor if he found out.

But we can't hide forever when this baby inside me starts showing.

Warm tears build in my eyes and next, I feel them streaming down my cheeks. I'm not sure why I'm crying. Perhaps the hormones have kicked in.

I've felt so happy these past two weeks, and this bombshell will nuke the hot and casual fun Balor and I have every day.

I don't want anything serious, and I *don't* want to get married yet. I know he feels the same about wanting to be casual.

A knock on my door is followed by my father's voice calling out to me. Heart pounding, I close the test stick inside my hand and tug my sweater sleeve down.

"Estella, can I speak to you for a moment?" Dad's Russian accent sounds thick and troubled.

"Of course." I clasp my hands behind my back and manage to wedge the pee-stick inside my pants.

"I am going on business trip."

"Where? For what business?" I snap, my baby worry spilling out of me before I can stop it. "Dad, Balor lets you freelance on the side, but you can't just—"

"It *is* for Balor." His right eyebrow raises at my tone.

Balor is sending my dad on a trip, but he didn't tell me.

Even though I'm Balor's personal assistant, I'm privy to projects the other team members in the command center are working on. Balor has sent IT specialists out of town here and there. And always mentioned it to me in the course of our conversations about projects.

Balor lights up talking about his work and how he built a state-of-the-art network, security systems, and firewalls. Computers are not my jam. I wish we had more in common like Eoghan and Jillian, who are both lawyers. I've learned that each of his brothers' wives is very different from their husbands.

That tightens my throat. Will I be forced to marry Balor? All his brothers have babies, and two wives are pregnant. Is that how those marriages went down?

"Where are you going exactly?" I ask my dad and shove everything else out of my head.

"Tokyo."

I go breathless at how far away he'll be. We've only

been apart a few days here and there since we went to Sydney.

"How long will you be gone?" I ask.

"I am not sure. Depends on my progress. Two weeks, at least."

My stomach flips at the idea of being alone for so long...

Wait, I won't be alone.

Did Balor plan this on purpose?

"What are you doing there?" I fold my arms.

His eyes narrow on me as he hesitates. "I am not sure what I can reveal."

"I work for Balor, too."

"As his assistant." Dad won't be happy that I took the part-time job at the school because that's where I met Wes, and Dad thinks he'll go looking for me there.

But he hasn't.

Dad would prefer I organize Balor's closet all day. The assistant job was always supposed to be temporary. Dad knew all along I wanted to teach again next fall.

"Dad, are you telling me everything?" I argue, even though I'm keeping the job at Fredricks a secret. "What's going on?"

Over dinner, he used to clamor on about his projects at the bank. A bank isn't the mafia. Perhaps, he's protecting me.

"Let me clear what I can tell you with Balor."

"Never mind." I wave my hand. "When do you leave?"

"Tomorrow night."

I go breathless. "Oh, that's very little notice."

"Do not worry, my Ella. This building is secure. You promise me you will take Ubers and not the subways or walk too far on your own?"

"Dad, I've not heard from Wes. It's been more than eight months."

His shoulders relax. "Good."

I'm emotionally scarred from that relationship. Bad memories of him beating me flash back sometimes, but I don't feel like I'm in danger anymore.

Two weeks without my dad watching over me means I can spend more time with Balor.

We *really* need to get to know each other better. I'm having his baby.

I truly don't know what his reaction will be. He said his busy schedule prevented him from having a relationship, and that went double for kids.

But I feel we're in a relationship. He got over that hurdle. Hopefully, he'll be happy about the baby. Especially if he cares about me.

"We should go out tonight." I smile to show Dad I'm happy and not stressed.

Although now I have something else to worry about.

Dad cocks his head and glances around the room. "It is Saturday night. You don't have a date?"

I lower my gaze at him. "Don't you think I'd tell you if I had a date?"

Dad hovers over me. He's six foot, stocky with a long face and a snowy-white beard over pocked, acne-scarred skin. His blue eyes under dark hair make him handsome. "You know you can tell me anything, Ella. It upset me to no end that you kept so much of what that animal Wesley did to you a secret."

"I was embarrassed. I thought it was my fault. And I thought…" My throat gets tight. "I thought he'd stop. I thought I could manage the situation myself."

He cups my chin. "Do you promise never to keep something like that from me again?"

"I promise." I let him fold me into a hug, the smell of his aftershave calming me.

"No man will ever raise a hand to you again." He

squeezes me. "I will make sure of it. And now that I am valuable to a man like Balor O'Rourke and his connections…"

My heart pounds, feeling how tangled my circumstance has become. Dad promises to get Balor involved if a new boyfriend hurts me.

Visions of being paid off, made to go away because I'm carrying an illegitimate mafia baby turn my stomach.

If Balor is the one to protect me, who will protect me if he breaks my heart?

CHAPTER THIRTY-SEVEN
ELLA

Dad's flight left at eleven p.m. Sunday night. Balor texted me that he had family obligations all weekend, but that he was looking forward to seeing me Monday morning.

I mentioned Dad's trip to him and asked why he hadn't said anything to me. He said it was a last-minute swap with another developer who couldn't go.

Monday morning, his car arrives out front to pick me up. When I get to his house, I tiptoe upstairs and find him like I usually do every morning.

Three more pregnancy tests showed positive, but my doctor is still backed up with appointments, so I must wait for an official diagnosis.

I'm guessing I got pregnant when we were in Los Angeles. Which means taking the low-dose pills shortly after was for naught. Or Balor has really powerful swimmers.

And gah, I could have hurt my baby! I flushed all the pills right down the drain.

I find Balor on his stomach, his naked body twisted in the sheets. His round ass gets me every time. The cool skin when I grip it makes me smile. Him, too.

Eyes closed, he turns over. "That better be my butterfly," he murmurs.

"I'm not the housekeeper."

"You're keeping me..." He stops and clears his throat. "What time is it?"

"Time for me to blow you."

"Oh, thank God. I jerked off so much this weekend."

When he's not hard and dying for my mouth, where I might not get a straight answer, I'll address why he sent my father to the other side of the world without telling me.

And then the baby news…

Right now, I just want to feel his cock slide past my lips.

Fisting his hard, swollen cock, he says, "God, baby, I need your mouth on me."

I lower my tongue and take a swipe at the pearly drops of pre-cum on the crown.

"Fuuuuck," he groans, low and so very male.

My womb holding his baby meows for him.

I'm ravenous for him to spill down my throat. He gets his most primal fucking my face.

I suck him into my mouth and take him in as deeply as my jaw will allow.

He strangles a moan when my wet lips release him to lick up the sides with my hands around the base of the stiff shaft.

The heat of his maleness makes my core tingle. With his legs spread wide and the controlled rhythm of his hips, he makes love to my mouth.

He threads his fingers through my hair, which I no longer spray with products or wear up in a clip because Balor always unravels any style I work hard at.

As he gets close, he pulls harder, wrapping the long strands a few times around his palm like it's braided nylon rope and he's a bull rider.

Balor, the bull rider. He's got the body for it. But he's so smart, he'd outwit a two-ton bucking beast.

"You suck my cock so good, Ella," he hisses. "My sweet little assistant loves sucking her boss's cock. You really had me convinced you were a whore. I'm so fucking lucky because you wrap those gorgeous lips around my cock like one, but you're mine. No one fucking touches what's mine." He groans and his hips move quicker as I bring him to the brink of orgasm.

He shoves himself even deeper into my mouth,

keeping my head steady while he thrusts inside me, hitting the back of my throat.

I gag, my eyes watering, but I don't care. It gets me off nearly as much as it does him.

Balor's visceral moans almost sound pained. He's dying to come, but he's being a brat. He wants to keep feeling my mouth around his cock.

I suck harder, increasing the pressure as he fucking loses it on me.

"Christ, I'm coming," he roars, his voice broken and with the accent, it's so sexy.

His cock spurts ropes of hot cum on my tongue. I cup his balls to milk him further, sucking down every drop.

It's too much and I cough it back up, coating his cock.

For a man who only let paid, professionals get him off like this, he loves my inexperienced mouth around his dick.

Maybe because my mouth has only been around his dick. Wes did me missionary once a week and that was it. No foreplay. Just mumbled he wanted sex and to get on my back. He stopped kissing me, too.

Now I feast on the power Balor gives me. How I own him in these moments.

He's a mafia billionaire who answers to no one. I, however, have to get to school. Even if it means I don't get the pleasure of his cock in my pussy right now.

"Jesus fucking Christ, Ella. You are so fucking sexy." He lifts me from his throbbing dick and pulls me on top of him.

His cock leaks and messes up my shirt, but I don't care.

"I missed you this weekend." He kisses me. "I couldn't stop thinking about you."

His confession gives me an opening. I consider the time, but I'll die if I don't get this out.

"I missed you, too." I take a deep breath. "Balor, how

do you feel about me?"

His eyes pop open wide, his breath shallow while he's silent.

Finally, his lips part. "I like you."

"Oh." My heart seizes.

Those words don't reconcile with the guttural comments of how I'm his. And now no other man is to touch me. I wasn't expecting him to use the L-word. I don't know if I love him. I've never been in love.

But something's at stake now.

Cupping my face, he says, "What's wrong?"

With a tight throat, I whisper, "I'm pregnant."

He blinks, a hint of restrained emotion tightening his jaw. "Okay. When did you find out?"

"Saturday."

"I spoke to you Saturday, you didn't mention it." He sounds hurt.

We hadn't been spending time together on the weekends. He's usually working. We're not open as a couple as far as my father.

"It's not something I would have told you on the phone."

"Does your father know?"

"Of course not. I wouldn't tell him before you."

And he'd certainly know if my father knew.

CHAPTER THIRTY-EIGHT
BALOR

I've denied that I fell hard for Ella long enough.

I thought I wouldn't ever let myself get so tangled and unraveled. Boy, I was so damn wrong, it scares the hell out of me.

Yet, here I am.

This is my moment, a moment I'd only ever gotten secondhand when my brothers announced they were going to be a father.

I never considered to ask how the news hit them.

This one feels like a searing crossbow into my chest.

But every muscle unclenches. Any breath I'm holding loosens. Any doubt I had about how I feel about Ella crystalizes in front of my eyes.

I'm pregnant.

She's mine. And I love her.

"Are you sure?" I ask because that seems like the logical response. "About the baby?"

Swallowing, she sits back and only now it feels crappy that she just sucked me off. We're talking about this in the shadow of my orgasm.

Fuck, that question of how I feel about her makes sense. I couldn't put an answer into words. So I said something lame. Don't my actions speak louder? Like telling her how much I missed her?

"Three at-home tests came up positive," she says, pinching her sweater. "I have an appointment with my doctor at the end of the month. They asked my last period date and based on that—"

"When was your last period?"

"Before I left Sydney. I'm not very regular. My cycle fluctuates. The pills were supposed to help that, too." She bites her lip and then looks up at me. "It's yours, Balor."

I grip her face, shock rolling through me that she thinks I would even suspect it wasn't mine. "Of course, it's mine."

Considering she told me she wasn't on the pill when I fucked her in L.A. where I pulled off the condom and filled her with my cum out of uncontrollable lust, this pregnancy is my fault.

"My brother, Darragh, will arrange to have you examined by a colleague right away. Today." I reach for my phone, but she stops my hand.

"I don't want to be a bother to your family." She sounds like doesn't want my brother to know.

"I just want to make sure everything is okay. That you're okay." I hold her against my chest.

"I feel fine. Just...emotional." She looks up at me. "And really dying for sex."

"Can you play hooky from school, little girl?" I tease her.

Smiling, she says, "The negative part of working for a school is that calling out messes up the day for a lot of people. Including the kids." Her lips close around my jaw. "School will be closed for the February break soon."

"Okay. Good." I get out of bed and get my thoughts under control.

It's not Darragh I'm worried about. It's Lachlan who plans to kill her father.

Fuck, Corvin is my child's grandfather.

This poor kid won the gobshite grandfather lottery. My da is no prize. I have to live with pretending what I saw that night didn't happen. That I didn't see him beat my mother. That I've forgiven him. But I've kept his secret because I honestly don't know what my brothers would do. The sheer audacity of Da's arrogance to lay a hand on the mother of seven fucking sons, five of whom he groomed to be killers just like him.

I was only sixteen at the time, and after witnessing his violence against Ma, he pulled me aside.

"Do yourself a favor, don't get married. Don't have kids. I got enough sons who will carry on my name. Women are fucking trouble. Pay one to suck your dick and be done with them." The alcohol on his breath dulled the meaning of his words, and I told myself he didn't mean it. *"You're the smartest one, Balor. We had you tested. You'll do great things."*

After he stumbled from his bedroom, I ran to my mother to help her, troubled by the disgusting mix of my father's compliment with his confession. It made me want to throw up, and I questioned what was true and what was drunken babble.

Ma held her head high, wiping the blood from her nose, and sternly made me promise not to tell my older brothers.

To this day, I've kept their secret, privately holding a grudge against Da. And upset at myself for being too small, too afraid to intervene.

It's only been tempered by the way he's been taking care of Ma since her illness intensified.

I have to come to terms that I'm saving Ella because I couldn't protect my mother that night. But it confuses me if what I feel for her is real. Or some transference that will blow up in my face later.

"Balor, do you have anything else to say about this?" Ella knocks me out of my thoughts.

I'm shocked where they went. Had I been bottling all that up?

"We can wait for you to see your doctor."

Her eyes go glassy. "Nothing else?"

My heart seizes. Is she expecting me to tell her I love her? Or to propose? Right here, right now? "No. So long as you're feeling well and don't need anything."

"Okay."

"Was there something you expected me to say?" If she gives me an opening, maybe I *will* propose.

If she's pregnant with *my* baby, we *will* be getting married. Full. Stop.

Her body tenses. "Fuck off?"

A wave of anger floods my veins. I clench my fists and take a deep breath before I respond. "Fuck off? Are you serious?"

She flinches at my harsh tone and hops off the bed. "What are we doing?"

"According to you, we're having a baby." I smile to get her to smile.

"I thought you'd tell me again how you don't want kids. How you don't want a relationship and—"

"That was before. Now it's the complete fucking opposite." I don't mean to sound so gutturally angry, but how can she think I'd tell her to bugger off?

"We don't have to get married." She steps farther away from me. "I don't want to get married yet. I'm only twenty-seven. I didn't plan this."

I stand there, still naked, my dick not quite flaccid yet. "I know you didn't plan this. And if you haven't bled since we were first together, I take responsibility for pressuring you to take me without protection."

"I said yes. I'm responsible."

"These can't be our wedding vows," I joke as the idea of marrying her shines brightly with no shadows or clouds in my thoughts, nothing haunting me about the decision.

"Seriously, you don't have to marry me."

"Seriously, that's not how this works in my world."

She steps back. "You can't force me."

"Wanna bet?"

CHAPTER THIRTY-NINE
ELLA

Since we're running massively late, we put the baby talk on hold. Balor showers alone, and I quickly cook our breakfast, making egg sandwiches we can eat in his car on the way to my school.

Balor stays quiet during the drive. The time factor hijacked our little stand-off. He thinks he can *force* me to marry him. I assume it's not the end of the discussion.

My mind races with so many scary thoughts. The worst is being held captive in his townhouse by a guard with no chance to escape. Triggers from Wes screaming at me that I couldn't see Hannah or Val ever again make my stomach turn over.

How did I get here?

"Are you okay?" Balor squeezes my hand. "Your face just drained of all its color."

Which must be noticeable since I inherited my mom's light-bronze skin tone. "I assume it's the…you know."

His jaw tightens as his eyes stray to the new driver, Denton. With no partition, because his Rivian isn't a limo, nothing we say is private. And when Balor doesn't finish my sentence, that I'm pregnant, I take the hint that he doesn't want anyone to know either.

"When you're done with school, I'll pick you up and we'll spend the rest of the day at home."

"Home?" I squeak.

"My home." His lips part as if he's ready to declare it my home, too.

But he doesn't.

These few hours, however, will give him a chance to arrange for my confinement. Whether literally with chains or through pressure and manipulation.

I just smile and rest my head on his shoulder as I often

do in the car. He cups my face and presses a kiss on my forehead. "We'll figure something out. But Ella, I told you even before this. You're mine."

Nodding, I take a few deep breaths.

We arrive at Fredricks Elementary and Balor studies the building differently from the other times he dropped me off. I'm carrying his child.

Game changer.

Balor taps my knee. "Let me get the door."

I usually let myself out, but his possessiveness and protectiveness take over.

When the door opens and his hand reaches in for me, I grasp it.

"Do you have a safety-resource officer?" he asks, helping me out of the Rivian.

"We do," I answer to ease Balor's mind, but leave it at that.

Wes had that job for a while. He's a sergeant now and works somewhere else. It's the only reason I felt safe going back.

Once I'm safely on the curb and Balor gives the school a glance to make sure it's not ready to combust into flames, he lets me go.

"I'll be here at noon." He presses a kiss to my lips. "Ella, I—"

Shaking my head, I say, "Balor, there was a reason I asked how you felt about me *before* I told you about the pregnancy tests. Don't dig yourself into a hole with words you don't really mean."

He bristles at my tone, but gnawing on his lower lip, he just nods. "Consider all the other words I've said to you. How I miss you when you're not in my bed. And my physical reactions to you. Or how I grab you when you wake me up every morning."

Closing my eyes, I admit, "I know. This caught us off

guard. Please, can we take it slow?"

Rubbing his jaw, he says, "I don't think slow is a speed option when it comes to things like this. "

It's all happening so fast, but I nod.

He kisses my forehead again. "I'll see you in a few hours."

A mother with one of the students in the special ed program passes us and does a double take at Balor.

"That's Jory's mom. He gets very agitated during drop-off. Let me help her." I turn away and hoof it to the school's entrance under a burgundy portico.

I take Jory from his mom, who always looks guilty.

"I've got him," I say and head to the back of the classroom to look at the huge saltwater tank filled with exotic fish swimming in a donated aquarium.

A few crabs on the bottom scurry across the green and white gravel. Tapping on the glass makes the crabs move back and forth faster and Jory laughs, getting them to move. I hum a soft melody while he watches all the movement.

Soon he's calmer, and we join the rest of the class.

The day passes without incident and when the head teacher announces for aides to get the kids ready for dismissal, I check my watch, surprised three hours flew by so quickly.

No, it's only been two hours.

Did Mrs. Seyfried mess up? Get the kids in a frenzy for nothing?

I sheepishly step toward her. "It's only eleven."

Smiling, she says, "We notified the parents last night. The classrooms on this floor need to have the water turned off so the city can do some main work nearby."

With Jory safely in the hands of his mom, I do something incredibly stupid. Dark and reckless. I go home. And don't tell Balor where I am.

CHAPTER FORTY

BALOR

"What the fuck do you mean, she's not there?" I bark at Denton over the phone.

Of all days for a breach to go down. This mess required my attention in the command center and forced me to spend hours focusing on and dealing with a deeply threatening situation, so bad that Shane is still scrambling to recode and swap out motherboards on my servers.

I've hacked into nearly every camera in this city and stored the feeds, filling up a football field sized room of humming machines holding petabytes of data.

We get breaches all the time from the feeds, amateur geeks hacking into them and creating fast-spreading viruses that, like the strong Hudson River current, drift into our network, banging on our firewall.

I sent Denton to pick up Ella and bring her here to see all this action. Most days, my techs keep their heads down and except for the occasional burp or fart, they don't utter a sound, making this place dreadfully boring.

Today, the command center buzzes like the trading floor at the New York Stock Exchange. I figured Ella would get a kick out of seeing all the activity.

Only, Denton got to Fredricks Elementary and found it closed. The students, teachers, *and* their aides all gone.

Ella finished up work early, left, and didn't tell me.

I stare from my glass office above the datacenter floor, watching the chaos below me, trying to stay fucking calm.

Calls to her phone go to voicemail and her location is no longer pinging. With my data feeds down because of the breach, I can't look up the cameras near her school to see what direction she went after dismissal.

Two more hours pass, and I've gotten no message back from her while Denton circles the neighborhood checking

coffee bars, restaurants, and shops.
   Ella has vanished.
   With my baby.

CHAPTER FORTY-ONE

ELLA

Hannah and Val stare at me in my father's living room, their jaws dropped. Their astonishment is split between my baby news and that I've temporarily stopped talking to the father.

Who's a hacker for the mob. Something else I had to delicately confess. Hannah's worried eyes kill me.

Balor's been calling me, and I had no choice but to turn off my phone and pop out my sim card so he can't track me. But it's only a matter of time before he shows up here.

I've lit a fuse that will no doubt explode spectacularly in my face.

"He's going to force me to marry him," I mutter, pacing.

"And that's bad, why?" Val asks, shaking her head.

"What do you mean, why is that bad?" Hannah jumps off the couch. "She's a person. She's free to do whatever she wants."

I smile weakly, knowing when you mix in a dash of mafia into that cocktail, it paralyzes rational arguments.

Val stands and grips my shoulders. "Ella, honey, do you love him?"

"We've only been *seeing* each other for two weeks." I bite a broken nail. "If seeing each other is the right word for screwing our brains out."

"Did he ask you to marry him?" Hannah throws that out there.

"No. But he made it seem like I wouldn't have a choice if he did."

"Of course, you have a choice," Hannah cries out. "What you also have is an opportunity."

I stop dead in my tracks and stare at her.

"Opportunity?"

CHAPTER FORTY-TWO
BALOR

"Opportunity?" I mumble to myself.

What the hell is that gangly woman filling my Ella's head with?

Bugging and wiring Corvin's apartment with cameras was brilliant. Only, I never thought I'd be sitting perched on her roof with rappel gear, listening to the woman who's having my baby get advice from a tribunal of BFFs telling her she has options.

There are no options.

We're getting married.

Maybe not today. But this ring in my pocket, a four-carat, near-perfect round cut in a halo setting trimmed in more diamonds will be on her finger by nightfall. My brothers bought their rings at Crest Diamonds, but I know a secret about the owner. One that if Lachlan knew, Archer Crest would be dead before Corvin.

It piques my curiosity if Shea's issue with Trace is related to what she went through with Archer right after he'd broken her heart last summer. It was around the time Trace provided extra security work for her.

Not wanting to give Crest Diamonds a penny of my money, and after five minutes of research, I made an appointment with a top private jeweler and just asked for something obscenely big and expensive.

"You have an opportunity to negotiate," Ms. Gangly says.

I zoom in on her and say to Shane who's listening from the command center, "Find out who this is."

"I don't want anything from him," Ella argues, and my nerves relax.

She never struck me as a gold digger or even close to it. Even flat-out told me she doesn't want to get married.

"I think it's in your best interest to come to some kind of agreement," the blonde jumps in.

"I need dossiers on these two women," I mumble to Shane, pinching the bridge of my nose.

"Ropes are secure, sir," Marcus, a climbing instructor who trained me to tackle Kilimanjaro a few years ago has his specialty gear fastened to his bird so I can rappel to the corner balcony of Snow's living room. "Ready when you are."

I could bust my way into Ella's apartment through the lobby, but guards carry guns these days. I don't want to get shot, and I certainly don't want to kill anyone.

I just need to get to Ella. And this is way more fun than any other route to her.

"I got the drone footage. It's just three women including Ella." Shane rattles off the names. "What's the end goal here, Balor? Are you really going to kidnap her?"

"It's not kidnapping," I grit out. "She's just confused."

"You really are an O'Rourke," Shane snickers. "I held a slight doubt, some hope even, that *you'd* be too cerebral to fall down the same insanity well your brothers had when it comes to women."

Funny, I thought the same about Eoghan, but he dove into the deep end over Jillian and went over the edge worse than any of my brothers. I cringed at the shit he was doing.

Glancing around, I smile, thinking he didn't go this far. I may have won the insanity prize.

Sure, we're alphas and possessive, but we're also competitive as shit. I think this one even beats Lachlan who killed Katya's fiancé at the altar.

Would I murder someone if forced? I've never taken a life. Never needed to. I destroy lives electronically. It's more fun that way. I can fuck with a breathing soul for the rest of their life.

Once someone is cold, and in the ground, the revenge is over.

Ella's father crashes into my head. Lachlan has the go-ahead to kill him once we get his code.

Now, he's the grandfather of my child.

CHAPTER FORTY-THREE

ELLA

"Negotiate how?" I cross my legs in a wing chair in front of the large expanse of patio doors in the living room, with Hannah and Val seated across from me.

The winter sun floods the room and warms me. I suddenly want to be on the patio to get air, but it's still very cold outside.

"You like him, right?" Val asks.

"Of course I do. I really like him. I'm...crazy about him." My heart pounds, thinking how crystal clear that revelation hit me seeing Jillian at his door, thinking she was there to fuck him.

I swear, I felt claws come out of my knuckles.

"Then what's the problem?" Val asks, again taking the gentle, nurturing approach.

"People who date for years have babies without getting married," I say to hear the words come out of my mouth, picturing every syllable infuriating Balor. "Why should I?"

"What is it about getting married that frightens you when—" Val stops and blushes. "Wes... You're still triggered by what Wes did to you."

CHAPTER FORTY-FOUR
BALOR

Hearing Ella is crazy about me thrills me, but that thrill quickly circles the drain hearing that prick's name brought up.

Wes...

Her ex.

The man who abused her. This bastard has her skittish about committing to me.

Shaking my head, I say into the microphone on my wrist to the Exfiltration Specialty Team Marcus assembled. "Stand by."

I resisted doing this sooner, but I had no choice. Now something's at stake.

I find the email I was copied on to Eoghan's office with Ella's work papers to see her driver's license.

Estella Reyes.

I found out a while back, she doesn't have the same surname as her father. The one smart thing he did to protect her.

The address on her ID is not the same as the building I'm about to rappel down. And I have an uneasy suspicion the old address is where that asshole who abused her lives.

She agreed to live with this prick. Yet she ran away *from me.*

As I run the address to get homeowner details, my fingers tense seeing the name materialize.

Michael Wesley Brennan

Ella wouldn't tell me his last name. Now I have that— *and* his address.

But the name hammers into my brain and it hits me like a bullet to the chest.

Sgt. Michael W. Brennan is Riordan's informant.

I.e. A dirty cop on the take from us.

Something I don't get involved in other than background checks. Which didn't include looking for an arrest record, because, as Ella pointed out, cops protect their own.

And my family doesn't exactly look for Boy Scouts to work for us.

Assuming this is the same guy, I hack into Brennan's employment records.

Yep.

Michael Wesley Brennan

And the address on Ella's driver's license matches his.

It's the same guy.

"Fuck," I roar and bang on the armrest to the bird. "Marcus, collect those damn ropes and get us the hell off this roof."

CHAPTER FORTY-FIVE
ELLA

Val and Hannah are quiet as I stare out the windows of the apartment. I can't avoid Balor forever. And I don't want to. I just want a handle on what *I* want before stuttering and letting him decide for me.

My girls comforted me, but they haven't really helped me figure anything out.

Ever since my abusive relationship, my thinking is often skewed by guilt and fear.

The few dates I went on in Sydney were for the sole purpose of pushing myself. I needed to not only sit with a man and not be afraid, but also test myself and not go along with whatever he suggested, whether it be the restaurant, the movie, a drink, or even going home with him.

Yet that all went out the window with Balor. A complete stranger. Who I somehow knew deep in my bones wouldn't hurt me.

The only time Balor hurt me was when he left that hotel without saying goodbye. I'd known we'd part ways. Just not like that. Even then, he still had given me more than he ever knew. I left the hotel that day having reclaimed a piece of myself that Wes stole.

Hannah comes up behind me. "I know I've been giving you a hard time. But you should call him. Let him know where you are."

"I will." I want Balor in my life, but my traumatic past is controlling my thoughts and decisions.

The phone for the apartment chimes with a call from the guard's desk below. I spin around and look at my friends, as they stare back at me with curious expressions.

"Did Balor reach out to either of you?" I point from Hannah to Val, ready to hand down sentences for being a traitor and giving him the green light to storm the castle.

No's sound off around the living room.

"Hello?" I say into the wall-mounted phone.

"You have a floral delivery from a Mr. Maverick."

I want to cry, remembering Shane called Balor by that cool code name. My rebel sent me flowers.

"You can send it up. Thank you."

"It?" Val asks. "Send what up?"

"Flowers." I shake my head, smiling. "The oldest trick in the book."

One that Wes never once bothered with. He spewed hollow apologies and excuses that never meant anything.

A knock on the door a few minutes later makes me jump toward the foyer. I look through the peephole and see a man in a cap, holding a vase of flowers.

Already in the vase? I've seen teachers at Fredricks get flowers. They come in a box, or wrapped in brown paper, assembly required.

I open the door figuring the guards let him up, and also, my best friends are here.

"Ella Reyes?" When he says my name, my blood runs cold.

Balor thinks my last name is Snow, like my dad.

It's a small thing, but my heart starts pounding and the hair on the back of my neck stands up.

"Wes," I mutter, terror racing through my veins.

I try to slam the door, but the man is already inside. Another man follows him with two vases, one in each hand. Then another man. And another. And another, who has several vases filled with flowers on a flatbed cart.

They file into my living room while Hannah and Val jump up and help place the cut crystal glass vases on every surface.

The living room smells like a florist, the air perfumed with red roses, yellow roses, pink roses, white roses, then more red roses, and next... *Baskets* of flowers, but I don't know the names. Calla lilies maybe? Snapdragons? With carnations in every color and Gerber daisies.

Good Lord, Balor bought out an entire florist and had them all delivered to me.

But where is he? There's no card on any of the arrangements.

How did the guard downstairs know it was from Maverick?

The delivery men file out, and I wonder how much they got paid for this stunt.

Balor is filling my house with all these arrangements just to prove he can throw his money around. His billions are the last thing I care about. I tried to return the expensive jewelry I bought on my ridiculous spending spree, but he insisted I keep it.

Disappointment floods me that he's not here. I want *him*, not jewelry or all these flowers.

Money has never been an issue for my family. Not that we're rolling in it like the O'Rourke family is, but my father has plenty of money. I've never seen Dad's bank account, but we live in this expensive apartment and maintain Mom's house in Connecticut, though I've not been there in more than a year.

As I close the front door, I spot another startling, huge, beautiful bouquet in the hallway, this one made up of at least one hundred roses. Thinking it's on a stand, I reach to grab it, but it has legs.

Human legs.

I gasp as the flowers are lowered.

"Hey, butterfly." Balor smiles at me. "You haven't been answering your phone."

I hold my chest, that *this* is his response.

Not yelling at me. Or hitting me. Dragging me around by my hair.

"Can I come in?" Balor emptied a florist for me, maybe more than one, and here he stands at my door, waiting for me to invite him in like a vampire.

Eyes fluttering, I stand back. "Of course."

His steps halt, noticing my friends lined up. "Alo. I'm Balor O'Rourke," he announces his name proudly.

"This is Hannah and Val. My... My best friends."

Balor puts down the massive arrangement and shakes each of their hands. "It's nice to meet both of you. I'm glad Ella has friends who will help her in a crisis."

"We always have our girl's back," Hannah says, signaling she's the one to win over.

Val's jaw has hit the carpet staring at Balor. "Is that accent real?" she says on a breathy moan.

"Aye," Balor replies with a panty-melting smile.

She can't ask me to set her up with any of Balor's brothers. They're all married. Except for the one who's in Ireland at the moment. At least that's what I'd overheard.

"We'll get out of here so you two can talk," Hannah says, dragging Val by the elbow. "You okay, Ella?"

"I am." I sniff, those damn hormones making me weepy.

Val looks woozy and knocks into a wall.

"I got you." I help her.

She hugs me, and I catch Balor's warm smile over her shoulder.

The door closes and the silence in the room thickens. I stay facing away, collecting my thoughts, and getting my nerves in check.

Heat envelops me as Balor presses his chest against my back.

"I was worried," he whispers with nothing but sweetness in his voice.

It's genuine and about as non-threatening as I've ever heard.

On a shaky breath, I turn around. "I know leaving the school without waiting for your driver was—"

His mouth covers mine, his voice raw. "Please don't ever do that again. I was freaking out."

No yelling. No hitting. No dragging.

Balor holds me and kisses me.

"*I* freaked. I'm sorry. I had to figure out what I want. Me."

"I get that, butterfly. But this is my baby, too. I want a say."

"I don't mean the baby. I would never keep a baby from his father." Except Wes, but I don't voice that. "I mean us. I want you to want me for me. That's why I asked you how felt. And all you said was you *liked* me."

"I told you, words don't do justice to what I feel for you. But just as you feel it's too soon, so do I. Just as you have things to work through, so do I." He kisses my hand. "All I know is when you're not with me, I feel empty. That's a start, isn't it?"

"It is." I cover the hand he placed on my stomach, keeping it there, loving how that feels.

"Please let my brother set you up with a doctor right away."

"Come on. Let's talk." I take his hand and we sit on the sofa. "I worry if your family knows I'm pregnant they might pressure you to...put even more pressure on me."

"You don't know them," he says and bites his lower lip. "And the pressure is more about being responsible adult men."

"I don't want to be a responsibility."

"You're making it so I can't win here. If I blow this off, I'm an ass. If I push you to commit to me, I'm a jerk."

Jerk... I laugh, remembering I called him that in my head the night we met.

"You *are* my responsibility, Ella," he continues when I

don't respond. "But don't confuse that with being a burden. Those are two completely different things. I'm thrilled..."

"About the baby?"

"Aye. I wasn't expecting it. But most single men aren't expecting news like that."

Negotiate. Like Hannah said. A successful negotiation means both parties get something. What can I give up? What can I live with to get what I want in return? What do I even want?

"Aside from me seeing a doctor right now, how do you want to proceed from here?" I ask.

"I'm glad you asked." Balor reaches inside his pocket and shows me a velvet cube.

CHAPTER FORTY-SIX
BALOR

I came here to propose. I *want* to propose. I planned to ask her to marry me and give her every possible reason why she should say yes.

Her friends encouraged her to negotiate.

Forcing the ring on her blows my wad, and I lose any leverage I have to keep her in my life.

Her. Not just her and the baby. Her. *Ella*.

"This was where my mind went this morning after I dropped you off. Even before you..."

"Pulled the disappearing stunt?" she says with her eyes slipped close. "I'm sorry."

I kiss her mouth. "First of all, you don't say you're sorry to me. You never have to be sorry. If you've done something that upsets me, I'll tell you. But you never have to apologize."

Shaking her head, she says, "I don't want to be treated like glass, or given all these passes. I expect to be held accountable if I've done something wrong. Just not with..."

"Never." He pulls our foreheads together. "*Ever*. This ring is a promise. It will be here waiting for you. I know what I want."

"And what is that?"

"You."

"Can we wait until I see my doctor?" She sounds guilty, like if she's not pregnant, I'll want out of this relationship.

Not likely...

"Will you let me go with you?" I ask.

"Of course." She softens. "What about my father? Did you send him to Tokyo on purpose?"

"If on purpose, you mean so you and I could make a go

of what we had the last couple of weeks? Aye. Sort of. I did need a developer over there."

And we needed to audit his keystrokes.

That's the bigger picture I need to lay on Ella. She needs to know exactly who her father is and that he will be punished in some way.

Several of my brothers have to contend with an in-law they don't care for. That's life. Snow is mine.

Now I must convince my brothers to let him live so the woman I'm falling for doesn't hate me and take away my baby.

***

"I don't want you staying here alone," I say, glancing at the flowers. "I want you with me. Can you give me that right now?"

Nodding with a smile, she says, "I want that, too."

I take her in my arms, and it's the most whole I've felt in hours. "I'll send someone to pick up the flowers."

"They're so beautiful. You didn't have to."

"Aye, I did. It's not that I gave you a meadow's worth of flowers. I will always pull out all the stops to show you what you mean to me." I cup her cheeks, tearstained and swollen from stress.

"Me, too. And I'm so…"

I stop her with a look. "I accept you're sorry for taking off on me today. I understand you're stressed and confused. Let's go spend time really getting to know each other better."

"I want that, too."

She lets me help her pack, and I smile at all the clothes I bought her because I recognize the labels.

Blushing, she takes out the jewelry cases. "I'm going to return these."

"You'll do no such thing." I pack the up the cases. "In fact, later, I want you to wear these. And nothing else."

SHATTERED VEIL

I whisk her home and we race up to my bedroom. With her suitcases lying strewn across the carpet, I'm balls-deep in my woman wearing a chunky emerald necklace that matches my eyes.

"This... This is how I want you. Every night. Naked, but draped in jewels I bought you."

It's not who we are to the outside world. I wear jeans and she loves leggings. This is how I get to show her exactly how much she means to me.

We both come in a rush and take a nap from the high-octane afternoon. With the sun setting, we wake up and make love again.

After, I leap from the bed, adrenaline pumping through me, until I trip over her luggage.

Laughing, I show her the second closet in my bedroom. "Put anything you want in here. Consider it yours."

She tilts her head from the bed. "Here's one condition I have."

"Can I add blow jobs to these stipulations?"

"Sure." She slips into my T-shirt and bounces toward me.

"What's your condition?"

"I want *that* closet." She points to mine.

"I say we share it. There's a spare room on the other side we can bust into."

"You'd break down walls for me?"

"You've broken down mine."

She gasps and holds her head. "Oh no."

"What, baby?"

"The money. I left it in my closet at home. In a shoebox. I want to give it back to you."

"That's *your* money." And I wish she'd think of this as her home.

Baby steps.

The biggest pun in the world.

Stress returns to her face. "What are we going to tell my father?"

"When we have a plan, when we know what *we* want, *we* will tell him. If it was just a marriage proposal, I'd speak to him myself. But I will always respect you. And with a wee-one in the picture, I won't devalue you to your father by leaving you out of the conversation."

I consider the little wins to get the ultimate prize.

For the mother of my baby to love me.

"I worry my father is dangerous, Balor," she confesses softly.

I laugh. "Not as dangerous as my brother Lachlan."

CHAPTER FORTY-SEVEN
ELLA

Say less, Balor...

Balor arranges for me to meet Lachlan on Saturday.

He keeps his warm hand on the small of my back as we enter the children's dance studio on Mayfair Street, but that does little to assuage my fear of his older brother.

The Enforcer.

I'm utterly terrified at the sight of him, wiping away the excitement I'd felt all day when Balor said his enforcer brother needs a favor.

From me.

Six-six, full of tattoos, and with a scar across his right cheek, Lachlan O'Rourke stands perched like a hunting owl, ready to strike if anyone gets too close to the petite woman with a blonde braid who's clearly pregnant. Seeing the name Lachlan tattooed on her neck, there's no mistaking that she's his wife.

Even though I have a bun in the oven myself, Balor isn't here to introduce me as the soon-to-be mother of his child. He promised to keep it our secret until we see my doctor.

Lachlan strides toward us while we linger near the glass door that chimed loudly when we ambled in. He starts the conversation with, "And when are *you* due, little one?"

I gasp, holding my stomach. "Balor!"

"He didn't say anything. I've come to know the signs." Lachlan folds massive arms across a chest so wide he blocks several little girls in tutus behind him from my view. "I'm wondering why I had to guess."

"Because it's between us right now," Balor answers.

"I didn't have that option," Lachlan argues. "Da outed us right away."

"Thanks for returning the favor." Balor sounds miffed.

"Can you not tell Kieran and Riordan?"

This secret he's agreeing to keep weighs on me. What I'm asking.

"Keep important news from our king and his underboss?"

"Never mind." Balor flushes with frustration. "At least let *me* tell them at our next meeting."

"King?" I ask, my stomach turning to ice with worry that everything Balor agreed to as far as us taking this slow will be smashed.

By a king no less.

Balor lowers his head. "My oldest brother. To the people in this city, he's referred to as King O'Rourke because he's the head of our family."

Lachlan's eyebrows pinch together as a steely gaze continues to drift between Balor and me.

"Balor said one of your wife's students has special needs?" I speak up, acting bravely in hopes of some respect.

It's certainly not out of sanity.

Lachlan's menacing grin drops suddenly at the mention of his wife *and* the precious angel who I heard is having difficulty with the dance lessons. "Aye. I'm grateful you took the time to help my wife even if you didn't come here just to share baby news."

"No problem," Balor says with snark.

Ignoring them and chalking it up to a sibling dynamic—something lacking in my life—I immediately pick out the little girl struggling among the eight perfectly poised mini ballerinas lined up at the ballet barre.

"Let's do snack time," Lachlan's wife says, eyeing us at the door.

By the letters tattooed on *his* fingers, I learn her name is Katya.

These two must have an interesting story.

The little girls rush over to a table set up in the corner. A woman, I assume a mother of one of these cutie pies, pours cups of juice and places them next to paper plates filled with cookies and cut-up fruit.

Katya glides up to us while holding the little girl's hand. I see hints of attention deficit disorder from the way she's agitated. The faint crusting around her ears suggests a chronic infection might be the source of balance issues.

"Hi, are you Ella?" Katya asks me in a voice so sweet, I could bake cookies with it. But she also sounds real, genuine.

"I am. Nice to meet you," I say, smiling then crouching down. "And who is this? What's your name?"

"Her name is Lia. She's non-verbal," Katya says. "I can tell she hears me. She just gets...lost."

"Not anymore. Hi, Lia. You have a beautiful name." I shuck off my coat and hand it to Balor. "I got this."

CHAPTER FORTY-EIGHT
BALOR

Holding Ella's coat, her perfume hits me in the chest. I smile, watching her take the little girl's hand over to the snack table.

She's going to be an amazing mother. What the hell kind of father will I be? Especially if I had a monster for one. All I have to go by is Kieran, whose twin sons are toddlers, and he can't stop hugging and kissing them.

The kind of affection we never got growing up, only Shea-Lynne.

Ella sits across from Lia, engaging with her without getting too close. She smiles and eats the cookies, getting Lia to eat as well. Ella speaks, pointing around the room, and Lia follows her hand gestures.

"She can't stop begging for cock, right?" Lachlan whispers to me with that deep baritone voice of his. "From the hormones and all."

I roll my eyes, but I'm still a man with an ego to maintain. "Oh yeah."

"I knew it." Lachlan smacks my arm. "I didn't see a ring on her finger."

"I haven't given it to her yet."

"Why?"

"Because we're taking it slow."

"Not when a kid is involved. Kieran won't allow you to—" He stops when I glare at him.

"Careful how you end that sentence. You can pummel me, but I can cut off the electricity in your house."

"And put my wife at risk?" He stands over me.

I push him away. "Stop with that hovering. It doesn't work on me."

"I'm just preparing you for what I know Kieran will say. We can't have a woman walking around Astoria pregnant with your wee-one in her belly without at least a diamond engagement ring on her hand."

He's not wrong. It goes against everything we stand for as far as our treatment of women.

"We're seeing her doctor in a couple of weeks. Just to make sure everything is all right. I'd hate to make a big announcement and then disappoint people in case…"

"In case what?"

"Her home tests weren't accurate." As the words fall from my lips, my chest tightens at the idea she's not really pregnant.

It confirms how much I want this.

"She's with child. I've inherited Da's knack for sure. Of all the things to inherit, right?"

"So long as you don't hit—" I stop, flinching that I almost spilled the secret I've been keeping about my father.

"And when the doctor confirms, you'll marry her?"

"Aye. I'll ask her when we're ready."

"You've done background checks and dug into her past?" Lachlan scoffs. "Everyone's got secrets and skeletons. Katya knows my past sins." He looks up, his eyes blinking, like he's running through all the people he killed.

It's a fucking encyclopedia.

"I have all I need to know about Ella. I did more digging, however, on her ex. The prick who abused her," I say, tasting acid on my tongue and rage in my veins.

"Yeah? Who is he? I'll kill him after I kill her father for you." He shrugs. "Or before. Dealer's choice."

"Down boy. I sent Snow to Tokyo. Shane is tracking all his coding activity and his postings to the dark web." A thought comes to me. "What if you just torture him at the black site until he gives me the password to his online vault? We can threaten to hand him over to the FBI."

Even though I'm sure he fears the feral cyber community more than the Feds. They're still recovering from his holiday stunt. That, and I've impregnated his daughter. I have a ton of leverage over this man.

At the same time, getting Ella pregnant *and* falling head over heels for her throws a wrench in any plans I have to hurt Snow. In any capacity.

"I'm not sure the level of punishment is up to you," Lachlan says, rubbing his chin.

I wish that weren't true, but it is. "I'll speak to Kieran," I say regardless.

"The ex. Give me a name. I'll pick him up and—"

"He's a cop, Lachlan." I pinch the bridge of my nose. "And not just *any* cop."

"Who?"

"Michael Brennan." My hands curl into tight fists of fury.

"Riordan's informant?"

"He used his middle name with Ella. She knows him as Wesley." I watch Ella with Lia. "There aren't two Michael Wesley Brennans on the force. I checked the records, hoping there was. So yeah. The one and only."

"What did he do to her?" Lachlan cracks his knuckles.

"All those tattoos you see on her arms and legs cover his sins," I say with murderous thoughts running through me.

Never mind me, Lachlan's neck turns that shade of red when he's about to strike. "He's dead."

"Wait."

"He can't keep breathing." Lachlan shrugs. "It's simple. She's carrying our bloodline and he hurt her. I'll handle it with Riordan."

If I don't say anything, Wes will be in the morgue by sunrise. I grab Lachlan as he goes to walk away.

"Wait. Don't say anything to Riordan yet. I don't know

if Brennan cataloged all the sins he's helped us bury."

Deep inside, my visceral instinct is the same as Lachlan's, to gut the fucker. Just not if it will take down my entire family.

Seeing someone suffer on a daily basis always felt more satisfying than murder, and I have the tools to do it. I can hurt Brennan more effectively. Like putting his name on the rotation for random drug tests and then falsifying the records to keep him off the streets.

"You're putting me in a fucked-up position. I'm already keeping your kid a secret, now this, too?"

"Let me do some surveillance on Brennan first. These guys plant tripwires, Lach. They leave instructions to third parties to deliver evidence if they wind up dead or missing."

Lachlan thinks about this and finally nods.

"Once I know our family's clear, *then* Rior can cut him loose and you can gut him," I add, knowing that could be just as dangerous for us. "I promise."

Lachlan pats me on the back and struts to the snack table, where a few little girls shriek in glee at the sight of him. They stand on their chairs and literally jump onto my brother's back.

They pound on him, calling him the monster. And he threatens to eat them. He carries them, three at a time, back to the lesson area. With such gingerly grace, he lowers them in front of the ballet barre one at a time. The girls roll on the floor hysterically laughing at him.

If I didn't see this with my own eyes, I'd never fucking believe it. But it puts a smile on my face. He's looking forward to being a father. And to a little girl, who he'll be gentle with, of course, but he'll also make sure she's a badass.

Ella works with Lia one-on-one, following Katya's steps. Before snack time, I'd seen Lia strangling the bar and kicking her feet wildly. My Ella has the little girl focused and following the lesson, moving to the steps in perfect pace.

The metaphor strikes me. I've been barreling down the highway at a fast and furious speed. Ella forced me to slow down. Smell the roses. Like the ones I bought her. Thanks to her, I get to watch a little ballet rehearsal. Just breathe and live my life for me.

Measured and graceful looks better on me. Because of her.

Ella points to the ballet barre hanging on the mirror, signaling she wants to stay for the rest of the lesson.

I nod happily and take a seat on the wooden window bench to watch. I should be dissecting every keystroke her father is typing a world away. But here, watching Ella with a little girl who needs her…

There's nowhere else I'd rather be.

CHAPTER FORTY-NINE
BALOR

Monday morning in my shower, Ella grinds her ass against me. She moans louder when my cock slips between her cheeks and rubs against her tiny hole.

I did that last night on the floor of my bedroom. Took her there, roughly. We fucked most of the weekend — our first weekend back together — and I loved it.

I hate not having her in my bed every night, but her father comes home soon.

Where the hell should I send him next?

Her hormones drive her to suck my dick in the middle of the night, prompting me to roll over and sink deep inside her, coming so hard. I spill so much seed that it seeps out and splashes against my balls and her thighs.

Wet and slick from the water and my bodywash, our drenched hair sticks to our faces. I can't get enough of her.

My hands come up from behind and massage her tits, squeezing these pert nipples I dream of sucking all day. Mostly because it drives Ella insane.

She gets more desperate for me every second and to ease her ache, I slip my hand between her legs. We're both drenched from the rainwater showerhead above, but my fingers know the texture of the silky juices deep inside her pussy.

I pump one finger in and out of her wet cunt and watch her head lower with a groan.

"God yeah," she whines. "Right there, Balor."

I work her clit with two fingers and run my tongue across her shoulder, nibbling on the tattoo there. "Are you needy for your boss's cock this morning?"

Her head bobs up and down, riding my hand. "Please!"

I'm slowly getting used to fucking without a condom, but I need her on edge because I can't last too long when

I'm bare inside her wet cunt.

"Turn around, butterfly." When she does, I stroke her chin and say, "Open for me."

Her jaw drops and her eyes light up when I hold my hand in front of her mouth.

"Suck. Suck yourself off me."

"Yum." She smiles, taking my fingers into her lush mouth.

"Yum, indeed. The only thing better is when these tangy juices mix with my hot cum."

Her hands close around my stiff cock, turning whatever languid veins I have left hard as fucking granite.

"I need to fuck you." I lower to the shower floor. "Sit on my cock."

She blinks, the water hitting her eyes. "We're like animals."

I don't disagree. Ella lowers herself onto my cock, and I still stretch her even after all these weeks of fucking this tight pussy.

Every inch she sinks onto me triggers my pulse to throb harder.

"Stop torturing me and fuck me," I groan, pulling her down until I'm balls-deep.

"Oh, Balor," she cries out my name, and I go feral for it.

Using my shoulders for leverage, Ella moves up and down on my shaft, the heat from her cunt scorching against my skin.

"Yeah, baby. Ride me. Ride my cock. Ride it like a slut." My cock turns to utter steel for her as I pump into her tight cunt, while she fucks me faster and faster.

I cup her tits. They are by far the most gorgeous set of perky, round breasts I've ever seen. She moans louder when I grab them during sex.

Her hormones are on fire, and some places on her body

are fucking ripe for my touch.

"I'm gonna come," she moans. "Any second."

"Come for me, I want to shoot my cum all over your face."

Her eyes fly open and then roll in the back of her head as she contracts around my cock with the force of a vise.

I hold on for dear life. And it's so fucking hard because when she loses her shit on my cock like this, it sends me spiraling.

To increase the pressure, I grip her hips with bruising strength and grind my cock harder inside her.

Now her eyes open and lower to mine. Locked in a stare, she fucks me through the last waves of her orgasm using my cock.

I grip her head and pull our mouths together. "I'm fucking crazy for you, butterfly. I can't get enough. Don't want to get enough."

"Me, too." She throws her arms around me.

But I'm seconds away from coming. I lift her up and quickly pull my legs out from under me to stand.

I need *both* hands to wrap around this fucking soda can of girth while I jerk off until ropes of cum splatter her face.

"Open your mouth," I groan. "Fuck. Fuck. Fuck, Ella." I spill my cum onto her waiting tongue.

I hate that I've done this with escorts and thought it was the hottest fucking thing.

But to shoot my load into the willing mouth of a woman who wants me for me, who opens for me because she's dying to taste my cum, has me climaxing harder than I ever have in my life.

"Don't swallow." A truly filthy idea comes to me, and I kneel in front of her. "Kiss me."

Our tongues dance together. "Spit it back into my mouth. Right fucking now."

She does it with no hesitation and incredible force.

Then kisses me even harder, wrapping her legs around me.

I lift her against the wall and fuck her again.

***

We dress in a hurry since she has to be at school by nine a.m. With our morning sexcapades, it's a nail-biter making it on time every day.

But since the gala, things have been incredible. We fit, we work, and we're perfect together. She has me on a schedule because I'm accountable to her. To be present for her and her needs and not work around the clock like I used to.

When Corvin comes home, the rubber meets the road as far as how he'll react to the news that I'm not only sleeping with his daughter, but that I knocked her up.

"We should probably just fuck in the car," Ella says with amusement, as we hold hands in the back seat.

She smooths her skirt and when I notice, she says, "You spent so much money on all these clothes for me, and now in a few months, I won't fit into any of them."

"Then I'll buy you more," I say, kissing her hand that I can't wait to see with my ring.

"Hopefully, I'll lose the baby weight quickly and still get some use out of these."

"Unless you get pregnant again right away," I say this absentmindedly like my brain has figured out we're starting a family.

That won't just be one child.

Not hearing a response, I look her way and smile.

"Assuming…"

"You're going to be one of those men counting the days until we can have sex again?"

Her vocalizing a somewhat distant future that depicts us still together relaxes me.

I offer a truthful answer. "Probably."

She smiles. "I'll probably be counting the days with you."

Up in the driver's seat, Denton shifts, taking my eyes off Ella.

I've always used a driver who doubled as a guard for years, not because I'm cheap, but because I could never keep my eyes off my iPad, or phone, or other device to do my job.

I worked around the clock, sometimes sleeping on the sofa in my office at the command center. Too many close calls forced me to realize I needed help in this area.

But Ella has normalized my sleep hours. By being with her all night instead of work, I was forced to delegate shit so I can have a life. With her.

There is no life without her.

We reach Fredricks Elementary, and I check the time.

Ten minutes to spare...

"Circle the block, Denton." I pull Ella on top of me.

She gasps when she settles on my erection. "Whoa."

"If you're going to be a cock tease, you're getting fucked in the car."

CHAPTER FIFTY
ELLA

Jory, my student for the rest of the school year, throws his usual tantrum when he has to wait his turn to pick his paint.

It's tough for any five-year-old to learn this kind of patience. For Jory, though, it's downright excruciating. I feel for the little guy. We sing songs while the six other students in Melissa's developmental learning class debate over which color they want today.

She also only lets them have one color to teach decision skills.

That and to figure out who's guilty if a kid ends up with a different color smeared on their face or tangled in their hair.

Thoughts of Balor and the things he does to my face and hair with his cum heat my core. But I push that away to stay present with Jory.

I particularly loved dancing with little Lia on Saturday afternoon. I stayed the whole class and told Katya I'd like to help out again. Balor's sister-in-law is the sweet, gentle music that tames her beast of a husband.

Spending time with her, I see a future where she's my sister-in-law, too, and it feels solid and right. As an only child, I always longed for a big family. But I also knew kids who grew up in mega-sized families and hated it. They would have preferred to have their parent's attention all to themselves.

Grass is always greener, I suppose.

Little Lia from the dance studio comes to mind, and with a few minutes left during the lunch break, Jory and the others go off with the lunch aides. I head into the admissions department to speak to a counselor. Fredricks Elementary offers several spots a semester to eligible students for free. I don't want to insult Lia's mom, but Jory will be moving up to another grade next year, and I would love to work with Lia.

Sure enough, two spots are open, and the counselor holds one for me. I'd worked here for three years while getting my special ed certification. I'm so grateful they didn't hold it against me for quitting after the Wesley debacle.

My phone rings before I leave the office, and with no kids in my charge at the moment, I reach for it.

But as I leave the office, I slam right into someone.

Even before I look at his face, I tremble in fear.

"Hello, Ella," Wesley says my name roughly, and the emptiness in his eyes reminds me of the monster he tries to hide. "Still clumsy I see."

I shiver at the reference, an excuse I'm sure he mentioned when someone caught sight of my bruises.

My phone is still ringing, and I glance at it.

Balor

One click to answer. One word from my mouth: *Wesley* and this man dies.

Power is...intoxicating.

"I'm talking to you." His loud voice turns heads.

Those eyes search the office secretaries watching us and he cracks a smile.

"Did you get your clothes? I figured you'd want them." He's all menace and delusion.

"You figured I'd want clothes I wore while you..."

His jaw ticks. "Care to finish that? We had our troubles."

"Trouble?" I laugh nervously.

"Yeah. You. You were trouble. For *me*." He bares his teeth like a wolf.

"Then let me and my troubled ass get out of your way." I back up and skirt around him.

Until he grabs my arm, stopping me.

I stare at the ugly, violent hand holding my arm.

You're a dead man for touching me. I belong to Balor O'Rourke, I think with satisfaction, even though I'm shaking.

"It's good to see you again," Wes says, his gaze holding mine.

"I'm late for class." I yank my arm from him and walk away, hearing that sickening sentiment in my head over and over.

CHAPTER FIFTY-ONE
BALOR

By the usual looks I get from Kieran and Riordan at the Thursday meeting, I relax, knowing Lachlan didn't blab about Ella being pregnant.

Eoghan sends a quirky smile my way and sits back, crossing an ankle over his knees with a wink, like he's ready to ask for popcorn when I make my announcement.

Motherfucker.

As if he has anything to jeer about after the fucking disaster he created in Las Vegas because of Jillian.

Kieran ends his call, and the meeting begins. Lachlan once again boasts about his rather gruesome black site kill last night, making my stomach queasy for the first time in a very long time.

Is Ella pulling my center away from this crazy life?

I breathe in and out until Kieran asks me for an update. I report the progress I made with the drone weapon testing using the custom chips.

I used Lachlan's house to launch a few prototype drones since he lives on Astoria Harbor. I flew them up and down the tributary to test speed and agility.

Ella came with me. She and Katya seem to be getting friendly. It sparks warmth in my chest knowing she's comfortable with my family. Heck, if she can handle Lachlan without passing out and Eoghan yelling at her, she can handle anything.

"Is that all, Balor?" Lachlan asks, practically stifling a laugh.

"What the fuck is so funny, Lachlan?" I bark.

"Nothing." He turns icy.

"What's going on between you two?" Kieran asks, looking from me to Lachlan like a peacekeeper.

Dragging this out is wrecking me. It's not that I got a

woman I'm falling for pregnant. It's the unfortunate baggage she comes with. And none of it is her fault.

"Ella is pregnant," I say, just to get it out there.

"Congratulations." Kieran sits back. "When are you marrying her?"

Except that...

I exhale. "We're...figuring that out."

"I would figure that out soon. *We don't have babies in sin*, I heard Ewan say once." Kieran lets out a soft chuckle, mimicking his best friend.

"She's my assistant. That makes things sensitive. Plus, her father..."

"Aww, fuck, Snow. That's right," Riordan says, shaking his head.

"I wasn't on board with killing him." I slide a glance at Lachlan. "I have the means to keep people in line without burying them six feet under. And with this new..."

"We won't kill him," Kieran gives the order. "He's going to be family. And like you said, his attack wasn't personal against us."

"How is your audit on him going?" Eoghan asks, his elbows now on his knees.

"He's done the work I've asked him to do." Well, I hope he has. "When it all comes out, I plan to tell him that I know the global attack was him and demand the ransomware code he used as assurance." I stare at each of my brothers. "He knows who we are. He knows what we can do to him."

"And if not, then I'll bring him to Dunbar Valley to change his mind," Lachlan warns.

"I can live with *that*," Kieran says, nodding to Lachlan.

"I'm trying to get this woman to marry me, you brats. Do not ever fucking say any of this to her. Do you understand?" My eyes fly to Eoghan. "And do not say anything to Jillian. These women... They look out for each other."

I consider the pack of she-wolves I had to impress two weeks ago.

"It's sensitive all right," Kieran says.

"Do you love her, Bale?" Riordan asks.

I sit back and throw a hand over my mouth. Love wasn't part of the plan with many of their marriages. In that respect, I'm not an anomaly.

Her father is just one hell of an albatross hanging around my neck.

"Well, do you, Bale?" Eoghan asks, sounding sincere and eager to hear my answer.

"I'm crazy about her. We have a good thing going right now. I like her in my bed. I like waking up next to her. She takes care of me. I fucking love that. She doesn't want anything from me, and I respect the hell out of her for being strong. She's staying with me in the townhouse while her father is in Tokyo. She also…" I pinch the bridge of my nose. "I'm treading lightly because of the abusive ex."

Do not say his name, Lachlan!

"Have you figured out who he is?" Lachlan asks instead in a voice that sounds alien.

Christ, he's a terrible actor, but no one picks up on it.

"I'm handling it. It's been almost eight months since she's seen him. It's why she's hesitant about our relationship. She wants to take things slow. So do I. I want to make sure she actually loves me first." I hold my breath. "And we'll get married when we want to, okay?"

I direct my pushback and faint hope for a blessing mostly at Kieran.

He gives a curt nod. "Keep me posted on your relationship with her. Any woman we open our homes, hearts, and beds to is a potential risk."

"I get that," I say quickly. "Remember, I'm the one

you've all been calling these past two years to delete your shit from public cameras, change shit on websites, hack into *gynecologist* records..." I kick Eoghan and yell to get my point across "I did it all because I understand the risk."

No one dares to yell back at me.

We finish the meeting and by the time I leave, everything feels normal. But when I head to my car. I find Lachlan leaning against it.

Here we go...

"You seriously need to tell Riordan about Brennan."

"I know, Lachlan."

"This cop knows where the bodies are buried, so to speak." He means the black site, which I've often seen guarded by an unmarked cop car.

I never asked questions because paying off the police isn't my responsibility. Just hacking into their computers when needed.

"I say we just end the fucker right now. Bring him to the black site, I'll get him to admit if he's got that tripwire you were talking about. I do this all the time, Balor. Dead men in shallow graves don't snitch." His deep jagged-sounding voice speaks to who he really is—the man I'm not sure his wife sees. "Riordan found Brennan, he'll find someone else. Only *we're* indispensable, Balor."

Shaking my head, I blame myself for not vetting Michael Brennan's police record deeper when Riordan brought him up. I don't even remember off the top of my head when Riordan made contact with him. That kind of stuff is so far in the background compared to my computer work.

"If his last breath is on us..." I stick my finger in Lachlan's massive chest. "I end him."

I give Denton the rest of the afternoon off and get into my car. I want to drive myself, but instead of going to the command center, I head straight to Ella's school.

I get there and park the Rivian. The weather still brisk, I pull on a jacket when I see Ella in the playground with a little boy, something I want to see better up close. She mentioned Jory, the student she's assigned to as a special education aide. Watching her with kids is my new favorite pastime. She's so gentle. So patient. So loving.

I never thought about having kids. The trauma of witnessing Da beat our mother burrowed into me like barbwire, and my hang-up of only wanting to bang escorts was born. All ideas of relationships and a family were dismissed. How stupid of me to think love wouldn't find me.

Fate put Ella on that plane. Opened the floodgates for me to act on the feelings I never let go of after our first night together. Her father is just a damn thorn in my side because I don't really know him. Or what he's capable of if cornered. Was the Christmas Ransomware Virus just a tease of what he can really do?

He hid his background under a shatterproof veil. Once I confront him, he has to come clean.

With my eyes on Ella and Jory, I walk right into the roughly textured bars of the school's wrought iron fencing, and it knocks me out of my thoughts. I step back and laugh at myself. I'm obsessed with the mother of my child.

Now I get what Eoghan went through last year.

Movement across the courtyard catches my attention.

Several other people gather on the side closest to the school's entrance. I assume they're parents and not sure why someone would be leering from all the way over…

My blood runs cold in my veins as my gaze sharpens. It's a man, and from what I can tell he's staring at Ella. Or Jory?

Is that the boy's father?

Taking out my phone, I snap a photo. Zooming in, I shoot it through my facial recognition app.

When it pings, I want to throw up.

Michael Wesley Brennan

My feet move before I tell them to.

I end him...

A threat from Ella's past was easy to brush off considering his involvement with Riordan. Something I didn't think I'd have to face. God, was I wrong. Here he is, watching Ella. *My* Ella. The mother of my fucking child. And it ignites a fury that will rage out of control.

I hike toward him, not sure what I'll do. My gun is in the car, per the school's firearms rules. Brennan is tall and looks thick and husky. But I'm strong with power and muscles from my martial arts training. Most people don't realize that I can do a lot of damage.

Brennan turns his gaze to me, and a flicker of recognition flashes across his face.

He knows who I am. Good, but it's not likely he knows why I'm heading toward him clenching my fists, looking like I'm ready to choke him. Instead of confronting me, he ducks into a dark-colored sedan and peels away.

I spin around to see if Ella noticed, but she's already back inside the school.

CHAPTER FIFTY-TWO
ELLA

On Saturday, Balor drives us to East Hampton where his sister is hosting a bridal shower for Jillian, even though they're already married.

I felt so honored that night at the gala when she included me. Technically, she put Balor on the spot, but the man didn't even flinch.

If anything, I did. I wasn't prepared for him to come around so completely.

"This is a first," Balor says through the comfortable silence. "A bridal shower."

"None of your sisters-in-law had a bridal shower?"

"Sisters," he corrects. "We don't use in-law. Once you have our name, you're one of us."

"That sounds a little eyebrow-raising, no?" I fold my arms. "Especially if you say my brother and sister are getting married?"

He barks a laugh. "You're right. Fortunately, though, we don't talk to outsiders much."

"Did your parents take you on trips growing up?"

Balor barks another laugh. "With eight kids?"

"I figured your family could afford it."

"Money-wise, sure. But it would have been a security nightmare."

"Wait." I turn to him. "You've never been to Disney?"

He shrugs. "Nope. Kieran is planning a trip with Isabella next year when his sons are older."

"Did you travel anywhere?"

"On my own, sure. After college."

"And not with a woman?"

"No."

I reach across the console to hold his hand. He not only squeezes it back, but he kisses my knuckles. With his lips wetting each one, I know my next tattoo.

B.A.L.O.R.

On each finger like Lachlan has on his hand for his wife Katya. What a hoot! Me having the same kind of tattoo as big, scary Lachlan.

"What about you?" Balor asks me.

I don't mention my tattoo idea because he'll tell me I can't get one when I'm pregnant.

I sigh. "We rented a lake house one summer in Maine, the year before my mother died. It was pretty great. Campfires, roasting marshmallows, learning to swim in the lake, boating, sunsets."

"Damn, butterfly. That sounds amazing."

"Oh, and catching fireflies." I exhale. "Then my mom died, and Dad just lost all interest in traveling."

"I'm sorry. So, uh, no Disney for you either?"

I shake my head and pat my stomach. "Someday, though. Right?"

"We've got a lot to make up for." There's an edge to Balor's voice, and everything always circles back to Wes.

I haven't told him that my ex showed up at school, and my nerves are too on edge about it.

It's been eight months. Wes can't possibly want to put everything on the line by harassing me now, can he? If Balor finds out, I worry Wesley won't live to see another sunrise. That will spark an investigation.

Balor's ability to use cyber skills to cover his family's crimes rival that of any police department, probably even the Feds. But there's always a chance something will fall through the cracks.

I can't be the reason his family faces retribution from law enforcement. So, I keep quiet. I'll tell Wesley I'm seeing someone if he bothers me again. I'll tell him I'm *pregnant* if I have to. Surely, that will make him not want me anymore. I pray he's smart enough not to fuck with the well-being of another man's child.

We reach East Hampton in little more than an hour, with Balor pulling over a few times for pee breaks I needed from all the water I've been drinking. Without a wince of annoyance, he turned off the highway with ease each time and walked me into every rest area we stopped. A donut shop once and a fast-food restaurant the second time where when I said I had a craving for fries, he bought me some while I used the restroom.

His sister's home is a spectacular waterfront architectural wonder with multiple rooflines and classic cedar shakes. Expensive cars and sparkling SUVs line the paved, circular driveway, and balloons billow in the breeze, tied to lampposts.

I spot a catering truck parked on the street. Because it's March, the party is indoors.

"When are they having their wedding party?" I ask Balor as he parks behind a black Escalade.

"A couple of weeks," he says to me over his shoulder.

Typical male doesn't know the exact date.

"I need the date." I check my makeup in a compact while he checks his phone. "I need a dress, a card."

"A card? For what?" He turns his head to me.

"To put a gift inside," I answer.

"Gift?"

I sit back and drop the compact into my purse. "You're kidding, right?"

"We don't exchange cards." He gives a scan of the property, where I spot three men in suits standing on the covered porch.

It makes me wonder if his ignorance of gift etiquette is a mafia thing or a wealthy thing. No, it's got to be a guy thing.

"Do you mean with each other? Or other people?"

"What other people?"

"Never mind." I wave him off. "I'll talk to Katya."

Balor smiles and says, "You like her, don't you?"

"She's a sweetheart. I also appreciate her letting me work with Lia."

Balor gets out of the Rivian and then comes to my side to collect me. Leading me to the front door, he keeps his hand on the small of my back.

This is the first time we're being open about our relationship. My father is coming home soon. He calls every couple of days, but mostly texts because of the time difference. I wonder how he'll take the news of our relationship.

I stop outside the stately front door as a new thought hits me, something we need to be on the same page about.

"Do any of your brothers know about Los Angeles?" I ask.

Now he flinches. Eyes fluttering, he says, "Aye."

"Oh? And do they also know that you left me there? Had your bodyguard pay me off?" Shame heats my neck.

"I remember everything about that afternoon." Balor's jaw ticks. "I left you in that bed. Left you dripping with my cum."

"Why?" It's a topic we've skipped over.

"I didn't think I could walk away from you so easily. I needed Trace as a buffer." His confession rocks me.

Did he immediately feel I was different?

"I was also appalled at myself for begging to cum inside you without a condom." He places a hand across my abdomen. "That's when we made our baby, though, right?"

"I'm thinking that's when it happened." I lean into him. "As thrilled as I am about it, I should have told you no. You were a stranger. That was very irresponsible of me."

"I think it just means we were meant to be." He smirks.

"And it's good I didn't have to get my father involved

to track you down."

Balor's head tilts. "How well do you really know your father?"

The question straightens my spine because I know my father is shady. "He's a programmer. An IT guy."

Balor purses his lips and without saying another word or knocking, he opens Shea's front door for me.

I step inside ahead of him but turn to ask him another question. "What did you tell your family about me and my dad?"

Balor hugs me. "I've cleared up everything with my family about who you are. And most importantly, what you mean to me."

When I turn back around, I freeze seeing so many people in a living room with vaulted ceilings staring at us.

Balor's about to say something when a stunning woman with dark hair approaches us. She throws her arms around Balor and his hands wrap around her waist. Smiling, he kisses her on both cheeks.

I think this is Jillian's friend, since I assume one of his brothers' wives wouldn't greet him this enthusiastically.

"Ella, this is my sister Shea-Lynne."

Ooops, I was wrong. "Sister as in…"

"My actual sister. My blood." He beams at her. "And my best friend."

That stings. I thought I was.

"Before you came along," he corrects when he spots my smile falter.

"It's so nice to meet you, Ella. A beautiful name for a beautiful woman." Shea leans in and hugs me. Whispering in my ear, she says, "And congratulations."

Heart spiking, I stiffen. "Thank you."

"This is Jillian's day. You'll have yours soon. I promise." She hugs me again.

With his arm around my waist, Balor says, "You know

this means you're next, Shea."

Her eyes immediately fly to Trace Quinlan, standing a few feet behind her. He's been assigned to protect her. And his eyes, and pretty much body, are *glued* to her.

"Not if this Neanderthal has anything to do with it. I have a better chance of licking the glass of the Mona Lisa than getting a man in my bed the way Trace Quinlan is up in my grill."

Shea's voice drips with venom but raw vulnerability seeps through. Mentioning licking glass and a man in her bed has Trace looking ready to combust.

"I'll talk to him," Balor says, pressing a kiss to my cheek, then heads in that direction.

I consider telling Shea to just lick Trace and get *him* into bed, but since we just met, I think it's best to save that comment for the next time I see her.

CHAPTER FIFTY-THREE
ELLA

Fredricks Elementary closes for the week of Spring Break. I'm thinking not much will change for Balor and me, other than I don't have to rush out the door so early. Surely Balor will be busy with work as usual.

Only, I wake up to a blindfold lowered in front of my eyes and next, I'm lifted over a man's shoulders, my ass in the air. I assume it's a man, and I assume this man is Balor.

"What are you doing?" I pound on his back.

"I'm kidnapping you," Balor says with a husky drawl.

"What time is it?"

"Early. The sun's just coming up."

"Where are you taking me? I need—"

"I packed everything for you last night after you fell asleep."

Kidnapping with toiletries. Not too bad.

"Let me dress you." Balor helps me slide into a long, wool dress and suede boots.

He even piles my hair on top of my head, masterfully twisting the band the way I do it to make a perfect messy bun.

He brings me to the bathroom to let me pee and brush my teeth. Kissing me, he says, "It's because I know you'll feel better. I love how you taste, twenty-four-seven."

Then I'm lifted again, and cool air hits my skin.

I gasp. "Coat! I need my coat."

"Already in the car, and already warmed up."

Warmth surrounds me, and the mint scent of Balor's air freshener tells me we're in his Rivian.

"Balor, this is amazing. But please let me grab—"

His fingers pinch my mouth. "I grabbed everything for you. I've been watching you."

Through a camera at times, I suspect.

"I know you're routine. I packed everything you need."

"My phone?" I reach for it, not that I can see the screen.

"In my bag." He revs the engine and kisses my nose.

Twenty minutes later, the car slows to a crawl, and then picks up speed. I catch the sound of a gate.

"This is killing me!" I screech.

"Just another thirty seconds, butterfly." He makes a sharp turn and then stops again, cutting the engine.

His hands wrap around my head. "Kiss me."

"No problem." I lean in and his mouth devours me.

"I've never wanted lips as badly as these."

Licking mine, I say, "Same here."

"Are you ready?"

"I think..."

"Look."

I slip the red satin blindfold off, and shock rolls through me. Before I process what the hell is in front of me, my gaze darts around the small airport. More like a private airfield.

"Uh oh," I mutter.

"Problem?" Balor nuzzles my neck.

"No." I take a deep breath. "Which plane is your brother's?"

"None of them. Eoghan and Jillian took it to Vegas again." He brushes my cheek. "Don't you see it?"

I look more carefully, and the sleek jet parked on an angle is pure white, the bright sun rising behind it in the east. But across the body of the plane are...

"Butterflies." I hold my mouth. "They make planes that you can rent with pink butterflies?"

"No. And this plane isn't a rental."

My gaze slides to his. "Keep talking."

"It's mine." He grips my hand. "Ours. Yours, really. I had the butterflies added just for you."

Blushing, I don't know how else to process this. I'd gone from being made to feel like rat feces on the bottom of someone's shoe, to being adored by a billionaire mafia man who just bought me a goddamn plane.

"Is this some kind of early April Fool's joke?"

"Not at all." He waves off an attendant coming to collect us. "I have another confession."

My heart drops. Did he sleep with someone else? Before we met again in that restaurant with my father? Or recently before we committed to each other? I have to be strong. No one's perfect. "Go ahead. Tell me."

"My brothers and I are competitive." He smirks. "Between the plane, the dresses, the jewelry, and your initial escort fee, I've spent more than five million dollars on you."

The amount stuns me. "I don't want to keep the escort fee. How can I keep a plane?"

Balor thinks about that. "Consider the plane as a way to escape me if I act like a jerk."

I can't see him being that big of a jerk. "Your brothers do crazy things like this?"

"In their own way. Given their own circumstances. Kieran tore up his entire front lawn to plant his wife's favorite flowers. Riordan ran into a burning building to save Priscilla. Lachlan…" Balor stops and turns red. "I'll spare you his crazy stunts. Darragh wanted nothing to do with us, but moved his whole life home so Ana could reconcile with her father. Eoghan threatened to leave us if we didn't accept Jillian, who was a prosecutor and tried to throw Ana and Cormac in jail."

"What? For what?" I shriek.

"*That's* a long story."

It's making sense now why Balor had to buy a plane.

"All my brothers did crazy shit. I wanted to make a statement."

I glance at the plane, and I should be insulted. But it's not uncommon for men to buy huge rings to impress friends and family, as well as the bride.

"Where are we going?"

"That's another surprise." He winks and gets out of the car.

The back cargo door pops open and I see through the rearview mirror that he's handing over his leather duffle and a white leather tote. Not the suitcase I'd packed to stay with him.

Balor opens my door, and I take in his charcoal wool car coat and dress slacks. "Ready?"

"That's an understatement." I let him take my hand and lead me up the airstairs.

The sharp smell of leather and thick carpet combined with some other airy scent my brain will categorize as new-plane smell hits me.

"Is this plane...new?"

"Aye." Balor smiles. "Not custom built. I picked it out from a few available."

"When?"

"The other night, when you were asleep."

"You left me—"

He presses his lips to mine. "Of course not. I bought it online."

"With what? PayPal?"

"I wired the money."

"You bought this sight unseen?" I spin around.

"I have a pretty good eye." He takes my hand and leads me toward the cockpit.

"Do you know how to fly the plane, too?"

"No. But…" He knocks on the door.

The cockpit comes into view and the number of gauges boggles the mind. "Wow."

"This is Arden, the pilot," Balor says, looking smug.

"Your pilot."

"Hi...Arden."

"Hello, ma'am." He tips his cap.

"Wanna tell me where we're going, Arden?" I ask him, since Balor doesn't want to tell me.

"That's part of the surprise."

My throat tightens. "What?"

"You pick, butterfly. These are your wings." Balor kisses me.

"I don't deserve this," I say on a shaky breath.

"Yes. You do. You're my woman. I want to do all this for you."

"Why?"

"To prove to you how I feel."

I back into a seat near the door. "It's just so much."

He lowers in front of me. "It's not. You've just been conditioned to think that."

Maybe he's right. Looking around the plane, I think of Jillian, Katya, her sister, Ana, Priscilla, and Isabella, Balor's brothers' wives. With those stories of what their husbands did, it comes into focus. They're not celebrities. They aren't supermodels. They just had something about them that made their husbands fall for them.

By talking to each of them at the bridal shower, I discovered how different they all were. And down to earth.

Is it possible that Balor and I just connect as well as they did? I feel how we fit together.

This extravagance is how he shows what I mean to him.

I deserve this the same as all the O'Rourke wives.

Good Lord, I'm going to be one of them.

"Ready, butterfly?"

"Absolutely." I smile and say, "Let's figure out where to fly this thing."

***

The answer is obvious.

While heading south, Balor and I shower in the private bathroom suite.

Feeling fresh, I go through the packed bag and dress in a casual pair of jeans and a light lavender sweater.

Looking out the windows, Balor says, "Are you sure you don't want to go to Paris, or London, or maybe Italy?"

"No." I press my back into his chest while we curl up on one of the leather sofas. "Not right now. This is perfect."

"You're perfect."

Looking down, I smile. "The Gulf of Mexico looks so amazing from up here."

"Sure does," Balor answers, talking on his phone. "All taken care of? Great."

"I can't believe this!" My heart kicks up to a crazy beat. And I don't think it will ever stop.

***

Five days later, we climb back into the plane wearing mouse ears, beads, and for me, a pair of Tinker Bell wings.

"That had to be the fastest trip around the Magic Kingdom," I say about our guided tour on a golf cart and skipping the line for every ride we missed the first day, because all we could do was walk around and stare in amazement.

Balor rented an Airbnb in an exclusive high-rise that overlooked the park.

We also hit Epcot, Universal, Sea World, and finished with a visit to Cape Canaveral where we met with astronauts and got to sit in a spacecraft!

Now I'm ready to go home and sleep in Balor's bed.

"Did you have a good week?" he asks, brushing the hair out of my face behind the headband.

"The best. You?"

"Amazing. Because I got to spend this with you. Now,

and not with seven brats and my cranky da." He kisses me.

"I won't tell Shea you called her a brat." I sink into Balor's arms and close my eyes because it's dark and there's nothing to look at outside.

"We should be in New York in four hours, folks," Arden announces from the cockpit.

We eat takeout on the plane from a restaurant with a six-month wait for a reservation. After we finish, I'm so satisfied, I just nod off.

I wake up, and Balor is helping me into his Rivian, which he left at the airport. Twenty minutes later, we're back in his townhouse, climbing the stairs.

This didn't feel real. And yet, it was the five best days of my life.

So far.

***

That night we make love and wake up Friday morning and fuck again. Naked, sweaty, writhing, clawing at each other, and grunting like animals. The sex also gets more intimate between us each time.

"Christ, this is so hot. Fucking you while you're pregnant with my baby," he growls into my ear. "You're so wet for me, Ella."

We've been going at it like this all week.

I've been taking as much of Balor as I can get. I'm going home tomorrow. I don't live here. Balor is my boyfriend and we're having a baby. That's how my mind sees it, even if packing my clothes will bring tears to my eyes.

My father is due home Saturday night. I have to be there.

Balor grips his headboard with one hand and squeezes my ass with the other, fucking me with the force of a freight train, groaning and growling.

"Fuuuuck," he roars and spills inside me. "God, that

was so good. We're so good together."

I wrap my legs around him tighter. "We are."

"Are you happy?" he asks, nuzzling my neck.

"Of course I'm happy."

"I don't mean from the plane I bought you, or all the good sex," he says wryly, sneaking a look at me.

"Oh. Then no. I'm not happy."

"Brat. On your hands and knees."

Biting my lip, I flip over, ready to beg for his cock in my ass, when my thoughts are cut short by someone pounding on Balor's front door.

"Who the fuck is that?" Balor bites out, looking at his phone. He stares at his security camera app and mutters, "Uh oh."

"What?" I say, choking on sobs building in my throat, thinking it's Wes. It's all been too good. It had to come crashing down.

"Get dressed. *Right now.*"

"What? Who's at the door?" I pull on my yoga pants, waiting to hear my ex's name fall off Balor's lips with venom. Right after he used that mouth to give me immense pleasure.

He just stares at me stone-faced. "It's your father."

CHAPTER FIFTY-FOUR
BALOR

There's only one reason a father pounds on a man's door the way Corvin Snow is beating on mine right now.

He knows.

Either that, or he's the stupidest motherfucker on the planet if this has to do with *anything* other than me sleeping with his daughter. For that, he gets a pass.

My brothers are fathers now. I get it, and pity the men who will show interest in my nieces in the future. Lachlan's daughter in particular.

I roughly throw on jeans and a T-shirt. Once Ella is fully dressed, I grasp her hand and walk down the steps with her.

I now get the massive flaw in the design of this townhome. It doesn't have a vestibule. The front door, made of all glass inside black-leaded panels, gives a perfect view of the stairs to anyone standing at it, as Snow is now. I should have put a curtain panel on the door or changed it to a full wooden craftsman door.

Too late now.

I won't hide my relationship with her. I will offer a bare-bones apology for not telling him sooner that I met her on the plane and that my interest started on that flight.

That's the damn honest truth. It was *always* her.

"Let me handle this," I say to Ella.

"He's my dad." Her voice is even, not demanding, and perhaps it's because she doesn't know how he'll react.

If he's smart, he'll be fucking thrilled a *billionaire* mafia boss loves his daughter and will protect her for the rest of her life.

Love…

Fuck, I do love her. Staring her father down, it's so clear to me. While I want to admit that to her first, if it diffuses the situation, if Snow is so off the rails in anger, I will use my admission to calm him down.

"Please, let *me* handle this." I kiss her forehead, knowing he can see me.

Her eyes are nothing but pools of panic. She ran circles around what Wesley had done to her. Managed him. Managed her father. Managed her job. All to keep her secret. God, that must have been so fucking exhausting for her.

I reach for the doorknob and make a point to look Snow right in the eye. He's not the man I'm trying to destroy right now. He's the father of the woman I love. A man she loves. A man who I've seen no evidence of hurting her.

My only beef is that he didn't kill Brennan when he found out. But when she came to him for help, he gave her shelter for six months. They were in Australia all that time and putting a hit on someone twenty-thousand miles away would leave a trail.

Even for him.

He had other things on his mind, though. Like robbing the richest people on the planet. He didn't steal from us. But he damaged our firewalls.

Which begs the question I consider for the first time, where is all that money he stole?

"Corvin," I say, leveling a stern glance at him. "Can I help you?"

His eyes fall on our linked hands and then up to Ella. "Estella? Do you have something to tell me?"

Everything inside me screams to take control of this. It's what an O'Rourke does. But seeing her father's expression, I realize I can't devalue Ella. Even to her father.

"I do." She glances my way. "I planned to talk to you when you got back *tomorrow*."

"I took early flight."

"Come in, Corvin. Let's discuss this." I turn my back on the man, expecting him to follow me.

Something hits me in the back of the head, and I whip around. Hundred-dollar bills lay scattered all over my kitchen floor.

The money I paid Ella.

"What in the hell is this?" He shoves the old note I wrote and left for Ella under my nose.

My scrawling mess speaks to how out of my mind I was that night:

Butterfly, I'll pay you another twenty grand to suck my cock again -Balor.

"Dad, I can explain." Ella steps in front of me.

"Explain how this man mistook you for a whore and paid you all this money?" He points to all the cash on my floor. "What else did you do to my daughter that you paid so much money?"

"Dad!" Ella shouts. "Talk to me. I'm right here. I'm an adult. I led Balor to believe I was an...escort."

"And it was not hard to convince him since that is who he *fucks*, Ella."

I go rigid at how easily Corvin spills my kink. The mastermind hacker knows me inside and out.

At least my sexual preferences were only escorts. *Were*. I'm done with all that.

But this mess with Covin... I need to clear it up immediately.

"I know, Dad," Ella keeps talking. "He was just a handsome stranger on a plane. I wanted to live out a fantasy. After so many months, I wanted to feel something. Something that didn't terrify me."

"*Exactly*," Corvin snaps through clenched teeth. "After what you'd been through with Wesley, how could you be so stupid?"

Snow's anger and insults might be rooted in parental

terror, but *no one* speaks to my woman like that.

"Do *not* call her stupid or any other derogatory name. It will be the last thing your tongue ever does. Got it, Snow?" I seethe and claim her hand. "I know exactly what she's been through. And now that it's out in the open, we're going to have a conversation about that motherfucker and how we punish him. Something *you* should have done." I roughly poke him in the chest. "I caught him watching her at school."

"What?" Ella shrieks.

"School? What school?" Corvin cries out.

"Dad, I took that part-time job at Fredricks. I *want* to teach. Not be a personal assistant."

"He was school resource officer there. That is how he and Ella met," Snow says, seething at me.

Rage heats my blood that Ella didn't tell me this, that she let me walk into that fury without warning.

"And why didn't you do anything about him?" I yell at Snow.

Ella steps between us. "Stop. Both of you. I love…" Her breath staggers. "You're the most important men in my life, and I know you both want me safe. Can we please discuss this without blame?"

"No problem." I kiss her forehead, "You're mine now. I will handle Brennan."

"I… I saw him one day at school, too," Ella confesses. "That was it. Once. Before break. I should have told you." She clears her throat. "Balor, I worry he can make trouble for you. For your family."

"My *family* can handle it." I level a gaze at Corvin, reminding him who he's fucking with.

"None of this changes the fact that you slept with my daughter, who I asked you to hire and protect," Snow keeps fighting me. "You breached my trust."

"I will apologize for any perceived trust you think I've

broken," I argue. "But Ella is an adult. This didn't happen again right away. What happened between us originally was two consenting adults in one moment of time. I admit, there was a miscommunication about who she was. Once it all came to light, I put my feelings aside to give her a job, like you asked."

"Dad…" Ella breaks in. "I'm crazy about Balor. He's everything I want in a man."

When her eyes drift to me with a quivering lip, I know she's about to pour gasoline on this fire…

CHAPTER FIFTY-FIVE
ELLA

Since my father is still steaming mad anyway, I go for the kill shot.

"Dad. I'm pregnant. Balor is the father."

"And I've asked her to marry me," he says to either avoid a punch in the mouth or to bring my father over to his side and force this marriage on me.

"And when is this lavish O'Rourke wedding that I will be asked to pay for?"

"As if I'd take a dime from you," Balor sneers.

Signing my death warrant, I mutter, "Dad, there's nothing planned yet."

"Thank goodness. You will say no!" Dad blurts.

"She asked to wait," Balor clarifies, tugging my hand before he turns back to my father. "And it's up to her. Not you, Snow."

"Estella, I cannot allow you to marry into a family like his. You do not want to live your life in danger."

"She *was* in danger." Balor advances on my father. "Not anymore. I'll deal with Brennan."

"I would think that man disappearing will cause your family some problems, O'Rourke," Dad says Balor's last name bitterly.

Balor's throat muscles tense before my eyes.

"And you're forgetting, I am not without my traditions," Dad continues. "I decide who she will marry. I did not see the horror Wesley inflicted on her. And that is pain I will take to my grave. Not anymore."

"She's carrying my child," Balor says through clenched teeth. "That gives me a say."

"I will not let you force my daughter into marriage like your brothers."

Balor's eyes turn black with rage. "How dare you."

I step in front of my father. "Are you insane, Dad? What the hell are you doing?"

"What is best for you."

"Right now, what's best for me is for *you* to not be murdered by the father of my baby." I push Dad toward the door. "Come on. Let's go home and talk."

"Where the hell do you think you're going?" Balor bites out from behind me.

I turn around, and the pain in his eyes flays me.

"Balor, this isn't how we wanted my father to find out. About us. About the baby. I have to get my suitcase." I rush up the stairs, different emotions attacking me. When I turn around with it in my hand, Balor is standing there. "Please, let me go home and talk to my father."

My throat tightens, and I wait for the:

If you walk out that door, we're through.
You're nothing without me.
I will kill you.

Those insults in Wesley's voice ring so clearly that it's a complete shock when I hear nothing. I open my eyes and see Balor standing over me, anguish in his softened eyes.

"As far as I'm concerned, *this* is your home now." He gets closer. "Your father and I agree about one thing, your ex is toast."

CHAPTER FIFTY-SIX

ELLA

After I pick up all the cash from the floor, I leave it on the kitchen island. I'd been meaning to give the money back to Balor anyway. Now he has it.

"I don't want this," I tell him. "I just want you."

Balor angrily stares at the suitcase in my hand. My words mean little if my actions lead me to desert him.

His face looks pained as he carries my suitcase for me to the Uber waiting outside. He shoves Dad's bags aside with force, signaling his anger. Only in the last week did Balor really feel like my boyfriend. Heck, more than that. He bought me a plane!

We got so close, and to have it torn away so abruptly has me twisting inside out.

"I'll come by your apartment later," Balor says and points to my father. "Then you and I will have another go at a reasonable conversation about what I intend to do with your daughter, who's carrying *my baby*."

Dad stiffens his spine. "I had planned to tell you this on Monday, Mr. O'Rourke. But I am offering my resignation."

"Dad, no!" I tug on his coat, my nails digging into his expensive cashmere.

But given how this went down, it's not fair for Balor to keep him as an employee. One who clearly doesn't respect him. Or his family. Sure, Dad appreciated the protection. Just not as a family member, which might mean extra concessions on my father's part to maintain loyalty.

"Your contract says you owe me one week's notice," Balor bites out. "You still work for me. I sent you to Tokyo to sabotage the factory that sent us those faulty batteries. Shane and I will go over your coding reports and the business records you stole. If it's satisfactory, I will release you from your contract," Balor sneers.

"Balor, I..." Guilt swamps me.

"You... Are not quitting," he says with a strained voice. "Nothing's changed, Ella. I agreed to wait until you see your doctor. But you are mine and I'm yours. Right?"

"Can I have until Monday to talk to my dad about this alone? Please?"

I'd planned to leave later eventually. This shouldn't feel so jarring, but it does. I'm being ripped away instead of just going home on my own.

I hate it.

"You're twenty-seven. Not seventeen," Balor whispers to me. "I'm me. Not Wes. I will not hurt you. Ever. You will be showered with affection and always protected."

My throat goes thick. "But you're forcing me..."

"Fine." He backs away. There's only so much a billionaire mafia boss will grovel or plead. On the street in front of neighbors no less. "We'll talk more about this on Monday. I have to work all weekend anyway."

Because I kept him from the command center for five days.

I think that's it, but then he presses his lips against my mouth.

"You and me, butterfly. You were on that jumbo jet and in that seat for a reason." He grips my chin and kisses me again. "Monday."

Nodding, I get in the Uber.

My father is already inside, all the words said between him and Balor finished. I can't see how he works for Balor after this horrible fight.

How stupid of me to think Dad would be happy Balor and I were together.

The car pulls away from the curb, and I turn to my father. "Please remember, Dad, Balor *will* protect me from Wes."

"That is why I did not want you back at that school!" he shouts.

I cover my head and rock. "Don't yell at me."

"Oh, Ella." He slides his arm around my shoulder and rests his head on mine. "I am sick with worry over that man. You left me little choice to deal with him. You kept everything from me."

"I know." And yet, when I tell him about Balor, he's just as angry.

"Don't you see how Balor is different?" I sniff. "He bought me a plane."

"With dirty money. His brothers are murderers," he whispers sharply because we're not alone. "What is it you think I do all day for them? The things I cover up!"

Waving my hands, I say, "I don't want to know. Balor has never hurt anyone."

"This is true. Or he has managed to cover it up. Even from me."

"How well did you know Balor before you agreed to work for him?"

Dad scoffs, "Enough."

"And that he used escorts?" The ache in my chest grows.

Dad's gaze drifts to me. "Yes. It surprises me he'd change his ways."

"For me," I snap. "For ordinary me? Is that what you're saying?"

"I am. But not for the reason you think. Mafia marriages are out of duty."

Several of the wives were forced.

"Trophy wives with plastic surgery and blackeyes under caked-on makeup." Dad's words shatter me. "I thought you'd had enough of that."

Nothing about Jillian's shower last weekend hinted at anything my father is describing. Certainly not the blackeye part. Every wife was well dressed, of course, since they are wealthy. But no one looked plastic. I watched every single wife with her husband. I saw love. I saw respect. I saw worship in those men's eyes.

I know all those signs.

Because that's how Balor looks at me.

And I just left him on the sidewalk. What's wrong with me?

"Dad, I'm going to a doctor tomorrow. Any doctor. I just want to confirm this pregnancy is real and to make sure everything is all right. Then I'm bringing the rest of my things to Balor's house on Sunday." I smile for the first time, relieved that it's all so clear to me. "I expect you to level with me this weekend about what your plans are. Where are you going to work? That apartment is expensive. Balor *will* be my husband, that means you—"

"I will not take charity from him or anyone." My father sits back and takes out his phone. "I will have new job by Monday."

CHAPTER FIFTY-SEVEN
BALOR

I receive a download link from Corvin Snow late Friday night.

Fuck, he's going to disappear again. He has to know I'm Maverick and that I know he's Iceman. This erratic behavior can't be because of Ella.

In an emergency meeting I called at my command center, Shane and I confirm Snow did what we asked in Tokyo.

Hacking into the network he corrupted, I analyze the code he used with Shane looking over my shoulder.

"Fuck, he's sophisticated," my second-in-command says.

"It's old-school Russian cyber warfare," I mutter, but smile. "Here. Right fucking here."

Like a bombmaker, cyber terrorists leave a signature in their destruction. Asking Snow to fuck with an adversary, I tricked him into revealing his secret ingredients. Which he did to show off.

"That's it," Shane says after receiving it from me. "But holy fucking shit, Balor. It wiped out my test network."

"What?" I jump from my seat. "It got past your firewall?"

"This one did." Shane sounds rattled.

"That means he's made his code more powerful." I pace back and forth. "I want everyone looking at that code. How does it compare to his December ransom hack? How did he fuel it to make it worse?"

This is what I'll be doing all weekend. Fuck…

"And shields up, every one of them. I pissed off a madman." Knocking up his daughter might have been the least of it.

Lachlan and Riordan stroll into my office.

"Who did you piss off?" Lachlan asks.

"Snow." I look at Riordan. "Tell Kieran all our systems will be slow this weekend. I'm throwing up as many layers of protection as I can."

"And when were you going to tell me Michael Brennan is Ella's ex?" Riordan folds his arms.

My eyes slip closed. "I'm dealing with a lot here, Riordan. I'm dealing with a madman who can crash fucking planes, or land them on my townhouse, a man whose daughter I got pregnant, a woman I'm crazy about, who was beaten, burned, and stabbed by a man *you* trusted to be an informant."

"*You* vetted him," Riordan bites out, then exhales. "And I'm sorry for all you're going through. What can I do to help?"

I sit back down and shove my hands into my hair. "Nothing. Shane and I have the network protection covered. I have something resembling the ransomware code. It will take all weekend to break it down. You and Lachlan need a way to cut Brennan loose without him retaliating. I caught him watching Ella at her school. I charged at him like a damn bull, but he took off. He had to know who I was."

"Then he knows how fucked he is?" Lachlan shakes his head. "The prick is dead. I'll do it tonight. Do you want Snow iced, too?"

"We're not killing Snow," I mutter.

"Why? He can destroy everything we've worked for," Lachlan argues.

"Riordan!" I snap. "Help me out. What the fuck do I do?"

I truly don't know anymore. I only know that I love Ella. I want to marry her and raise our baby. But her father will be a dark shadow I have to keep looking for over my shoulder for the rest of my life.

Riordan glances at the large monitor Shane and I use to share screens. "We agreed, Snow doesn't die. We send him to Dunbar to let the animals there teach him a lesson. Brennan doesn't die either, not this weekend. Can you get another team to unmask all *his* shit, and find out what secrets he has buried that can hurt us?"

"Aye," I say.

"You two know how to kill a guy's boner." Lachlan stomps out the door.

Riordan shakes his head at our brother. "I'll piss him off even more when we do execute Brennan."

"How?"

"I'll have my wife do it. She's been aching to kill a scumbag like Michael Wesley Brennan again."

CHAPTER FIFTY-EIGHT
ELLA

"You're definitely pregnant," the doctor at the walk-in woman's clinic says, pressing a wand on my abdomen. "Based on your last recorded period, I put your conception window as mid-January, and your due date as October 5th."

It's one thing to find out I'm pregnant, but hearing a due date slams reality into me.

"Congratulations," Hannah whispers to me.

I'm so glad she's here, but miserable that Balor isn't. That I deprived him of this happy moment.

"Thank you, Doctor." I wipe away a few tears.

"I'll have my RN call in prenatal vitamins and start you on your maternity plan." The doctor shuts off the machine and gives me a towel to wipe up the gooey ultrasound gel.

I'd rather be wiping Balor's cum off me.

He called me last night and we talked for a while. I told him how I felt. He did the same. But we're both just spinning our wheels over the same argument.

"Doctor, is everything is all right? Does the baby look okay?"

"They're fine."

"Great. Wait, *they*?"

"You're having twins."

Hannah slaps a hand over her mouth. When the doctor leaves the room, she paces. "Holy shit. Knocked up by the mafia boss with twins!"

I can't move. Doctors really should prepare you better for news like this. I felt nervous and anxious before. I'm downright terrified now.

"I guess we have a lot to celebrate when we go out tonight." Hannah closes the privacy curtain so I can get dressed.

The last thing I want is to go out. But staying home with my dad or lying alone in my bedroom is the breeding ground for my dark thoughts and depression.

My tears fall more rapidly. This news makes me feel even worse that Balor isn't here. Sniffing, I call his cell.

"Hello?" A female voice answers his phone.

My heart jumps into my throat. But I've been down this road before. With Jillian. With his sister. He's surrounded by women. Why someone's answering his phone, though, stumps me.

Unless it's because it's me and he doesn't want to talk to me all of a sudden?

"Who's this?" I struggle to recognize any one of his brothers' wives' voices.

"It's Petra. Who the fuck is this, and why are you calling Balor?" The vitriolic voice sends a numbing sensation through my body.

"This is Ella. Petra? Who the hell are you, and why do you have Balor's phone?"

"Because he's in my shower. Look, I refuse to share him with another whore again."

In her shower. This has got to be some kind of...

"I'll be right there, Bale," she purrs. "That man loves anal sex in the shower. I have to go. Bitch, don't call him again."

The call drops and so does my phone.

CHAPTER FIFTY-NINE

ELLA

Every call to Balor the rest of the day Saturday goes to voicemail but it doesn't allow me to leave a message. Every text fails like I've been blocked.

Hannah and Val circle me as I sit on the floor in my bedroom crying.

"Where's your dad?" Hannah asks.

"I got a text that he's meeting with someone about a new job." I hold up my phone. "That's how I know my phone is working."

"We're still going out, right?" Hanna asks. "I got us into the VIP section of the club. You deserve a night out after all this."

I *should* get an Uber and start pounding on O'Rourke doors, but that's how women get labeled psycho.

"There has to be an explanation." Val rubs my back.

"A woman answered his phone. Balor is never without his phone," I mutter.

"Did you hear him in the background?" she asks, while Hanna shakes her head.

"What are you saying?" I stand up. "That I imagined a woman telling me the man I love just fucked her and wanted a second round of anal in the shower?"

I go dizzy because that's *our* thing. Only, it was his thing with escorts, first.

When my friends each open their mouths, I remind them, "Balor screws escorts. *She's* an escort apparently because she said she won't share him with *another* whore."

My friends gasp in unison.

"This is my fault," I whine and gulp down more tears. "He asked me to stay. I didn't. I ran home with my daddy like an idiot. Balor is insatiable. I was in his bed every night. I understand he has needs."

"Now you're talking like a mafia trophy wife whose husband fucks around," Hannah says, looking nervous. "You're not marrying him after this."

I turn away and fix my makeup to go out. I need to shake this stress away with some dancing, loud music, and bodies bumping into me, so I don't have to think or feel this pain in my heart.

***

Out on the street in front of my father's building, I bundle against the cold.

Leaving the twenty-grand at Balor's house means I have no money to move out on my own anyway. I'm stuck living with Dad until I return to full-time teaching at Fredricks.

I should be able to afford one of those micro-studios.

With two babies?

I dump my head in my hands. If I don't hear from Balor by tomorrow, I'll talk to Katya, and explain the baby situation. Put myself at the O'Rourke's mercy.

"Two Ubers?" I say when more than one car pulls up.

A man gets out and struts up to me. "Sorry, my buddy has groceries in his front seat. Can I take you in mine, same price? I'm just getting started and can use the reviews."

"Me?"

"Who else?"

Hannah and Val, plus Val's sister, Thea, who just showed up, are climbing into the backseat of a sedan that can only fit three people.

I consider calling out for one of them to ride with me, but I want to keep calling Balor. And I might ask this driver to make a detour to Astoria.

Knocking on doors like a psycho isn't looking like such a bad idea after all.

"You know the address to the club, right?"

"Yes, ma'am. Just need to program it. Give me a minute."

The other car pulls away and I relax.

Before my besties notice I'm not with them, I dive into the other car. Taking out my phone, I text Hannah that I'm right behind her.

The rear passenger door facing the street opens and it's like it happens in slow motion.

Wesley gets in. Smirking, he turns to me. "Hello again, Ella."

I reach for the handle to open the door, but it's locked. "Open this door!"

"Go!" Wes barks at the driver.

I hold onto the door as the car tears away from the curb, thinking this isn't an Uber.

Wesley planned this. I inhale, trying to center my thoughts and think of a plan to escape. Maybe it's time I face my fear with him. What can he do to me that I haven't already endured? I survived once. I'm stronger now.

Only, I'm carrying Balor's children. I can't tell Wes I'm pregnant. He's so evil, I can't imagine what he'll do to me.

"Where are you taking me?" I ask him, trying to remain calm like I don't care and I'm not afraid of him anymore.

"Where you belong. With me. Forever." He turns to face me with glassy eyes. "Ella, I'm so sorry. Please. Please give me another chance. I know your father knows what I did. And I'll apologize to him, too. Prove to you that it will never happen again."

The harder I fight Wesley, the harder he'll fight back. I have to trick him somehow.

"Can I have time to think it over?" I sniff. "Please, just ask the driver to bring me back to my apartment. Please?"

"Fuck, man, I love when you beg me." He grips my face, startling me. "Will you crawl for me?"

His touch makes my stomach turn. "Um."

My heart pounds. I squeeze my phone in my hand. Even if Balor doesn't want me anymore, I know I could message Katya and her husband will get me out of this.

"Answer me!" Wes hollers.

When I struggle, an acrid smell fills the car's interior. Wesley's large hand presses a thick white towel across my face.

I pull on his veiny hands and kick, screaming into the towel as he smothers me. The sickly-sweet smell drags into my lungs and then everything goes black.

CHAPTER SIXTY

ELLA

Water splashes in my face, and I gasp a breath. Head pounding, I crank open one eye and my world tumbles out of control.

Wesley fills my vision. In his police uniform. As if I need the reminder.

"Hello, *Estella*," the breathy way he says my full name turns my blood cold.

I lift my head to scream, only to realize I'm tied to a table. Flat on my back with my hands over my head. When I try to kick, I realize my legs are tied to each corner as well.

I shiver and realize I'm stripped down to my bra and panty.

"My clothes! Where are my clothes?" I bellow, twisting against the bindings.

"The clothes some *other* man bought you?" he grinds out, sounding furious.

"I don't know what you're talking about." I play dumb.

How much does Wes know about my life now?

"I have all you need right here." He picks up the box that was left on my doorstep, the one he dropped off.

The idea he got into my father's apartment has me thrashing on the table. "Stop. Stop it. Help!" I scream.

"Relax, Ella," he says, scrunching his nose.

"Don't tell me to relax," I snap. "Where the hell am I? How long have I been here?"

"I can't say where you are." He smiles. "But you've been here for three days."

Breath whooshes from my lungs. *Three* days? Is Balor looking for me? My father? Combined, they're a deadly duo.

"You are a stupid, stupid, dead man, Wesley," I grind

out.

"You belong to me. Did I not make that clear?" His fingers grip my shoulder. Sharp nails like talons dig into the tatted skin. "And what the fuck is this?"

"It's a tattoo to cover where you engraved your initials into me like a monster."

"I branded you as mine," he screams.

"I am *not yours*," I scream back. "You're a damn cop who knows the law. You can't own another person."

"You're tied to a table in my basement, so maybe the situation says otherwise."

"Where's my phone?" I wiggle against my restraints. If it's nearby, and I can get my hands free, I might be able to drop a pin where I am.

If Balor isn't looking for me now, eventually, he will. Right? I'm still having his babies.

My father will realize I'm missing and ask for his help.

"Your purse is at the bottom of the river." Wes smiles and holds up my phone. "Don't worry, I kept this little souvenir."

"My wallet, my license? Why—"

"You're not leaving this house anytime soon. You don't need money or your license. You. Are. Mine." He tosses my phone on a wooden table, raises a large hammer, and smashes it. Pieces go shooting off in all directions.

Killing my last hope that anyone will find me.

Except…

Balor knows about Wes and will find his address, which isn't too far from Astoria.

River…

"You threw my stuff in the river. What river?"

"Hudson River." Wes grimaces. "Upper Hudson River. We're at my dad's house upstate."

Oh crap.

"When you say, I'm not leaving here…"

"You caught on." Wes paces. "I still have to work. When I'm gone, you'll stay here."

"You'll untie me?"

"I don't trust you not to run away," he says.

"Wes, you work long shifts. And then there's the drive." I look at him with pleading eyes. "Surely you won't leave me all day like this."

"Not just all day." He smiles. "All week, too."

I swallow, thinking this has to be a nightmare. "You're going to keep me tied up, all week. No food, no water, no way to go to the bathroom?"

"I'll put out bowls of food and water and a wee-wee pad. It's only until you've atoned for your sins."

"*My* sins?"

He takes out a photo from his back pocket. "You've been a very bad slut."

Eyes flickering across an ultrasound photo, I see my name printed in the top right-hand corner.

"Where did you get that?"

"Your purse!"

"Now you know I'm *pregnant*, Wesley. The father is a dangerous man. Are you insane?"

Wesley takes out his gun and presses the barrel to my forehead. "Who's dangerous?"

"Wesley, please. I'm having a baby."

His Adam's apple bobs up and down, anger transforming his face. "You let that fucker dump his poisonous seed inside you?"

I close my eyes. "Please, Wes."

"You won't be pregnant by the time I'm done with you." He digs the gun harder into my skull, and I have to breathe through the pain. "And you're going to pay extra for letting another man touch you."

I shiver at the thought of him, or anyone, hurting my babies.

"You're sick, Wesley. But it's not your fault." I try to use sympathy as a ruse. "Just untie me. We can talk, work this out."

He ignores me and takes out another phone and texts someone.

"Who... Who are you texting?"

"The doctor."

I heave, bile rushing into my throat. Gagging, I struggle to sit up to swallow down the stinging acid.

"Wesley, my acid reflux," I gurgle out.

I'm sure he remembers those times when I bolted out of our bed, choking, to get to the bathroom. When I woke him, interrupted his sleep, and he kicked me while I lay huddled in a ball on the bathroom floor.

"Choke on it. Like that guy's cum."

I will myself to breathe through my nose, yanking my neck up. Through watery eyes, I see him smile at my pain.

"If you hate me so much, why the hell do you want me?" I cry.

"I don't hate you. I love you. You just need to be taught a lesson."

"A lesson?"

"On how to act. Be the wife I want and need."

"Oh, being a normal human being isn't your thing, I forgot."

"Don't fucking sass me. You're tied to a damn table. I can put you in an unbelievable amount of pain." He smirks. "Oh, right, I plan to do that anyway."

My fractured mind wonders if he's bringing a butcher here to give me an abortion. My babies? Oh, God. Balor. I'm so sorry. Where are you?

"Wesley, what is the doctor for?" I ask quietly.

"To laser off these tattoos." Wesley takes out a knife. "I'll have to find new places to carve my initials into your skin."

"Why?" I scoff. "If I'm never to see the light of day again."

"Oh, you'll see the light of day. I'll even let you see your father. And when you do, you will be perfectly behaved. I'm going to beat the will to fight me right out of you." His smile makes my stomach turn. "There's no way to escape me this time, Ella. I thought I could trust you, but you ran away from me. Never again. I also used a contact at the State Department. Your passport has been invalidated. Can't leave the country this time with your crooked old man."

And with no driver's license... Even if I did get away...

"Fuck you." I pull violently against my restraints. "You're fucking insane."

Wesley grips my face, squeezing so hard my eyes feel ready to pop out. "And just for that, you won't get any anesthesia to laser these tats off."

Terror rushes through me, but I refuse to just give in. I'm not going down without a fight this time. "You don't know who you're really messing with by doing this to me."

He stares at me, lips curled in a feral snarl. "Do it. Say his name. The man who knocked you up. That fucking nerd."

"Then you know it's Balor O'Rourke and what his family can do to you."

Shaking his head, he says, "Oh, I know the O'Rourkes pretty well."

"I would expect you to know criminals operating under your nose."

"I never met Balor, but I know Riordan O'Rourke."

Lips trembling, I stay silent.

"Do you know how I know them?" he asks.

I just give a slight head shake.

"I've been on the take from them for years. They trust

me. I've kept their asses clean. That murderer brother of theirs should be in Rikers. In the psych ward." Wes paces around the table, face going red. "I make sure all the dirty, bloody trails he leaves behind gets cleaned up. They have a warehouse *where they kill people*. Like the roach motel. Sleazeballs go in and never come out. Not in one piece anyway. Who do you think patrols that location and keeps other cops away?" Wesley goes on. "Me. I'm more fucking important to them than you and your bastard child."

"That's not true," I scream.

Balor is in the shower waiting for me...

"You can lie to me all you want. One thing I do know about Balor is he only fucks whores. He doesn't want a family. He has no use for you or this kid. I'm doing him a favor. Riordan O'Rourke tells me everything. And pays me well for my silence."

"And killing his brother's baby is going to keep you in his good graces?"

"You don't fucking listen. Balor O'Rourke doesn't want you. He wants his whores back. He doesn't want kids."

Is any of Wesley's rant true? If he's known the O'Rourkes for years, can he make these assumptions about how Balor feels about kids? But what about his Irish-Catholic brothers shrugging off losing one?

I'd only met them a couple of times. I was so fucking wrong about Wesley. Clearly, I can't rely on my own judgment.

"You're next, I promise," Balor's sweet sister had whispered into my ear, the sincerity rattling through me.

But she's their innocent treasure who doesn't work for them. Shea has nothing to do with their business.

All while my life is over.

Wesley's phone buzzes and he smiles. "Oh good, the doctor is here."

CHAPTER SIXTY-ONE
BALOR

Three days not hearing from Ella.

I'm raw with pain and wired with enough rage to level this entire city with a dirty bomb.

I've been unable to leave my house, craving her scent that I smell on every damn piece of upholstery. I told my housekeeper to not touch my bed or even go near my bedroom. I can't work, my hands are cramped from fisting them so tight. I can't eat, except for the food that Jillian and Shea force on me.

If I thought my sleep sucked before, this is much worse. At times spots form in front of my eyes and my breathing shallows out. Darragh is stopping by tonight to give me a B12 shot.

"We tracked her down!" Shane bursts into my home office with Eoghan on his six.

Several of my most trusted tech experts are working around the clock to find her. All while I'm a useless, melted-down mess.

Eoghan has practically moved in to make sure I don't drown myself in the toilet bowl.

"Where?" I go to stand but feel dizzy and sit back down.

"It wasn't easy."

I grab the tracker device from Shane's grasp. "What the hell is she doing in Beacon, New York?"

Where the hell *is* Beacon, New York? I never fucking heard of it.

"Her phone's SIM card isn't pinging anymore. But..." Shane takes a breath. "I used that tracker you put in the back of the phone, under the case."

Something I never told her about. "And?"

"I got a read on it. But it's fading. Dying."

"Why? *Fucking talk, Quinlan.*"

His jaw tightens as he says, "Her purse is at the bottom of the Hudson River."

I stagger back into a chair. "Jesus fucking Christ."

"That doesn't mean she is." Eoghan comes up next to me and rubs my shoulders. "Hold it together. We'll find her."

"I was also able to track her movements on the day she disappeared," Shane says. "She went to a clinic in Manhattan. Saw a...gynecologist."

My head snaps up. "The day she went missing? Saturday?"

"And my team is scouring cameras to piece together where she went after that appointment." Shane lays a laptop in front of me. "This video is her going into the clinic."

Seeing her stroll into that building alone tears my heart out. I miss her so damn much. It stings more because she was angry with me. I was supposed to go with her to see the doctor. Instead, she went to a clinic without me.

And didn't tell me.

She didn't want me there.

That meant she planned to tell me it was over between us. It feels like broken glass in my mouth when I try to swallow that down.

"There's more information on her visit, if you want it, Balor." Shane eyes me with a wary, flat smile, cautious of my reaction. "I dug further into her records."

"She told me she wanted to see the doctor and confirm the pregnancy before we made an announcement," I say the words as fear paralyzes me. "She is pregnant, right?"

The idea she lost the baby or wasn't pregnant in the first place, even though multiple at-home tests confirmed it, has me reeling.

"She's preggers all right." Shane cups my shoulder and

bends down to whisper in my ear. "She's having twins, Balor."

Twins. Ella is having twins. We're not strangers to twins. Darragh and Cormac are twins. Kieran has twins. Now...me. The guy who didn't even want a relationship.

"Oh, we got more footage of her. I'm pairing my laptop." Shane grabs a remote and switches on my large-screen monitor across from the desk. "Here she is going into the doctor, and coming out. She walks home to her father's apartment. We got her on a series of cameras."

A montage of her movements, stills and grainy videos, eat at my sanity.

"She gets home, but then a few hours later, here's what happens." Shane fast forwards. "Here she is, getting into a car."

"A car?" I stand up.

"From what I further pieced together, an Uber was called to her father's building."

"One Uber?" Eoghan says, hiking up to the screen. "I see two cars."

"Guys, shut the fuck up with the commentary." They forget I'm the real expert. "Let me just watch the fucking video."

It plays, and every second destroys me. She's dressed up to go out with her friends. I see Hannah, Val, and a woman I don't know by the other car. Why did they make her go alone? Was she planning to go somewhere else?

"Shane, did you track this other car's license plate?" Eoghan snaps.

After more glaring, Shane says, "Stolen car."

My phone rings, and I lunge for it. Seeing the caller, fury floods my veins.

Why is *she* calling me when...

I swipe to answer. "What?"

"Some thanks I get," Petra huffs.

"Thanks for what?" I bark.

"When are you coming over? I got rid of that little girl for you, like you asked."

"What?"

"Your text!" she cries out. "You said you were forwarding her calls to me. When she called, I did as you asked. Said you were in the shower and we just fucked and that you don't want anything to do with her."

I stagger into my seat. "Petra, I never sent that text."

"It came from your number." Her breath hitches. "You aren't coming over?"

My stomach twists painfully. "Petra. No. In fact..."

Something hits me, and I snap my fingers. "Shane, do a scan on this phone number. Petra got a text ghosted from my number. Get one of the guys to see where the fuck that text came from. It's also looking like my calls from Ella only are being forwarded to her."

"Got it." Shane reaches for the phone, but I speak into it one last time.

"Listen to me carefully, Petra. Do not hang up, or it will be the last thing you do."

Shane takes my phone and leaves the room.

"What's going on?" Eoghan crouches in front of me. "Talk to me."

His wedding celebration with Jillian is on Saturday. He's completely and utterly obsessed with his bride. Barely leaves her side. But he's been here all day, every day.

"Someone ghosted a text to Petra from me that said if Ella calls, to say I'm in the shower." I shift in my seat. "My calls from Ella are being forwarded to her."

Eoghan's jaw drops. "You can do that? All that? Ghost texts? Deep-fake call forwarding? How the fuck do we trust anything we ever see, Balor?"

"I'm going to have to re-program our phones to enter

codes, two-step verifications. Just us. Family. Until we know…"

Family…

Corvin Snow.

I shoot up from my seat. "Where the fuck is Ella's father?"

CHAPTER SIXTY-TWO
ELLA

Pain. Blood. Fury.

My skin burns from the laser. All I do is cry.

Wes and this so-called doctor argued over giving me the topical anesthetic. Wes told him I cheated on him and was carrying bastard twins. I didn't get any.

The doctor also told him it would take several treatments to fully remove the tattoos, but Wes paid him enough to accelerate the strength of the laser and finish today.

My skin is peeling away, bubbling up like a volcano. But it's not lava that oozes from each of the wound sites. It's blood. My blood.

"I'm pregnant, you bastard! Won't this amount of extreme pain and strain on my system cause me to miscarry?"

The doctor looks at me feebly and says, "It depends."

"On what?" I snap.

"The strength of the fetus."

I'm carrying an O'Rourke. Two. I pray that means they should be fine.

Should…

Otherwise, Wesley will figure out another way to torture me and kill my babies.

I haven't given up hope that their father will save us…

CHAPTER SIXTY-THREE
BALOR

Camryn knocks on my office door. "Balor, the other team is trying to find Mr. Snow. But I did some digging of my own and found some data you need to be aware of."

"Come in." I wave to her. "Talk to me."

"Under his Iceman profile, he messaged someone on his dark web page about Maverick. You. It was triple encrypted, but I hacked that easily," she says proudly.

"What did the message say?"

"He figured out you knew who he was and that you planned to kill him."

My blood runs cold. "How?"

"He put a listening app on your phone," she says grimly.

The chill turns to a fiery rage. "God damn it!"

Camryn straightens her spine, showing no fear of me. "If you give me your phone, I'll find the app and remove it."

Without thinking twice, I unlock it and hand it to her. "Here."

Camryn takes it, her face lighting up from my trust. "There's more," she says, rocking on her Keds.

I roll my eyes. "Hit me."

"We're locked out of Iceman's Swiss bank account."

"He took out our hook?"

"Looks that way."

"Or…"

Before I fly out of control, I say, "Or…"

"I found an alias of his. He's been traveling back and forth to places like Monaco under this name." She shows me a fake ID. It's him, all right. "Right before we lost access, I tracked hundreds of deductions from that Swiss account, all wired to different hotels where *this guy* was a registered guest."

Monaco.

Las Vegas.

Atlantic City.

Macau, China.

Connecticut.

Gambling.

Or the Swiss account is closed because he's broke.

"And he's trying to get a fake passport to leave the country."

Nerves snake down my spine. Snow is disappearing again. And he's taking Ella. Fucking carrying my children!

I thank the Lord every day she was on that flight. Even with this pain gutting my insides, I wouldn't give up the chance to have her in my life.

"He's also wanted in Australia now. Under the Snow name," Camryn says. "He never paid the rent on the house he and his daughter were living in. World Trade Bank had been including a housing stipend in his paychecks, but he kept all the money."

"I assume that's why he stayed behind in Australia and sent Ella to New York alone." I look up at Eoghan. "I want Snow's debts settled. *Today.* I will not have anyone come after Ella."

"Done." He crooks two fingers to Camryn to sort through the payees.

And then I'm going to kill Snow myself.

Riordan rushes into my office, yelling, "Jesus, fuck."

I stand up. "What now?"

"I just got a text from Michael Brennan." With shaking hands, he shows me a photo that makes my stomach revolt.

Ella is lying on a table wearing nothing but bra and panties. Pools of blood cover her skin and there are wide gashes on random spots on her body.

The attached text says:

Taken care of, just the way you asked. I'll need extra money this month for pulling this one off. You're welcome.

"Why does my informant have your girlfriend? And why is he saying *I asked for this?*" Riordan's eyes swim with anger, his voice sharp as a blade.

"You mean, my fiancée," I utter the way I heard my brothers saying 'my wife' with such visceral, primal steeliness in their voices.

"What's going on, Balor?"

"Someone is sending fucking texts from all of us to Brennan and…" I can't even say Petra's name. "Others. Shane is looking into it."

I grab the phone and stare at the picture, willing away the urge to vomit. I search the photo, my brain scanning for clues around her. But I can't tear my eyes away from these massive gashes on her shoulder, her thigh, her hip… I freeze and look at her foot.

Her tattoos. The tats she got to cover his scars.

He's carving them off!

"Shane!" I yell.

"What?" he answers loudly from the other room. "I'm looking for Snow!"

My eyes glance at this horrific photo. Sent from MB1 as Riordan has him saved.

Brennan.

Ella's purse sits at the bottom of the Upper Hudson River.

Near Beacon, New York.

"Fuck this." I stomp to my laptop and look it up myself, my wrists screaming in pain.

I hack into Dutchess County records and have to sit down.

Brennan

A *Mason* Brennan owns a house in Beacon... Right on the Hudson River.

I flip over to Brennan's police records, and I tighten even further seeing his father's name was Mason Brennan. Has to be the same guy.

Now we have the address.

I scour that house in Beacon for a Wi-Fi signal and curse, finding none. But I locate a doorbell camera across the street. After hacking into it, my heart plummets, seeing Ella dragged from a sedan and into a beat-up house three days ago.

It's the same damn maroon Camry that picked her up in Manhattan. The driver of that car isn't Brennan. Just another fucker I will find and kill.

Riordan drops his head close to me. "Talk to me. What's going on?"

"Michael Brennan. Our..." I cringe, but can't blame my brother for what turned out to be a fucking coincidence. "Your informant—"

Rior's face contorts. "Don't call him that."

I spin the laptop around and show Riordan. "Brennan's got Ella."

"Motherfucker. He's dead." Riordan shrugs with no emotion. "*I'm* killing him. Priscilla can watch me. How dare this motherfucker—"

"Someone's ordering our enemies around like puppets, pretending to be us." I'm not defending Brennan, only reassuring my brother so he doesn't think he's being massively betrayed.

And fly off the handle in a fit of rage that could come back to haunt us.

"Who? Who can do that?" Riordan asks.

The texts that came from my phone.

Taken care of, just the way you asked.

Ella's calls to me were forwarded to Petra's phone.

Snow is the only other person I know with these techno skills to ghost my phone and break my custom-built firewalls.

Petra was at that fundraiser where he could have made the connection with her when he saw her talk to me.

Fuck!

Fury flooding my veins, I pull my phone out and dial. "Petra, did you call a Wesley Brennan or a Michael Brennan for anyone?" I bark into the phone without a hello.

"Um…" Petra's voice goes shaky.

"Tell me before I send a drone to *blow up your fucking apartment*."

"Balor…" she sniffs my name. "I got a text I thought was from you with instructions."

"*Instructions? You, too?*" I snap. Someone is trying to keep Ella and me apart. "You didn't mention that a few minutes ago."

"You didn't ask and information at this point will cost you." Her tune changes because she realizes she's been duped, and I don't want her.

"How much?"

"One million."

"Talk. I have your account information."

"I can forward you the text. It looks like it came from you. It gave me all these instructions." She clears her throat. "One was to call a Wesley Brennan, saying I'm speaking on behalf of your brother Riordan because you and I are together and Wes can now take back his little whore. I was told to use those exact words. That his little whore was a bonus payment for his continued cooperation with the O'Rourkes."

My eyes fly to Riordan. "What does the rest of Wesley's message say, Rior?"

His blue eyes lower to his phone and with them closed,

he says grimly. "She won't be a problem for Balor anymore."

Only one other person can fake all of this. Or *would*.

Corvin Snow.

And he wants her away from me, so much that he'd give her back to a monster.

For what?

Shane jogs back into the office. "I found Snow. Surprise, surprise." He smirks. "His car's license plate tags just pinged one of our secret transmitters. He's on the New York State Thruway."

I bet that prick is headed to Beacon where Brennan is holding my Ella.

We *have* to beat him.

"Rior, I need the helicopter."

My brother nods and gets on the phone.

Next, I call Lachlan.

"Yo!" he answers.

"I need you. Snow's working with Brennan. He kidnapped Ella. He's torturing her, Lach." I can't hold back my emotion, not even with him.

"I'm on my way."

CHAPTER SIXTY-FOUR
LACHLAN

In the soundproof compartment of Kieran's helicopter, Riordan, Balor, and Eoghan sit at a table looking at blueprints of Brennan's sprawling riverside ranch.

They have the hard part.

My part is easy peasy.

Shoot. To. Kill.

I'm in the front compartment with my second, Griffin, and Riordan's second, Connor Quinlan.

Fuck, we'll miss them.

I hated leaving Katya, but she practically shoved me out the door with those dainty hands.

"Go bring back my future sister! She's carrying *your blood*, Lachlan."

How my wife knew that would spark my lust for revenge impressed the hell out of me. Ella is pregnant with my family's bloodline. Balor hasn't said that he loves her, but I know he does. That look in his eyes is the look I've seen on each of my brothers these past couple of years. Except Cormac. But his time will come, I suspect.

Right now, the man who hurt Balor's woman has to die.

It's her father, Corvin Snow, I'm silently struggling with. He betrayed us and that *should be* an automatic death sentence.

Movement next to me spins my thoughts in another direction. Darragh, who's here as a medic, rubs his fingers, his face tense. He and I both know how Balor feels conflicted about Snow, especially since we have that murdering snake Alexei Koslov as a father-in-law.

Darragh is all-in now with our family after years of pretending we didn't exist. Since coming home, he's slowly turning into one of us. Each month he gets a new tattoo.

"I see Snow's car," Camryn, one of Balor's hackers, reports from the cockpit with the pilot, igniting my fury fuse to get this party started.

I press on the headset we're all wearing, and then speak into my microphone. "Pilot! Hover over that car. Get me within shooting distance."

When I stand, Balor blocks me. "We're not killing him. Not yet."

"I'm *intercepting* him," I utter in a deep voice, the demon in me taking over.

"It's a crowded highway, Lachlan," Riordan says. "The plan was to intercept him *at the house*."

"Not enough time. He's got a lot to consider, and I won't keep Ella in danger or pain one second longer. The conditions we're going to put on him are not stipulations that selfish prick will agree to immediately."

"We still haven't figured out where we're landing," Riordan says, pushing a hand through his hair. "The airport is miles away and then we have to rent a car. But we're all packing fucking Uzis."

"We're landing on the fucking front lawn," I bark.

"Still subtle, aye, Lach?" Darragh pats me on the arm. "This is a medical emergency. Land as close to the house as you need. In the back preferably." He points to the blueprint. "There's a lot of land between the river and the house. I'll deal with fallout from the authorities."

"Get me on the ground," I say.

"Lachlan, what are you doing?" Balor grabs my jacket.

"I'm going to carjack Snow and talk to him on the ride to Brennan's house. Let him know his *options*. Give him some time to think about it."

"Carjack him?" Balor screeches. "He's driving ninety miles an hour!"

"Then I suggest someone find strong enough rope to lower me onto the fucker's hood!"

CHAPTER SIXTY-FIVE
ELLA

"You have to stay still and stop screaming," the doctor says, leaning over me. "Please, hun. I'm sorry."

"Give me something for the pain, please," I whisper.

"He won't let me." The doctor's jaw goes tight. "Do breathing exercises. Close your eyes and try to leave this room."

"My babies," I cry, shivering so hard, that my teeth rattle. "Don't hurt my babies."

He swallows, and I feel his hand on my thigh.

A gun cocks, the tinny clicking making me look up through warm, salty tears.

"What the fuck are you doing to my girlfriend?" Wes asks low and sinister.

"Checking to see if she's bleeding," the doctor barks.

"Are you a gynecologist?" Wes asks.

"No. You know I'm a—"

"Touch her cunt, and you die."

The doctor straightens, holding the laser. Facing Wes, he says, "I'm still a fucking doctor."

"You have a one-star rating on all medical review sites with multiple allegations and judgments against you. Why do you think I called you?"

Because a reputable doctor would tell Wes to fuck off.

"Wesley, please. Let him give me something. I promise, I'll... I'll be a good girl for you. Please. You're right, Balor doesn't want a wife or children. I'll... I'll give them up for adoption. Just don't...hurt me anymore. Please? I'll do whatever you want."

Wesley's jaw ticks like he expected me to keep fighting him. "I knew you'd come around. Give her something, quack."

"I have to set up an IV," the doctor says, sweating.

"No. You're not putting anything in my veins."

"I can prepare a local." He tosses the laser into a dirty duffel and stomps to the suitcase he brought.

I've always held doctors in high esteem. Balor's brother cemented my view of a handsome, polished doctor, above reproach and committed to the sanctity of life.

How do people like this quack lose their way?

"Do you have a lighter to sterilize the needle?" he asks Wes, sounding annoyed.

"You didn't bring antiseptic?" I yell.

"I was told not to, and—" He doesn't get out another word.

An ear-piercing eruption of gunfire follows, and I scream. The doctor's head explodes, my skin coated with blood and flesh.

Through the smoke, a giant man cloaked in black emerges, the gun still pointed.

Wesley jumps, his gun waving at the now kicked-in basement door.

"No," he yells, but a thud silences him.

Through squinting eyes, I see him on the ground, several men pointing guns at him.

Then all I see is…

Balor.

CHAPTER SIXTY-SIX

BALOR

Riordan storms up to Wesley first. *"On your fucking knees."*

Griffin Quinlan cracks him on the head with his Smith and Wesson.

The prick's trembling jaw scans the room and all the guns pointed at him. Wisely, he drops his gun and lowers to the cement.

More shouting dissolves into the background as I take in Ella. My brain tries to process everything. She's half-naked, covered in blood, both her own and from the other victim. A guy who tortured her on this table is dead on the floor with his head blown off.

All her tattoos are now a graveyard of bloodied, chewed-up skin. Her wrists are raw from the coarse ropes. Cursing, I cut her free with a knife, but I don't know what to address next.

With her arms no longer bound, she grabs me and cries. "Balor, I'm sorry."

"Jesus fucking Christ, for what?" I hug her so hard.

"I had no idea. About anything. All the trouble I've caused."

I push my lips against hers. "You're not trouble. You're mine."

I scoop her up into my arms, but she's shivering so hard, I press her body to mine and try to warm her.

"I need a blanket!" I yell. "Get Darragh in here. *Now!*"

I'm responsible for what happened to Ella. Bringing the women we love into our family's world puts them in danger. I sat on the Wesley connection to us. I should have told Lachlan to kill him the second I figured out Ella's abusive ex was Riordan's informant.

After kissing her, I draw our eyes together. "Listen

carefully, Petra *did not* answer *my* phone. I was nowhere near her."

I debate telling Ella that her father set me up, too. Connor Quinlan has him in his car out front. My eyes will never unsee how my psycho brother, Lachlan, dropped onto Snow's hood and got him to pull over. My heart was pounding out of my chest, and all I could think was one wrong move, and we are breaking Katya and Ma's hearts.

"I should have known that call was fake or staged." Ella shakes her head. "I was stupid and upset."

"No. That's a sophisticated ghosting trick. No regular person would—"

"Are you calling me regular?" The humor in her voice eases the tension as tears gush from my eyes.

I lower her into a nearby chair and kneel in front of her as Darragh rushes in with his medical bag and a warming blanket.

"Ella, my brother, Darragh, is here. He came all this way just to take care of you. Can he do that? Examine you?"

"Really?" She nods, her eyes flooded with tears. "I'm so sorry for leaving with my dad Friday morning."

"It's okay," I say, kissing Ella's forehead. "None of this was supposed to happen. We were supposed to—"

"I went to a doctor, Balor. Alone." She lowers her head. "I know you wanted to be there. I should have waited for you."

Darragh and I gently wrap a blanket around her. My brother begins checking her vitals and dressing her wounds. Ella's teeth continue to chatter, but her eyes stay on mine.

"And what did the doctor say?" I hold her hand, smiling softly at her. Even though I know about the doctor, she's fragile, and I want her to know I'm in support of any decision she made because she's done nothing but act in good faith.

"We're having twins." The *we* in her response wrecks me.

Right here, I know she's mine.

"That's perfect, baby. You're perfect." I kiss her forehead. "So perfect for me."

When I rise to my feet, my clothes are blood-stained, mirroring all her wounds. It rocks me with a fury I've never felt before. These red splotches make what she's been through real.

"I got her," Darragh says, and I step back to let him take care of my woman.

A few feet away, Wes is tied up, and Riordan has his gun to the fucker's head.

I walk up to him with the knife still in my hand. "Have anything to say to Ella?"

Pride is toxic. He's struggling and decides with a shrug. "Do whatever the hell you're going to do."

I consider if Brennan has a tripwire, something that will go off if he's killed. Evidence that will automatically be sent to the FBI about my family if he disappears.

"Oh, we will. You're dying tonight." After a glare, I point the knife at his throat. "How fucking dare you touch what's mine."

I look back to Ella. Darragh is focused on tending to her many, many wounds, Eoghan taking my place next to her. I hate that she's exposed, and Wesley's scummy eyes are looking at what belongs to me. That fucking quack we killed damaged so much of her sweet skin, we can't even cover her up properly without putting her in more pain.

Watching her wince and seeing her squeeze Eoghan's hands as Darragh treats her wounds, all I can think is I would take her pain from her a thousand times over if I could. There's only one way to do that. I draw my fist and smash it into Brennan's nose with a gratifying crunch. He falls over, screaming in pain, his blood splattering my aching hand.

I stomp his shoulder, feeling it dislocate with a satisfying pop, and when Wes tries to guard his face, he can't. He can't move that arm.

This isn't me. This isn't me.

I don't have the stomach for this, but I will that nonsense away because it's who I have to be for Ella. For our family. There can never be a shadow of doubt in her mind that I can't protect them with my bare hands.

The scent of blood fills this disgusting basement and competes with mold and wet cement.

Wesley gurgles on his own blood. With my good hand, I squeeze his neck to crush his larynx.

"You choked her like this, didn't you? How do you like it?"

I feel the air trying to pass my tightened fist around his neck. He kicks uselessly until his eyes roll into the back of his head.

I allow this scumbag one desperate gasp to watch him suffer more. My specialty. The more he whines and cries and pisses himself, the more it fuels me to keep going.

His suffering thrills me more than I ever thought it would. But it's for her. Ella. The woman I love, who's having my babies.

Every groan and screech from Wesley's fucked-up face and shaky voice only ignites images of how he beat up Ella. How he caused her pain with no regret or remorse or mercy.

My hand is on fire, but I keep hitting him, even when he stops moving.

Griffin Quinlan pulls me away. "Mate, the plan."

My right hand's a bloodied mess and with crimson splatter all over my clothes, I turn back to Ella.

Jaw dropped, she breathes heavily. But I see no fear in

her face witnessing what *I'm* capable of.

This is for you, butterfly.

Only you.

Wesley is a wheezing puddle, and to kill him would put him out of his misery. I won't. Not yet. I want him to suffer even more.

And Griffin is right, we have a plan.

"Bring him in," I say, wiping the sweat from my forehead, feeling blood smear across my skin like a warrior.

"Bring who in?" Ella says, looking around.

Connor Quinlan drags in her father, his wrists chained up. Snow's dark hair is all over the place, a mess, but without a single bruise on his body.

A purposeful move. A courtesy for the woman I love. I have something worse for Snow. Something much more painful.

"Dad!" Ella cries out. "Balor, what are you doing?"

"Tell her, Iceman." I glare at him. "Tell her *everything*."

CHAPTER SIXTY-SEVEN
ELLA

My father is a global cyber-terrorist.

As I shiver in the blanket, my arms and legs bandaged, Balor makes Dad stand before me to confess his many crimes and sins.

My head is spinning.

Perhaps he didn't intend to hurt anyone, but according to Balor, his cyber-attacks during Christmas week resulted in the deaths of hundreds of people across the globe. His ransomware virus may have hurt them indirectly, their deaths circumstantial, but he's still responsible.

Dad made millions in ransom but blew it all on gambling and settling past debts. Those 'jobs' he was doing were not developer side gigs. Those were trips to Vegas, Monaco, Macau China, and even Lisbon, Portugal. Desperate to feed his addiction, he often left me in the apartment in the middle of the night to sit at Blackjack tables in Atlantic City or Mohegan Sun.

I learn that he even sold my mother's family home in Connecticut over a year ago and didn't tell me. Mom's old clothes, her cookware, and her recipes were in that house. Her wedding dress!

All gone!

The loss of my legacy tears at my soul.

But nothing is worse than finding out he orchestrated this whole abduction scheme with Wes to get me away from Balor because the O'Rourkes discovered his secret identity.

A terrorist named Iceman.

When Dad sees all my injuries, he pulls away sharply and tries to kick Wesley. Lachlan takes the chain from Connor and yanks him back like a dog, so hard that he falls.

Balor brings a knife to Dad's throat.

"Now tell your daughter who ghosted my texts to Petra. And who gave the instructions of what to do with her," Balor snarls.

Dad's jaw trembles. "It was me. But I had no idea it would result in *this*. Ella, you have to believe me. I'm so sorry, honey."

"Still think Wes is better for her than me?" Balor shouts.

"Mr. O'Rourke..."

"Cut the fucking mister act."

"Despite the outcome, I did not intend for my ransomware virus to hurt you or your family. It... It spread farther than I intended."

"Like the atom bomb," I mumble.

"What, my love?" Balor turns around.

"The tests at Los Alamos. They expected a detention of seven megatons. But the bomb replicated itself over and over, reaching over fifteen. It couldn't stop." I take a breath, spewing what I learned in my physics classes at Yale. "Like a virus."

"Da, Ella." Dad gives me a small smile. "You understand."

"Then why did you agree to work for Balor if you knew he would be looking for you?"

"To cover my tracks. And... To hide. I meant what I said when I told you, they would protect us." His sad eyes take in all the guns aimed at his head.

Protection one day, a death sentence the next.

"Then why did you team up with Wes to take me away from Balor?"

"Wesley promised me he would never lay a hand on you again." Dad chokes up. "He's one man I thought I could control. I am no match for the mafia."

"Your father also figured out we reverse-engineered

everything he did." Balor's lips twist into a hateful sneer. "And he planned to disappear. Leaving you with a monster."

Dad just lowers his head.

"All clear, Balor," Camryn says to Balor. "No tripwire on Brennan."

"Thank you, Camryn." Balor whispers to me, "Your father's fate is up to you, Ella."

"What?"

"He's your father and despite his despicable lack of judgment, I believe he loves you."

"You'd let him live?"

"For you? Aye."

After a moment, I take a breath and speak, "A dead man can't atone. A dead man can't make up to me the hole I'd have in my life if he breathes his last breath and takes all his sins with him. I'll hate him forever, and I don't want that hate in my heart, Balor."

He lays sympathetic eyes on me. "I know, my love."

"I love you, too," Wes mumbles, his voice choked with blood.

"You're dying in five minutes." Lachlan kicks him in the head, drawing more sickening moans. "Shut the fuck up."

What are they waiting for?

"Dad..." I call him in a shaky voice. "This is an impossible choice for me. Tell me, tell me you love me."

"Of course, I love you, Estella. Everything I did, I did for you."

"He's broke," Eoghan chimes in. "But there is a small account for you, Ella."

"Please. Let my father live," I say with a shaky breath.

Balor kisses my forehead. "Then he lives."

"Thank you." I know the massive sacrifice I'm asking, and it speaks volumes to how much this man loves me.

Straightening, Balor turns to my father. "You were told the rules in your car on the way here, but I'm going to repeat them, Snow, for your daughter's sake. You're going away for six months to deal with your gambling addiction. When you get out, someone will shadow everything you do for the rest of your life. You will be injected with a tracker. You will be stripped of your identity and given a new one by me, for your protection. I will control everything you do. You are not to leave the city without permission. You will have access to your grandchildren, *my children*, but visits will be supervised. You never have to work another day of your life. I will pay for your apartment, and you will get an allowance. I will have eyes on you 24/7, Snow. That's the price you pay for your life. It buys you time to make up your sins to the woman who will be my wife."

Dad goes ashen at Balor's demands. A man who lived like a millionaire is being reduced to a groveling peasant.

"There is one more price I'll exact for next one million breaths," Balor scoffs a wry laugh. "After this, we're going straight to the command center, and you *are* handing over the keycode."

Dad visibly swallows harshly. "I..."

"Keycode?" I ask.

"His viruses, like the one he infected the world with three damn days before Christmas are locked in his private server. A vault with all his sins." Balor looks at my father. "You're handing it over to me, Corvin."

Making Balor *aka Maverick* the most powerful hacker in the world. I trust Balor would never in a million years hurt innocent people.

Dad's composure crumples a little more with every passing second. But he brought this on himself.

"Give us the passcode and your six months will be in a cushy rehab center in sunny Malibu," Balor continues.

"Or a torture camp in Ireland. Your choice."

"I'm headed to Ireland soon," Lachlan says. "I'd love to continue our...chat."

Dad just heaves.

"And in case you think you can get around my restrictions." Balor takes a gun from Lachlan that looks plastic and moves to my father's side. "There's one piece of insurance I need from you."

Lachlan smiles, unlocking the chains on Dad's wrists. He smooths them like a prima donna, but when his gaze fixes on the ravaged state *I'm* in, he drops his hands.

I'm draped only in a blanket over my bra and panty, gauze and tape crisscrossing the wounds all over my body. Darragh says they will hold until he brings me to his hospital for proper treatment and skin grafts.

"What? What is my final payment, Mr. O'Rourke?" Dad's tone ticks up with anger now.

To my shock and horror, Balor shoves the gun at my dad.

Clicks go off around the basement, echoing against the musty cement walls. Everyone points their gun at Dad. Except Darragh, who keeps tending to my wounds like nothing else is happening. And not Lachlan, who has his phone out.

"Call me Spielberg," the enforcer says, smiling widely, recording my father.

Eoghan glances at the view screen. "Put a filter on it, and you're Scorsese."

"Shut the fuck up, you two." Balor shakes his head.

"What... What am I to do with this gun?" Dad asks.

"Kill the man who hurt your daughter." Balor points to Wes on the floor, still writhing.

Dad fumbles with the piece, making me wonder if he ever held a gun.

"No, Mr. O'Rourke." He tries to hand it back. "I will

not deny you the pleasure of proving to my daughter—"

"*I* have nothing to prove to her. She knows I love her. You will kill Wesley and we will have it on video, so if you ever, *ever* betray me, her, or my family again, that video goes to the FBI." Balor balls his hands into fists, wincing through the pain of beating Wes' face. "This is my insurance if you think you can outsmart me. Kill that man. And keep in line. I'll spare your life and keep your dirty secrets. All of them."

My heart shatters for my dad, but he's made so many mistakes. He's lucky to live. He's lucky he'll see my children born and get to hold them.

"Dad, please. Do what they say. Nothing should be more important to you than me!"

His lips tremble. "But my sweet Ella? You want a murderer for a father?"

I swallow and look around. "I'm marrying into a family of murderers. Proudly."

Balor blinks at me, and a smile ghosts his lips.

This is what it took, brat?

"For the record, I've not murdered anyone," Balor says to me instead. "Trust me, how I ache to finish off this scumbag. I brought him to the brink. Your father needs to know we own him." He turns to Dad. "Now kill this motherfucker so I can get the mother of my children *the proper fucking medical care she needs!*"

"Dad, please. Do it for me. Do what you should have done six months ago. You had the power when I told you. Don't let Wesley ever hurt another woman like he hurt me." I hate putting this shame on him, but I'm breaking the chains of feeling guilty over the abuse and holding others accountable. For once!

Nodding, my father lifts the gun. More skilled now. He was faking it. With eerie precision, his fingers stretch in the trigger well.

"Get close enough so his blood soaks into your clothes," Eoghan, the lawyer, says. "DNA evidence."

I assume they would figure out a way around the obvious duress my father is under. Sadly, he would never make it to trial.

"Dad?" I call out to him.

To my surprise, he turns to me, to all of us, holding the gun.

"Hey," Lachlan yells and tosses his other gun to Balor.

The men in the room advance on Dad. Riordan, Eoghan, Darragh, and the Quinlans, who look more bloodthirsty than anyone.

"I got it," Balor says, pointing a gun right back at my father. "What are you doing, Snow?"

"Estella. I am so sorry."

"Dad... For what?"

I rise from the chair, the blanket falling to my feet. "Dad?"

I worry he'll shoot Balor just to make his brothers kill him.

Death by O'Rourke.

"Goodbye, my Estella," he whispers.

Then...

He puts the gun into his mouth.

And without any further words, my father pulls the trigger.

CHAPTER SIXTY-EIGHT
BALOR

"No!" I dive for Snow.

Griffin and his brother Connor hold me back. Snow's lifeless body crashes backward into the metal shelving units lining the walls.

A second later, his body collapses onto the floor next to Wes, who's now balling.

Ella runs to her father, but I catch her. "I'm so sorry. I'm so fucking sorry," I whimper into her bruised shoulder.

"You asshole!" She breaks from me and kicks her father's lifeless body. "You selfish prick."

I scoop her up and hold her, but she winces from the many open wounds.

Griffin dashes upstairs with Darragh at the sound of someone outside, who no doubt heard the gunfire. We landed the helicopter on the wide expanse of property behind Brennan's house.

A helicopter, a car with a smashed hood, gunshots, and two dead bodies means a massive clean-up effort.

I have every confidence Lachlan's team will fix this.

"Ella, look at me."

She's shaking and looks dizzy. "How could he?"

As someone who has a selfish-as-fuck father, I can use my healing journey to help her. She'll always have me.

"Ella, I need to do one more thing, but I'm not sure how much more you can handle."

"What? What else do you..." Her eyes drift to Brennan. He's still alive.

In the end, I'm glad it will be me. I glance at Eoghan who's watching us. His gaze is a mixture of relief, sadness, and happiness that this shitshow is over.

His gaze turns to the gurgling mess on the floor. Straightening his back, like it's his duty to once more kill someone for me, he lifts his piece, but I stop him.

If I thought it would help her, I'd let Ella kill him. But that kind of revenge will only damage her further. My brothers have all killed someone, except me and Darragh.

He's a doctor. It's not the same thing.

It's my turn.

"Eoghan, no." I push the gun barrel toward the floor.

A look passes between us and for a second, we're back in Boston the night I got pummeled and he killed my attackers. That was his first time. This is mine.

I'm the murderer now.

Nodding, Eoghan grabs my shoulder with a meaty hand. "It will be okay," he whispers.

"Ella, you might want to turn away. I won't fill your head with any more nightmares that I—"

"You? You've not given me nightmares at all. You've made everything better for me."

I kiss her forehead. "Still, you can turn away."

"Tell me, will it make it better if I watch?" Her question silences the room. "Will it give me the closure I need?"

"No," Eoghan answers. "I shot a man who tried to rape Jillian and she watched. She has flashbacks and panic attacks."

This is something he never mentioned.

"Eoghan, hold her for me," I say. "I kill him. Not you."

He immediately takes my Ella into his arms, tucking her head against his chest. "Just a few more moments, lass. It will all be over."

My first kill will be for the woman I love. The first and last.

I take the gun and with the clearest head I've ever felt about anything, I stomp over to Michael Wesley Brennan and unload my clip into his chest.

CHAPTER SIXTY-NINE
BALOR

A few days later, I bring Ella to her father's apartment. I see it as his and not hers because she lives with me. She will live with me, forever.

The kind of disaster we found ourselves in requires a lot of cleanup. Dealing with this apartment is one.

Lachlan's team took Brennan's body, chopped it up, and buried the pieces farther north of Beacon in several open fields and lakes. His parents are dead, and it turns out his father probably murdered his mother. Wesley was an only child and the end of a line of serial abusers.

Good riddance.

The police department will look for him since he's an active member of service. He'll just end up being one of the millions who are never found.

He's dead, and I have the love of my life at my side, pregnant with my babies.

Today, we're collecting the rest of Ella's things from the apartment and will meet with a realtor about selling it.

It's mortgaged to the hilt and was about to be sold at auction in a foreclosure. But Eoghan stopped it and paid back the bank so we could sell it free and clear. Hopefully at a profit, money that will go to Ella to spend as she chooses.

Ella chokes up at hearing all these messy financial details when Jillian brings us the paperwork.

I press my lips against Ella's forehead. "I settled whatever your father owed. It's a clean slate."

"I'm so sorry," she whispers.

"Nothing to be sorry for. None of this is your fault. All I want is for you to be free of this."

Nodding, she walks around, touching items here and there. "I don't even know what to keep. My mother's gone. Now he's gone, Balor."

Elegant souvenirs from around the world decorate the living room. Leather-bound books sit unread on the shelves in lower bookcases that stretch from one wall around the fireplace. I peeked at Snow's closet; his suits were both tailor-made and designer brands.

He could have sold off all this to pay his gambling debts. Instead, he chose to terrorize the world. And left his daughter in ruin.

"Hmmm," Jillian says, looking at her phone and reading a text. "Oh boy, your brother is going to lose his shit."

I glance at her. "Why? Did you like a post from a guy?"

"Please don't get me started on that." She shakes her head. "His credit card got denied again. I had to give him mine. You can guess which embarrassment he hates more."

"Something tells me Eoghan would happily change his name to Diamond for you."

"Only because it's my dad's name and he didn't have a son." She smiles. "There's plenty of O'Rourkes and—" Her phone rings, and with an eye roll, she answers it. "Hi. Slow down. What's going on?"

I stand, worry crawling all over me. Instinctively, I finger my phone, but get nothing other than a blank screen. Quickly, I power off and then power on. But nothing.

It's fully charged, but the phone is dead.

Jillian has stopped talking and is tapping her screen, troubled.

"What happened?" I step closer. "Is your phone working?"

"Yes, but my call with Eoghan just dropped." Jillian shows me her cell screen. "I'm trying to call him back but it's going directly to voicemail."

My face drains of all its blood.

"Guys, what's wrong?" Ella moves beside me. "You're scaring me. You're both white as sheets."

Any other time I would blame my cheap Irish skin, but Jillian's ma is from Ireland, too.

"Jillian are you on our data plan yet?"

She shakes her head. "No."

"Ella, butterfly, is your phone working?"

She slips it from her purse. "Yeah?"

Jillian's phone rings again.

"Eoghan, I'm here. What's going on? Uh-huh. What phone is this, babe? Your burner?"

The burner phones work. Because they run on the federally protected spectrum that uses military satellites.

Mine is at my house.

"Can I talk to Eoghan, Jillian?"

"Yeah, oh Balor. It's bad."

My throat tight, I say, "Alo?"

"All our phones are dead, except the burners," Eoghan speaks calmly. "Even Darragh's and he's fucking livid because he's a doctor. What's going on?"

I glance around, the worst pit in my stomach making me sick. "Check the bank accounts."

"What?"

"You heard me."

"Which one?"

"All of them. Mine. Yours. You manage them, Eoghan."

"Aw, Christ." Eoghan jostles the phone after tapping. "What the fuck?"

"What it is?"

"This can't be happening."

"Balor, what's going on?" Ella slips an arm around my waist.

I close my eyes and hug her close to me.

I'm fucking blind without a laptop. "Ella, love, where are your father's computers?"

She stumbles back. "No, it can't be him. He's..."

"It's okay, baby. It might not be," I say, though my gut strongly doubts it. "I just need to check."

Nodding, she says, "He works in his office. I'll get the key."

I watch her dash away. *Mine.*

"Tell me what you see, Eoghan," I say into the phone.

"I'm getting all these notifications on my phone, Balor," Jillian screeches. "All our checks and wire transfers are reversing as insufficient."

"Tell me what you see," I repeat to Eoghan, my voice even.

"One-thousand-dollar withdrawals. Over and over."

"Interesting..."

"There are hundreds of them," Eoghan says. "Our banks are processing these withdrawals, draining our accounts. Whoops, Lachlan's account is empty. Better fix this or he'll go to the bank and shoot someone."

"Nah, he'll slit their throats. More fun and easier to get away with."

All while a cyber code is circling the globe looking to hurt my family.

Hurt. My. Family.

My family is losing millions by the minute and that bastard Snow is dead. He won't know how happy we are. Unless he made it to the pearly gates and is watching me fuck her every night.

But he'll see how dirty his daughter is for me for all of eternity. That could be his hell.

"Balor, what is this?" Jillian looks shaken. "There aren't any fraud alerts."

No fraud alerts. Either what we're looking at isn't real, or Snow disabled the alerts because that would have given me time to stop the withdrawals.

Or slow them down.

"I have the key." Ella returns, waving a silver key.

It hits me. *Snow is the tripwire*. His death unleashed this destructive virus that is bankrupting my family.

I follow Ella down a hallway to an office. She unlocks it and lets me inside. It smells of cigar smoke. A Mac-Air laptop sits closed on his desk. Could the code be on that laptop? Or some other device buried ten feet deep in another state? Or sitting on the bottom of the ocean?

No, that's not possible. This is an active link on a loop to keep making these withdrawals. It needs a live Wi-Fi signal for the commands.

It has to be on this laptop in front of me.

"Jillian," I call out from the office. "Ask Eoghan for a link to one of the accounts that's being drained. And give the link to Ella. I cup her cheek. "It's going to be okay. All of this can be reversed."

I put a safety net around the URLs for each of our accounts. Added a layer beyond the banks' shitty firewalls.

Someone broke through our walls.

My walls...

Snow.

Iceman.

I approach the Mac-Air slowly like I would a bomb.

Just opening it, I lose my breath.

There's no passcode. Just a photo of him and Ella as wallpaper. I ignore that, for now. She'll need my support to deal with this death, and with the loss of him in her life. The life he chose to show her and not who he really was.

My fingers go to work, and I hold my breath looking for this laptop's IP address. But without the data we collected on Snow, I don't know if this is the vault without tearing it apart.

Digging through folders, my heart stops at one with my name on it.

O'Rourke Ruin.

I click it and find a link to a bank account. It takes seconds for me to break into it, and I choke seeing the account growing before my eyes.

$1,000.00
$1,000.00
$1,000.00
$1,000.00

On and on.

He expected me to find this sooner. Or didn't expect the code to spread...

The bomb replicated itself over and over, reaching fifteen megatons. It couldn't stop. Like a virus.

Possibly his coding lost control of this one, just like the one he'd launched at Christmas.

Clicking on the profile my fingers freeze over the keyboard.

Estella Reyes

An account he opened for her. She doesn't use Estella.

"Here, I have one of the bank accounts." Ella comes around and gasps seeing her name and a swelling balance.

I pull her onto my lap to keep me calm. "Stay with me. Help me."

"I don't know what that is." She takes a deep breath. "That's not me."

Days ago, Eoghan said he found an account for her. But we never imagined it would be the scene of the crime of the century.

If Wesley knew about this money, he never would let her keep it.

"It's okay, baby." I believe she had no idea.

She's twisted into the fabric of my soul. Every fiber

rings true and pure. Plus, for me, it's child's play to figure out how and when this account was opened.

Baby. Child. I cup her stomach.

"Even if I weren't in love with you and having your babies, I'd strongly advise my father not to attempt to ruin the mafia!"

"I worried Wesley had a tripwire that upon his death, evidence would go to the FBI or something," I say. "But he wasn't that smart. Or tech savvy."

"But my father was. What does this thing want? How do we stop all those withdrawals?" Ella whacks the screen. "Balor, this is *your* family fortune."

"I know, baby." I press my face into the back of her shoulder, then dig further into this laptop, reverse searching by date. Looking for files updated around the time of Christmas.

Shockingly, there's a folder with one file dated three days before Christmas.

I smash ENTER and a dialogue box flies open.

PASSCODE: XXXXXXXXXXXXXXXXXXXXX

"I don't suppose you can hack that?" Ella asks, her voice shaking.

"I'm not sure."

"It's like he wanted you to try to stop it."

"And possibly fail. There's jamming the knife into your gut, and then there's the twisting that hurts worst."

"Entering useless numbers—"

"Or letters, or characters."

"Oh my God, how many possibilities does that make it?"

"21 spaces to fill?" I start to type in every failsafe code I know for that total of characters.

It's not a random number. It's a passcode program used often, but Snow would never code it with known passcode breakers.

"Balor, Kieran is calling you," Jillian says from the office entryway.

"Tell him I'll call him back."

"Your brother, the king," Ella whispers.

I scoff. "He'll never hurt me and even if this can't be fixed and we end up broke, or worse owing millions in transaction fees, he won't have any power to hurt me."

"Balor, I'm so sorry." Ella holds back tears.

"No need, baby. We'll figure this out." I give her a little squeeze, but she flinches. The many wounds on her body are still inflamed.

Each night, I gently massage every spot with ointment to help her heal. My kisses and soft-spoken words telling her how much I love her are meant to mend her heart and soul. I'm the only man in her life now.

She shifts in her seat and tugs at the bralette she's wearing because the tattoo under her ribcage...

I freeze as my mind buzzes and lands on the answer.

"Ella, you said your father suggested that tattoo under your ribcage."

She stiffens. "Not the location, but the saying."

The Russian alphabet always freaked me out. I'd spent time in Moscow and had figured out some of the letters in order to use their keyboards. I didn't love her father's poison etched into Ella's skin, but it's her heritage.

"The tattoo meant so much to him and for some reason that butcher with the laser carved *that* one off me first."

I stand up so fast, that I nearly launch her across the room. "What?"

My eyes devour her body. Those letters that represented some random saying, she didn't even understand, had been removed from her body first.

Fuck, that can't be a coincidence.

"Ella, my love. Can you remember exactly what that saying said?"

"No. It's some Russian proverb. Dad always said it in his native tongue."

"Do you remember it?"

"I don't know." Her pained face kills me.

I gently kiss her swollen cheek. "Breathe, baby. And think. It's in your head. Push it forward."

She struggles, mangling the rough language.

"You're doing great, butterfly. Keep going." I watch more money pour into her account.

Several words smoothly come off her lips, and my cock hardens at how the language sounds in her voice. It's so fucking ironic. The Russians were our biggest enemy for years. I'm the third O'Rourke to fall head over fucking heels for one.

Even if my Ella is undeniably American, her roots are Russian.

"Say that into your phone, baby." I activate the voice tool and hold it up to her.

She repeats the saying, clearer now. Snow must have said it to her over and over. It was in her brain. She just needed to find it.

Using my chi training, I'm forcing myself to be calm with every fiber of my being. With every trained muscle to function at its highest level for complete and utter smoothness in my actions.

Otherwise, I will fucking detonate.

Ding.

I blink at her translated words:

fortune favours the brave

Slowly, I count the characters. 22 without spaces.

The code wants 21.

That stops my heart.

Fuck!

Looking closer, I see the translator spelled *favours* in British English.

"I think we've got it, butterfly." Slowly, I type the proverb, using the American English. Something perhaps to throw us off.

A screeching buzzer whines at a decibel that rattles my fucking eardrums.

Then the screen goes completely black.

CHAPTER SEVENTY

ELLA

We breathe a sigh of relief when Balor's phone pings, coming to life again with missed calls and messages.

We watch the computer screen come back to life. All the bank withdrawals shift into reverse, emptying from the account in my name.

Balor explains that my father used a veil code that also jammed the O'Rourke phones, so Balor couldn't make calls or hack into the banks to stop it.

He stays glued to Dad's laptop for an hour, digging through all his files, and with Eoghan on the line, they confirm every penny is accounted for.

One by one, each brother calls him like the night we were stuck in the snowstorm.

When Balor hangs up with Kieran, he shuts the office door.

"We have to talk." His voice is flat and unemotional.

He was told to end his relationship with me, I know it. He'd started talking Gaelic over the multiple heated conversations, yelling and slamming his fists on the desk.

I've been holding it together. And now…

Now it's over. And I can't blame him. How do I know this won't happen again? How do I know next week there aren't more tripwires planned and another set of withdrawals won't start all over?

I walk with pain searing up my leg, wearing a cumbersome aircast because Wesley carved away the rose tattoo on my ankle. Just to be a dick and hurt me, since I'd had that one when we met. That one didn't cover his sins, but he wanted to make new ones.

"It's okay, Balor." I put my hands on my stomach. "These are your babies. I won't keep them from you."

"What are you talking about?"

"I gather your family is livid with me. And I don't blame them."

"Whoa, whoa, whoa. They're livid. But not with you, I promise." He strokes my cheek. "They're furious with me. I hired your father and put us in this position because of my own thirst for power. I knew I should haven't touched you, but I couldn't resist you. This is *my* fault."

But it's not like Kieran will put a hit on him.

Right?

"How did my father do this? I want to understand your world better, Balor."

Because he's going to be in mine for the rest of my life.

"He was feeding that bank-draining virus code a PIN every couple of days to keep it from launching. When he killed himself, it triggered the withdrawals."

I shake my head. "He could have been hit by a car! How freaking reckless!"

"I know, butterfly." His eyes slip closed and for a second, I see him wiping away a tear. "Ella, come look at your dad's laptop."

"Balor, no offense, I know this is your world, your beating heart, but I don't ever want to see another computer again." I'm ready to close all my social media accounts, too.

"I located your father's ransomware code."

My heart stops. "You did?"

"In another file. Along with an email from a hacker in Japan."

"What?"

"Your dad planned to sell him the code for one billion dollars."

One. Billion. Dollars.

"Do you know who this guy in Japan is?" I ask, keeping my lunch down.

"I sure do."

"Okay. Why are you looking at me so funny."

"The code is tangible property, according to Eoghan, and not abandoned, in legal terms. We found his will, too. You're the sole beneficiary, Ella."

My father was cremated, his ashes sitting in a box here in the apartment. Balor and Shane declared him dead, falsifying a death certificate.

"The code is mine, technically?" I stare at him. "And you'd hand it over to me?"

"Absolutely. It's not mine." He swivels in my father's chair, looking back at the laptop screen.

I glance around. Dad left me nothing but debt. Debt Balor is paying off for me. I could sell this code and have one billion-freaking dollars?

That means I can pay Balor back. Pay his family back. Earn my respect back. Be Balor's equal.

"Is this Japanese guy a *good* guy like you?"

"No," he scoffs. "Not at all. He's linked to the destruction at the Fukushima Power Plant in 2011. When the tsunami hit, he struck the power plant, hoping the chaos would cover it up."

"Then no freaking way am I giving him the code, selling it, whatever. I'm not giving it to anyone." I've seen what that code can do.

"Not for one billion dollars?" He gently leans forward, resting his elbows on the desk. "You need to think about this very carefully. You'll be independent and won't need anyone. Not even me."

It's an easy decision. My pride isn't for sale.

Is Balor testing me? Living in a mafia family requires loyalty. I get it.

"There's nothing to think about, Balor." I stand tall. "Where is that code? Delete it."

"I'm not deleting it. It's not mine. It's yours." He clicks something and sheets of paper spit out of my father's printer.

I grab one of the many sheets. Garbled letters, numbers, and symbols I don't understand make up my father's ransomware code.

My ransomware code.

"Balor, I don't want this. I want you. I want us."

He stands, eyes lowered. "You'd rather have *me* than one billion dollars?"

I move closer and throw my arms around him. "I'd rather get one billion dollars the old-fashioned way."

"The oldest profession in the world?" He grinds against me.

"Been there. Done that. If we're getting married—"

"*If* we're getting married?"

I flash the obscene engagement ring that I've been wearing since Balor brought me home. I refuse to take it off. "This means you and I *are* getting married."

"I won't force you to marry me, butterfly." He pulls out of my arms and scoops up the printouts. "Especially not in light of this."

"I'm confused," I whisper.

His hands shake, curling the pages back, one at a time. "I had planned to steal the code from your father. That's why I hired him. Not to use it the way he did. Not to hurt strangers." Balor hurts his enemies.

His brothers *kill* their enemies.

"Now you have it." I don't bother asking why he doesn't sell it. "What's mine is yours."

His jaw tightens. He's already rich and knows that with this code in the hands of someone truly evil and not just mischievous like my father—trying to bankrupt the O'Rourkes excluded—the world will never be safe.

"Then you know that what belongs *to me*, belongs *to you*." He sits down again and pulls me onto his lap. "My money is your money. I can also spend any amount of money on you I want."

He already bought me a plane. I can't imagine how he tops that.

"Last chance, butterfly."

"Not *a* chance, Maverick. This butterfly has happily tangled her wings inside your web. Forever."

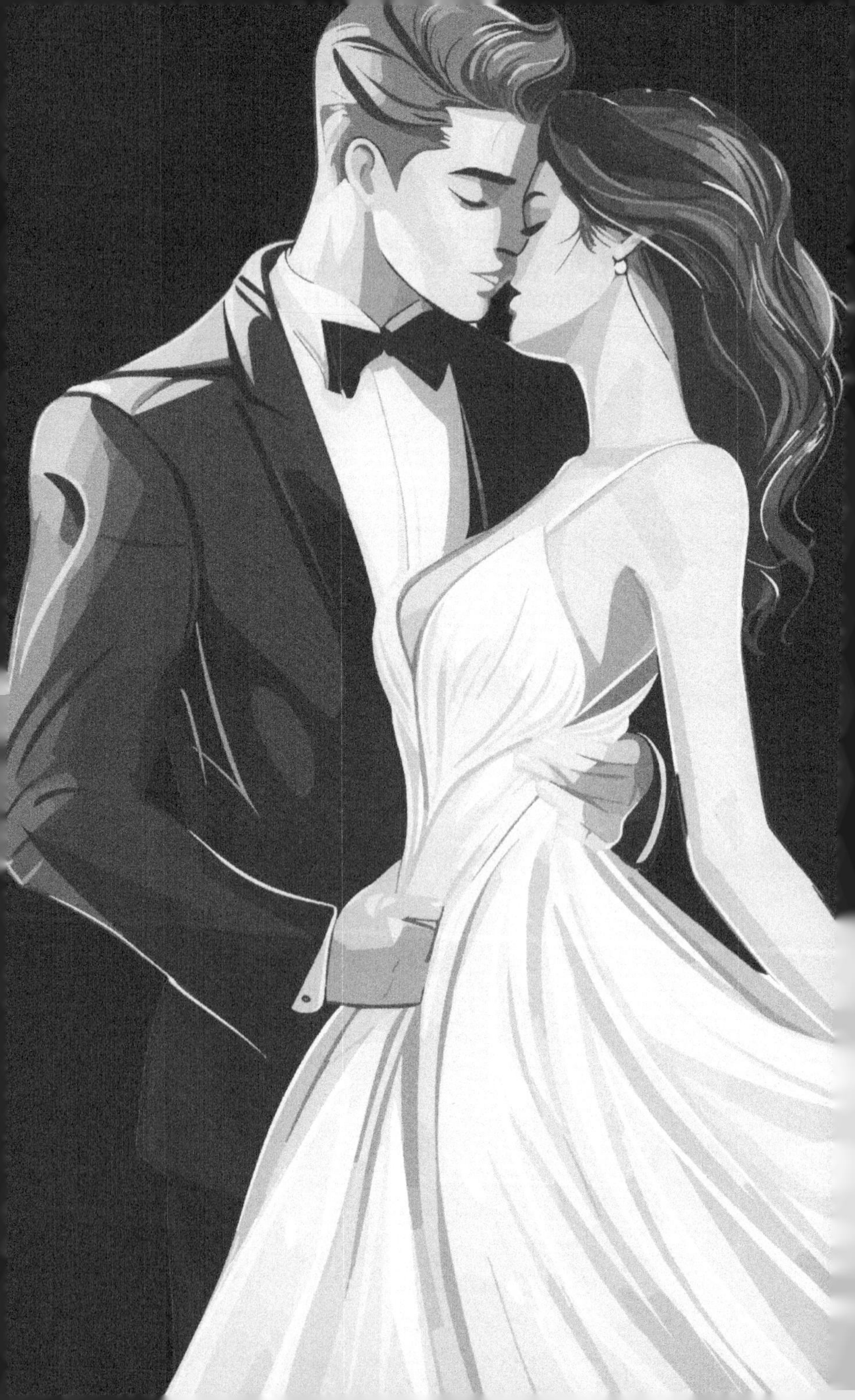

EPILOGUE ONE
ELLA

Jillian offered to postpone her wedding ceremony that following Saturday for me. It didn't make sense for the shadow I casted on the O'Rourkes with my father's sin to stretch any further.

It was the least I could do to bless Eoghan and Jillian moving forward with their party, and not inconvenience hundreds of people, especially those who flew in. The sad talk of the party is that Balor's parents didn't make the trip.

Saturday is beautiful, and Jillian stuns in a lace and crystal mermaid dress with a train that must be close to ten feet long.

Shea, my soon-to-be sister, stays in lockstep with us the whole day, helping me get around. I'm grateful it's still chilly out, since I'm wearing a long-sleeve dress that covers most of my bandages. I continue to heal while I'm being prepped for skin grafts.

Looking around the wedding, like most single women, I think about what I want mine to be like. It's a race on two fronts. To heal enough to wear my dream wedding dress and to not have a basketball tummy.

But my dream of wearing my mother's gown is dead.

Balor, dressed in a finely cut suit, keeps a gentle hand on my waist at all times. It's the one place that doesn't hurt. Every flinching pain reminds me material things don't matter. I'm alive.

That Balor had never killed anyone had been a badge of honor he'd held on to. Proud he never had to commit that kind of sin. He proved his value early on to his father with his technical skills and wasn't forced to do their dad's dirty work on the streets like his brothers.

He ended that streak for me. I would have preferred

my father to kill Wes and then spend his life making up for his sins to me. But he selfishly took that away from me.

Instead, Balor made the sacrifice, and will live with that kill on his conscience for the rest of his life. To further reinforce what we have, he tattooed my name along his collarbone. Since he mostly wears button-downs open at the neck, it's visible.

It's like I branded him and he's mine. When I asked why he chose that location, he admitted that Lachlan got his wife's name tattooed above his dick. "You know you own my dick. Now you know you own my heart," Balor said.

I told him about the tattoo I want on my fingers. He loved the idea, but asked me to wait. My health comes before his possessiveness.

Next week, I have my first appointment with a therapist to make sense of my mixed feelings. How a lifetime of love from my dad weighs against a couple of years of betrayal and one utterly horrible day.

"You look tired, baby," Balor says, a few hours into the celebration.

Any other time, we might be getting busy in the bathroom, but I'm not ready. My body isn't ready. My heart? It's all-in. I've moved into his townhouse, and soon we'll start decorating one of the spare bedrooms into the nursery.

The babies are absolutely fine. Tough O'Rourke genes.

"Let's get you home," Balor says, taking my hand.

"We should start saying our goodbyes." I suck in a breath, considering that can take an hour.

"Ever hear of the Irish exit?"

I laugh. "Literally?"

"No one will judge. They know what it took for you to be here." He presses his lips to my forehead.

His words carry a few different meanings. What it took

for us to be together.

Luck, patience, trust, and shattering the veil to Balor's heart.

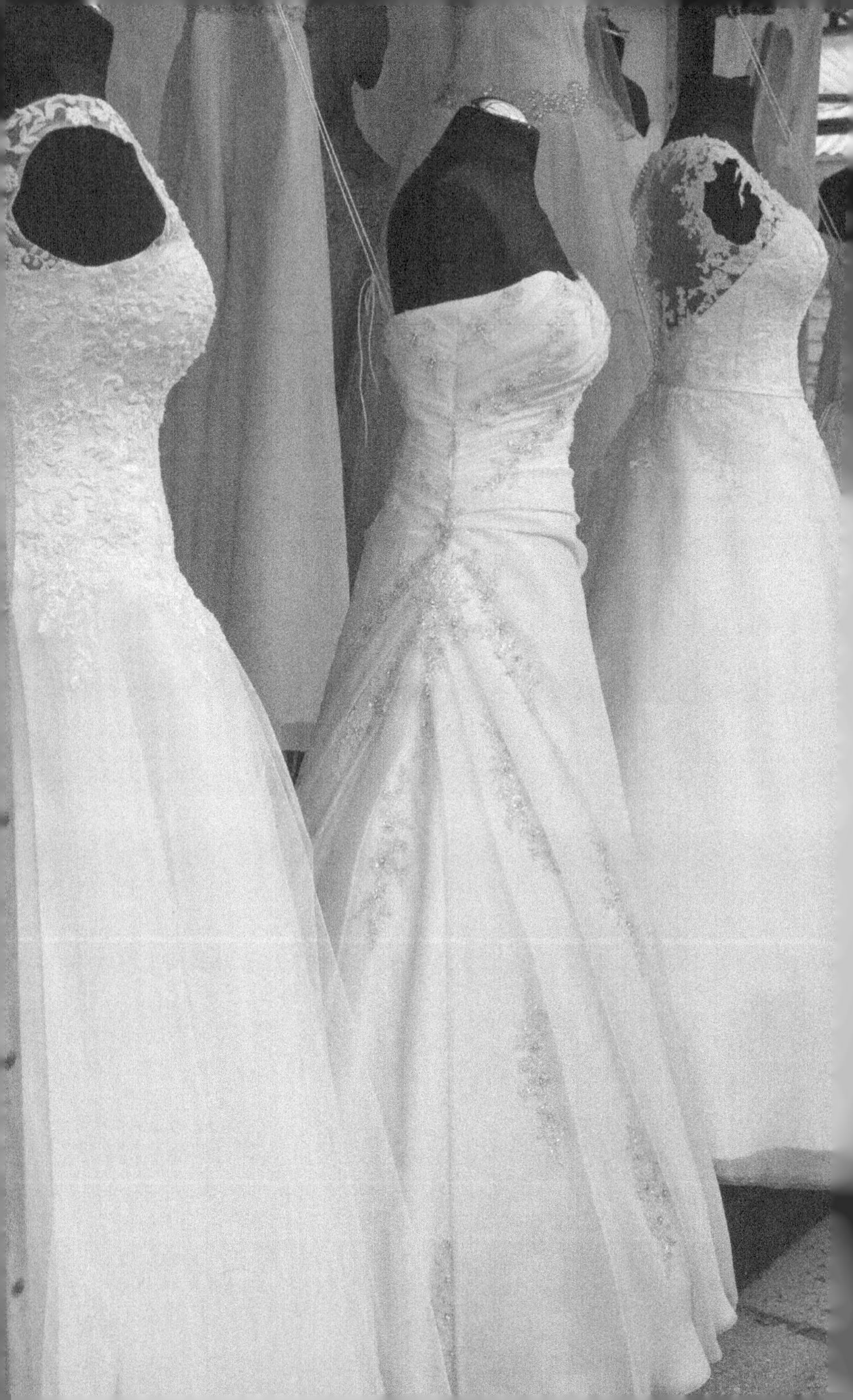

EPILOGUE TWO

ELLA

Wedding dress shopping is supposed to be fun. No, a ball. The bomb. The shopping event every woman dreams of. Not for me, since I can't wear my mother's dress.

"Let's find something that looks similar," Jillian says, fingering dresses on a rack while I stand idly by in a short, white satin robe.

She came with me when my two besties were *both* busy. Odd.

Hannah and Val came to visit me at Balor's house, stunned at what happened. But they support my decision to marry him.

"I don't want to love something other than my mother's gown. It feels like a betrayal," I whine.

And I want Balor right now. But I've slowly gotten used to being alone while he's at work. And I've even been going out alone, walking around Astoria and enjoying the warm spring we're having.

The other day, I walked to Katya's dance studio and worked with Lia some more.

I glance around the dress shop, considering Jillian's suggestion. I need to pick something. I'm keeping her from Eoghan, which means that psycho stalker husband of hers will show up any minute.

A monstrosity of a dress, a ballgown overload, catches my eye. It can't be any further from my mother's dress, and it's so gaudy, so loud, so over the top, it will get all the attention, and no one will really see me.

Perfect.

"How about that one?" I motion to it.

Jillian looks horrified. "Here. How about this one? It looks vintage."

My heart rate ticks up and a shred of excitement

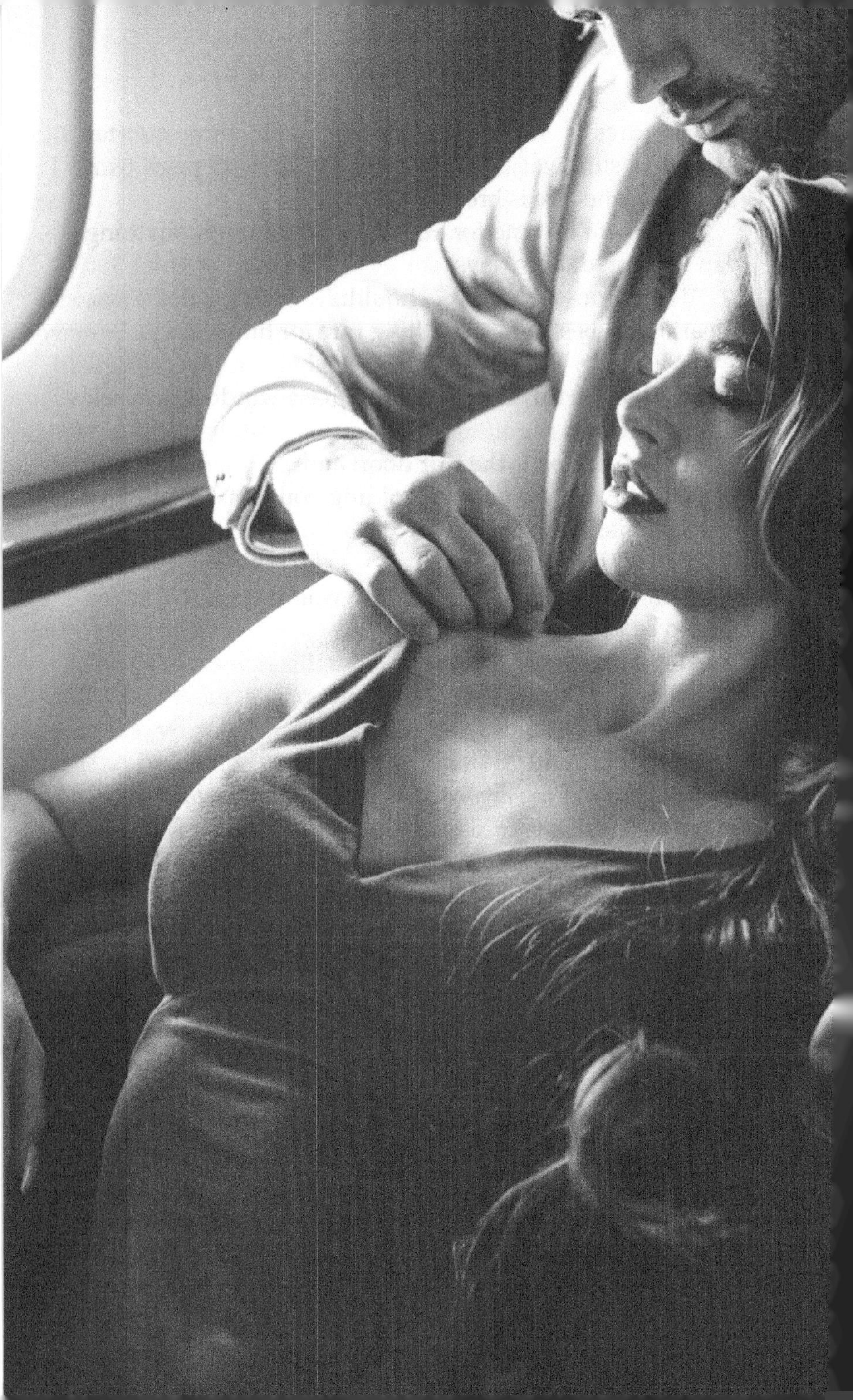

EPILOGUE THREE

BALOR- ONE WEEK LATER

"Give the woman's mouth a rest," Lachlan says, passing Ella and me on Kieran's jet.

"We're on our honeymoon." Ella defends how damn inappropriate we're getting.

We're taking things slow in the physical department while she heals. Every day she gets bigger with my babies, and I love her body more every day. She's so inextricably mine.

"Must be nice to have a honeymoon. I didn't get one," Lachlan complains.

"Because you stole your bride on her wedding day and then had to hide her from her father."

"What?" Ella slaps my chest. "Get out!"

Lachlan narrows his gray eyes at us.

I stand up. "How is Katya feeling?"

She's due next month, but likely won't make it given her size compared to Lachlan's.

"Not good," he growls. "She's going on bed-rest the moment I get home."

I blow out a breath when he turns around and struts to the front of the plane. Smooth as satin, he takes a seat next to Darragh.

Shea naps in a captain's chair in the row behind them. Denton and Trace sit a few seats away.

I turn away, but notice Trace watching my sister.

Aw, fuck, I've seen that look in a man. Is he insane?

I'm about to give him a talkin' to when my wife snags my arm, and I sit back down.

My sister is an adult. Just as I argued for Ella to make her own choices, Shea should get the same consideration.

We land in Ireland, a small airstrip in Dunbar Valley. Lachlan, Darragh, and Trace practically surround Shea like she's a celebrity. They leave in one hired SUV, while Ella, Denton, and I wait for another.

"Are you sure you don't want to go with your brothers and Shea?" Ella asks, touching my face. "I can wait for you at the hotel."

I chuckle to myself. Hotel. "No, you don't leave my sight around here."

She glances around the hangar. "It's dangerous?"

"Dunbar Valley is a torture camp. It's mostly criminals. My father recruited assassins from the place back in the day." I tense up. "When Lachlan was eighteen, Da sent him here."

"To train as an assassin?" Her voice squeaks.

"And to be punished. This place is privately run. Someone dumps you here with instructions, you get whatever treatment your sponsor paid for."

"Your brother Cormac is here." She clutches her chest. "What did he—"

"There's time to explain that." I have to ease her mind because Lachlan is bringing him home.

He doesn't think I know.

"But my brother, *no brother* will ever hurt you. You're an O'Rourke. You are one of us now, Ella."

She blushes as I help her into the SUV that arrives for us.

A twenty-minute ride later, I take out that red satin mask from my leather duffle.

"What is that for?" Her eyes widen.

Smiling, I slip it over her eyes. "I have another surprise for you."

"Balor," she says breathlessly. "First a plane. Then you put me on the deed to your house."

"Our house. Our children are living in a house that both their parents own." He kisses my nose.

"You do so much for me. You've given me everything."

"It's nothing compared to what you've given me. Peace. Love. And the motivation to stop hating myself for only wanting one way to get off."

I slide the mask on and put my arm around her.

The sun is ready to set over the green knolls of the vast property of our *lodging*.

Even I'm impressed. But I keep my excitement in check.

I open the car door and help Ella out.

Denton, who's my bodyguard now, and mostly looks after Ella, takes our bags from the back.

Before the stone steps, I remove the blindfold.

Ella blinks and spins around like she doesn't believe what she's seeing. "We're staying in a castle?"

I smile. "You're *my* queen. You deserve to spend our honeymoon being treated like royalty."

The staff slowly filters out a side entrance, and stand in front of the massive, ten-foot-tall dark wooden door. That's the downside of honeymooning in a castle. There's a household who will hear us have sex if Ella is ready.

We climb the steps and the valet, the head of the household, introduces the staff. Ella greets them all like she *is* royalty.

"We're tired from the flight," I say, steering my wife toward a set of dramatic carpeted stairs.

"Dinner is warming up for you, sir," the valet says.

"We'd like dinner in our room tonight." I turn to Denton. "My guard gets free reign. He goes where he wants. Eats when and where he wants."

"Absolutely, sir. On both points."

"Aye," I say, thickening my accent.

In our bedroom, a classic medieval bedchamber updated with electric lights and outlets, I put our bags away. I smile at the USB ports in the wall and plug in my laptop.

I don't travel without this thing.

In the sitting room outside the sleeping area, Ella and I eat a dinner of roast chicken, potatoes, and steamed figs.

That night I make gentle love to my wife all night.

The next day, we take a walk on vast grounds, enjoying the warm sun on our skin.

My phone rings and I plan to ignore it, but I also catch Denton running toward me.

My veins turn to ice. Something happened.

Ma. I planned to see her and my father tomorrow. Lachlan and Shea went today. God, am I too late?

"Lachlan," I say into my phone choked up.

"Problem."

Odd way to start a potential death notification.

"Talk to me."

"There's been a siege at Dunbar."

Now my legs go weak. "Damage assessment."

"There was a new batch of terrorists dropped off last month. No one fucking told me."

"And?"

"They escaped."

I close my eyes and look around. We're almost fifty miles away, but Denton's panic makes sense.

"Let's get back to the castle," I say through clenched teeth. My arm winds around my wife. "It's okay," I whisper, even though this castle stands out like a sore thumb. "Listen Lach, Ella and I will be at the airport to leave in—"

"We're not leaving. We can't," Lachlan drawls, his voice deadly.

"Fuck. What about Cormac?"

"He's with me. With us. Darragh and I."

"Wait?" My legs go numb. "What about Shea-Lynne? She was with you."

"She's with Trace."

Trace… Who's ex-military.

And there are terrorists crawling around Dunbar.

"I'm glad Trace is with her, but where are they?" I ask, fury igniting in me.

"Shea and Trace are missing. He kidnapped her."

Read Illicit Temptation, Book 3 in the Astoria Royals Special Edition Series.

DEBORAH GARLAND

ASTORIA ROYALS ON AUDIO!

Love growly, alpha Irish accents?

The Astoria Royals Series is available on audio.

More information, samples, and downloads are available on my website:

STAY IN TOUCH WITH ME

My newsletter followers get not only a good laugh each month, but also updates on new releases, sales, and giveaways.

Sign up at my website:

Or Follow Me on Amazon:

DEBORAH GARLAND

You can stalk me on other platforms

TikTok

Goodreads

BookBub

Facebook

Instagram

HERE'S DEBORAH

Deborah Garland is a 4x Award-Winning and Amazon Top 45 Bestselling author of emotional and funny, steamy romances!

She lives on the beautiful North Shore of Long Island with her very patient husband and their mischievous pug. She had to learn how to make her own Cosmopolitans and right now there's a bartender who will NEVER see her again. She eats cheap mac and cheese with expensive red wine, her heroes are ALWAYS over six feet tall, and they fall, hard, HARD for the girl.

Made in the USA
Monee, IL
22 October 2024